PLOUGH THE SEA

Robert Wilder

PLOUGH THE SEA

G. P. Putnam's Sons
New York

To

A Lovely And Gracious Lady

LOUISE FRANCIS TERRETT

With Devotion

HE WHO PLAYS AT REVOLUTION PLOUGHS THE SEA.
—attributed to Simón Bolívar

I.

OF the day and hour nothing can be known. Only the year as it was marked by some Spanish soldier in the boredom of his watch. On a broad parapet of the squat fort he had taken a knife or short sword and cut the date into the side of one of the four towers which studded the corners.

1588. He had dug the numerals out in the spongy stone and then added one word. *Cristo!*

What quiet agony of loneliness had possessed him as he chiseled The Christ's name? Or, possibly, it had merely been an irreverent curse of irritation at being posted in this strange land so far from home. None but the man, dead these centuries, could say.

Beyond the harbor entrance, which the long guns of the fort commanded, lay a tropic sea of deceptive softness. When the soldier turned and gazed landward a solid matting of jungle rose to the mountains which were in the color of green jade. To the northwest the Windward Passage separated this island from the great, curved lizardlike shape of another. Beyond that lay the loose scattering of the Islands of the Indies.

He has no sense of history, this unknown soldier, nor of his place in it. He stares seaward and does not know that in this year, at Corunna, the greatest fleet ever assembled was preparing to sail against the heretic Queen, Elizabeth. That Drake and Howard waited at Plymouth for the first topmasts of the armada to stand on the horizon. That before the year's end the back of Spain's power would be broken and this small garrison, with others of Philip's empire, would be by-passed and isolated for decades while British and French buccaneers roved the southern oceans.

The great mills of the centuries would grind out the years. Wars would rage across the seas and over continents and eventually the pennant-decked cruise ships would sail past this fort, and leggy girls in vivid shorts and halters would pose for snapshots before the tower in which he kept his watch. Now and then a crew-cut college boy would take a knife and scratch into the date and word cut by a lonely sentry and keep them fresh.

Could he have returned on this Sunday morning, a little over three hundred and seventy-three years later, this Spanish man at arms might have looked down from his post on the wall to a stone-flagged court below. He would have gazed with uncomprehending wonder as a file of a dozen men shuffled up from a dungeon cell. They shaded their eyes against the harsh light and moved haltingly at the bayonet-prodding of a guard until they were close-packed. These were no soldiers. At least, they wore no uniforms. There was no spirit in them and the cotton garments hung as from angular racks on wasted bodies. They coughed, hacking weakly, slid their feet and seemed to lift them in a stiff, macabre dance from the hot stones. They neither looked at nor spoke to each other, for they were without interest in things beyond or outside themselves. One or two made a sign of the cross, but the motions were mechanical and without conviction.

The guard now went among them, stripping the loose, pajamalike coats away, bundling the thin garments in one arm and carrying them to a wooden tub. The naked backs rippled and twitched as though a sudden chill had touched them, and the skin was a bluish-white, the color of chalk water.

A door on the opposite side of the courtyard creaked open and for a moment a man stood partly framed. As he stepped out he stooped a little to clear the lintel.

He wore a uniform of sorts although it was without insignia. The shirt, carefully tailored, bore the sharp, vertical creasings of meticulous pressing and folding. It was open to the second button at the throat. The trousers, loose fitting, were tucked into laced boots which were polished to the color of mahogany. Between his fingers he held the half-smoked butt of a cigarette. He drew upon it, inhaling deeply, and then dropped it almost absently while the smoke trailed in lazy tendrils from his nostrils. Cradled in one arm was an instrument at which the shade of the Spanish soldier would have gazed with puzzled interest. It was like no firepiece a man could imagine and yet the barrel, the curious design, the unmistakable sheen of blue steel, marked it as a weapon of some sort.

The man walked slowly forward, a thumb flipping a small catch at the side of the thing he carried.

At the sharp, metallic click the backs of the huddled men stiffened and their scrawny shoulder blades drew together as though they would cover their nakedness or make a smaller target. One man fell upon his knees and began to sob convulsively. His abject figure swayed back and forth in a helpless misery. The others ignored him, keeping their faces to the wall.

A guard strode over and impatiently kicked the trembling buttocks upright.

As though on signal the bells of the city's many churches began to toll. The throbbing notes sent the pigeons swirling from their roosting places on ledges and in the eaves. A stately procession of sound enveloped the day, vibrating on the soft wind.

The man halted. With both hands he held the thing he carried waist high. A finger tightened within the trigger guard and an insane chatter filled the court. Steel-jacketed hornets bit into shaking flesh. Where the rifle was held for a moment too long its spewing fury all but cut one of the condemned in two. The man moved it back and forth as he might have played a garden hose. Then it was over. Brass cartridge cases, ejected as they had been fired, lay scattered about as bright ornaments in the sun.

The man carrying the submachine gun turned and walked back toward the open door as though he had merely stepped outside for a breath of air.

Within the room five officers, one a colonel, snapped to attention as the executioner entered. He ignored them and went to a basin of water on a stand. A captain took a fresh linen towel from a drawer and stood with it, waiting. No one spoke.

The man washed his hands carefully in the water. He dried them, one finger at a time, then the palms and finally the backs and wrists. Inadvertently he dropped the towel and the captain bent quickly to pick it up. For a long moment the man stood, softly kneading the knuckles of lean, sensitive fingers. There was about him a curious air of detachment and a brooding, dark sadness in the eyes at this moment but, oddly enough, it was somehow contradicted by the faintest of smiles about the lips. It was a handsome face, almost ascetic. More than that. It had the serene beauty of an untroubled saint, certain of his place in Heaven. So, also, it had been slyly whispered by those who knew of such things, had been the expression of Torquemada during the hot fury of the Inquisition.

The man walked to where a narrow barred window looked out upon the courtyard. He stared pensively. A soldier was sloshing buckets of water over bloodstained stones. The fallen bodies were being dragged away, hauled by their heels to where a chute, cut through the stone, led to the water below. There the sharks cruised and waited and by now there would be a furious churning and a crimson dye would spread and finally dissipate itself on the outgoing tide. From a shirt pocket he took a cigarette. The captain held a match, already flaming in anticipation of the need. The man smiled a faint acknowledgment as he took the light and then turned to face the others.

"*Una copita, eh?*" The accent was rude. "Relax, *hombres*." He spoke this way, sliding from Spanish to English, unaware he did so.

There was a guarded relaxation. The colonel went to a cabinet and withdrew a wicker-covered bottle of unopened rum. He set a single glass upon the table and twisted a wired cork from the bottle's neck.

"For all of us, Pepito." An indulgent smile accompanied the order.

"Of course, Excellency." The colonel brought additional glasses. He filled five and took up his own. The others stepped forward in accordance with their rank and picked up theirs.

"*El presidente!*"

The colonel barked the salute and tossed the rum down in a single swallow. The others, making a chorus of the toast, drained their drinks.

For a moment, which lengthened uncomfortably, the man regarded them all with a mildly alert curiosity. They knew why, and yet none was embarrassed. Satisfied, he also poured out the rich, dark rum and drank it slowly with satisfaction.

He studied them. The uniforms, brilliant with decorations from his hand. Unnecessary spurs of silver on hand-crafted boots. The gold braid, fresh as newly minted coins. This was his vanity, to appear among them as a common soldier with no mark of rank and yet to command their immediate obedience. Loyalty was another matter. It shifted with the winds of chance, blowing this way and that as opportunity offered. He indulged himself in no illusions.

His nod was brief, impersonal, and he turned and walked again through the door, followed by the colonel.

Where a heavy bridge spanned what had once, long ago, been a moat a black Cadillac waited. The chauffeur stood, holding the car's door open, as he had been standing from the moment the man alighted half an hour ago. Four crisply uniformed members of San Rafael's police were at attention beside their motorcycles. As the door was closed softly behind the man and the colonel they kicked their machines into action. Because it was Sunday the exhausts were muffled. One pair swung out ahead of the limousine. The other two fell in behind. The car rolled down a slight incline to the highway.

Beyond the ancient fort, lying along a graceful crescent of land embracing the bay, the city of San Rafael sparkled against a mountainous backdrop. It was as modern as though recently planned and laid out. Broad *avenidas*, brilliantly lighted at night, cut straight and true across a grid of streets. A corps of sanitation workers kept them immaculate and shining. A fleet of new buses rolled silently and on swift schedules through the city and to outlying districts. Buildings imaginative in design, and with the use of much glass and balconies, seemed open to the sun. Hotels, constructed with American capital, rose in colored tiers along the bay. Winter tourists lolled about huge swimming pools in the warm, cloudless days, and yachts were moored within a new marina.

Seen at night, from the air, San Rafael was a dazzling, multicolored jewel on the dark sheen of the Caribbean. A park, three miles in length and fronting the water, was a tropical garden. Here the palms bent toward each other with rustling whispers, and flowers grew in great clusters of purple, yellow and scarlet. The park's sidewalks were of black and white mosaic and there were nightly concerts in the bandstand, which was fashioned as an enormous seashell of coral pink. Dominating the park was a bronze statue of heroic proportions. From this eminence the man looked down upon his people with a gesture of benediction.

There were smaller images of The Benefactor at avenue intersections and in the midtown plaza; busts in marble and bronze. These had been erected through the subscription of civic and political groups, paid for with the pennies of schoolchildren and youth organizations. They all bore upon a plaque the same, simple legend:

JORGE OJEDA
"THE BENEFACTOR"

Nothing more was needed. One had only to look about; to regard this shimmering city, and see indisputable evidences of the man's beneficence. Within the memory of many the paved streets had been straggling trails of dirt over which the people walked or drove their dusty burros. Now there were the buses; clean, well lighted, with the latest air brakes and automatic doors. This was a miracle barely exceeded by that of Creation itself; to be whisked from one end of the island to the other on the fine highways and across broad city streets for a few centavos.

To the outlying villages The Benefactor had brought the light of electricity where only smoky torches had been the illumination for centuries. It was true not everyone wanted or had need for the globes which burned so brightly. It made no difference if a man lived with his entire family in one room. The inspectors came. They counted the adults and children and upon this basis a man purchased so many bulbs. His bill for the electricity was based upon this and not on the current used. Even when the children died or the girls married and moved away, the bulbs, to the number of those originally purchased, must be replaced. If he had new children he must buy a bulb for each.

No longer did the women go to the creeks and there gossip and pound their clothing with stones in the weekly washing. In each community there was a laundry. Clothing was dumped into gleaming machines to be whirled clean and dried. It was also true that only a certain brand of soap powder could be used in the machines and every family was assessed a fixed tax to maintain the laundry. Miracles, it was pointed out, were expensive.

Many schools were built and to each came a teacher. Often he had nothing to do because the *escuelas* were frequently built in places where there were no villages—at highway intersections, atop a small hill commanding a road. Unlike most schools these were made with walls of thick concrete and had slits for windows, and the teacher was usually joined by three or four assistants who wore uniforms of the *Joventad*, a youth society. For these schools everyone paid an education tax.

Now and then there were small grumblings but those who uttered them had to be careful with whom they talked. Too often had a man spoken his mind only to find himself given a job far back in the mountains where the mines brought copper and other metals from the ground. Very few returned but their families received a piece of paper which declared the man was engaged in important government work.

Once there had been a small rebellion over such a little thing as a match. On the island only a certain kind could be purchased. These were tiny tapers of wax in colored boxes. They were not always suitable, for when carried in a man's pocket on a hot day the wax became soft, the matches limp and would not strike. Tourists from ships and the air lines were warned to leave their mechanical lighters and tabs of foreign matches behind. After a few halfhearted complaints, they accepted the regulation and later bought dozens of boxes of the government matches to take home as souvenirs. When the country people refused to use the matches, soldiers went through the villages, stamping out all fires and fixing a tax upon everyone. Trucks came with matches and the people all lined up to purchase a fixed quantity. After that no one objected again. It was explained the money went into a fund for the poor and everyone knew the poor must always be helped.

Because of the things accomplished by The Benefactor tourists now came in great numbers each winter. They bought baskets, rough native woven fabrics, carvings and slyly obscene figures worked in wood and stone. They spread the Yankee dollars with careless enthusiasm in the stores, bars and night clubs. When they hired a car and drove through the country they all exclaimed over the number of schools and their heavy construction.

In many things San Rafael had yielded to the paternal concern of the man. One had only to walk through the market district and, remembering how it once had been, marvel at the change. No longer did the country-women sit along the curb with their small heaps of pottery, peppers, beans, corn and fruit. They all had numbered stalls, open-air booths for which they paid a fixed rent. This, however, they agreed was actually no more than had been pinched from them in the old days by any roving policeman with a hand out for the *mordida*. Some of the old pleasure in the market was gone. It was no longer possible to gossip and exchange comments; to haggle and barter with each other, trading this for some of that. There were re-signed shrugs and small sighs for the change, but everyone agreed it was better. The man had told them so and so it must be. The stall rent was paid promptly into the hands of a collector at the beginning of each market day and unless this was done, the booth remained shuttered and the woman sent home. For she was not allowed to sit or stand upon the sidewalk. The rent, as with all taxes, was administered by The Benefactor, for the relief of the needy in remote provinces of the island.

Everything, it seemed, yielded to understanding with time. There was that matter of identity cards. At first it had seemed a thing of a nuisance, an expense for which there was no explanation. The cards, bearing a fingerprint and the photograph of the holder, were issued at Government House. They must be carried at all times by every adult and shown to the police upon demand. To a people inherently casual in their habits, who moved from village to village to visit for months at a time with friends or relatives, this was a stupid authority. Who could always remember to carry a card? How did a man and woman get the pesos necessary for a photograph and the stamping? For one who ignored the order there came a swift punishment. He was put to work on the roads or rented to the holders of the big sugar estates. He swung a machete from the coming of daylight until dark, clearing the jungle, or was sent to far places in the mountains where he worked in the mines. Then it was explained, in words coming from the man himself, how only the good people were given cards or had the privilege of carrying them. Those with criminal records were issued cards of bright yellow. So it became a matter of pride and gave a man a social standing to carry on his person a white card. They were solemnly displayed to all by the members of the families whenever a boy and girl were married. For a few centavos additional duplicates of the cards, stamped so, were issued and these were tacked on the walls of the house so every visitor might know immediately that here lived people of probity.

All about everyone, as The Benefactor had said, they could see the evidence of his concern. Fine-looking police in blue trousers, scarlet jackets and white helmets directed traffic and made it possible for a man to cross the street without being run over. Police, tightly disciplined, were everywhere on motorcycles and in squad cars for the protection of the people. There were fine buildings to be gazed at, parks to be walked in and the careless, shiftless way of life was gone. There was a purpose in everything and it was not enough just to sit in the sun because the feeling of this was good. There was no unemployment. A man did not have to look for work. A department of the government found it for him. And, although it might not be work for which a man was fitted or in which he took pleasure, he was made to understand he could not be absent or change employment because of a whim.

All of this had a curious effect upon a people in whose veins flowed

Spanish, Negro, Indian, a little French and English blood. In this combination there was laughter, music and a happy indolence. Fruit hung ripe for the picking, fish were heavy in the island waters, shelter was no farther away than the thick palm fronds which could easily be thatched to provide a cover. Sun blessed the island for most of the year. It was good to lie in, drinking a little rum, smoking some tobacco, making love to a girl. Sometimes, those who thought about such things had the feeling they were all marching in step and some of the good laughter was gone and could not be recaptured. Men no longer smiled so quickly. There was a purpose, though vaguely defined as such, and a man looking at the shining streets, the brisk flow of traffic, was sometimes uneasy although the feeling was not one to which he could put a name.

Among the buildings there was a fine one of stone. It was a modern prison with gleaming, electrically operated cell blocks, diet kitchens, workshops. This was proudly shown to the visiting Congressmen from the United States who came frequently on trips arranged by the government. It was a monument to The Benefactor's concern for even those of evil temper; an example of great humanity.

No one ever mentioned the Presidio, the ancient fort with its time-stained battlements, its dark cells and subterranean dungeons. Tourists who were thrilled over it as a place of history and asked for permission to inspect it were now told that its age made it unsafe. For that reason and that alone the man had closed it to the public some years ago.

The devout and superstitious whose way took them past the fort always crossed themselves hurriedly and averted their eyes until they were well beyond the scarred walls. The families of the men garrisoned there never talked about the place and without knowing why, they felt ashamed their men were posted there. It was marked, though, how the *julia*, the black truck of the police, often rolled over the drawbridge with its back door locked and a uniformed guard riding on the step. Through the wire grating at the rear could be seen the heads of those who sat on the narrow benches inside. The *julia* never brought anyone out; just the driver and the guard, who now rode on the front seat. They never laughed or joked as did men when a job is finished.

The Cadillac rolled slowly along the street of the markets now. Boys and girls, barefooted, trotted alongside the car holding in their outstretched hands offerings of guavas, mangoes, bunches of wild grapes and cups of the tiny strawberries which grew in the hills. They carried these things on bright green sections of freshly cut banana leaf. They laughed as they ran, making a game of it, hoping to be noticed by the man. It was too much to expect he would actually accept the gifts or order the automobile halted. It was enough to see him and know they were seen even though he gave no sign.

Slowly, reluctantly, they dropped behind and then stood in the middle of the street staring after the car until it took a turn at the intersection with the Avenida de Independencia and disappeared.

The man smiled softly to himself. "Back there," he spoke quietly, "one among those children is my assassin, Pepito. I may have even looked into his face. That is a strange thing to think on, isn't it?"

The colonel said nothing. Words were not expected of him.

"Valdez and the others who died this morning from standing too long in the sun without their shirts were impatient. They could not wait for one of those boys back there to grow up. Because they were in a hurry they were careless and for that they died."

He dug with long fingers into a shirt pocket and took out a cigarette. The colonel made no move to produce a match. Ojeda chuckled and struck one of his own and then a hand dropped to the officer's knee with an approving squeeze. He nodded his satisfaction.

"I trust you a little, Pepito." He inhaled deeply of the tobacco. "Not too much, you understand. But I put some confidence in you because, when we are alone this way, you do not bow too low. That was what first made me suspicious of Valdez. He always looked me straight in the eye when talking. It is a thing men sometimes do. They exaggerate their sincerity and honesty. Look, they say. I meet your gaze with a straightforwardness. Could a traitor do this?" He smiled a little. "I would tell such men yes. It is an easy thing to do. I, myself, have done it." He leaned back and scratched his head against the cushion. "Do you know how I really found out about Valdez and his conspirators?"

"I wondered."

"His wife." A soft bubble of laughter exploded within Ojeda's throat. "For a long time I have felt this thing about her. In her mind she has become fascinated by the idea of becoming the woman of *el presidente*. Not, you understand, because she is inflamed by lust, for she is an indifferent bitch at love-making. Greed makes her hot. She thinks of jewels, of Paris gowns, of an estate and trips abroad on the presidential yacht; of the Riviera and the envy of the women there. But, she has a husband and it is necessary to rid herself of him first. How better to do it than by posing to me as a true patriot? So, she betrays Valdez twice. Once with her body in my bed and then with her tongue as she gives me his name and those of the others. This is because she loves me, you understand, and wishes to perform a great service to her country. I shall give her a decoration, I think. Something gaudy and of value with diamonds and emeralds. It may inspire the wives of other conspirators. Let us make a thing of special design and be sure it is expensive. Create an order of some martyred saint. They always have a fine and solemn sound. The Order Of Saint Something or Other. Talk it over with Bishop Mendoza. It flatters him to be consulted on such matters."

A great wall, stretching in two directions until it was lost in a curvature of the hill, was broken by enormous gates of finely wrought iron. Sentries stood at attention on either side and as the car approached, a noncommissioned officer stepped from the gatehouse and snapped a sharp salute as the Cadillac rolled past. Ojeda nodded to him.

"Should you ever find yourself in my position, Pepito, put your faith in your sergeants. Never mind the officers. Without the help of the sergeants no revolution can succeed. Let the captains, the colonels and the generals scheme and draw their plans. In the end they have to depend upon the noncommissioned men for the army's support. Without that they have no army and without an army there is no revolution. It is something to remember."

"I will keep it in mind, *presidente*." The words were dryly spoken.

The road to the palace atop the hill wound and twisted itself upward skirting terraced gardens which dropped in a series of huge steps. Each was a shelf of carefully cultivated beauty, commanding the services of a head gardner and his assistants who had no other responsibility beyond a particular ledge of brilliant color. Viewed from the palace the effect was that of a magnificent cascade of flowers, stunted cedars and azure pools flowing in perfect order to the elevation's base. San Rafael spread itself below and beyond lay the Caribbean with its splotches of purple, green and blue; the reefs on either side of the harbor's entrance making a great ruff of lacy white.

Ojeda turned his eyes from the scene as the car and its escort drew up before a baroque palace. Guards were motionless at both ends of the flight of marble steps. Two mastiffs, as disciplined as the soldiers, waited. Only a small ripple of their coats betrayed an excitement and they waited for the word from Ojeda which would release them.

When the car's door was held open the man made no move to leave. He studied the colonel.

"Is it possible, Pepito, you are a man without ambition? Never have you asked me for anything; an estate, a promotion, a source of revenue. It is in my mind to do something for you. What is it you would like?"

Colonel Juan de Cespedes tapped a fingernail on his teeth. He whistled softly and the tiniest of smiles kindled a light behind his eyes.

"Make me a sergeant, *presidente*." The request was voiced gravely.

Ojeda's sudden shout of laughter startled the guards and sent the dogs into a frenzy of impatience. They raced toward the car, rearing high against the windows, barking furiously, eager to be a part of the fun whatever it was. The man reached out and pulled affectionately at the ears of one. A great tongue wrapped itself over the hand in a wet caress. The laugh subsided to a small chuckle and then died altogether. For a moment the eyes of *el presidente* considered the impassive features of the one he called Pepito as a term of warm regard and understanding he shared with no one else. It was difficult to know with what degree of lightness the request had been made or how it should be taken. Finally Ojeda shook his head.

"A general, Pepito. Be satisfied with that." He touched de Cespedes lightly but with a strange gesture of warning and bent his lean body to leave the car. "We shall make the promotion in the morning."

II.

O NCE she had worn a great beauty, shrugging gracefully and without question beneath it as she might have accepted a bright scarf laid across her shoulders by a doting servant. Now, what was left was fragile and faintly yellowed by time as a delicate piece of lace. Sometimes, when she looked at herself in the mirror, she thought it was a little sad.

She was all but hidden within the woven shell of a huge, wicker chair drawn into a plot of dappled shade at the garden's end. She sat, not primly or stiffly but with an unmistakable dignity, for it was not in her nature to lounge carelessly even when alone. On a latticed arbor, laced and threaded with flame vine scarlet in its intensity, and grapelike clusters of pale blue wisteria, a large *macayo* hung upside down by its taloned feet. It shrieked with an angry petulance, calling the woman's attention to its extraordinary position and the remarkable ease in maintaining it. It was a heavy bird of brilliant plumage, the feathers tinted with sharp yellows, crimson and green. It rolled a bright eye toward the chair as it screamed harshly.

"Silly bastard." The unemotional comment was made in French, vaguely and indefinably accented. "A silly bastard."

Delighted with this evidence of attention the parrot screamed again and began to swing itself back and forth on a thick vine until a small shower of violet-colored petals floated down to fall on the woman's lap. She brushed them away idly with a small, delicately boned hand. The skin seemed almost transparent and veins were faint tracings.

She examined her hand, turning it from palm to back and smiling a little ruefully at its wrinkled surface. It was curious, she mused; she didn't actually feel any older. But, this was a thing of the mind. The degeneration of the body could not be denied.

It occurred to her that this thing one called the soul was continually affronted by the flesh. It grew old and withered before one's eyes. Even in youth the body was a source of mortification to man's soaring spirit. It must be washed or it stank. It must evacuate itself upon a stool and its parts cleaned by a hand which rebelled against the grossness. It was a prey to all manner of ills. Cut, it bled and then formed scabs. It itched and must be scratched as any monkey's belly. Boils erupted upon its surface and leaked a noisome pus. It became, by turns, too hot or too cold and was a helpless victim to the ecstasy generated by a man's touch. It was forced to assume positions completely without dignity upon a toilet seat or in copulation. Its demands upon the soul's tolerance were never ending. This set her to wondering a little about Heaven and whether the soul could possibly transport with it the familiar shape of the body. She hoped not. It would be better to flow as a trail of vapor, a breath of wind or an unseen fragrance.

On a mahogany taboret, inlaid with mother of pearl, there was a bottle of amber-colored rum, a glass and a small pitcher of water. Beside these things, centered on a narrow silver tray, was a darkly rich panatela. In circumference it was no larger than a cigarette but almost three times as long. She reached for it, moistened one tip with a touch of her tongue and then held a flame to the blunt end until it was evenly fired. She drew upon it, inhaling deeply with a sensuous pleasure, and allowed the smoke to dribble from half-parted lips with her eyes closed.

Madame Cleo Dessaline was ninety years old and she had yielded nothing but her youth to time. Her prejudices and opinions were as fixed as they had been at twenty. The gown she wore was of flowing crepe, gathered into a high bosom in the style of the Empire. Small sandals of soft, gold-tinted leather were on her feet and her white hair was arranged in curls and ringlets. She used only the faintest trace of coloring on her cheeks and this was a carmine paste, sent to her from France in tiny china pots. It had been compounded to her order seventy years ago, perfumed with a private scent and the formula kept on file in Paris. Her skin was clear, though no longer tight, and it had taken upon itself a limonite tint, the color of fine meerschaum when infrequently smoked.

She opened her eyes, half turned and poured a small drink of rum. The label on the bottle bore a curious resemblance to the way she had looked as a girl. The figure held a tray on which were filled glasses. Beneath the drawing, in fine script were the words:

La Belle Dessaline.

In block letters, at the top of the label, was the inscription:

She held the glass to the light and watched the sun's rays sparkle through the liquid. Then she sipped it slowly and with appreciative satisfaction.

It did not occur to her that to a stranger she would have presented the slightly startling spectacle of an old woman tippling alone and smoking a strong cigar. These were the things she had been doing for years on a Sunday after Communion and her soul was purged.

The *macayo* screamed again, this time a note of warning. Madame Dessaline glanced down the shadowy length of the arbor and watched as her granddaughter walked through the tawny light toward her. Ferris. Madame Dessaline thought this was a ridiculous name. She had never known a girl named Ferris. To her mind it was only another evidence of the peculiarities of the British. Their unadmitted ego so frequently manifested itself in the preposterous habit of burdening a daughter with the mother's family name. If her son had married a French girl it was certain the child would have been more properly called.

The girl was coming from the pool at the back of the garden. In her hand she carried a jacket of white, absorbent cloth and a rubber bathing cap. The suit she wore was little more than a diaper and a narrow bandeau holding full, hard breasts. The sun had tanned her to a dark, resin color. She was a lithe, vital animal; a sleek cat that had been warming itself on a pad. Watching her Madame Dessaline tried to remember how it had felt to be twenty-two. But, she concluded, what Ferris Dessaline felt at twenty-two could have no possible relation to the sensations of Cleo Dessaline at the same age. It was impossible to imagine Ferris permitting her fine body to be laced into stays; fainting with maidenly delicacy in a moment of minor crisis; blushing when spoken to by a gallant young man; tapping a suitor lightly on the wrist with a fan as a rebuke to his impetuousness. Madame Dessaline and Ferris were of different planets. It surprised the old lady, sometimes, that they were able to communicate with each other in the common languages of English, French and San Rafael's bastard Spanish. Or, for that matter, that they could be nourished by the same foods, breathe the same air and walk upon the same ground.

Ferris Dessaline took the island of San Rafael as though it were her own. She strode upon it with a breezy freedom and drove a bright red Mercedes through its streets with a reckless and proprietary air. Moored at a slip at the Yacht Club's basin was a speedboat, lean and wicked-looking as a garfish. In it she cruised the coves of the island or roared out through the harbor entrance to sea, cutting wide circles about an incoming cruise ship or a plodding freighter. Half naked she seemed to ride the craft as a mermaid upon a sportive dolphin. The few eligible young men of San Rafael were treated by her in a carefree, almost amused, manner. She beat most of them unmercifully on the tennis courts and golf links, outswam and outfished them. Oddly enough, they appeared to suffer no embarrassment. She was coldly contemptuous of The Benefactor's police and the traffic squads managed to be engaged with other duties when she roared down the *avenidas* or parked in restricted zones.

Watching her approach now Madame Dessaline thought how beautiful she was and, in a way, envied her the freedom of this age. Even had she wished to try, Madame Cleo could not have adjusted herself to a world so radically changed. Even here, on this remote island in the Caribbean, a noisy vulgarity had intruded and she could accept no part of it. Upon the rare occasions when she ventured into the startlingly modern business sections of San Rafael she rode in her carriage with driver and liveried footman, and a maid on a small, folding seat facing her. She refused to enter a store. The item or items which she wished to examine, and possibly purchase, must be brought to her by the proprietor and not a clerk. The old, established merchants humored her in this. The employees in newer shops merely regarded her with astonishment and Madame Dessaline struck them from the list of those to whom she gave her custom.

Beneath the arbor Ferris halted to snip a blossom from one of the vines and tuck it behind her ear. For her grandmother she had a genuine affection. She was even secretly awed by the old lady's refusal to accept the twentieth century. This, she understood, was no frightened withdrawal to a musty corner but defiance. She turned her back on it as she might a rude tradesman. A few old and trusted friends still inhabited Madame Cleo's world. They were drawn from the families whose homes occupied the green hills. They came to her teas, her small receptions and occasional dinner parties as part, Ferris thought, of a secret ritual, the observances of which were known only to themselves. They were characters in a period piece, animate figures from a waxworks. In their manners and speech there was a stately elegance. They were immutable in a transitory world. These were the landed people, the holders of vast estates in cane, timber and tobacco, and they all lived in quiet apprehension of this upstart who called himself *el presidente*; a man of dubious lineage who appropriated what he wanted at the point of a bayonet. Socially they ignored him, hoping their quiet disapproval would, somehow, cause him to vanish.

The Benefactor made no effort to propitiate, reassure or cultivate and enlist the support of this stubborn, resentful core of aristocracy. He let them think what they would. If his background was veiled in mystery he permitted it to remain so.

The island society was liberally marbled and there was a complete range of color degrees from white to the deep blue-black of Nigeria. Few families of standing on San Rafael cared to examine too carefully their own genealogy. French and English buccaneers had landed here and mated casually. Soldiers of the early Spanish garrisons had taken native Carib girls on the hot, white sands of the beach or in the tangled scrub. A Negro slave had later planted his seed in the results of those unions. Sturdy English stock, members of Royalist families who had fled the American colonies during the Revolution, settled here, married or consorted. Members of old French houses who had run from the black fury of Haiti found refuge, a new life, wives and mistresses. The men had taken the black, the white, the *mestiza*. It was even rumored, maliciously of course, that the clear-featured daughter or wife of a Bourbon or English squire had not been above finding pleasure in the great, corded strength of a plantation slave. Yankee trading ships had dropped anchor in the port. Crew and officers had gone ashore to carouse with the waterfront girls and propagated. Many restless and unhappy soldiers of the Confederacy had wandered from their defeat and settled here. The fertile seed of life was divided and split again and again. Nourished by the warm sun it had proliferated without end. Out of this hot cauldron had boiled the few families of wealth and property. They took the land and its bounty as a birthright. There were wide-flung *estancias* on which were bred fine cattle; plantations in cane and indigo, distilleries from which flowed the bright rum; mines yielding copper, gold and silver. The sons and daughters of the fortunate were sent to France and England for their education.

The concept of an island republic was maintained in an uneasy state of balance and the scales were frequently upset by men of ambition. The President and the legislators were voted into office by a minority—the owners of the large estates, the mines and plantations. No sooner was an elected representative seated but someone schemed to oust him. There were constant upheavals, small revolutions, a scattering of gunfire in which a few peons were killed or wounded. One president was thrown out and another took his place. These abortions of government were intramural. The entrenched and the opposition were always members of an established family. No interloper intruded. If General André Laurentrec threw General Garcia out of the palace it mattered little, since both were *patrons* and gentlemen. They could be counted on not to steal too much or bear too heavily upon the privileged. They tapped sources of graft which did not impinge too directly on the landowners, finding new revenue in customs duties and taxes on the disenfranchised. These interludes of violence were tolerantly regarded as events of a sporting nature. The victor always gave a great ball for the vanquished; if he didn't display a petty nature and have him exiled or shot. If exiled the defeated was graciously permitted to take his family and loot with him. If shot it was done with full military honors.

"The Benefactor" had ignored the etiquette of the situation. He had come to power, springing like an unexpected genie from a lackadaisical revolution against the too-open looting of a senile general. By what now seemed a sorcerer's magic Ojeda had made the small, badly equipped army his own. He marched upon the capital, lined General Romero and his cabinet against a wall and had them shot. He then executed Romero's opposition and the island of San Rafael was his.

Now no one knew what to expect. No less, certainly, than the worst. Ojeda had put into operation plans for a general reduction of the great estates and a division of the land among the people. When he wanted something he took it: a mine, a distillery, an interisland shipping line, a refinery, all utilities, supervision of private bank deposits together with the banks themselves.

In the beginning there had been a show of resistance. The owners of the huge estates forgot their private differences and pooled their resources. Arms and a small counterrevolutionary force were gathered on the Gulf ports of the United States and were smuggled into San Rafael. Guns were put into the bewildered grasp of field hands and they were assured it was their duty to fight for liberty. They took this to mean that they wouldn't have to work any more and promptly fled to the hills with the rifles of revolution.

As dispassionately as he might have planned a campaign against the breeding pools of malarial mosquitoes Ojeda rounded up the revolutionists and their leaders. They were shot without trial as being dangerous to the peace and security of San Rafael's republic.

The peons, after exhausting their ammunition on the wild pigs, monkeys, small deer and each other in the mountains, drifted back to the capital city with their empty rifles already fouled and rusting through neglect. They surrendered to the police with many expressions of polite gratitude for the small vacation and waited to be told what to do. They were either recruited into The Benefactor's growing army or sent back to the fields to work for the glory and profit of the state.

Ojeda courted foreign capital and investment, particularly American. The island and its population was a bastion of democracy against the creeping blight of Communism. He wangled several million dollars in aid from the United States and expected more.

Whenever there seemed to be a wary or penny-pinching reluctance on the part of Washington to provide additional grants of money a surprising thing happened in San Rafael. The Communists demonstrated. An easily repaired corner of a minor public building was destroyed by a bomb. This same angle had been blown up so many times that only a very small bomb was needed. The segments broke away like pieces of a jigsaw puzzle but they made a fine scattering and several persons were always hurt by the flying masonry. These provided excellent photographs for the Associated Press. Placard-carrying students marched down the *avenidas* shouting their slogans: LONG LIVE THE SOVIET UNION. DOWN WITH YANKEE IMPERIALISM. The demonstrators gathered in front of the American Embassy and stoned the gates. They were always careful not to do any real damage to the residence itself. But there they were, hurling rocks and epithets at American property. The Associated Press photographer also took pictures of this. When they were printed in the United States, who could be so complacent as to deny that a Red threat existed on the country's doorstep?

In screenplay sequence The Benefactor's troops were shown quelling the Moscow-inspired riot. Screaming agitators were hauled into waiting *julias*. Grim-faced soldiers of the Republic of San Rafael held them at bay with bayonets. The American Embassy advised its Government that without Ojeda's strength and determination the Communists might occupy this island of strategic importance in the Caribbean. Moscow's guns would be trained on Miami or Palm Beach. It was only a matter of self-preservation, therefore, that The Benefactor be provided with additional millions, new weapons and some of those fast jets from the Air Force. Members of Congress thereupon crawled out from beneath the beds where they were hidden and promptly voted San Rafael more money and military aid.

Then, from Buenos Aires, Montevideo, Santiago and Rio came wounded screams. This small, insignificant island, it was pointed out, was receiving more American dollars than any of the real, good neighbors to the south. How come?

The Kremlin told everyone that Yankee gold supported a dictator, ignoring the true democracies. Peking warned all of Southeast Asia what was in store for them if they permitted themselves to be enslaved by American aid which was only a ruse, a wholesale conspiracy by American taxpayers to subjugate them and saddle the world with the Francos, the Peróns, the Batistas and Ojedas.

No one was really happy except Jorge Ojeda—*el presidente*, The Benefactor. He invited the American ambassador to lunch as proof of good relations and solidarity against The Reds.

It was not quite true that *el presidente* ignored San Rafael's old, established families. Once a month, on a Sunday, a reception was held on the grounds of the presidential palace. These fetes were attended by a select few of the more important Americans on the island; a group of Ojeda's ranking officers, their wives, sweethearts and mistresses; a few civilians of *el presidente's* selection. With a quiet humor few suspected of him Ojeda had impressive, engraved invitations delivered by hand to the dozen or so

[17]

families who occupied the ancestral homes on the hills. These were always politely refused by servants at the doors of the residences acting on the orders of their masters or mistresses. The couriers gravely returned the unsoiled envelopes and cards to *el presidente's* secretary. They were carefully put away, to be used again a month later.

On this Sunday morning Ferris Dessaline strolled to where her grandmother was seated, perched herself on the arm of a chair, dug a pack of cigarettes from her jacket, lit one and eyed her grandmother with a friendly wink.

"*Que tal, chica?*" This was an easy impudence. "You look like an old rip, sitting there swigging rum and smoking seegars!"

"They settle my stomach. Communion always unnerves me. Confession, also. On Fridays I never seem able to impress Father Bernado with my small sins. He gives me such insignificant penance. I become quite discouraged at times."

"Why don't you try taking from the Bishop?" A long, brown leg swung with limp grace. "Maybe he can come up with something new."

Madame Dessaline ignored the flippant suggestion. They had reached a guarded state of truce in matters of the Church. Although her mother had embraced the faith when she married André Dessaline the daughter had refused to consider this binding on her. She and Bishop Mendoza frequently indulged themselves in long argument which the priest seemed to enjoy despite her heretical challenges. She had told him she would as readily put her trust in voodoo drums as his Latin chanting. She declared she saw no difference between the mysterious rites in the hills and the goings-on in his cathedral. They both had the same ends in view. A chicken's blood and the cup of wine had much in common. Miraculously, Madame Dessaline thought, the Bishop wasn't offended. He came to tea frequently. Ferris suggested this was because her grandmother made such large contributions to the Church. It was one thing to have a dutiful daughter of the faith. It was quite another to have one who was reverent, wealthy and generous.

Ferris took a long drag on the cigarette. "I'm going to *el presidente's* fiesta today."

"Why?"

If Madame Dessaline was surprised by the declaration the emotion was concealed with a bland question. She moistened the panatela's tip again in the rum and watched the *macayo* as the bird made an attempt to stand on its head.

"I don't really know; curious, I guess." Ferris had expected a sharp protest. "You don't mind?"

"I suspect he is an outright murderer who uses the safety of the Republic as a cover for his deeds. He is also an opportunist and a reckless freebooter. Do those things excite your curiosity?"

"In a way." Ferris was honest. "As the movements and habits of any predatory animal are interesting. That's why we go to the zoo. I wonder why he doesn't just sack San Rafael, as any pirate would, and clear out with the swag. That's what most of his predecessors did. Why is he different? Why does he stay when he must know any number of persons would be delighted to kill him if given the chance?"

Madame Dessaline permitted the smallest of smiles to touch her lips. "Simply stated: I imagine he enjoys the sensation of power. Most of us find it irresistible."

Ferris shook her head doubtfully. "I don't believe it is that simple. I shouldn't think it would be enough. If I get a chance I'm going to ask him." She stood up and shrugged into the jacket.

Madame Dessaline's eyes brightened with quiet amusement. "I'm at an age when gossip remains almost my sole vice. Ask him for me if it is true he is charging San Martin, Morillo and Torralba and the strumpets they brought with them a thousand dollars a day, American, for permitting them to stay in San Rafael." She laughed softly. "That I would really like to know. It is an ironic jest."

It was a matter of rumor, freely circulated and generally believed, that The Benefactor was charging his reluctant guests this extraordinary sum and that they had, unwittingly, become semi-prisoners of *el presidente's* wry humor. The trio had fled to the Republic for sanctuary. Two, Morillo and Torralba, from countries in South America where they had ruled and looted for years as ruthless dictators until ousted by a counterrevolution. The third, San Martin, had barely escaped with his life from a neighboring island in the Caribbean when the army revolted. With each of them came a small entourage and their strikingly blond mistresses. Ojeda had accorded them no formal welcome. They were permitted to remain on San Rafael but at the price of their purses and dignity. He treated them with an amused contempt, restricted their movements on the island, accorded them none of the protocol they expected and charged them outrageously while they brooded and made elaborate plans for a triumphal return to their own countries.

"Why don't you come with me and ask him yourself?" Ferris picked up the bottle of rum and inspected the familiar label. "I wonder why he has never appropriated the Dessaline distillery; this house and the estate with it?"

"Not because he is unaware of their existence, you may be sure. I suspect he wants to digest what he has already stolen before gobbling up more. It is characteristic of the feral nature. No thank you. I prefer to remain here, swigging rum, as you say, and smoking my cigar."

The girl bent and touched her lips lightly to her grandmother's cheek. "I'll remember everything that's said and done and give you a full report over *la cena*." She turned and walked toward the house, through the darkly tangled beauty of the garden.

Madame Dessaline watched her, admiring the free stride and confidence of her bearing, the unaffected acceptance of a striking beauty. André Dessaline and his British-born wife had both been killed in an airplane accident in the mountains when Ferris was four years old. Since that time the two of them had come to depend much upon each other although neither would have admitted to this fact. Ferris had been sent to school in New York and, later, in France. She had returned willingly to San Rafael and expressed no desire to go abroad again save for an occasional flight to Miami for shopping during the winter. She apparently was not restive under the insular restrictions of San Rafael. Madame Dessaline wondered, sometimes, why she hadn't married or even expressed a real interest in a man beyond how well he could shoot, play tennis, ride and dance. A little vaguely Madame Dessaline wondered if her granddaughter was what, in her day, had been described as a *good girl*. Then, sensibly enough, she decided it was none of her business.

The *macayo* shrieked its irritation over her lack of attention and began to tear at the wisteria blossoms with a wickedly sharp beak.

"You are," Madame Dessaline repeated, "a silly bastard." She tipped the rum bottle to refill her small glass.

III.

HE stood for a moment, studying his reflection in the long glass. Behind him the manservant made a few unnecessary touches with finger tips at the shoulders of the white silk jacket and then stepped back with a quick smile of pride as though he had created both the man and the clothes he wore.

"It is all right, *joven?*" Jorge Ojeda turned to face him.

"Yes, Excellency." The valet canted his head slightly in an attitude of critical appraisal and then nodded. "It is well."

Ojeda walked to where the doorlike windows were open to the afternoon and stared down into the garden. Servants were moving unhurriedly, arranging the tables, the chairs and brightly striped umbrellas for the guests who would be arriving soon. For some reason they always seemed delighted by these fiestas although they meant extra work. He never understood why.

"Do you like being a valet?" He spoke without turning and wondered to himself what had prompted the question.

"It is better than being a soldier." The man shrugged. "Anything is better than being a soldier." He filled a small glass with the pale, straw-colored sherry and brought it to Ojeda on a tray. "Do you like being *el presidente?*"

There was no insolence in the question. They frequently spoke to each other in this fashion when there was no one to hear.

"Sometimes." Ojeda sipped the wine, savoring its fine dryness. "It is better than having someone else make the mistakes." He peered into the glass. "When we used to lie in the hills with only a few men and rifles, a machine gun which didn't always work and some grenades not to be trusted . . . did you dream then we would be here, in the palace?"

"I used to dream of women. That is all. A fine, plump girl to keep me warm at night. It is better to dream of the things you know about: a girl, a drink, a full belly."

Ojeda finished the wine and put the glass on the tray.

The man brought a box of polished ebony and ceremoniously held back the lid. The box was lined with cedar and half filled with cigars. Ojeda studied them critically and finally selected one. His fingers moved over the silken texture of the fine wrapper and his eyes noted the slightly mottled color with its flecks of green. He pressed it, feeling the thick firmness.

"Did you know my father was a cigar maker?"

"No, *jefe.*" The man held a light, cupped within a shell of his hands. "You have told me many things but not that."

Ojeda had to bend slightly as he took the fire to the cigar's end although the man's arms were stretched high.

"By hand, as these are made." The fragrance of the Havana clouded about them. "Not in a mold or by machines, you understand, but with the mind, the heart, and sensitive fingers feeling for perfection. Each one was a little piece of art and he the artist. He coughed a great deal as he grew older and died of consumption. Most of the cigar makers did."

The valet carefully replaced the humidor on a table and refilled the glass with *Manzanilla* which came to them in casks from Spain. It was his habit to listen and go about his duties at the same time. They both understood this was no calculated rudeness.

"Have you ever been in Tampa, *joven?*"

"I have never been any place but San Rafael, *jefe.*"

"It is in Florida. That was where my father made cigars. He sat at a little bench all day, bent over it as a jeweler works. To his left were the stacks of leaves with the center stems removed. They were slightly dampened always to keep them soft. These were the binders and wrappers. At his right hand were the long shreds, the *bonchero*. He worked with his fingers as a musician playing upon his instrument. They use a knife, a crescent-shaped tool sharp as a razor blade. With it he would cut and trim so quickly, so expertly the movement was a flash of sunlight. He was proud of what he did. Never did he make a second; *de segunda clase*, you understand? A mistake which, because of its imperfection, is sold cheaper. He was an artist."

"And he died coughing the blood from his lungs?"

"That is the way it was. That is how he died."

"It makes a man wonder." The valet made the statement absently as he glanced about the room to see that everything was in order. "It is something upon which to think, *verdad?*"

"What does? What makes a man wonder?"

"Whether such perfection is worth the price. Is it right a man should spit out his lungs because he sits all day at a bench making cigars of the first class? Machines do not cough up their blood and the cigars look as good and taste as well."

"Machines have no heart, no pride in their work. There is a difference."

"Not enough to die for. I wouldn't think so."

The valet drew up a deep chair, placing it within an oblong of sunlight where it fell upon the floor through the window. Then he stood behind it, stiffly at attention because he had an unadmitted pride in serving *el presidente*. No one had told him to do this and Ojeda, noting the gesture, smiled to himself.

"Will you sit here for a while, Excellency? It is early."

Ojeda nodded and settled himself comfortably. He heard the man move across the room and close the door softly. He was alone. In a little while he would have to go down and receive his guests. Until then it would be pleasant just to sit here. Half-forgotten things had been recalled by the mention of his father. He shut his eyes, allowing memory and fancy to play their tricks. It was as though an unseen hand began moving little pieces of his life around, joining them together the way one did with a puzzle. Pictures, scenes and incidents emerged without any continuity although each had a relation to the whole. The mind behaved as a hummingbird, darting from plant to plant, never quite satisfied but finding a little nourishment and stimulation in each.

He was a boy at the age of sixteen and the year was 1930, a time of great depression which no one understood but which gripped them all in a quiet terror. The city was Tampa and a district of it was known as Ybor City. In this section the customs, habits, and even the speech were alien to the brisk city which enclosed it. To this place had drifted the men and women of several nationalities. They had come legally or otherwise from Cuba or in small boats across the Gulf from Mexico's eastern ports. There were Puerto Ricans and a scattering of families of Spanish and Greek descent with strains of African Negro in them. The blood lines had crossed and recrossed so many times no one could be sure of anything save they were all casually lumped together as *spicks* or niggers by the illiterate whites and even those who should have known better. A curious form of speech, used only among themselves, had developed over the years. It was compounded of English and Spanish and variations in dialect of both. Along the Texas border, in the towns on both sides of the Rio Grande, they call a similar blending of languages *pochismo*. It is part English, part Spanish and words will be coined to combine the elements of each. Such a phrase as "lunch counter" becomes a *loncheria* because the sound of this falls more pleasantly upon the ear. The game of miniature golf when it flourished was spoken of in a coined diminutive as *golfito* and an automobile became a *caro*. So it was that here in Ybor City the idiom and accent were almost unintelligible to those who lived beyond the crowded blocks of the neighborhood.

Ojeda could remember no other home but this although his father had told him he had been born in Key West. He was a man who talked but little and then rarely about himself. He never said by what means they had come to this city or why. During the years until he was sixteen Jorge Ojeda had been sent to a parochial school, a dingy building seemingly grim of purpose, where the Sisters were unsmilingly zealous and unrelenting in their determination to impart an education to reluctant children. The playground was a large square of concrete surrounded by a high wire fence. Such games as tag and baseball were noisy and bloody affairs, with skinned knees, cheeks and elbows from the abrasive surface regarded highly as badges of prowess. Early in his school days Jorge learned that to survive it was never important to fight more than one boy. You picked out the biggest, the toughest, and went at him in a flying tangle of arms and fists. It wasn't necessary to win. The mere fact you fought the leader was enough to engender a respect. This one beating saved you from a hundred lesser engagements. It was a small kernel of knowledge he put away to be remembered as he grew older.

In the evenings there were games of stickball in the narrow streets beneath the yellow electric lights, and a gathering on the corners to watch the men as they went into houses where phonographs blared and girls sometimes stood half naked in the windows behind soiled lace curtains. It was a time to watch the automobiles from uptown come to the district and park in front of a restaurant which had achieved a fame outside the neighborhood for its *paella* or lamb cooked in a Greek style with olive oil and white beans. Sometimes a dime could be earned by being first with an offer to watch the car while the tourists were inside. Then, also, there were errands to be run for the girls who waited outside the small cribs and wanted a note delivered to their pimps in the poolrooms or for a package of cigarettes from a store on the corner. As a boy grew older he grew wiser in many things. The most important of these was that there is little room for compassion in the world which surrounded him. To survive you must be tougher or smarter. It was better if you could be both. The rewards of small dishonesties were in direct proportion to the acts. A thief who broke a window and snatched a handful of gaudy trinkets, imitation diamond rings or cheap watches was usually caught. Salvatore Oretega, who sold pints of whisky from the back room of his store, was sent to jail. The men who brought it to the beaches by the boatload were big enough to make their deals with federal officers and were not bothered. The little whore who solicited on the streets was picked up but Fat Mama, who owned three big houses patronized by the men from uptown, went unmolested. Growing older Jorge Ojeda decided this was a natural and logical scheme of things. Time after time he saw it proved. The world was filled with slobs and only an idiot would want to be their brother.

The Ojedas occupied three rooms over the shop where Jorge's father and two assistants made the cigars. These were bought by the wealthy and before the year of 1930 they seemed without limit. The hand-crafted products, made with care and of the finest tobacco, were packed in boxes of twenty-five and sold for that number of dollars. They were shipped to a standing list of customers all over the country and never placed in the hands of jobbers or any of the retail stores in Tampa.

It was a time, in those days before 1930, when life was simple. Those who wanted work had jobs. The girls and women were employed as maids, cooks and cleaning women in the hotels and private homes. The men were gardeners, porters, drivers of trucks, laborers in the freight and express offices. Innumerable small businesses flourished in the district of Ybor City; shoemakers, restaurants, small grocery stores redolent with the odors of cheese and sausages, olive oil and peppers. No matter that the neighborhood contained half a dozen mixed nationalities. They pooled their fiestas and holidays. A street was roped off for dancing. Sidewalk stalls were temporarily set up on the curbs and they sold everything from *tacos* to fried fish, purple and green iced cookies, soda water and a concoction of rum, pineapple juice and slices of green lime floating on the dark surface. Everyone knew about prohibition but few paid any attention to it and the authorities rarely intruded into these purely local celebrations.

Ojeda's mother was a woman well over six feet tall; a Haitian who habitually wore brightly colored shapeless dresses which fell in a straight line to her ankles. She never wore shoes, indoors or out. Two hoops of gold hung from her ears and her head was wrapped in a yellow bandana. There was such a great dignity about her that no one ever whispered or snickered at the barbaric appearance she made when striding down the street to market or when, returning, she balanced a huge basket piled with her purchases atop her head. It was whispered she could cast spells and when, as she sometimes did, she cursed a tradesman in her argot French of the island, the man would tremble because the unfamiliar speech must be the words of the devil. She was much sought after by girls who wanted love charms made or furtive men who wanted to get rid of a shrewish wife. It was said she could make a doll, stick a pin in it, and the victim for whom it was intended would die of a great pain in that very spot. No one ever actually saw her do this. To the girls who wanted a love charm she would laugh, a rich pleased sound, and say there was one ready-made between the supplicant's legs.

Jorge could never remember that his mother had ever held or kissed him; although this must have happened. Yet, he did not recall her as a fierce or indifferent woman. She sang often to herself or to him and laughed when happy about something. But, and he understood now he had somehow been dimly aware of this at an early age, her laughter was inspired by things within herself. It bubbled from some secret well and had nothing to do with what someone said or did. There was about her the containment and confidence of a strong animal forced by circumstances to herd with a lesser breed. She tolerated them; nothing more. And held herself with a stately pride, splendid in her black majesty.

He could wonder now what tied his mother and father together for they seemed to have little in common beyond the food they ate, the bed they shared. Yet there was no sullen resentment, no outbursts of furious anger. They never fought as did the neighboring men with their women or drank themselves into a screaming rage born of desperation over finding themselves trapped. There was a silent communion understood by themselves alone. In the evenings his father would come upstairs from the shop. He carried with him always the spicy fragrance of the tobacco with which he worked. A little smile would light his features as he watched the woman in the kitchen, her bare feet making a soft, slapping sound on the linoleum as she moved from stove to table. At the sink his father would pour an old jelly glass half full of rum, add a few drops of water and stand sipping it while his eyes followed her movements with a quiet pleasure. Then they would eat and the meal was taken in silence, but it was a silence of understanding and not of constraint. Now and then his father would ask him small questions about school; what he was learning, how he had spent the day. The queries were made, not in a tone of parental authority, but with the casual interest of a man who meets a friend after a period of separation and asks what he has been doing.

After the meal they continued to sit about the kitchen table. His father read the newspapers; one in Spanish and one in English. Jorge would bend over his schoolbooks. His mother, when the dishes were washed, took her place in an uncushioned rocking chair. Beside her, on the floor, was a pile of slender reeds with dabs of color here and there along their length. With them she would weave a basket, the colors miraculously meeting each other at just the right places and forming a design. She sold these to a man who had a little shop down the street or traded them for a piece of bright-colored material to be worn about her neck as a scarf.

The woman had never called her son by his name. She spoke to him saying: Boy. It was her name for him and not a thing said angrily or with impatience. Sometimes, when he came home early from school, he would take a seat on a high stool in the kitchen and watch with interest as she put together the things for their supper. Her big hands working deftly with a rough stone mortar and pestle, grinding the spices into a pungent mound. When they were to have the chicken, cooked with tomatoes, peppers, oil and saffron rice, the killing of the fowl became almost a mystic rite which he observed from his perch on the stool.

His mother was contemptuous of the plucked and dressed chickens in the market and would buy only a live bird. This, in itself, was something in the nature of a ceremony. She would select one from a tethered bunch held by a countrywoman who brought them to the district each Monday. She examined its eyes and pried open the beak. She studied the color of the feet and pinched it here and there, pulling away a few feathers to test the tenderness of the skin. When she was satisfied she carried the bird home, swinging it by the legs as she might a sack while the chicken croaked its dismal terror.

Ojeda smiled a little to himself now as he remembered her elaborate preparation for the killing of a chicken. Most women simply held a bird to a wooden block and with one stroke of a cleaver cut off the head. In an unprecedented moment of garrulousness she explained to him one day why this was a bad way to kill a chicken. It seemed that the fowl, mysteriously knowing what was about to happen, tightened itself against the stroke of the blade. This made it tough. The muscles never relaxed, even in death. The best way to kill a bird was to get it a little drunk first. With her fingers she would force the beak open and carefully pour a teaspoonful of rum down its gullet. This induced a state of indifference. The chicken was relaxed. When its throat was slit over the sink it was limp. "He jus' don' give no damn what happen'." The blood had spurted over her hands, dripping into a bowl. "He sof', tender an' good to eat now. He die real happy an'" that more than happen to mos' people." It never occurred to him to question her wisdom.

Only at such times, when he watched as she worked at the stove or above the sink, did he feel a cord existed between them. She would talk in her soft, musically cadenced speech, telling him stories of her girlhood on the island. These and the tale of the king Christophe who called himself King Henry and built a great fort and castle on the top of Cap Ferrieré. "No one call Christophe nigger. He walk upon the lan' lak Emperor. He kill a thousan' men, maybe, to carry the rock up that mountain to make a castle an' then he spit down on whole worl'. He shoot the big gun an' the white people go runnin'. An' "—she would break into great laughter—"the white say Whooee! Who that mans mek lak God?" She had stared at him intently then. "You go back to island sometime, Boy. You be king if you want. I gots the feelin'."

She had said this with such intensity that a small, cold prickle rippled over his skin and he wondered, for a moment, if it was true she could peer into the future and see what waited there.

Until he was sixteen and the terrible blight of insecurity and fear struck everyone like a killing frost he felt his life was full and rich. There were beaches of powdery sand from which to swim and the summers were long and filled with a delicious idleness. A neighbor, a squat Greek who also wore earrings of gold, was a fisherman and owned his own boat. With his two sons he combed through the Gulf's waters with a seine for the shrimp as they traveled in great shoals. Now and then he would invite Jorge and they lived, ate, worked and slept on the stubby craft for two or three days at a time. They cruised in waters with such fine-sounding names as Boca Ciega Bay, Long Pine and Mullet Keys and once, as far north as Tarpon Springs where a colony of Greek fishermen, their boats splashed with vivid colors, took sponges from the bottom.

Beyond the limits of the city there were great stretches of piny flatlands dotted with palms, towering pines, scaly oak and clumps of scrub palmetto. There were dark and mysterious reaches of the Hillsboro River to be explored where the trees were draped with Spanish moss and it was easy to pretend they were the skeletons of Spanish soldiers still wearing their tattered coats of mail. There were squirrels and rabbits to be hunted with a single-shot rifle of twenty-two caliber or a hawk to be knocked down as it rested on a high branch. It was a time when the body grew tough and lean, the legs tireless, the mind inquisitive, alert and filled with a thousand fancies and dreams.

Once a week he went to a residential district known as Seminole Heights where he had a job. He earned a dollar for a day's work and was given his lunch in the kitchen where he ate with the Negro cook. He mowed the lawn, trimmed the hedge, watered the flowers, washed the car and did whatever odd jobs came to the mind of his employer, who was a widow by the name of Mrs. Waters. He would wait for her at the back door of the house, knowing what was to be done and eager to get about doing it. Mrs. Waters, though, liked to tell him, reading the chores from a little book as though he were a strange boy coming to work for the first time. She called him Georgie. Once he had politely tried to correct her. The name was Jorge and pronounced *hor-gay*. Mrs. Waters had laughed with a bright tolerance. Jorge, she pointed out, couldn't possibly be anything but Georgie and it was a ridiculous eccentricity to imagine spelling it as he did made Jorge anything but "jor-gee." So she continued to call him Georgie and he, because it was now something of a game, always said *hor-gay* under his breath. They got along splendidly with this arrangement.

A mile or so away from the Waters' home was a deep, clear sulphur spring. From the center the water roiled gently as it flowed from somewhere deep in the ground. The pool was a couple of hundred yards in circumference and the owner had put up a fence, a few benches and bathhouses where, for twenty-five cents, clothes could be changed. Through the fence he could see boys and girls his own age diving from the boards, swimming through the water which was so clear each detail of the bottom could be seen. They lay about on pallets in the sun and their skin was tanned to the color of the tobacco leaves with which his father made the cigars.

This Saturday he had brought a bathing suit with him to work and in the late afternoon, when he had finished his chores, he went to the springs and put his twenty-five cents down on the counter of a little booth where a man sold tickets. The man had regarded him intently.

"You a nigrah, boy?" He asked the question softly.

"No."

"You suah as hell look like a nigrah to me. What's youah name?"

Jorge told him, pronouncing it carefully in Spanish.

"Ef you ain't a nigrah you got to be a Mex with a name like that. You oughta know damn good an' well you ain't allowed to swim here with white people. Now why the hell don' you jus' git along an' cause no trouble." He pushed the coin back across the ledge.

Jorge felt the hot, salty scalding of tears in his eyes and he bit upon a lip to keep his mouth from trembling. He had never thought of himself as a Negro nor his mother, black as she was, as one. She was French. Haitians were darker skinned than other people but they weren't Negroes. Negroes were Africans and their people had been slaves.

"I'm Spanish. Spanish and French." He didn't want to argue or explain. He wanted to leave this place and put behind him the indifferent contempt he could see in the man's face. "My name's Ojeda. No Negro has a name like that." He thrust his hands into his pockets so the man wouldn't see how they were shaking. "Don't you know the difference?"

"Ah know Ahm goin' to have to run youah ass down the road ef you keep standin' theah an' givin' me an argument." The man was angrily impatient. "Now take youah money an' git on about whatever you got to do." He flipped at the quarter and it spun out to fall upon the ground.

Jorge Ojeda wanted that quarter. He had worked hard to earn it. It lay there at his feet and he could not force himself to bend and pick it up. Beyond the ticket window he could see the boys and girls as they laughed, chased each other, tumbled into the water. Daily exposure to the sun had tanned them until their skin was actually darker than his. No one had ever questioned his blood before; even on the streetcars or buses where seats were marked COLORED and WHITE he had sat where it had pleased him. He turned to stare at the man.

"You goin' to pick up that two-bits?" There was a wicked hatred in the man's eyes now.

"No, you son of a bitch. I'm not going to pick it up." He made the answer quietly. "I wouldn't pick it up if it was the last quarter in the world." He turned from the window.

Every instinct told him to run. He heard a crash as the man within the booth overturned the chair on which he had been sitting. He walked slowly with his head up but he was crying now and could almost taste the vomit in his mouth as his stomach retched and heaved. He walked, waiting for the blow which would send him sprawling.

"You nigrah bastard." He heard the scream of fury behind him. "Ef Ah evah catch you aroun' heah again I'm gonna stomp youah black guts out. You heah me? You heah me, you mulatto son of a bitch?"

He wouldn't look back. He couldn't see the man as he stood just outside the booth yelling his rage, held there by an indecision he couldn't understand. The voice and what it shouted grew fainter and he knew the man wasn't coming after him but there was no satisfaction in this. He wiped at his eyes with a forearm. Drawing it away he studied the skin as though seeing it for the first time. It had a color. Of course it did. Everyone's skin bore a tint. Some was fair, creamy white and pink as that of a baby. There was freckled skin, yellow skin and skin with the appearance of watered milk. A boy he knew, Domingo Crispin, had skin the color of leather but he was not as dark as Jorge's mother who was undeniably black.

He pinched the skin on the back of one hand and watched it whiten where the blood was shut off. When he released the pressure it returned to normal. He couldn't find a word for this particular shade. It sure wasn't black. It wasn't brown, either. Maybe it was sort of an olive color or that of a russet apple. What he sought for didn't lie in the skin. Negroes were all colors. They were black; sometimes as black as shoe polish. They were tan, the shade of watery coffee or cocoa. He had never seen Negroes with red hair and freckles. What had that man seen in him he couldn't see? Why had he suddenly called him a nigger bastard? He felt his face, fingers moving inquisitively across lips and nose. There was nothing there; no heavy, flaring nostrils, no broad, flat structure, no thickening at the mouth. What had that Cracker son of a bitch found in his face he was unable to detect? If he was really a Negro that was one thing and it could be lived with once accepted. But he had never thought of his mother as a Negress even though she was black.

He hitched a ride on an empty ice truck and dropped off downtown. He began walking with a purpose, strolling and turning to study his reflection in every window. He stood on a scale in front of a candy store. Without putting in a penny he stared at himself in the circular mirror. He saw nothing he hadn't seen a hundred times before. He appeared no different from anyone who was behind him on the sidewalk. He studied them in the glass. Stepping from the platform he began moving again through the late afternoon crowd of shoppers and people coming from the early movies. He had walked here times without number before, familiar with every block and crossing. Now he experienced the sensation of being a stranger, an alien. Doubt and a fear he had never known had suddenly become his companions. Once, he caught himself on the point of stepping from the curb into the street as three men, talking earnestly and moving abreast, blocked his way. Instead, he slowed his pace imperceptibly and an unreasoning panic gripped him. Suppose they just kept walking? Suppose they looked up and saw a fresh, nigger son of a bitch who wouldn't move out of the way? A lump of terror, a sickening clot against which he swallowed helplessly, lodged in his throat. If they pushed him from the sidewalk he didn't know what he would do. He wanted to run but there was no strength in his legs; only an itching, cold sweat on his body. He almost screamed: Don't. Please don't. For God's sake, man, don't do it. At the last moment one of the trio glanced up. Without breaking his stride or losing a word of the conversation he automatically dropped in behind a companion and left a passageway for Jorge Ojeda, whose knees were on the point of collapsing. He cried softly to himself and there was no one to know or hear.

Now, everything he did on the way home assumed an importance. At a corner drugstore he turned in, went to the soda fountain and took a seat. Along the length of the counter there were people bent over their sodas or talking casually to each other as they lifted mouths from straws. He ordered a coke and waited fearfully. The soda jerk, in white jacket and with an envelope of cap on his head, flipped a glass in the air, scooped it in shaved ice and drew the coke indifferently. Jorge put down his nickel, reached out for the frosted glass and his hand shook so he couldn't lift it. He thought, I'm going to puke right here. He slid from the seat and almost ran from the store.

At the Greyhound Bus Terminal he tried to assume an air of purpose. Pushing through the revolving door he went to the WHITE section of the waiting room. At the newsstand he bought a pack of salted peanuts. At the rear, ranged on the benches which were marked COLORED, the Negroes waited beside their bundles and paper suitcases tied with string. They sat there in what seemed to him a dark, numb patience, neither talking nor showing any interest in their surroundings. For them now he felt a strange compassion, an understanding he had never known before.

He took a seat on a bench on which was stenciled: WHITE ONLY. Now, for no reason, he was ravenously hungry; greedily starving. He filled a palm with the salted nuts and chewed as though he had had no food for days. He ate with a ferocious compulsion and dropped the crumpled glassine bag on the floor at his feet.

"Boy!"

The voice, the authority in it, all but jerked him from the bench. He looked up in wide-eyed terror. A uniformed guard was glaring at him.

"Damn it, boy. Don't you have no more raisin' than to littah th' floah like that? Pick it up now an' put it en th' trash can like it belongs." He shook his head and walked away; a man weary with the careless habits of travelers.

In none of these things did Jorge Ojeda find a cause for elation. An illiterate Cracker with a mysterious instinct had seen something which, apparently, no one else saw; something about which he had never before thought. It had happened today and so, could happen again tomorrow or at a time when he would be completely unprepared and defenseless. He would have to make up his mind how it was going to be. Ybor City, with its mixture of bloods, was no test. Here, outside, was where he would have to face it. What was he? No, that wasn't the question. What did he want to be? That was simple; so simple it made him ashamed. He wanted to be Jorge Ojeda, a boy whose parents were Spanish and French and who lived in Ybor City because so many countrymen, also, lived there and not because his mother was black.

He climbed the dark staircase to the rooms above his father's shop and the flight had never before seemed so long and, at the same time, so short. He stood for minutes outside the door before putting his hand to the knob.

His mother turned from the stove, a wooden spoon at her lips. She blew softly upon the rich sauce and tasted it with approval. Then she smiled, not at him but over what she had made. There was, though, a warmth in her eyes which was for her son. Then, without a word of greeting, she went back to her cooking.

His father sat at a table working an awl through a leather belt on which he was fastening a silver buckle. He smiled and nodded with a gentle pleasure. Always he was happy when working with his hands. He was a frail man whose height was shortened by a hunched manner of standing or sitting. It was a posture resulting from years of bending over a bench. They looked much alike, this father and son, and there was a bond between them although neither could have given it a name.

"You're late." The man spoke to him in Spanish. There was no rebuke in the comment. A spasm of coughing which shook him with an uncontrollable violence had the dry, rasping sound of reeds being broken. He held a handkerchief to his mouth, glancing apologetically over it at Jorge and the woman.

"It is cold." He carefully balled the cloth in order no one would see how it was stained. "There is a draft at my bench. I must move it." He bent his head quickly and occupied himself again with the belt.

When supper was put upon the table they ate without talking but in a quiet spirit of companionship as it filled the small room as a warm glow. Jorge caught himself glancing at his mother's hands as she served their plates. Somewhere he had read or heard that the half-moons on the fingernails of a Negro were always a deep purple. He didn't know whether this was true but hers were light crescents. He watched the way she held herself and studied her face. The skin was black. There was no denying this. But her features were sharply and clearly drawn, as fine as his own or those of his father.

He kept his head bent over his plate, for when he asked what he must he didn't want to meet her eyes. His mind fumbled and sorted out the words. Then the question came simply, as it should.

"What are Haitians?"

The woman probed within the small iron kettle, set on an asbestos mat on the table. She spooned out a section of the fish, cooked in a hot red sauce, for herself and appeared not to have heard what had been asked. His father, though, looked up at him with a troubled frown.

"Do you not study of such things in the school? Did you ask the question there and what were you told?" He waited for Jorge to reply and when the boy only averted his head he continued. "Haitians are natives of Haiti as Spaniards are of Spain, Indians of India, Frenchmen of France."

"That ain' what he mean, Papa." She, who had apparently not been listening and had not lifted her gaze from the pot's contents, spoke softly. "Lak you know th' thing what make you cough ain' jus' a col'. Lak you say it ain' there an' it go away." She put the square of fish on her plate. "Someone call you nigger today, Boy?"

He nodded unhappily and because her voice was gentle, so filled with sympathetic understanding, he was afraid he was going to cry. More than that. He wanted to leave his chair and go to her side. There was an almost frightened desire to press against her, hiding there in a flight from a sudden loneliness. There was about her a huge, imperturbable strength and in it lay shelter from this misery.

"Nigger's a word." Never had he heard her voice so gentle. "It ain' a person, Boy. One black man say to other: Nigger, you're crazy. But it ain' th' same word lak white mans use when he say: Nigger, come here." She paused for it wasn't often she talked beyond a few sentences. "Now, en my islan' the black people come first as slave. They have English to masters an' French, also. Then they have big fight an' white masters get kill off. Slave turn out to be master. But of what? No one sure. Ol' Christophe, the way I tell you in story once, make himself King Henry. No one call him nigger then. They say: Yes, Your Majesty. Yes, Sir, Your Majesty." She laughed but there was no scornful satisfaction in the sound. It had a rich, gusty good humor. With a gesture which caused Jorge to look up in surprise she reached over and put her big hand on his. "You got th' look of Papa, Boy. By mystery you don' have no color lak mine. You can be what you want. Whatever it is, whichever away you want to go—white, black or mixed up with some of each. It for you to say. But, don' try to be black wit th' black an' then go to be white wit th' white. You ain' nothin' then. Be one or th' other an' don' feel no shame in what you decide. If you wan' say I'm all white, I ain' had no black woman for mother, I don' feel no hurt. I onerstan'. It ain' no real, good worl' to be black in lessen you gots th' pride in what you is lak Christophe had." She patted his hand and then took her own away. "You gots name Jorge Ojeda. Spanish name. Looks lak Spanish mans. Be Spanish mans. It maybe better fo' you that way." She paused, feeling her way. "Now, then; lak today, maybe, you find mans who got feelin' lak fox. He know chicken there even though can't see 'im. He goin' to say I smell nigger." She shrugged. "That a chance you take."

"This is not good talk to have between us." The man objected and his unhappy eyes rested for a moment on woman and boy. "I do not like what I have heard here tonight. Things are as they are. Jorge is blood of us both. You have been the best of all women for me and I do not want you hurt. In love we made him and he is what he is."

"Papa." She reached over and laid the back of her hand against his cheek. "You talk lak boy mekin' wit girl." Her laughter was throaty, pleased and tender. "Sooner or later what Boy asks come out. He gots to live with it not us." She began to eat with a hungry pleasure, her fine, square white teeth crunching through the hot crispness of a hard roll. "Boy gots to ask himself: What am I? Black or white. What I wants to be? Nothin' wrong in mans askin' himself that. It wrong only when he don' mekin' up mind."

And Jorge Ojeda, called nigger that day for the first time, made up his mind. Watching his mother, feeling the inarticulate sadness of his father, knowing what it was to walk Tampa's white streets in fear and cringing a little, he had already denied and betrayed them.

IV.

AND so, a time was now upon the land when those who had little had less and those with a great deal fretted and worried about how they would keep it. A frightening paralysis locked the spirit of a nation and the only treatment suggested was that of patience.

In the small shop where he had once worked in an easy fraternity with his employees, the *tabaqueros,* fashioning the fine cigars purchased by the wealthy, the man Ojeda sat alone and wondered what had happened. Dust gathered upon the floor and shelves. The boxes of smooth cedar wood were stacked and empty in a corner. No one would pay a dollar for a good cigar any more. They smoked the cheaper ones made by machines. Sometimes, he would move his hand over the surface of the smooth table. It was as a parent might caress an unhappy child, reassuring it wordlessly. How well he and the men had spent the hours here; they had used their skill with quiet pride. Even *el lector,* the one who was hired to come each day to read aloud from the Spanish newspaper and periodicals while the men bent above their work and listened, was honored to be associated with such craftsmen. Because of this he frequently added dramatic flourishes, pauses and a change of voice to his reading. The men listening, but never breaking the easy rhythm of their work, would murmur soft exclamations of astonishment over a particular bit of news or information. There would be a chorus: "Ay! Ay! Ay!" Muted but filled with a wonder that such a thing could be. Their hands moved with deft precision.

There was only the memory of other times and better days to bring Ojeda here now and he came each morning because he could no longer bear the empty rooms above. He had looked for work but had found nothing for which his delicate fingers were fitted. Also, the cough was worse and it shook him as a skeleton might be dangled on a wire. His skin had taken on a pallor; a waxy surface of a candle. Who would hire such a man? The boy, Jorge, had found a part-time job as a cleaner of toilets and basins, the mopping of a tile floor in one of the city's hotels. The woman did small bundles of laundry and traveled miles to do day work as a cleaning drudge. On what they earned and a pittance doled out from the treasury of the club to which he belonged, El Centro Español, they existed in a numb misery and went to bed each night hungry and awoke to the desperation of another morning.

In this helplessness a man could only sit at his empty table and stare vacantly through the window which had gathered a grimy crust. When the coughing came he would have to grip the table's edge for support, for its fury all but threw him from the chair. In the old days the passers-by would frequently stop and stand, gazing with rapt attention as cigars were made before their very eyes. Now no one halted and few even passed on the sidewalk outside. Often, when the humiliation of having his woman and son work to support him was an acid, burning away the soul, his hand would reach for the *chabeta,* the bright, sharp knife with which the tobacco leaves had been shaped. How simple it would be. Draw it with a steadiness across the throat and let the misery of his life fall in a crimson trickle upon the floor. Always he pushed the knife away. The terror of the unknown. The agony of purgatory for this mortal sin. He would be cast like a piece of meat into unconsecrated ground and no priest would speak the words for his soul. He was held from the act by this fear.

So, he coughed and spit and lay his head upon his arms on the workroom table. And then, one day, the woman had come home and had found him on the floor. The breath in him was but a tiny whistle. At the hospital the doctors had shaken their heads. They had said maybe. If he could be sent to the dry air in a faraway desert. If he could be fed well and taken care of. Then, maybe, for a few years more. They took him away to a ward of isolation, for even a poor cigar maker could not be left to die upon the street even in a time of depression. Because he had no will to live and the fever had burned away his lungs he died in a short time and his place in the ward was taken by another.

The club to which he had paid dues for many years and where he had played dominoes with his friends over cups of coffee with a little rum provided a good funeral. There was a hearse and a black limousine for the mourners, a priest, and later a headstone to mark where Tomas Ojeda lay. When they lowered him into the slit of earth the woman did not cry and the boy stood beside her until the shovelfuls of soil began to thud upon the coffin. Then they turned away in silence and went home.

In the quiet rooms the great, black woman who had loved this man and borne him a son rocked back and forth in a chair. She chanted her lamentation in a voice which slid from a minor key to the wild, shrill, keening note of a sea bird. What she sang in her grief was as old as Africa. It had sounded there and in the hills and peaks of Haiti and the words were those a white man would not know or even begin to understand. Listening, the boy Jorge was frightened and felt the dark unknown close about him. This was the time of a black woman's grief and he had nothing to offer in comfort. For three days she did not eat or sleep nor even know he sometimes stood beside her. Then the blankness lifted from her eyes. The rocking halted. The mystic threnody was stilled. She went to the stove, made coffee and drank its scalding bitterness.

Because he must keep the small job he had, Jorge had gone each day to the washroom of the hotel. A period of mourning was a luxury not to be risked. Too many others were eager for this work of cleaning after the filth men made. He did what he was supposed to do and was silently contemptuous of those who would walk away from an unflushed toilet. Even a dog, a mongrel cur, sometimes scratched the ground to cover what it had left. Not man. He left his dirt for others.

On this evening when he came home and climbed the worn staircase he heard his mother singing. There was a different note in her voice. It was as she had sung when the man was alive. She was in the kitchen and he noticed first the long dress of yellow with purple flowers imprinted upon it. A bright turban was wound about her head and the earrings, the golden hoops, swung and danced from the lobes of her ears. In the iron pot she had cooked a chicken and there was rice with its red beans and a plate of the long, dried, purple chilies to be crumbled over it all. There was even a small bottle of dark rum. She poured some for him.

"You man now. You take your drink lak Papa used to."

He drank the rum, adding a little water from a tap at the sink as his father had done. Then they sat down to the meal and ate without talking. When they had finished, the woman crossed her arms on the table and sat with her head bent for a few moments. Then she raised her eyes and he had the curious feeling they were strangers.

"You go 'way now, Boy." She spoke quietly and without emotion or emphasis. "You go to mek life of your own without black woman for mother." It was a soft order not a complaint.

"No." The rejection came automatically. Then he had time to think and was ashamed because he knew what he had said was without honesty. "Why?" This was added defensively and they both understood.

She smiled a little because he was young and her son and she was wiser than he knew.

"You be Spanish man lak Papa. It be no good to you to have black woman for mother. In the school you be smart an' learn things. You read books lak Papa. What you do when you grow up? You find good job like

Spanish man. You look at white girl to marry. Then someone say, He nigger bastard. He gots black woman for mother. You gots life spoiled 'fore it commence. You go now an' no one ever know. Go far away, Boy. Forget Haitian woman. You be Jorge Ojeda, Spanish man."

"What will you do?" He would not degrade the moment nor cheapen her honesty with a hollow protest. "Where will you go?"

She laughed. It was a sound rich and earthy. "We talk true between us now, Boy. Papa gone. He don' come back. We ain' mek th' sadness no more. I a woman need a mans to fill her. I gets 'nother mans. Not lak Papa, maybe. Today, when I go out to buy chicken, I see Jamaica mans again, black lak me. I see him before." She chuckled deep within her throat. "He mek sign lak goat to me but I pays no 'tention 'cause Papa live in that time en am good woman to Papa. He stay in house down street en gots job on dock wit steamer. I go to live wit him. He big nigger en do good for me. You onerstan', Boy? I gots empty feelin' for mans. Can' sit all times thinkin' 'bout Papa. You onerstan'?"

He understood what she was doing and why. She opened the door for him and always he was to wonder if he would have put his hand to it. It had been made simple, elementary. She wanted a man again. He would only be in the way. He could never know if she lied because of a great and unexpressed love for him or if the things she had said had been a truth. She was a female and felt the need to mate again. He was the cub grown and must leave the cave. Because he was young and incapable of making such a decision for himself she, out of a deep wisdom, left him no choice. He could go without shame. He could even go feeling abused if it was easier that way. He had not rejected her. She had abandoned him. He never really forgot her although they saw each other for the last time that evening. He went to work in the morning and when he returned in the late afternoon she was gone.

With her she had taken nothing but the collection of scarves, the dresses, a few cheap pieces of imitation jewelry and a hairbrush with a silver back which Tomas Ojeda had brought home as a present on a long-ago birthday. He sat for a long time in her chair and cried softly to himself because he was lonely and a little afraid. But he cried also because he was grateful to her and was ashamed at having been ashamed of this woman's color and the fact he shared a despised blood.

A dealer in secondhand furniture reluctantly paid him fifty dollars for the contents of three rooms. This, as he explained hurriedly, was more than he could afford; more than the stuff was worth. He would have a hard time disposing of it and would undoubtedly lose everything on the deal because no one these days had money with which to buy anything. He was making such a generous offer only because he had known Tomas Ojeda and now wanted to be of help.

Jorge, listening absently, his eyes roving over the shabby, familiar things, wondered a little why the man persisted in debasing himself with these cringing lies and protestations. Why the hell wasn't he honest? He could have liked him if he had said: I'll only pay you fifty dollars because I know you need the money. I can squeeze your nuts and no one will give a damn if you scream. Take it or leave it but I know you'll take it because you have to. Instead of this honesty he whined and lamented the bad bargain he was making out of sentiment.

"You want to take something with you?" the dealer suggested. "For a dollar or so you can have a keepsake? No!" He was made intoxicated by the magnificence of the idea. "I will give it to you. That little clock, maybe. Take it as a gift. A present from me who often drank coffee with your father." He stood back, raising his hands in astonishment over the notion of such generosity.

Jorge shook his head. He wanted to tell the man to wind the clock and stick it up his ass. Instead, he said nothing.

"Where is your mother?" There was a sly, wise gleam in the man's eyes. He knew what the big black woman had done. Gossip had run as a wind up and down the streets. The neighborhood was too closely integrated for such a scandal to have gone unnoted. "Suppose she comes to me and demands the things back? I could lose the money. You are, after all, only a boy and without authority for such a transaction."

"You know where my mother is." Jorge's contempt was a lash. "She lives with a Jamaican man two blocks away. You know that. Why do you ask, because you drank coffee with my father?" The coldness of the words was frightening. "Give me the fifty dollars and take what is here. There is no one to care."

In dirty bills the dealer counted out the money and placed it in Jorge Ojeda's hand. He was made nervous by the open hatred he could see in so young a face.

"I will come tomorrow with a truck." The man wondered why he knew a fear and tried to ease it. "Until then use it as your own. Sleep in the bed tonight if you wish. Make use of everything; the stove for coffee, the radio and the chair for sitting in to listen. Take your time. I am in no hurry. The day after tomorrow will suit just as well." He backed away a couple of steps.

Jorge turned from the dealer and his sweaty face. At an army surplus store he had purchased a barracks bag, one of many left over from the war which had been fought when he had been three years old. Into it he had stuffed his possessions: the twenty-two rifle and a box of shells; the socks, sneakers, a few shirts, extra pants, the good shoes and the best suit. This last he folded carefully in a paper sheath.

Wrapping the heavy cords, which closed the bag's tucked throat, about his wrist he slung the bundle over one shoulder and walked from the room. He went down the steps and into the street without looking back.

The secondhand dealer, watching him from a window, thought it was strange a boy of this age could leave what had been his home without so much as a second glance or betraying an emotion. There had been no hesitation, no apparent fear of what lay beyond these walls and the well-known streets where he had grown and played. He was tall—the man studied the figure—tall as was his father but without the stooping carriage. Even now, in adolescence, there was the suggestion of power in the frame and easy set of the broad shoulders. He would be a big man. He was at the corner now and the unhurried stride carried him into the next block without hesitation. It even seemed to have a purpose. The man knuckled one side of his nose and stared after the boy. This Jorge Ojeda displayed no haste. He was not running in a desperate effort to hide himself from the gaze of curious neighbors. His feet struck the pavement with a firm confidence. The dealer speculated for a moment on the destination of this *joven*. Then he shrugged. It was of no importance save, perhaps, to Jorge Ojeda himself.

In those days there was a straggling tide of men upon the nation's roads. It flowed and shifted, rising and ebbing in uneven and purposeless movement. It was a vagrant and ragged wave of humanity, detached from the mother sea, seeking a beach upon which to break itself and so put an end to the aimless wandering.

Of all of those who had left the order of a routined way of life behind them, taking to the highways, the rivers, the endless miles of prairie and desert, the men without ties or families were the fortunate ones. They awoke each day only to their own helplessness and bewilderment. They did not have to see them written in the tired lines of a woman's face or hear them spoken in the hungry crying of a baby. A man alone could ask for work or beg for food and these things did not score his soul as they did that of a man with a family. There was a difference; a thing hard to define. But it was there. A man alone could go to a back door and say: I'm hungry. If you have chores to do I will do them in return for the food. Give me something to eat. I need that and the knowledge someone gives a damn or that there is a place for me in this world. He could speak these words without flinching beneath the suspicious eyes of the man or woman of the house. It was different when he must say: I have a wife and children who have no place to sleep, no roof for shelter, who have not eaten well for days or weeks. When he confessed those things he was naked. He was saying I have failed myself and those who depended upon me. I have created love and life but

I am unable to sustain either. I am helpless and must have your charity for them. This is a world with which I cannot cope. I am no longer strong, confident or even a little brave. Those who trusted in me lean upon the wind. They need help and I cannot give it to them. This was the ultimate humiliation.

Those were some of the things which Jorge Ojeda learned as he walked and listened and sat, sometimes, around a fire at night with a small, pathetic and rootless group who had no place to go. The man of the family always moved a little out of the light so his face could not be clearly seen. When he spoke there was no strength in his words.

Draw a line eastward from Tampa across the peninsula of Florida and it will end at a place on the Indian River around Melbourne, Eau Gallie or Palm Bay. Between the points lies a gently rolling country of lakes, long stretches of pine woods, mirrored swamps where the gray cypress rear on their spiderlike legs in dark water and the white cranes sometimes rest at sundown. It is a pleasant, fertile land; fragrant and warm in a semitropical climate, with orange groves, truck farms, patches of scrub and tall pines. Mistletoe hides itself in the oaks and in the season there are bright clumps of holly and Christmas berries to sparkle in the sun. If a man must wander, footloose and jobless, it is far better to do it here than in the cold warrens of the city or upon prairies which hurt the eyes with their distances. A man with a knife and a simple understanding can make his own shelter. The scrub palmetto is at hand. By stretching a few light branches between a couple of saplings a thatched lean-to is easily made. With a few pennies for a hook and line, fish can be taken from the hyacinth-flowered rivers. Along the back roads there are weathered cabins and nearby patches of beans and sweet potatoes, a few orange and grapefruit trees to be raided at night. This is not stealing, for a hungry man must take what he needs and no one was really hurt by the pilfering.

As he walked, rested by a roadside ditch or caught a ride, sometimes, in a bouncing truck Jorge Ojeda had no sense of being among the dispossessed. He encountered lone stragglers along the way or migrant families. Most of them had come from the Northern states in their gasping Fords and Chevrolets which trembled and sagged beneath the weight of household goods and humans. They had sought Florida as others in the Midwest had started for California. They all talked hopefully of work in the groves or upon small farms, in the garages and stores of the little towns. Some were without direction and seemed to wander in dazed circles without any idea of where they were or where they wanted to go. Others talked of Miami, West Palm Beach, Daytona Beach, St. Augustine, Jacksonville, where a tourist population might provide some kind of a job. In them all he discovered there was a pitiful conviction that everything was going to come out all right. Some trusted in their God and to this end there were prayers and the singing of hymns when they gathered and halted for the night. Others were possessed by the notion that something wonderful was going to happen. A man would come along in a big limousine and say: You people all come up to my house and stay for a spell. I'll take care of you. They believed this. Perhaps it wouldn't exactly happen just that way. Maybe it would be the offer of a good, steady job; a house and a piece of land; a relative they had never heard of would die and leave them a fortune. These things were talked about with a wistful seriousness. It was, Jorge thought, that having been pushed so hard and so far whatever happened could only be better.

Since he was too young to have any real idea of what had occurred to the country—why men were jobless, why crops went unharvested while men and women were hungry and drifting—he asked questions. The migrants had no valid answers. It all had something to do with a vague place called Wall Street. In newspapers picked out of trash cans in the towns he read and tried to make sense out of the many words. He listened to radios in lunchrooms. There was so much talk, so few facts he could assimilate. From the experience of his father and the little cigar factory he knew how the blight could strike. It seemed impossible, though, such a thing could happen to the entire nation. He wondered also if these men and women with whom he sat, talked and sometimes ate ever had a chance for survival. Most of them seemed to have only a primitive ability; that of picking fruit, digging a ditch, carrying a thing from one place to stack it in another, turning the crank of a gasoline pump, ploughing a furrow, pushing a barrow, unloading a truck. Yet, and this he thought was a little frightening, they asked no more than the opportunity to do these things. They were satisfied to be the human fuel which furnished the power to turn the wheels. The supply was inexhaustible. They bred with the idiotic fecundity of rabbits with no thought of how the babies would be born or cared for in their world of desperate uncertainties. Instead of compassion and a kinship for and with them he began to feel impatience and even contempt. Because of this he tried to avoid people and in the evenings, when he saw small groups with their sprung trucks and cars pulled to the side of a road, he walked on and felt no loneliness.

He still had most of the fifty dollars from the sale of the furniture. At a J. C. Penney store he had bought a cheap but warm blanket. Woolworth's, for fifty cents, had provided a light frying pan and a small pot. In Winter Haven he found a rummage sale and for seventy-five cents had bought a knife, a Boy Scout ax and a canteen. He had everything he needed, for this was no wild and savage land through which he walked. If evening found him on a long stretch of empty road without a sign of cabin or fence he felt no uneasiness. It was simple enough to find a stand of pine where the ground was covered with the bronze, pungent needles as they had dropped and gathered into a thick carpet. If he hunted with care he usually found a squirrel or a rabbit to be killed with the twenty-two caliber rifle his father had given him on his twelfth birthday. The piece broke easily into two parts and was rolled inside the blanket. As reserve rations he had a square of salt pork, a sack of rice, some dried chilies and red beans. These things were ridiculously cheap at the country stores. A fire was easily built from the dead branches of a fallen pine. Water was usually at hand and if it wasn't he had the canteen. Since he had cut himself away from everything he had known, he felt no homesickness. Because he was without a destination, he experienced no sense of adventure; the interest and even excitement of going from one place to another. He thumbed a ride when he could—and this was often. He was young with an easy pleasant smile and a quietly reserved manner. In him there was no threat, no danger, and rarely did he ask for a lift that it wasn't given. Sometimes a salesman took him from one town to another. Now and then a private car carried him for a few miles more. As he rode, listened, watched, he began to wonder about many things. The country hadn't completely gone to hell as everyone said. New, shiny cars rolled on the highways. There were nice homes and well-dressed, busy people on the streets of the towns. He also discovered that strangers regarded him queerly and with a slight suspicion when he said he wasn't going any place in particular. They were made uneasy by a person who had no destination.

One evening he had made a fire, shot an incautious rabbit, skinned and dressed it, wondering why rabbits which fed on grass and small plants should stink as they did. He spitted it on a stick over the fire and leaned back, resting against a pine. Out of the gathering, hazy dusk a man, attracted by the fire, had wandered in from the road. He was gaunt and weathered, wearing faded overalls, and an Adam's apple stuck from a scrawny throat as a thumb. In Jorge he saw only a boy and without asking permission hunkered down to share the fire. He added a can of beans and some coffee from a paper sack to the meal. While the rabbit was roasting he took an automobile road map from a pocket and began to study it intently in the fading light. He talked as he scanned the sheet but Jorge wasn't sure whether it was to himself or to him.

"I might make Kissimmee, Campbell or Orlando tomorrow, maybe. That is if I can git a ride. It'd be quite a trip, seein' Orlando an' all." He glanced up for affirmation.

Jorge wondered what the man was going to do when he reached Kissimmee, Campbell or Orlando. The towns were much the same. There would be little chance of a job for a stranger. The police usually hustled an obvious itinerant to the city limits with a warning to keep going. He didn't ask the question.

"Where you a-goin', boy?" The man lifted the can of boiling coffee from the fire and then stuck his fingers into the hot liquid to test what was apparent. He jerked his hand back with surprise. "God damn but that there is sure enough hot." He sucked the fingers. "I ast where you were a-goin'?"

"Nowhere." Jorge broke some pieces of pine bark and tossed the fragments into the fire. "Nowhere in particular."

The man grunted. "That's a hell of a reason for walkin'." He regarded Jorge as though he wasn't too bright.

"Where are you going?" Jorge couldn't resist the question.

"I just said, didn't I? Kissimmee, Campbell, Orlando, or maybe to Sanford or De Land." This was a sure-enough stupid boy.

"What are you going to do when you get there?" Jorge was pleasantly interested.

"Boy, you ain't too sharp, are you? How do I know what I'm a-goin' to do until I git to them places?" He was impatient. "A fella looks around an' sees things. He makes up his mind and says: I'm goin' to Palatka. Then he's got somethin' in view. He ain't a drifter. Understand?"

Jorge nodded. A man needed a goal, if even only a geographical one. Hereafter, he decided, when someone asked him where he was going he'd say Jacksonville. This would give him a purpose in life.

When the rabbit was roasted they cut open the bean can's top and set it on the coals until the sauce bubbled. With the small ax Jorge split the rabbit, giving the man his half. They drank the cooling coffee from its container, passing it back and forth. It was black and bitter. They ate without talking and when the meal was finished it was almost dark.

The man belched and spit a piece of bone to the ground. Then he worked a long, dirty finger around the cavity of his mouth.

"You got a good little fire burnin' here." The man popped a tongue against his loose plate. "If you was to find some oak it'd keep fueled up till mornin'." He waited for Jorge to get up and search for the wood. When the boy made no move he sighed wearily. "Pine goes in a hurry. It's gone before you know it. I don't suppose you got a little tobacco, even one of them cigarettes would be tasty."

"No." He wished his visitor would leave. "No. I don't smoke much."

"That was a sure-enough tough rabbit. Now, the next time you hunt for a possum. They're greasy. I'll say that. But they ain't tough like a rabbit. That's because a rabbit runs like hell all over the place. A possum don't do much but hang up in the crotch of a tree. That's how come they're so fat. Ever think about that?"

"No." He was getting tired of the man's senseless chatter. "It's going to be too dark for walking soon." He made the suggestion hopefully.

"I bin thinkin'." The man made a whistling sound between his few, snagged and yellow lower teeth. "Say you an' me team up? We'd move in comfort an' style to where we want to go. Like we're standin' together beside the road waitin' for a pick-up ride. People in their cars would come along. They'd say to each other: Look at that there poor old man an' his son wantin' to go someplace we're goin'. We can't leave no homeless old man an' his young boy out here. They'd say: Let's stop our new car an' invite 'em in for a hitch ride to wherever they're a-goin'. You see what I mean? A fine-lookin' boy like yourself would make people feel charitable like an' old man by himself wouldn't. Understand?"

Jorge understood. This reedy-looking character in his dirty overalls wouldn't inspire anyone to stop. Also, there was a stench about him. Whoever gave him a lift would find an excuse to get rid of him in a hurry.

"How about it?" The visitor pressed the invitation eagerly.

"No."

The man was patient. "You ain't goin' to git far with no attitude like that." This was a moody reflection upon Jorge's future. "How old are you, boy?"

"Near seventeen." Jorge wondered why he bothered to reply.

The man watched as he cleaned the ax by chopping the blade into the sandy earth several times. The eyes followed every move he made as he opened the barracks bag, replaced the tool and pulled out the blanket. He swept together a level heap of pine needles and stretched half of the blanket to cover the light mat. The other half was turned back to use as a cover. The bag served as a pillow. When this was done he tossed the last of the pine knots on the fire and it sprang into warm, bright life.

"You goin' to keep all of that there blanket to yourself?" The man expressed a horrified astonishment over this unbelievable display of selfishness. "You ain't even goin' to offer a mitch of a corner of a good warm blanket to an old man who come upon you as a wanderin' stranger out of the night?" He stared mournfully. "All this stranger asked was a chance to be a good friend, sharin' half an' half with all his worldly goods to say nothin' of companionship an' a knowledge of things to be told about with good advice an' all." He waited for an indication of Jorge's melting.

"Why don't you go on and get started for Kissimmee or wherever it is you're going?" Jorge rolled himself into the blanket and burrowed down comfortably. "It's getting late."

"I never would have believed it." The stranger was not to be denied. "It just don't seem possible one human could be filled with such uncharity toward another. I heard about the younger generation. How they don't have no respect, no kind heart. But, I said, it can't be true. There's good in everyone, even in thoughtless young boys who got a warm blanket and a bag full of goods. When you find it ain't so, like I'm doin' now, it just takes the entire faith out of a man. It makes him wonder what the world's comin' to."

"Well, you wonder about it. I'm tired and I'm going to sleep. Now, shut up. If you want to keep the fire going and sit by it all night that's all right with me. Just stop talking so damn much."

"There ain't enough wood stacked to keep that there fire a-goin' all night." The complaint was mildly and reasonably voiced.

"Then go and find some more." The food, the warmth of the fire and the blanket made him comfortably drowsy. The old man was becoming a nuisance. "I didn't ask you in here. Don't you ever take a bath? You smell. I can smell you from over there."

"I got the asthmey. A man with the asthmey can't take the risk of washin' himself all the time. It sets a chill to the bones. Anyhow, I don't smell nothin'."

With half-closed eyes he saw the stranger as he foraged around for pieces of small dry limbs. He began to wonder about such a man. By what stages did you reach a state of whining resignation or this grotesque optimism that something better lay ahead in Kissimmee or Orlando? Hadn't there been a time when this putrefying old man had rebelled? In the strength of his youth hadn't he ever said: This isn't good enough for me? I want more. Maybe I even want it all and, by God, I'm going to go after it. If so, what had happened to blunt the will, the desire?

"Old man," he called softly, "what did you think about when you were my age?"

"My pecker." He sniggered obscenely and broke a few twigs to throw into the flames. "What else is there to think about when you're seventeen?"

"Didn't you ever look around and say: This is a big, fat world, I'm going to grab a piece of it?" Even as he spoke he knew he would get no real answer. "Didn't you ever get mad? Didn't you ever say: If I don't do it for myself no one else will?"

"The Lord will provide."

"Like hell He will." Jorge half sat up and stared at this squalid figure, balanced on unsteady heels and peering into the flames with rheumy eyes. "How long can an old man like you wait?"

"You ain't had a proper Christian upbringing, boy. That's the trouble with you. The Lord teaches charity. You just ain't got it. Otherwise, you wouldn't be lyin' there snug an' in comfort while I'm out here a-shiverin' in my asthmey."

"You're a damned old hypocrite. Why should I give you my blanket?"

[45]

"Because it's better to give than to receive."

"Whoever said that was a damn fool or wanted something someone else had." This was a pretty ridiculous conversation Jorge decided. "It's like saying money isn't everything. The only ones who say that are those who already have it. I never heard a poor man say it."

"The meek shall inherit the earth." The phrase was intoned with a quiet fervor.

"You're crazy." The boy made the statement without malice. "You're a crazy old coot and I don't know why I let you come in here to begin with."

"There ain't no need to call names just because your conscience bothers you." He was being patient.

"Do you know what I'd do if I was you, old man?" Jorge didn't wait for an answer. "I'd pretend to be looking for more wood to put on the fire. I'd walk around until I found a good-sized piece and then I'd come up behind me and beat me over the head with it. Then I'd take the blanket and whatever else I wanted. I sure wouldn't be sitting there on my skinny butt waiting for the Lord to provide."

The fresh twigs snapped and exploded as the flames licked over the pine's bubbling resin. The glow illuminated the stranger's features and Jorge saw he was laughing and a foxy amusement sparkled in his eyes. For the first time he betrayed an unsuspected humor.

"What's so funny about that?" Jorge was surprised.

"I studied some on just that." The confession was blandly made. "I said to myself: I wonder what kind of goods this here boy's got in his bag? I pondered on whether it was worth stealin' an' schemed to find out how to get you by surprise. Then I said to myself: Supposin' I don't hit him just right with the first crack? He's young, big for his age an' strong-lookin'. Like as not he'd beat the livin' tar out of me." The laughter was gone now and the smile with it. Nothing was left but a dejected admission of defeat and the knowledge of his frailty and humiliation. When he spoke again the words were so softly voiced as to be almost inaudible. "I don't know as I could stand bein' licked by a seventeen-year-old boy. I guess that would just about put an end to any ideas I got as to the kind of a man I was once. A fellow my age probably couldn't live without bein' able to fool himself a little. That's all he's got left most of the time."

Propped on an elbow Jorge Ojeda stared at this skeletal figure. Almost any other answer to his question would have left him unmoved. He had expected a pious, hypocritical declaration of honesty from this beaten old fraud. This would have made sense and he could have laughed at it. Now he was confused and oddly touched and this made him uncomfortable but he wasn't sure why. With a twisting motion he stood up. He hesitated and then with an impatient snort dragged the blanket across the few yards separating them. With a rough, indifferent gesture he tossed the covering across the old man's shoulders.

"There." He almost shouted, forcing an angry tone and an outrage he didn't really feel. "Take it, you loony old coot. I'm only giving it to you so you'll shut up and let me get some sleep. I'll probably never be able to get the stink out of that blanket. I might as well forget about it right now. Keep it. I'll get another one someplace." He glared down at the huddled figure and then turned away.

From his bag he took a sweater. Mrs. Waters, back there on Seminole Heights, had knitted it for him as a Christmas present. On him it hung loosely and without shape but it was warm and he pulled it over his head. Then he stood and looked down at his visitor.

The old man had said nothing. The blanket hung from his shoulders and spread in an untidy heap about the skinny loins. He was just sitting there, head bent. Then he blew his nose with the sound of a water-filled trumpet and wiped it with the sleeve of the dirty long underwear he wore beneath the overalls. Jorge kicked at his bag and then whirled about with startled surprise as he heard the man chuckle raspingly. The old fool was laughing. Damned if he isn't sitting there in my blanket laughing at me for being a sucker. Even as he thought this Jorge wondered why he wasn't furious over being tricked. The truth of the matter was he, also, thought it a little funny.

"I don't know what you've got to laugh about, you old fool." He worked to keep an honest amusement out of his tone.

"I got me a blanket, didn't I?" The statement wasn't complacent. Oddly enough, Jorge thought, it was a little challenging. A point had been proved. "I told you the Lord would provide."

"The Lord didn't have anything to do with it. I'm just crazy, that's all."

"That's what you think. It wasn't a thing but the doin' of the Lord that led my feet to this very spot an' got me a warm blanket to sleep in. Don't you believe in the Lord, boy?"

"Not the way you do."

"I'll admit He takes some nudgin' at times but He's up there, lookin' on, watchin' the sparries fall. You got to have faith."

"And end up like you?" The question was brutal. He meant it to be because he was embarrassed by what he had done. This was a shield against a further weakness. "A homeless bum wandering around until he drops dead some day on the road?"

"You don't have to be ashamed of what you done." The rebuke was mild but unmistakable.

Jorge was surprised by the intuitive expression of what was in his mind. How could this old man know what he was thinking?

"You got plenty of time to get as mean as you want if you're sure that's the way to get ahead. You start workin' at it now an' you can probably be the meanest son of a bitch in the world by the time you're growed. It's a thing that don't take much cultivatin'."

"Shut up and go to sleep."

He watched as the man curled himself into a small heap. His head was pillowed on one arm, the blanket drawn up to cover his face.

For a long time Jorge lay awake. The night, which had seemed a thing of dark silence, began to be filled with small sounds. There was a faint crackle in the brush where a little animal moved cautiously. A whippoorwill called plaintively and after an interval was answered. An owl hooted a mournful question and on the highway a car went past with the rushing sound of wind in a tunnel. When he looked up through the pines he could see patches of the sky, brilliant as though it had been dusted with sugar crystals. He had the feeling that all about him there was a continual, furtive movement as the small creatures of the woods foraged constantly for their existence. During the hours of the day they were unable to defend themselves against the hawks and so must move this way at night to feed and disappear.

He found himself thinking of the old man's words. "You got plenty of time to be as mean as you want if you're sure that's the way to get ahead." He wasn't sure what that meant and he didn't think the man did either. When you got that old and were fumbling around just to keep alive, the world and those who had what you needed must seem hard. They slammed the door in your face because they, also, were a little afraid. He thought of his father, a man of gentle disposition who had never raised his voice in anger. He had been without envy or ambition to be more than he was: a maker of fine cigars. He had given generously of what he had to less fortunate friends. A neighbor in trouble with his rent, the bills for a sick wife or child could always go to Tomas Ojeda and find sympathy and an open purse. But when the disaster struck his small business and ate away his heart, no one came forward and offered help. They let him sit alone and bear the humiliation of having a wife and young son support him. If Tomas Ojeda had been mean, mean in the sense this old man had meant it, he would not have died as he had. So, Jorge Ojeda decided, to hell with that. A man must make a cover for himself; an armor against those who would devour him. Without it he was as defenseless as a soft-shelled crab, as helpless as the migrants he had met along the road. But, and this struck him with a sudden force, it was really these inadequate ones who, by their very number, could overwhelm you. The hawks of the world were rare and could be spotted. The ants and the locusts moved in irresistible swarms. They were the threat because, individually, they were deceptively harmless. Step upon the ants, he thought, and you will survive the hawks.

When he awoke, the sunlight was filtering down through the high, green branches which moved softly in an easy breath of wind. His neck felt stiff and the side of his head, where it had rested on the stuffed bag, was sore from contact with the ground. It was a moment before he realized why. He spun over to his hands and knees. Save for a small thickness where his cheek had rested the coarse fabric of the bag was in flat, wrinkled folds. It wasn't difficult to see why. The bag's bottom had been craftily slit with a sharp knife. While he had slept a prying hand had slipped in through the gaping rent and the bag's contents taken out—article by article, piece by piece—the fingers halting at the point where his head lay.

He stood up slowly. From his wrist dangled a short length of the cord which closed the bag's throat. He had wrapped it there as a precaution just before he went to sleep. The stranger by the fire was one of the ants. This had occurred to him while he lay there thinking. Once the cord had been sliced away the same, cautious hand had pulled what it could from the bag's top. A ferret could not have worked with more skill and silence than had that old man. In his anger he, oddly enough, felt a certain rueful admiration for the cunning.

He stooped, picked up the bag and shook it. Only a couple of soiled shirts, balled up with some dirty socks, fell out. Everything else was gone: his one good suit, the shoes, rifle, pan, ax and extra trousers. These other things remained only because the predatory fingers had been fearful of awakening him. Abruptly he grabbed at the shirts and shook them. A tobacco can he had hidden there dropped from the folds and lay bright and red in the sunlight. He grinned. The old bastard had missed this. In it were the wadded bills, the remainder of the fifty dollars. He picked it up, snapped open the lid and looked inside. The money was still there. He put the can in his hip pocket and carefully buttoned the flap.

Turning he looked about the little clearing in the pines. Last night's fire was a heap of powdery ash. It stirred gently as a breeze caught it. The blanket, also, was gone. He grinned, thinking of the old man skittering down the road; a frightened crab, clutching his loot and moving as fast as his skinny legs would take him. He laughed. The idea of that scarecrow figure high-tailing it through the night was somehow funny because what he had taken would do him little good nor last for long. The suit and the pants he couldn't wear. The socks and clean shirts could not be sold or traded for something else. No one would really want them. The thing of value, the tobacco can with its money, he had missed. The theft had been as senseless as the act of a raccoon which will carry off any bright object simply because it cannot resist the temptation to an acquisitive nature.

He knew he should be sore but he wasn't. It was something learned and never to be forgotten. You stepped on the ants before they bit you. Or, and maybe this was a better idea, if you kept them fed and satisfied you might even be able to train and harness them to work for you. Once, at a carnival, he had seen a side-show act of trained fleas. They pulled little carts, turned the wheels of a tiny mill and marched up and down a ladder. He could remember staring at the insects with an almost frightened intensity. That night he had awakened with his throat strained as he fought to scream a nameless terror in a dream. The fleas, gigantic now, stood and watched as men and women performed for them. Because they multiplied so rapidly they had taken over the world and the order of things was reversed. Thinking about it now he wondered why it hadn't happened. Probably because man was smarter and so it was with mankind itself. Someone had to pull the carts, tip the ladders, turn the wheels, carry out the garbage, clean the toilets. These were the flea-men. The wiser and tougher had trained them to do these things. If they rebelled they were destroyed and more docile fleas found to take their places. So, it became a pretty simple matter to decide what you wanted to be—a performing flea or a trainer.

He walked from the clearing and into the hot, early sun of the morning and found himself whistling. He was hungry but filled with the buoyant spirit of his youth. He thought, I can go anywhere. I can start out now, right here, and go to New York or California. If I really want to work at it I can go to Europe or China. There isn't anyone or anything to stop me. More than that. I can be one of the men or one of the fleas. It's probably a lot easier to be a flea but I think I'd rather be a man. This may take some doing. He struck off down the road. Sooner or later he'd come to a filling station or a store and wait until he could catch a ride into town. He'd eat a big breakfast. Abruptly, he laughed and then halted. Low over a field a hawk was almost motionless in the air as it waited or watched for a lizard, a small snake, a toad or mouse. He wondered what fed upon the hawks? The larger hawks, maybe, or an eagle, or a farmer with a gun blew the hell out of them to protect his chickens. That was something to think about and when you came right down to it not even the farmer with the gun was safe. There would always be another farmer with a bigger gun who might want what the first farmer had—his wife, his money, his land. Where did it end? How did you make yourself invincible?

He turned at the sound of an approaching car, stepped to the road's side and waved. The driver slowed, inspected him and then stopped. On the car's door panel there was a sign; a checkered feed bag with the word PURINA on it. The man was a salesman.

"I'm going to De Land if that'll do you any good. Couple of stops on the way. Winter Park. Orlando."

"That'll be fine." Jorge smiled.

They rode in silence for a few minutes. The salesman lit a cigarette and offered one. Jorge shook his head and thanked him.

"You're out pretty early, aren't you?" The driver glanced from the road for a second to study him. "Where you bound for?"

Jorge wanted to shout with laughter because he felt good. Instead he kept his features grave. He was aware of the man's inquiring gaze.

"You got something in mind, a job someplace?"

Jorge nodded. "Yes, sir." He replied with respectful gravity. "I'm going to catch myself some fleas."

V.

ON that morning, leaving the small glade within the pines to hitch a ride with a traveling salesman, Jorge Ojeda had not even a vague notion as to where he wanted to go or what he should do once the unknown destination had been reached. Later he was to think about this and wonder why he felt no uneasiness, no sense of being alone and homeless.

The man made small, incessant talk as they rode. There seemed to be in him a compulsion for words. It was as though the sound of his voice somehow reassured him. Without being asked he told Jorge of his home in Dothan, Georgia; spun fanciful tales of life on the road; the girls, the booze, the farmers' daughters, stag and poker parties. Listening, Jorge only wondered why he bothered to lie or why it seemed important to him to impress a youngster in his teens.

The garrulous poultry feed peddler dropped him off in De Land. That afternoon he had walked about the community and up a long, sloping street to where the buildings of Stetson University were spread over a tree-shaded campus. Standing there he wondered what it would be like to go to college. What wonders of the world, its secrets and cultures, its reason, could be explained within these many classrooms? The treasures of man's mind and imagination unlocked in the library, the miracles of science and life itself explained in the laboratories. He stood there, filled with a hunger he had never before known, to understand, not what but why. It even occurred to him that these were strange things for Jorge Ojeda, son of Tomas Ojeda, a cigar maker of Ybor City, to be thinking.

Somewhere, within one of the buildings marked Elizabeth Hall, he heard the faint sound of a muted gong. A few minutes later young men and girls came through the doors and down the steps. They carried books, talked animatedly as they walked with a casual friendly exchange. They seemed not much older than he. How did they get where they were? He had no idea how you went about going to such a college as this. You sure just didn't walk into someone's office in a pair of rumpled khaki pants, a not too clean shirt and dirty sneakers with about forty dollars in your pocket and say: I'd like to go to college. There are things I want to know. Give me a chance to learn. Probably what he had been taught by the Sisters in the parochial school wouldn't be enough. He'd have to go to high school for a while first. Somehow he knew there wasn't time for that. He was in a hurry but he wasn't sure why. There was an urgent drive within him he couldn't explain.

A girl, pretty and wearing a loose sweater, plaid skirt and moccasins, trotted down the steps. She was alone. Her glance caught his and in his eyes she must have seen a wistfulness of which he was unaware. For a moment he thought she was going to stop but she didn't.

"Hi!" Her smile was bright, friendly and confident.

"Hello." He spoke the word almost shyly.

She continued on down the steps and across the street but she didn't look back to where this strange boy with a disturbing intensity in his eyes, a hunger almost, stood alone.

For a minute or so more he remained where he was. Back through the pines, the big oaks and magnolias he could see other buildings—the dormitories probably, and lecture halls. Then he began to laugh, quietly and to himself. It wasn't likely Jorge Ojeda would find any of his fleas in a college. Those who lived and studied here were probably preparing to catch some for themselves.

He went back down the long, shaded street to the town's business section. From a rack in front of a filling station he took a map. Again he laughed softly to himself. He thought about that scrawny old coot who had run off with his stuff. He also carried a map such as this and through its tracings he imagined places, such as Kissimmee and Orlando, filled with the wonders of creation. The boy at the gas pump, hearing the muted laughter, wondered what could be so funny about an old road map.

Squatting on his heels at one side of the station Jorge unfolded the sheet. The tracing of roads spread in all directions. A man, he thought, ought to see the Atlantic Ocean. It probably wasn't much different than the Gulf of Mexico but just the same, it ought to be looked at. His finger moved eastward. Oak Hill. Edgewater. Coronado Beach. Ponce de Leon Inlet. New Smyrna. Those were fine-sounding names; especially Coronado, Ponce de Leon, New Smyrna. The last, for some reason, made him think of figs. Maybe, that was where Smyrna figs came from.

Looking up he called to the attendant. "How do you get to New Smyrna?"

"Like you get to any other place. You walk or you ride." He snickered at his wit.

"You're too funny to be pumping gas. It's a real waste of talent. Is there a bus or a train?" He didn't really want to spend any of his money on transportation but he wouldn't admit it.

"There's a bus station down the next block."

Jorge folded the map and put it back in the rack. Then he walked until he came to the bus depot. He bought a ticket to the first stop beyond De Land. From there he would hitch a ride the rest of the way.

The route of the bus carried him through sparsely settled country and the destination called for by his ticket was little more than a general store and a couple of frame houses. He began walking; caught a ride of a mile on a mule-drawn wagon with spavined wheels. There didn't seem to be many cars and the few which did come along ignored his signal. He kicked through the short, wiry grass which ran parallel with a drainage ditch, and had about decided he would have to walk the entire distance when a Ford truck stopped for him. Piled and lashed in the truck's bed were crates of celery with Sanford stenciled on the boxes. He remembered it as one of the places that old man had talked about visiting.

Settled on the cracked leather seat with the driver he rode for a few minutes in silence.

"Where's Sanford?"

"Back country apiece. Near to the St. Johns River. Celery capital of the world. Anybody ought to know where Sanford is."

"I didn't." He half smiled. "I don't like celery anyhow."

"Can't 'bide the stuff myself. Sometimes just haulin' it makes me want to puke." The man took a paper sack of Mail Pouch chewing tobacco from a pocket and stuffed a wad into his mouth. As an afterthought he offered it to his passenger. "Want a pinch?"

"I never chewed tobacco. What's it like?"

"Damn it, try some an' find out, then you won't have to ask questions all the time." There was an unmistakable note of crabbed irritation in the tone.

"You mad at something?" Jorge made the query pleasantly interested.

"You're damn right. I'm mad at everything. I wake up mad and I figure to stay that way all day. That's the way to get ahead in the world. Don't take nothin' from no one. I only picked you up because I said to myself: There's another one of them young bums on the road. He'll do to be mad at until I find somethin' else." He allowed the truck to weave and slew recklessly over the road while he studied his passenger. "You one of them Norkins?"

"What's a Norkin?" Jorge was mystified.

"Boy, you don't know nothin', do you?" For some reason this display of ignorance seemed to cheer the man immensely. Some of his truculence abated. "Smyrna is filled with Norkins. You got the same kind of complected color."

For a sickening moment Jorge Ojeda experienced the same terror he had known walking down Franklin Street in Tampa on that day when the man at the bathing springs had called him a nigger. Was a Norkin some sort of a local name for a Negro or a person of mixed blood? Did this thing which he had thought safely behind him and all but forgotten now show itself unexpectedly? He glanced at the man. There was no fury, no contemptuous hatred in his expression and some of the fear drained away. Whatever a Norkin was it didn't mean Negro. This man wouldn't have picked him up in the first place if he had suspected he was colored. He wouldn't share the truck's seat with a nigger unless he was a helper. Even then he would have made the Negro ride in the back, balanced on the celery crates.

"They's some damn pretty Norkin girls." The driver had forgotten he was supposed to be angry at everything and everyone. He was flattered to find someone who didn't know what he did. "You get one of them kinda dark complected ones an' you sure got yourself somethin'. Norkins are some sort of Spanish. Anyhow, that's what they say. I knowed one once in St. Augustine when I worked in the F.E.C. yards there. She took up with a drummer, though, an' went off with him. I figured she gave him the clapps same as me an' so I didn't much care. She was a beauty, I'll say that for her."

Jorge relaxed. Whatever a Norkin was he, or in this case she, had some sort of an acceptable status with the driver. He wouldn't have talked about laying a Negro girl although he had probably done it often enough. It was supposed to change your luck; which was as good an excuse as any. He drew a deep breath and held it until the unreasoning fear subsided.

"What you goin' to Smyrna for?" The topic of Norkins had been exhausted.

"I thought maybe I could find a job."

The driver made a moist, gurgling sound of disgust. The slimy cud of tobacco interfered for a moment with his speech. He worked it around to a cheek.

"Ain't a damn thing to do in Smyrna you couldn't have done wherever it is you come from; except, maybe, shrimpin'. There's some orange pickin'. But you won't get it. That's what's runnin' this country right down the drain to hell."

"Oranges?" Jorge honestly puzzled by the vagaries of his chance companion's mind. "Shrimps and oranges?"

"No!" The man shouted his impatience at this stupidity. "The goddamned niggers, that's what. You just ain't thought about things the way I have. It's a matter of economical. That's what it is. You take a nigger now. He'll work for fifty cents where a white man's got to have a dollar. So, who get's the job?"

"Why does a white man have to have a dollar?" Jorge knew this was a dangerous question.

"Because he's white an' that makes him better'n a black nigger. That's the reason why. He's got to live up to bein' a white man an' that costs more. You sure as hell don't know much, boy, if you don't know that. How you goin' to keep a nigger in his place if you work side by side with him for the same wages? First thing you know he'll begin thinkin' he's as good as you. How'd you like that to happen? There wouldn't be no end to it. They'd be sittin' in the same café. They'd be walking right up to your front door. How'd you like your sister to be spoken up to by some nigger?"

"I don't have a sister." This didn't seem to be an unreasonable answer.

The man slammed his foot down on the brake and the truck's rear end all but lifted from the ground as the tires skidded to a halt.

"This here is as far as you go with me, boy." There was a cold finality in the statement. "I don't give no hitch ride to no nigger-lover an' that's the way you sound to me."

"I just said I didn't have a sister."

"That ain't what you meant. If you was older an' not so damn dumb I'd say you was one of them Bolsheviki agitators who come down here to stir things up in the South. But you ain't got sense enough for that. Just the same you get the by God hell out of this here truck."

Jorge opened the door and stepped down. He looked up at the man who was glaring at him.

"Thanks for the lift."

"You ain't welcome. If I'd knowed what I know now you'd never got it." He leaned toward the door. "You just wait till you try to find a job only to have the man say he can get a nigger to do it for less. You won't be so damn easygoin' then. You'll sit on your bare ass an' think about things."

The truck jerked forward with a slam of gears and Jorge stood and watched until it rounded a long curve. That's the way it is. That's the real hatred. It really isn't a matter of color. It's the economic conflict and maybe there isn't any answer for it. Not in the North or the South or any place. He wondered how it was to live with such fury.

It wasn't far from where the truck driver had put him out to New Smyrna. He crossed the tracks of the Florida East Coast Railway and walked up the main street. On an impulse he stopped a man and asked where he could find the public library. He followed the simple directions and at the steps hesitated. He had an idea the question he wanted answered was going to sound pretty foolish to the librarian.

At a desk there was a girl. She glanced up with a polite inquiry in her manner.

"Yes?" She smiled at his obvious shyness.

"I—" He laughed because he was embarrassed and the whole thing, somehow, seemed ridiculous. "What's a Norkin?"

"A what?" The librarian was plainly at a loss.

"I rode part of the way from De Land with a fellow who said there were a lot of Norkins in New Smyrna. Anyhow, that's the way it sounded. What was he talking about?"

"Oh!" Comprehension lighted her eyes. He thought she'd be a real pretty girl if she didn't wear those heavy shell-rimmed glasses. She took them off now and laughed, not at him but at the word. "He probably meant Minorcan."

Jorge understood he was supposed to know what a Minorcan was but he didn't. She saw the small frown of perplexity gather on his face.

"Wait a minute." She left her place at the desk and went to a shelf. After a moment she found what she was looking for and pulled out a volume. "Here. This will tell you about the Minorcans."

He took the book to a straight-backed chair at a long, bare table. It was a travel guide of Florida. Where she had opened it for him he saw there was a chapter devoted to the history of New Smyrna. In it were descriptions of old Spanish missions, sugar mills, the foundations of an old fort and a canal built by the Spaniards. Then he came to the part he sought.

> In 1767 Dr. Andrew Turnbull, a Scottish physician, brought 1,500 colonists to this site. About 1,200 of them were from the Island of Minorca, east of Spain.

This was enough. The Cracker truck driver had taken him for the descendant of one of these early settlers; a man, probably, with Spanish blood in him. He closed the book with an inaudible sigh of relief and then carried it back across the room to where the girl sat.

"Thanks. I thought maybe it was a dirty word at first. The way he said it, I mean."

"Do you live here?" She took her glasses off again. It was an unconscious gesture as a girl's hand sometimes strays to touch at her hair when a man looks at her.

"I don't know. I mean, I just walked into town. Why?"

"Oh! Nothing," she replied hastily. "I—I just thought if you had moved here you ought to take out a library card. It's quite a story." She smiled again. "Depending on who tells it. There was a rebellion against Dr. Turnbull. Some of the Minorcan colonists walked all the way to St. Augustine for protection under the Spanish flag."

"Well . . . if I stay I might do it. Take a card out, I mean." He made all of it sound unimportant because he liked the way her eyes lighted when she smiled. "I have to find a job. My name's Jorge Ojeda."

She understood the tentative offer he had made. It embarrassed her to realize she had removed her glasses because she wanted him to see her without them.

"I'm Jean Tolliver. I only work here part time. Three days a week. What kind of a job are you looking for?"

"Most anything will do for a starter." He was aware of the appearance he must make in the worn sneakers, rumpled pants and a faded blue shirt. "A fellow stole most of my things last night. I guess I look like a bum." He wanted her to understand.

"Well," she admitted, "you look a little creased in the wrong places. I wouldn't try to find a job in a bank if I were you." She thought there was a beauty in his face, which was a curious way to describe a man or a boy. "This isn't a very large town."

"I'll find something." He wasn't particularly concerned. "I guess Tolliver isn't a Norkin name, is it?"

"English. Jorge Ojeda could be, though." She pronounced it as he had, accented in Spanish.

He grinned at the suggestion. "I'll look around and see who can use a new Norkin." He hesitated and then nodded. "So long and thanks for the information."

"Good-by." This was almost primly spoken. When he reached the door she called a little hurriedly, "Come in again. Let me know how you make out."

He ate at a lunch counter. Fried shrimp, potatoes, cole slaw and a big slab of something called Key Lime Pie. The check was forty cents.

"You don't need a helper, do you?" he asked the counterman. "Someone to wash dishes or wait on customers?"

"There ain't no customers these days. You're the first one to come in here this morning except for coffee. I can't make a livin' for myself let alone a helper."

Jorge hadn't really wanted a job in the lunchroom. He asked because he thought he ought to get used to the idea of looking for work. From the café he walked down the business street to the river.

Rocks made of shell, which he later learned were called *coquina,* were piled along the water's edge. He sat on one and watched as an occasional mullet leaped in a silver flash and fell back with a plopping sound. Great oaks with their widespread branches hung with gray moss gave a warm shade to the river front. There were massed growths of oleander, pink, white and red, and tall magnolias with waxy green leaves and the creamy, fragrant blooms cupped within them. Above the day's soft whispering he could hear the muted bass note of the ocean behind the dunes across the river.

Almost reluctantly he stood up. He might just as well have a look at the Atlantic while he was here. For a moment he considered going back downtown and buying a blanket. He could sleep on the beach. If that old bastard hadn't stolen everything he could even live over there for a while. But that sure wasn't any way to go about finding a job.

He crossed the river on a wooden bridge and walked along empty streets half covered with windswept sand, and cut through the high dunes. There were scattered, weathered cottages and a larger frame building which looked as though it might have been a hotel. Everything seemed boarded up and deserted. He saw no one.

This was Coronado Beach. At least it had been marked as such on the road map he looked at in De Land. To the north he could see where an inlet led into the river and beyond that the slender, mellowed red brick of a lighthouse. He tried to remember something he had read about Coronado in school. Don Francisco de Coronado. A Spanish soldier and explorer. But that was in the Southwest, New Mexico or someplace like that. How did he ever get down here? Probably he didn't. Someone just thought it would be a good name for a beach.

He half stretched himself out on the warm sand which was lightly colored with a powdering of red shell. He gazed at the ocean, fascinated by its eternal movement. In a continuous procession the waves reared and fell forward. Just before they broke, in that second of curling at the top, they were green and translucent and now and then the shape of a fish could be seen. All about him on the dunes there grew an oatlike plant with a shock of golden buds. He broke off one and bit into it. Save for a slight saltiness there was no taste and he spit out the crusty fibers.

Watching the ocean, listening to its hypnotic sound, it occurred to him this was a strange place for Jorge Ojeda to be sitting. Before him stretched the immensity of this sea. Behind him was the ghostly silence of an empty collection of shacks and houses. He sat there alone but felt no loneliness and wondered why this was so.

For the first time he found himself wishing he knew more, had been able to study and learn beyond what the Sisters had taught. The mind should be a storehouse of treasure. From it, at will, a man could select the objects of his imagination and marvel at the wonders of this world. Suppose he knew for sure that Columbus, standing on the deck of his ship as it cruised this coast, had held his eye to a glass and looked upon this very spot where Jorge Ojeda now sat? It would no longer be a section of beach but a part of mankind's history and he was sharing it. Had Spanish soldiers in heavy armor walked this sand, and if so, it was possible Jorge Ojeda's feet had made prints above theirs . . . rubber sneakers fitting into long-vanished boot marks. For how many centuries had the waves broken here and whose ears heard the same sound he listened to now?

He lay back fully, shading his eyes with crossed arms against the sky's bright arc. He thought, I ought to be worried about how I am going to get along. I ought to be lonesome and even a little scared but I'm not. I should be wondering what is going to happen to Jorge Ojeda. How he is going to eat. Where he will sleep. What he will do when the little money is gone and he can't find a job. I'm seventeen years old and I have no trade, no skill and not much of an education. Instead of being troubled by all of this I lie here and think about Columbus or whether a Spanish soldier stood here or maybe made love to an Indian girl on the dune behind me. But seventeen, as his mother had once said about *nigger,* was only a word. You could have seventeen dollars or seventeen marbles. When it was an adjective applied to the years it became something entirely different. You could be old and wise at seventeen or young and an idiot. At the moment he felt neither seventeen nor seventy. He was simply Jorge Ojeda lying on a beach. He was ageless; without beginning or end. The reason, he mused, I am not uncertain or lonely or scared is because I know this is all part of something already planned for me. This was a conviction he would not speak of to anyone else. Even said aloud to himself it had a crazy sound; a real loony thing to imagine. The big, black Haitian woman could have said it with quiet simplicity and no one would have dared question her wisdom. Her son, now, drew upon an inheritance, the existence of which he had not suspected. It was mystical and as primitive as the sound of a drum; a sure feeling of destiny. Whether it was good or bad he could not tell but he was certain it was inescapable. Nothing he could do would hurry or delay the shaping of a pattern already drawn and waiting to be filled in by time alone.

The creaking of an ungreased cartwheel awoke him. He remained as he was for a moment. The sound was the cry of a small animal. He sat up, feeling the chill of late afternoon, and realized he had been asleep for several hours. Behind him the sun was a tangerine red and the ocean, which had been green and blue, was a shadowed indigo. Coming toward him along the beach was a wagon drawn by an old horse the color of sooted white. As he watched, the cart halted above the high-water mark. One of the two figures on the board seat dropped lightly to the packed sand. The other lowered himself with the slow, uncertain movements of age. From the tail of the wagon's bed the younger man began hauling at the heavy folds of a seine, drawing it out until it stretched a full two hundred feet on the beach. Lead weights were along one edge and round cork floats were spaced at the other. At each end of the long, gray net was a heavy wooden staff the thickness of a vaulting pole.

Jorge pulled himself stiffly to his feet and walked toward the wagon. The young man was stripping himself down to a pair of bathing trunks. His skin was tanned and polished by the sun until it glistened with the color of cordovan. Heavy layers of muscle were broad at the shoulders and flat on his belly. He glanced at Jorge as he approached, nodded but did not speak as he tossed shirt and faded dungarees to one side.

The old man was as gnarled as a brier root, as wrinkled as the shell of a walnut, and so dark in color that for a moment Jorge thought he was a Negro. He squatted on his hams and with thick fingers examined a rent in the meshes of the net.

"*Bastardo. Tiburon.*" He muttered to himself over the shark which had made the tear and continued to curse in soft Spanish at the damage which should have been repaired. As Jorge's shadow fell across him he looked up from beneath a crudely plaited straw hat. Despite his age the eyes were sharp, youthful and angry. "*Bastardo.*" He repeated the word.

Jorge smiled and, in Spanish, wished him a good afternoon.

The old man took the greeting in his native tongue as a matter of course. "*Buenas tardes, joven.*" He held up the ripped section as though it should also be a matter of concern to this stranger. Then he straightened up and his glance roved along the net's length.

"*Listo, Juanito?*"

The young man nodded that he was ready and hooked an arm about the pole at his end of the net. Watching, Jorge thought the old man was too ancient, too twisted and frail to hold, as an anchor on the beach, his end of the heavy seine while the young one took his out through the light breakers. In the water he would make a wide sweep which would bring him and the netted fish to shore.

"Want a hand with that?" Jorge made the offer to the boy, who seemed only a year or so older than himself. This was fishing as he had done it many times on the Gulf coast. "I'll hold or help you pull."

The boy shrugged. "There's no money in it." He didn't make the statement rudely or with an ungracious rejection of the offer. "Just some fish and damn cold water." He smiled to share a secret. "You can pull with me if you want. The old man would get sore if anyone told him he was too old to hold the beach end."

Jorge nodded and pulled off his khaki pants, shirt and sneakers, down to a pair of short underdrawers. The old man watched these movements critically but without comment. Jorge crooked an arm about the pole below that of the boy. Then, pulling together, they began to walk toward the water, dragging the net through the heavy sand as the old man followed.

"My name's John."

"John or Juan?" Jorge asked. He figured he had finally encountered a Norkin.

"Depends on who asks." The boy was indifferent.

"Mine's Jorge. Jorge Ojeda."

As the first of the small waves in the shallows swirled in and broke against their legs Jorge winced. It was cold. They bent forward, straining back and shoulder muscles, dragging the net into deeper water. Their toes dug into the smooth bottom and they were into heavier breakers. Beyond this point the unruffled swells flowed in against their waists and finally to their chests, lifting them gently from the water's floor. They were neck-deep before they heard the old man's distant shout. Glancing shoreward they could see him. The end of his pole was buried as an anchor into the beach and he reared back against the strain of the fully stretched net.

"He's stronger than he looks." Juan made the comment with admiration. "He's tough as hell and he must be eighty."

They were half walking, half swimming or treading water as the waves lifted and dropped them back with an easy rhythm. This was hard work, taxing all of their strength as they began to make a crescent sweep. The lead held the heavy net to the bottom and they must strain against that, the resistance of the water and the accumulating catch. They were turning into the shore now and the shelving bottom began to grow shallower. Jorge caught an occasional glimpse of the old man. He was braced, a solid figure, taking at this moment the full brunt of the operation. He leaned away, resting on his heels, as he fought against the pull.

Jorge and Juan were straining, half doubled over forward. Their toes fought for a hold in the bottom and their legs drove through the shallows. Just above the water's edge they dropped their pole. Then, with the old man working frantically at his end, they began taking the net in, hand over hand. Within the narrowing pouch at the center the fish threshed and boiled in their panic to escape. When this heaving pocket was clear of the water they rested for a moment, their breath coming in labored gasps.

"The old man used to take the outside." Juan choked a little on the effort of speech. "He damn near drowned himself one night but wouldn't admit it. I had to go after him. We almost lost the net." He turned and whistled sharply and the spiritless horse began walking slowly, bringing the wagon to them. "He still wants to go out," Juan continued. "Just to prove how tough he is."

"He's your father?" Jorge studied the old man as he came to where they stood. "Grandfather?"

"Father. Manuel de Cespedes y Catonia." Juan chuckled with an affectionate pride. "Isn't that a hell of a name for a fisherman?"

The old man joined them and they began sorting out the catch; the fish first and then the blue crabs which had to be untangled or shaken from the mesh. There were, also, a few small hammerhead shark. These were snatched up by the tail and tossed far up into the sand where, in tomorrow's sun, they would rot. The fish were whiting, fine, silvery mullet, pompano and small bass. The crabs half filled a galvanized washtub.

"Where do you sell the fish?" Jorge looked up.

"A market in New Smyrna sends over a truck. The old man boils the crabs. We smoke the mullet; keep some for ourselves and sell the rest door to door across the river."

The old man took a package of cigarettes from his pocket. He was the only one who wasn't wet. They lit one apiece and squatted, smoking with silent pleasure. In the darkening sky there was a fragment of a moon, strangely pale in the waning light.

"We'll make a couple of more hauls?" Juan made the question an invitation which could be refused. "Two ought to do it."

Jorge nodded. It didn't seem strange that he had become a part with these two; that he should be crouched here, sharing cigarettes with an old man and his son who, only a few minutes ago, had been strangers.

"*Como se llama, joven?*" The man spoke abruptly.

"*Jorge, señor. Jorge Ojeda.*"

The man inclined his head approvingly. "*Fuerte.*" He reached over and dug steel fingers into the muscles of Jorge's upper arm. "*Muy fuerte.*"

"He speaks English." Juan made the comment as though his father was not there or could not understand. "He speaks it as well as you and I do."

"Better," the old man commented blandly.

"He's a hell of an old man," the son continued, oblivious of or indifferent to his father's presence. "Wait until you hear him drunk sometime. He's got an old accordion at the house. He gets loaded on homemade scuppernong wine. Then he is something to hear. He sings gypsy songs."

"*Flamenco.*" The old man made the correction wearily. "You are an ignorant fisherman."

Juan winked at Jorge. "He says the Duke of Alba was his cousin. He says the de Cespedes were nobility of the Spanish court. They lived in a castle with a hundred rooms in Andalusia."

"Fifty rooms. One hundred servants." Manuel de Cespedes y Catonia made the revision of his son's statement with mild authority. "You are not only ignorant but without grace or manners." This, Jorge realized, was said in effortless and all but unaccented English. "Except," the man continued, "that I know better I would say you were a whore's bastard. Unfortunately for her, your mother was a great lady." He turned to study Jorge. "Ojeda is a fine name. An admiral in Spain's navy many centuries ago."

"He's either the biggest liar or the smartest man in the world." Juan shrugged helplessly.

"My father made cigars in Tampa." Jorge offered the information.

"The de Cespedes, father and son, are fishermen. Nothing more." The old man pinched the live coal of his cigarette out between his fingers. "The world turns swiftly." He stood up. "We have work to do."

They made two more hauls and on the last kept only the hand sized pompano and the mullet. The rest were thrown back alive into the sea.

"We take from God only what we need." The old man watched as the fish streaked away to deep water and safety. Then he turned to Jorge. "If you wish our house is yours." This he said in Spanish.

"I have no place to go." Jorge made the statement, not as a complaint but as a simple fact. "Thank you."

Standing in the wagon Jorge and Juan folded in the heavy net until it was piled high on the bed. The fish were in wet sacks; the crabs scraped, crawled over each other and made small bubbling sounds in the tub. The old man stood watching until everything was in order. Then he climbed to the narrow board seat, took up the reins and waited until Jorge and his son joined him there.

"We will spread the net to dry and then we will all have some wine." De Cespedes slapped the leather across the old mare's rump. "We will eat and get to know each other, which is as it should be."

In such a manner had their lives been joined and with the passing of time they became each a part of the other without realizing it. With the de Cespedes, Jorge Ojeda was a fisherman and they shared what they took from the sea by their labor. The cottage of grayed boards and shingles within the dunes was their home and they lived as men should without fear. The ocean at their feet supplied their few needs. They sold the market fish. The mullet they smoked over bay and oak fumes on long racks and the boys peddled them from door to door—not humbly but as men who had a thing of value to sell. With the money earned they bought their tobacco, the rice and flour, coffee and sugar, meat or a chicken for stewing on Sunday. On occasions they would purchase a jug of rum from a bootlegger and the old man would get out his accordion and sing the wild laments of the *flamenco* or quiet songs of love and unhappiness.

From Manuel de Cespedes y Catonia, Jorge Ojeda absorbed some of the quiet wisdom. He believed the old man to be what he said he was. There was pride in his manner, education in his speech. He lived in contentment which had no part with dumb patience or resignation. This was the life he had chosen and he never expressed regret or envy for any other. In

Juan, Jorge found a brother and they argued and sometimes fought as brothers will. But the fights were without anger. They occurred, as they do with strong, young animals, out of vitality or a trivial incident which gave them an excuse to pit themselves against each other.

Jorge went often across the river. There were girls to be walked with and made love to in the darkness. There was the library and from it he borrowed books and read them at home into the night's long hours by the light of a kerosene lamp. From them he learned much of history and of men and through them, although he did not know it, he achieved a certain grace of manner and speech. He grew strong; tough in his body from the heavy work, self-reliant and confident. He had no feeling he must hurry. This was an interlude. He would take it for what it was and nothing more. When the time came for him to move on he would recognize the hour. Of this he was certain.

Sometimes, when he and Juan were shoulder deep in the water, throwing their muscles against the surge of the waves and the net's heavy drag, he would smile quietly to himself and amusement would kindle in his eyes. Once, unable to withstand the impulse, he had shouted with sudden laughter. This was the work for which animals were trained, to be patient beneath the burden, to bend the back and carry the load without complaint or question. Juan had stared at him with surprised curiosity.

"What's so funny?"

Jorge shook his head. It could not be explained here or now. It had occurred to him this was one hell of an unlikely place for a man to catch and train some of the world's fleas. Without his realizing it, he had become one of them.

The years spun themselves out of the skein of time and were woven into a rich fabric, the pattern of which was companionship, affection, understanding and a measure of love as it can exist between men. Watching, listening sometimes while he pretended to be drowsing in the sun, the old one marveled at the quiet assurance which possessed this Jorge who had become a second son.

Unlike Juanito, whose head was filled with an urgent drive and fanciful dreams of a dazzling future in which beautiful girls, fine clothes, cars and pockets bulging with money figured, Jorge Ojeda had the rare quality of patience and confidence. What would be would come with time. It could not be hurried nor made to swerve from its predestined course. Everything he did and said reflected this conviction. Time, alone, would command. He waited for it and laughed softly at Juan's restive spirit. And always he was at the books which he took each week from the library across the river. Where Juan would sprawl on his belly, engrossed in the sporting pages of the Jacksonville *Times-Union,* this Jorge lost himself in history, biography, and the great story of mankind from the beginning as it was written in the Bible and taken by other men through the centuries. When Juan would scoff and ask, "What are you going to do with all that stuff?" Jorge replied confidently, "Some of it I will remember. Much of it I will forget. But, what I remember will stay with me because in the end I will have a use for it."

To piece out their small income both of the boys sometimes found day-work in New Smyrna or helping on the shrimp boats. But always they had enough to eat, a roof and the graying cottage for shelter. Beyond their world of the dunes and the sea tremendous events were shaping themselves. Violence, unrest, poverty and the chaos of the great economic upheaval kept the world in an uneasy state of suspension.

Out of their contact with the shrimp boats Juan and Jorge had moved without conscious effort into the smuggling of small loads of contraband whisky and rum. The craft made contact beyond the three-mile limit with a larger vessel and the illicit liquor transferred, to be carried ashore from the shrimpers' docks and sold to local bootleggers. From this they had graduated to hands aboard a rumrunner and later to a boat of their own, financed by a respectable businessman in New Smyrna who took his share of the profits and later sold them the boat outright for more than it was worth, and they were in business for themselves.

It had been a time of high piratical adventure which appealed to Juan's flamboyant nature. On the boat and in the islands he wore a gold ring in one ear, wrapped his head in a bandana and would have affected a black patch over one eye if it hadn't provoked Jorge to hysterical laughter. It was a game played in constant danger and for high stakes. No one, except the federal government, regarded rumrunning as an unlawful or disgraceful occupation. The law was flouted, laughed at throughout the land. They neither accepted themselves nor the men with whom they did business as criminals but matched their wits against them, the sea, federal officials, hijackers and larcenous agents who had to be bought off to look the other way when the cargoes were landed.

They had brought the liquor from Nassau, Bimini and Cat Key. The Bahamas experienced a time of prosperity unmatched since Southern privateers had run contraband past a federal blockade during the War Between the States. Cases of whisky, rum and brandy were piled high on Bay Street, in Nassau, where they were sold to the smugglers. The island's first families were engaged, indirectly at least, in the trade. There were fights, brawls and a noisy carousing in the bars and native slums "over the hill."

In Nassau they rented a house which they used as a headquarters during their stay on the island. It was filled with girls, music and gusty humor, for this was the age of laughter between them. Once, they had gone to New York and taken a four-bedroom suite at the Biltmore Hotel. When the two-week binge was over, the casual friends gone, they had spent almost twenty thousand dollars and it had all seemed like a great idea at the time. The old man, Juan's father, had merely shrugged at the whole business. He displayed little interest in the money which they now had. When they would bring him a case of wine, he would taste it with a skeptical expression but never admit it was superior to the vintage he made himself from the native scuppernong grape.

The years had changed both Jorge and Juan physically. Ojeda's once lean body had filled out. There was strength in the sloping shoulders, finely modeled hands and long legs. In his bearing there was an easy pride and confidence; an epée-like quality. Juan was almost as tall but inclined to a heaviness. He had, as always, the quick, easy laugh; the quality of making friends with everyone from a stray dog to a native boatman in the islands. His zest for this good life was insatiable and he displayed it in his women, liquor, food, and clothing and shirts which were tailored and made to his order in New York.

Now they both understood that the time of adventure was running out. With the election of Franklin Roosevelt repeal of the 18th Amendment was certain. There would be no place in the new scheme of things for the buccaneers of the rumrunning fleet. Neither was quite certain what they should do. The craft they owned could be converted into a charter fishing boat but this seemed a tame occupation. Juan, called Pepito by Jorge for reasons neither quite remembered, brooded moodily on this. To return to the placid life of a fisherman was unthinkable.

"When the time comes, Pepito," Jorge had calmly answered his continual questioning, "we will know what we are to do."

This night, heavily laden and without running lights, the boat crept through the narrow channel of the inlet toward a great sweep of darkness which was the lagoon. Her exhausts were muffled and the twin motors barely ticked over with a steady rhythm as they maintained steerageway on the rush of an incoming tide.

Within the glass-enclosed shelter of the cabin's overhang which sheltered the pilot and a hatchway leading below deck Jorge Ojeda strained his eyes to pierce the night. On both sides of this cut from the sea the breakers crashed and ran in foaming whiteness on the inlet's shoals. Far up on a spit of land, a dark streak against the blacker night, the lighthouse stood to flash its beacon. Along the channel itself there were bell buoys, their sound clear and reassuring. Neither Jorge nor Juan needed these guides. They had run this inlet channel so many times in all sorts of weather that they could almost smell their way in and make the course by instinct. There was no light on the compass or instrument panel.

An automatic .12-gauge shotgun and a Thompson submachine gun rested within easy reach on a shelf between them. Beneath a tightly stretched tarpaulin in the cockpit aft were tightly packed, burlap-wrapped "hams" of Scotch and Irish whisky, cognac and rum. Below, every square foot of space, including the small head, was similarly loaded. On the shelf, with the firearms and night glasses in a leather case, was an unopened bottle. Jorge took this now, tore away the foil and pulled the cork. He offered it to Juan at the helm.

"Pepito?"

Juan didn't take his eyes from the course but he accepted the bottle and took a long, satisfying drink. His hand on the wheel was as sure and sensitive as that of a jockey and he held the craft's bows true on the dark line of deep water. He half smiled and returned the bottle.

"Bien suerte."

Jorge drank and then recorked the bottle. It was the first drink either had taken since leaving the Bahamas. It warmed and revived them. Their faces were drawn and their eyes tired from the strain.

The only sound above the evenly turning motors was that of the running sea behind them as it hit the beach with a rolling crash. They were through the worst part of making in from the open sea. The water in the lagoon, which was called a river because it stretched for almost two hundred miles along the mainland, was quiet and with only the reflection of the stars upon it. The long, scrub-covered spit of Merritt Island lay portside. On the starboard a few lights showed, scattered here and there in the houses of a small town clinging to the river's edge.

"It's almost done, hey, big man?" Juan laughed softly.

Jorge did not relax. His gaze continued to search the water.

"When we're unloaded, Pepito. When the stuff is in the truck and the money in our hands. Then it is done for the last time."

The boat moved with a comfortable sluggishness now past the wooden channel markers where, by day, the pelicans roosted in solemn meditation. If there was to be trouble it would come within the next few minutes. A lurking Coast Guard cutter could pick them up in the glaring beam of its searchlight. They didn't really have to worry too much about the Coast Guard. They were mostly young men and did not take the Prohibition Act very seriously. Now and then certain financial arrangements with them were made and the boats looked the other way. There was, though, always the possibility of an overzealous officer and patrol who ignored the unadmitted truce between rumrunner and the Treasury Department. The firearms were not for use against the Coast Guard. If they halted a craft and confiscated its cargo it could, sometimes, be purchased back for a not un-reasonable sum. Neither side considered this to be dishonest but a natural hazard of the game. The guns were at hand because of hijackers; here and on shore. It had happened before. A light would stab out of the darkness, blinding them. A raiding craft would move alongside with armed, danger-ous men on her deck. They had once lost a full load that way. The second time it had been tried Jorge had turned the submachine gun loose with a cold fury. The searchlight had been the first target; the shadowy figures the second. Both had been raked with a deadly precision and they left be-hind them the screams of agony and then silence as they had raced beyond pursuit.

On the starboard side now there loomed the dark tangle of a mangrove island; a matted place of spider growth. Jorge reached for the machine gun and moved back into the open where he could command this place. Behind it could be lurking a hijacking boat.

Juan touched the twin throttles and the beat of the motors accelerated. A small wave began to cream about the bows. Nothing moved or showed itself when the sheltered side of the island was cleared. Jorge relaxed and heard Juan laugh softly.

"Injun like heap big firestick. Ug?" Juan's words were thickly burlesqued. "No gettum chance to shootem pale face. Too damn bad."

"Ug!" Jorge permitted himself this bit of nonsense.

Sometimes they whiled away the monotonous hours of the run from Nassau or Bimini with such foolish talk or spoke to each other in out-rageously corrupted Spanish in which they mixed English and Spanish words, howling with laughter at the effect. A simple meal, prepared and eaten while cruising, was made better somehow if it was interspersed with such a ludicrous sentence as: *Pase me los frijole beans on un plato con some of that there arroz rice, corned beef carne and salsa gravy.* Neither could have explained why such locutions were hysterically funny. Cer-tainly it would not have occurred to either that it was only because they were young, healthy animals who had become inexplicably yoked with a deep attachment.

The lights along the shore were brighter now. Juan picked up the shadowy outline of a nun buoy and spun the wheel to carry them past at a sharp angle. In five minutes more they would be at the mouth of a deep canal which ran inland through the marsh until it ended in a bog. Where the water began to shallow out there was a makeshift dock. There a truck and men would be waiting with cash for the cargo which would be quickly transferred and run north.

"This is the last one, *amigo*?" Juan asked the question regretfully. "We've had a hell of a time, haven't we?"

"As you say, Pepito," Jorge spoke thoughtfully, "we've had a hell of a time."

"What do we do now?"

"I have been thinking about something." Ojeda rested his arms on the shelf. "It is a thing to do together. We will talk about it later."

A tiny light winked on the shore and Juan cut the motors, allowing the boat to drift with a slowing momentum. Jorge went forward to throw a line to a waiting man.

All of this had been such a long time ago and yet, each detail, every small sound of that night, was distinct in Ojeda's memory.

VI.

THE knock on the door was repeated. He had heard it the first time but it had seemed to come from a great distance and without meaning to him or connection with the room in which he sat. This time it was sharper and brought him back to the day.

"Yes?" He half turned in the chair. "Come in."

Colonel Juan de Cespedes who, by The Benefactor's grace, would be a general in the morning, came into the room and closed the door behind him. He had changed into a uniform of dazzling tropical white. A row of miniature decorations blazed across his chest.

"I thought maybe you were sleeping." He crossed and without invitation poured himself a glass of sherry and selected a cigar. He lifted a couple of the medals with a forefinger. "How do you like them?"

"You are a beauty, Pepito. A beauty and a man of resources who bestows his own decorations. What are they for—love, bravery, loyalty? Where did you find them?"

"I had them copied from one of the books in the library. Sanchez, the jeweler, made them for me. I don't know what they mean. Who cares? They look pretty."

"You are a fine, white peacock of a man." Ojeda nodded approval. "A soldier of magnificence and great elegance. You give the place a distinction. Always you have had a flair. Even during the revolution you stood out. I wonder why I don't trust you completely, Pepito?"

"I don't think you ought to call a full general Pepito, Excellency. Even when there is no one to hear but the two of us, I never call you Jorge." There was a mild irony in the rebuke. "I bow to the office not the man. You have taught me much. I remember a time when I was only a dumb fisherman and then a bootlegger. Look at me now."

"I am." Jorge Ojeda studied him reflectively. "But I still don't trust you as I should."

Juan shrugged. "In your place I wouldn't trust anyone either." He lit the cigar carefully. "Today I am satisfied to be what I am. Tomorrow being a general will be enough. But the day after tomorrow I might wake up in the morning and decide it would be a fine thing to be *el presidente*. Then," he waved at a scarf of drifting smoke, "I would have to arrange to have you killed. Or, and I've got to remember this, you might learn I have become a man of ambition and have me shot the way Valdez and the others were. Why did you do that one yourself?"

"Because I trusted Valdez. We had been friends."

"You went to bed with his wife."

"That is what the wives of friends are for. Anyhow, with Valdez it was a personal thing. I would do the same with you, Pepito."

"I believe it." Juan was undisturbed. "Valdez I can understand. Besides, he was a fool to trust a woman with such a secret. But the others—they were men whose names you didn't even know. A firing squad would have done just as well for them."

"It was a necessary gesture, Pepito. Excuse me—General. I must try and forget you were once only a dumb fisherman and then a bootlegger."

"*Gracias, presidente.*"

"Anyhow," Ojeda permitted the sarcasm to pass without notice, "I made of the executions this morning a mirror in which I am reflected. Thick as are the walls of the Presidio, whispers pass through them. By now it is known *el presidente* himself gave out the punishment. It will lend the people confidence in The Benefactor. *Mira!* They will say to each other: *El presidente* is still one of us. He does his own killing when it is necessary and has not lost the common touch even though he lives in a palace. He is a man capable of anger even as you and I."

"Did you learn all this from the books you are always reading?"

Jorge shook his head. "As an untutored musician I play by ear. I do certain things instinctively. This was one of them."

Juan de Cespedes glanced at his watch. "Are you coming down now?"

"Who could resist making an entrance in the company of such a splendid figure as you?" He stood up. "I have been sitting here thinking about us; of your father and the net we pulled together and how, on a night when we decided the time had come to stop running whisky from the islands, we looked at each other and said: What do we do now?"

"You would have made one hell of an actor, Excellency."

"I was a better soldier."

"Yes," Juan agreed, "you were one hell of a soldier. No one can deny that. Of all the men I knew you were the only one who liked the killing; really felt good when he got a Jap in his sights and squeezed the trigger. Sometimes, I thought, for you it was like having a woman."

"You talk as a child. War is a simple matter. Only the retired generals who write textbooks make it complicated. You destroy the enemy or he destroys you."

"For fun?"

"It has an appeal. Men have found it fascinating for centuries."

He walked to the French windows and leaned against the frame, studying the scene below. It had taken on a form and order. The servants stood waiting. The colored umbrellas were huge blossoms. Silver buckets in which champagne gathered a frost sparkled in the sunlight. The long buffet was prepared and the chef, with his assistants in their loaflike hats of white, were at grave attention behind the table. Ready for the carving knives were roasts; the tender *cabrito,* the young kid of the goats; the saddles of the small, mountain deer; the turkeys, ducks and geese. The hues of the table delighted him. There were pink mounds of shrimp and crawfish. A huge, blue-black pit of caviar in sculptured ice. For the Americans, who thought champagne was only something for weddings or anniversaries, there was a bar with whisky, vodka, gin and rum.

"That night, after we had collected the money"—Juan reminisced and his voice carried a soft note of wonder—"it was thick in our pockets. Do you remember? All I thought about was the women it would buy, the clothes, the car, the whisky to be drunk."

"Instead, we gave it to the Duke of Alba's cousin." Ojeda did not turn and Juan could not see the quiet amusement in his eyes. "It was a time of fine excitement come to an end."

"How do you like that?" The years had not erased the perplexity of that moment. "We dropped it all in my old man's lap and said: Here, *viejito.* Take it. Lie in the sun and play your accordion while it lasts. Get yourself a woman. Get drunk."

"I often wonder if he did those things."

"He was the only one who didn't think you were crazy." Juan refilled his glass. "Remember? He looked at those rolls of bills and they had no meaning or interest. He said only: Where do you go?"

Ojeda left the window now and came to the table where he also refilled his glass and drank half of it.

"The Marine Corps." Juan would not be denied the incredulous thing which had happened almost thirty years ago. "*Jésus Cristo!* Of all the damn fool things. Parris Island. Pendleton. There were times when I never thought I'd make it."

[71]

"I was sure." Ojeda finished his wine. "Even in the Pacific I said to myself: This is a part of my destiny. The things I learn here will serve a purpose. I thought of the many men of history who had made a trade of fighting and how it had carried them far. There is always need of a good man in places of trouble and unrest. I told myself: I will be good at this trade of killing." He paused. "You see I was right. Look around you or at yourself in the mirror, Pepito. How many dumb fishermen become generals and pick out their own medals?" He made a motion as though to touch Juan de Cespedes on the shoulder with an impulsive gesture of affection and then changed his mind and the hand dropped away. "We will meet our guests. I sometimes wonder why they come or why I invite them."

"They accept because you invite them and you invite them because it pleases you to be *el presidente*. But," Juan regarded the tall figure quizzically, "not all of them eh? The ones from the big houses on the hills who have seen many *presidentes* come and go. They ignore the command."

Ojeda shook his head. "You must think me a man of small anger, Pepito. That is strange, knowing me as you do. If that was what I wanted they would come. I could strip them of everything. Houses, land, money, servants; even food and the privilege of walking San Rafael's streets. I could then say: Each Sunday from now on you will come and take back with you some small piece of what you have lost." He tapped the rim of the sherry glass and it rang with the tinkle of a silver bell.

"You would be afraid." De Cespedes made the statement without malice or emphasis. "You would be afraid to test the power so far. Suppose you did and they said: We would rather stand this way, naked, than to drink, eat and talk with you at the palace receptions. What would you do then?"

"You see?" This time Ojeda completed the gesture of a moment ago. He put his arm across the shoulder of an old friend. "I am right not to trust you completely, Pepito. You are beginning to think. The brain stirs a little as a man turns in his sleep before awakening fully."

"That is because I have become a general." Juan laughed. "Below that rank thinking is done for you. It is your fault. *Vamonos?*"

"Yes, fisherman. Let us go together."

The red Mercedes waited just within the gates of the official residence. Two sentries at rigid attention undeniably blocked the way although they somehow managed to give the impression they were unaware of the car's presence. Ferris Dessaline leaned back in the seat, a crooked arm resting on the wheel. Through the small window of the gatehouse she could see the sergeant of the guard as he spoke into a telephone. She waited without impatience. For so many Sundays now the invitations had been returned by the Dessaline servants that she had come without one.

The guard had been courteous, respectful but firm. The sergeant polite, understanding but also inflexible. This was a girl of shining beauty. Under almost any circumstances a man must regard her with pleasure and grant a request. The unconcealed admiration in his eyes told her those things. His words, however, had said that without an invitation no one was permitted to enter the grounds. He would telephone the palace and give the name of the Señorita Dessaline to a superior and ask for instructions.

She could see him now as he nodded and hung up the instrument. In the moment before he came out she wondered how it would feel to be turned away. It could happen. It might well happen.

"It is permitted, Señorita Dessaline." He saluted and smiled as though between them they had a secret.

She winked at him and the Mercedes slid forward, gathering speed, and took the first of the long, ascending curves with a low-slung grace.

As she drove, Ferris looked about with curiosity and pleasure. The Presidential Palace was not entirely new to her, for she had known the place as a child. With the children of Presidente Maldinado she had ridden docile ponies over the wide estate and the son of another *presidente* had kissed her at the age of six beneath an arbor near a fountain. Now for the first time since The Benefactor had seized power she passed through the gates.

Winding upward her eye was caught by unexpected vistas: a terrace; or a sheer drop, down which cascaded a flowered curtain of color. What she saw made her wonder about this man Ojeda under whose orders this beauty had been created. It contradicted so much he had done on San Rafael and argued a far gentler nature than he had displayed. This undisputed tyrant of an island—a tough, unswerving man of ambition, a murderer, if not by choice, certainly one by his own idea of necessity—had also an understanding of grace, form and a reserved magnificence. One would seem to contradict the other.

As she drove slowly she wondered why she was here. It was a thing to be gossiped about tomorrow and an act to be censored and disapproved of by almost everyone the Dessalines knew on the island. Curiosity wasn't enough to explain her presence. Or if it was only curiosity, then it was too much and not something to be satisfied by a formal exchange of polite words at a garden party. She had small patience with those who complained of boredom. It confessed a lack of imagination. So, as an excuse, this was ruled out. She braked the car to a halt and lit a cigarette, curious as to why she was lying to herself. She had come because she was bored and the idea of listening to and talking with this man had suddenly stimulated her imagination. She had seen him, of course. She had listened to his execrable Spanish when he spoke on the radio to the people he always addressed as *Niños*. He did this, she had to admit, without suggesting a hypocritical affection or paternal indulgence. He spoke the word children as a teacher might to a class and it carried discipline and authority. San Rafael, she thought with a small grin, must have more radios in proportion to its population than almost any other place in the world. Ojeda had seen to it that even the meanest cottage had a set. In remote villages where the transmission lines for electricity had not yet been strung there was a battery-operated set for each family. The radios had not been sold to the people but given as presents. That the money to pay for them had been taken in devious and unrecognizable ways from the *niños* themselves had, apparently, not occurred to them. The sets were *regalos*, gifts of magnificence from The Benefactor himself, who wanted them to understand all things. Through them came music and the words of *el presidente*. When he spoke, no one failed to listen. His words and wisdom were made available because of his generosity.

She stubbed the cigarette out in an ash tray. Even her grandmother's friends, who never spoke his name, admitted he was shrewd. A scoundrel, undoubtedly, and of an order with which they were unfamiliar but he was clever. There had been scoundrels in office before, but by comparison, they had reduced the presidency to a post of small pilfering. This Ojeda took what he wanted on a grand scale and made no effort to hide what he was doing. Dropping the Mercedes into gear she spun through the remaining curves toward the wide driveway before the palace. Again she caught herself wondering what it really was this man wanted. In a way he was a prisoner to his own ambition. San Rafael was a self-created Elba. To leave it for more than a few days would loose all the scattered forces opposed to him. He had to stay or perish. He had condemned himself to exile on this island. It was, she conceded readily enough, a small paradise of sun and flowers, a gem within the setting of a blue Caribbean. But it was this only if it could be left and returned to at will. Without this freedom it was a coral prison.

From Madame Dessaline she had heard the stories of other men who had occupied this office. Once in, they placated their opposition with bribes and inconsequential but fine-sounding positions in the Government. Thereafter they devoted themselves to the pleasures of being *el presidente*. They were thieves but genial ones with a robust capacity for life. They had large families and their mistresses and took them all on seasonal excursions to the French and Italian Rivieras, Switzerland, German spas, with vacations in New York, London and Paris. The presidential yachts grew in size and luxuriousness and official residences were scattered liberally about the cool reaches of the green mountains. By comparison, this Jorge Ojeda was a monk. She couldn't recall ever hearing his name mentioned in connection with a woman. He gave the few necessary State functions out of a diplomatic necessity and these Sunday garden parties once a month. Since it is the habit of servants to talk and what one tells another eventually reaches the ears of all employers, it was generally understood that life in the palace was only short of austere. What, then, were the rewards? Ferris shook her head. No ready answer came to mind.

Ojeda stood with a glass of champagne in his hand, listening to the many-keyed hum of conversation. The sounds rose and fell continuously as small waves. With him were Kent Glastonbury, Chargé d'Affaires at the American Embassy, and his vividly animated young wife, Christina. Ojeda had an open admiration for Glastonbury. By a miracle he had preserved an almost rakish manner and a sense of humor, rare qualities in a career diplomat. They got along famously, in Christina's words. She confessed she hadn't the slightest idea what the phrase meant. How did you get along famously? It was one of those ridiculous expressions used by the British to confuse the colonials. The Glastonburys came to the palace because they enjoyed the parties and not because it was part of their duty.

A servant brought fresh glasses of wine. Christina lifted hers.

"*Salud!*"

They both made the small gesture of salute in return. It was a good wine, dry and crisp.

"I wonder," Kent spoke, "why we Americans regard champagne with suspicion?"

"Because it tastes good." Christina was emphatic.

"That doesn't make any sense."

"I think it does." Ojeda enjoyed their irrelevancies. "Because it gives a pleasure to the palate it is immoral. Whisky isn't a particularly pleasant-tasting liquid. It is drunk more for the effect than for the pleasure it gives the senses of taste or smell. A man can get drunk on whisky without the guilty feeling of having enjoyed it."

"That's what I meant." The girl smiled at her husband.

"Then why didn't you say so?"

"I did but in fewer words. It's my New England upbringing." She bowed in Ojeda's direction. "*El presidente* has the charming volubility of all Latins."

"*El presidente* is as much an American as you are." Kent made the statement casually. "At least, he was born in the United States. Isn't that correct, Excellency?"

Ojeda wasn't surprised. This was an area in the Caribbean which the United States considered vital to its interests. Little went on which was not carefully watched by Washington. Certainly the background of everyone in island office must have been investigated and the information locked away. Too much money was being spent here. Washington would want to know into whose hands it fell. He was a little curious as to how complete the file on Jorge Ojeda was.

Past Kent's shoulder Ojeda saw one of his aides, Captain Ortega, escorting Ferris Dessaline across the lawn toward them. A few moments before, one of the secretaries had whispered to him. The guard at the gates had asked for instructions regarding a Señorita Dessaline who had arrived without an invitation. Ojeda had nodded his permission. Watching her now he wondered why she had come. Glastonbury followed his glance and whistled with soft astonishment.

"Is this surrender, Excellency? Do the walls crumble?"

Ojeda shrugged. "Reconnaissance, probably."

Captain Ortega made the presentation with stiff formality.

"*Presidente*." Ferris smiled. "I forgot my ticket."

"It is unimportant." He studied her gravely. "I am happy you wanted to come."

"Hello, Christina. Kent." She offered her hand to them. "How are you?"

"Surprised." Glastonbury was faintly mocking. "The natives in the hills will be restless tonight when they hear about this."

A waiter was at Ferris's side. She took a glass from the tray.

"If you're trying to embarrass me, it isn't working." She turned to Ojeda. "I came because I was curious about you. It was personal. Also," a small, impertinent smile crept into her eyes, "my grandmother wanted me to ask you a question. But that can wait."

"How is Madame Dessaline?" It was a mere politeness.

"Adamant, Excellency. When I left she was having a glass of Dessaline rum and smoking a cigar. She denies your existence as she does the validity of the Protestant faith. You cannot be, therefore you are not."

"And you?" He was aware of an inner radiance which transcended the surface beauty. "What is your opinion?"

"I'm a pragmatist. What I see I believe."

There was a constant shifting of scene as small groups gathered, broke apart and re-formed with others. Close together but at three separate tables sat the refugees, the Generals Morillo, Torralba and San Martin. With them, appearing as though they had been cut by the same lapidary from one block of flawless crystal, were three blond, extremely beautiful and perfectly groomed young women in their middle twenties. The generals, in full uniform and with their many decorations catching fire in the sunlight, appeared morose and suspicious. They drank their scotch and soda without apparent pleasure and stared moodily past each other without an exchange of words. Now and then someone would stop to speak or make a politely formal inquiry. When this happened the general addressed beamed and became voluble with an invitation to sit down. He would glance at his companions as though to say: You see? I am not forgotten. I have friends, supporters and those who care. I am not alone on this damned island. Alone again he peered glumly into his drink and watched the others with narrow-eyed sullenness. Their companions, on the other hand, made an almost desperate attempt at gaiety. They laughed with a tinkling merriment, leaned back and forth toward each other like long-stemmed blossoms in a light wind and talked animatedly in an effort to appear delighted with everything.

"Why do you suppose dictators in flight always take blond mistresses with them?" Ferris looked up at Ojeda.

"I think they are generally supposed to be more expensive than brunettes." He answered gravely, well aware of what was a deliberate insolence. "Few things of value are left behind."

Ferris was surprised and made a quick re-evaluation of this man. He was not easily thrust off balance and that was exactly what she had tried to do out of sheer perverseness.

"I'm sorry." She made the apology with unsmiling honesty. "I was rude. It was unnecessary."

"Whenever I see them together," Christina was being chatty to cover an awkward moment, "I can only think of those stone figures on Easter Island. There they sit and wait for someone to come along and explain them."

Kent took his wife's arm firmly. "Even for a wife of an undiplomatic diplomat you are often too much." He made a briefly amused salute to Ojeda. "I know you'll be glad to excuse us, Excellency. Ferris?" He nodded to her with a quick grin.

They watched as the Glastonburys moved away and were absorbed in the crowd. They were casually friendly with everyone and seemed to have an inexhaustible store of small talk.

"I sometimes wonder how Kent has survived the strictures of his post." Ferris glanced at Ojeda. "He must be unique in the field of diplomacy."

"He's deceptively efficient at his job. Would you like to sit at a table?"

"I'd much rather walk around. If it is permissible to monopolize el presidente."

They strolled slowly and she was aware of heads turning and curious stares following them as they moved. Ojeda made a slight, formal bow now and then in recognition of a smile or a spoken word. For the most part his face was a polite mask. Now and then Ferris saw someone she knew or vaguely recognized. Most of them were American executives of American-owned properties on San Rafael. The others were all strangers and she wondered where they had come from and what they did.

"You don't seem to enjoy your parties." She was interested. "Why do you give them?"

"Why did you come?"

They halted on one of the terraces. Below was spread the sloping perfection of the gardens and beyond them the shining city and the great, blue expanse of the sea.

"I'm not sure. I think I wanted to dislike you."

"Couldn't you have disliked me from a distance?" He was interested and with a flicker of amusement transforming his features. "Most persons find that as satisfactory and much safer."

She took a cigarette from a small case and he struck a match. Holding it he studied her upturned face. Their eyes held for a moment and then slid away.

"Off with their heads!" She drew upon the cigarette.

"You are trying to be outraged by authority or power." He laughed quietly. "I don't know why. The history of your family contradicts that. The Dessaline fortune was built with slaves. Men were beaten and frequently killed for rebelling against what the Dessalines took for granted. Why are you striking this phony attitude with me?" There was an abrupt harshness in his voice.

"I'm exploring. What are you? One of these days I'll inherit control of the Dessaline properties on San Rafael. When that happens I'd like to know how to cope with you."

"You can't. Not on that level." It was an unemotional statement of fact. "The best you can hope for is that the Government—"

"Come now," she interrupted. "Who is being phony? You mean Jorge Ojeda."

"All right. The best you can hope for is that Jorge Ojeda will have no need for the Dessaline properties or that he will be indifferent to your presence on the island. After today"—he bowed ironically—"that will be impossible."

"I guess that is a compliment." She was doubtful. "Anyhow it's basic. At the risk of being trite I must say you surprise me. I had an idea you would be all the things one associates with a freebooter—arrogance, rudeness. Except for your Spanish, which is atrocious, there is charm, persuasiveness and education in your speech."

"You're being pretty damned patronizing, Miss Dessaline."

"I suppose so, but what you just said is a little more in character. You were a sergeant in the American Marine Corps, weren't you? Just then you sounded like one."

He chuckled. "In my bad Spanish, *acaso es borra*? Do you think that is nothing?"

They began walking again along the graveled path which seemed to wander without purpose or direction through the carefully groomed woods. There was a mountaintop freshness in the air and a sense of isolation which created a quiet intimacy.

"A man learns to read." He spoke as though to himself. "With that the tool for an education is in his hands. I have tried to use it. My schooling was parochial and elementary."

She was surprised. "Why are you telling me that?"

He shrugged. "It's an expression of vanity, I suppose."

Their feet made a small crackling sound on the raked pebbles. She laughed suddenly and halted, turning to face him.

"I almost forgot. My grandmother wanted me to ask you if it is true you charge San Martin and the other generals a thousand dollars a day American for the privilege of sanctuary on San Rafael?"

"I think that is the figure."

"Why?"

"To remind me how expensive failure can be."

"I was sure you didn't need the money."

"No." Again he ignored the sarcasm. "I don't need the money."

"I was abroad at the time of the revolution. More and more your name began to appear in the reports. You were a captain in General Quatero's forces, weren't you? I heard, when I came back, how he trusted you completely. He spoke of you affectionately as his son who would some day succeed him. Yet it was you who betrayed and killed him."

"I had him shot. There's a difference." He was unmoved. "By General Quatero's orders General Romero and his cabinet were executed in the Presidio. Then, by my orders, General Quatero was put against the wall."

"Again, why?"

"Because he had what I had given him. A successful revolution and San Rafael. I couldn't see much of a future working for General Quatero. Anyhow, there was little difference between him and Romero as far as the people were concerned. They were only taking on a new rider."

"And you decided you would be better for your *niños?*"

"I have been."

"Like hell." She was close to anger. "No one is better off under a dictator; complete, unquestionable authority. I know that and so do you."

"It has been the traditional government of the island." He was unruffled. "Only the names change. Romero. Quatero. Ojeda. Why is mine so objectionable to you?"

She wasn't sure. "Maybe it's this damned pose of beneficence. The others were thieves but they weren't hypocrites."

"How do you know I am a thief?"

"Aren't you?" There was almost a shade of doubt in the question.

"I got rid of Quatero and took his job. Such things happen regularly in great corporations. Ambition in young executives is encouraged. Why shouldn't a man be ambitious in the matter of government? I don't imagine an assistant vice-president gets rid of a superior in, say, Standard Oil in the same way. But on San Rafael at the time, bloodshed was necessary. To have deported Quatero would have only turned an angry dog loose to nip at my heels. So, he was executed."

"And now you are *el presidente*."

They turned and began retracing their steps. She was a little baffled and uneasy, for what he had said was not all sophistry.

"Do you like being *el presidente?*" She was persistent.

"My valet—Jorge Ojeda's valet asked me the same question this morning. What I told him I will not tell you because, again, you will yell hypocrite. Liar. Like hell. And," he actually laughed at her, "other words more suitable to the Marine Corps than a Dessaline heiress. Of course I like it."

"Even though someone will probably assassinate you one of these days? Or another strong man will come down from the mountains and put you against the Presidio wall?"

"Even though those things may happen."

"The idea doesn't disturb you?"

"It doesn't worry me, if that is what you mean."

She was irrationally annoyed by a matter-of-fact acceptance of the things she had said. He made no effort to deny or dispute them.

"Haven't you ever realized you are as much a captive to San Rafael as it is to you? Or that in time you will sit somewhere in exile as do Torralba, San Martin and Morillo?"

"Why does that make you angry?"

"I'm not angry." She realized abruptly she was and her voice unconsciously raised itself. "I don't give a damn what happens to you. I'm curious, that's all; trying to figure what you get out of it. If you are as big a thief as everyone says, why don't you clear out with the loot? Take a blonde along as the others have done and enjoy yourself."

"You saw them back there. My generals in exile. Did they look as though they were happy? They have saved their lives. That is all. The price is their pride and the knowledge of failure. They fret and scheme how to recover what they lost. They dream of gathering arms and men and assaulting their capitals, of leading a victorious army. This, of course, will not happen. They will grow old and tiresome, making everyone weary with their stories of vanished glory. Their mistresses will become unfaithful. Their limbs arthritic, their memory vague—and they will be hungry. Not for food but for the taste of life as they once knew it. When the time comes and I have to make a choice, I will take the Presidio wall. It has been a long, strange walk up the hill. I am not ready to come down. This is my destiny. I would not change it if I could."

She stared at him. Somehow the word destiny as he spoke it did not sound foolishly grandiose. It was mystical. There was about him the quiet acceptance of certain things as they were and must be. Men and women had walked to the stake with this calm conviction and a serenity of purpose on their faces. She felt herself shiver as with a sudden chill of foreboding. It seemed to her she stood apart and watched this man as he walked alone in a shadowy distance.

"It was no simple thing for Jorge Ojeda to get where he is. One of these days I'll tell you some of the story."

It was a moment or so before she realized fully what he had said and the implication of the words that in time he would talk and she listen.

VII.

ON the balcony, which extended the width of the house and overlooked the deliberately tangled profusion of the gardens, Madame Cleo Dessaline sipped the bittersweet chocolate of her breakfast and broke open a small crescent roll.

With a seemingly laborious, swaying motion the *macayo* waddled out over a limb of a banyan tree and dropped heavily to the railing. He regarded Ferris with yellow, malevolent eyes and screamed a harsh fury.

"I wonder why he hates you so?" The old lady buttered a part of her roll.

"Because he knows I think he is a filthy creature."

The parrot screeched an angry agreement, stretched forward and deliberately nipped at her finger. She slapped it viciously. The bird yelled with a croaking laughter at having goaded her into the act. He moved out of reach, cocked his head to one side and stared at her speculatively.

"I'll wring his damn neck one of these days." Ferris lit a ciagrette and poured a second cup of coffee. "He knows it. He tries to provoke me."

"It seems such a waste of emotion to hate a silly bird. What's he like?" The question was added almost absently.

Ferris smiled to herself. Madame Cleo had the faculty of sliding from one subject to another without appearing to be aware of the irrelevancy. She would not speak the name Ojeda or dignify the man with the title of *presidente*. Ferris was supposed to understand they were no longer discussing the parrot.

"I'm not sure."

"Scoundrels are notoriously deceptive." The old lady made the generalization without emphasis. "Scoundrels and libertines."

Ferris leaned back in the chair and glanced up through the varnished leaves of the ancient tree. Sunlight seemed to fall as a bright rain over the branches.

"I am not sure he is either," the girl mused. "He is a man of curious shadings. He could be the charlatan everyone calls him or a person of almost unbelievable innocence. The chances are he is a little of both. It is hard to tell at a first meeting."

"Nonsense." The declaration was made with assurance. "Would a man of innocence fill a city with statues of himself and label them The Benefactor?"

"That is one of the shadings; one of the contradictions." Ferris nodded an agreement. "Talking with him you somehow get the idea he possesses a quiet humor and these municipal images tickle it. I don't pretend to know the real answer. He is no clown, no *farceur,* though. He is not without purpose."

"Obviously." Ojeda was damned for all time by the statement. Madame Cleo's finger touched the newspaper, folded on the table. "Your name is included in the guest list. You may be sure we shall hear about it before the day is over. You were imprudent and, I imagine, the presence of a Dessaline must have flattered him immensely."

"He didn't seem particularly impressed. It was quite a respectable gathering, semiofficial. Christina and Kent Glastonbury were there, among others."

"Americans will go anywhere." Madame Dessaline dismissed the United States Embassy. "They even attend the funerals of persons they don't know. In any event, now that your curiosity has been satisfied I hope you will not repeat the indiscretion. Adventurers and trulls."

Ferris rose, bent across the table and kissed her grandmother's cheek with light affection. "Trulls is such a wonderful word. No one but Cleo Dessaline would think of it. Actually, no one seemed a bit trullish. I had the feeling most of those there came because they wanted to. By the way," she remembered something, "it is true. The generals pay a thousand dollars a day each for the privilege of living on San Rafael. You wanted to know. He said it was to remind him of the price of failure."

"Ha!" Madame Dessaline was triumphant and seemed to find immense satisfaction in the news. "It is a tidy sum to pocket. What are their women like? Cheap doxies," she answered her own question.

"How in the world do you remember such words? Trulls and doxies. No, they are quite beautiful and, I imagine, very expensive. They must be extremely satisfactory in bed."

"I should hope so. There is little enough to do on San Rafael." The old lady was unperturbed. She sighed. "In my day it was generally believed that fornication was a pleasure reserved exclusively for the upper classes.

The others just bred; dumbly like cattle, blindly following an urge to reproduce."

Ferris stared at her grandmother and then shook her head wonderingly. The old lady frequently astonished her.

A maid came with the morning's mail. Ferris took it without interest and handed the small packet to her grandmother. Madame Cleo carried on an extensive intra-island correspondence with a large circle of friends. Even such a simple thing as an invitation to tea was carefully written in her fine script on crested paper. The telephone was an instrument to be used by merchants and servants and, of course, the Americans who would find life unendurable without it. Madame Dessaline would no more think of lifting the receiver from its cradle than she would caress a two-headed asp. To send her voice across a wire to some unseen person at the other end was a vulgarity and an offense. She would have been as likely to shout a greeting from her carriage on the open street to a stranger.

"What in the world do you find to write about?" Ferris watched as her grandmother carefully slit open an envelope.

"We are not without our resources." Madame Cleo made the remark sound darkly mysterious. "Resourceful and determined. À couvert."

"Well," Ferris was emphatic, "you had better keep it under cover or you will find yourselves on the end of a deportation ticket. He could do it, you know. Complete confiscation and an act declaring you and your friends undesirable."

"A citizen cannot be deported from his own country." The old lady was smugly emphatic.

"Perhaps not. But a citizen can be put against the Presidio wall. In your case, however"—she laughed at the idea—"I have a feeling that his sense of the theatrical would resurrect the guillotine and send you to it in a creaking tumbrel." She sobered. "I wish you would stop it." There was honest concern in the request. "You are too intelligent not to know how ridiculous and dangerous it is. You and your friends are no match for this man."

Madame Cleo appeared not to have heard. She glanced up from the letter with an expression of pleased innocence.

"Elise Pontrain is expecting another baby." She put the letter aside and opened another, talking of the first as she did so. "Ernesto is being graduated from a place called Prince Town. It is some sort of a college or university, I believe, in the United States. He is coming home for the summer. Elise would like to have you for a visit."

"Elise bores the living hell out of me."

The grandmother ignored the deliberate crudeness. "Ernesto would be perfectly acceptable to me as your husband. I think it is time you thought about marriage. Girls without husbands deteriorate rapidly in this climate.

It has something to do with the Tropic of Cancer." She uttered this absurdity with bland authority. "I never really understood it but any physician will concur. There is a decaying effect upon your glands."

"Ernesto Pontrain is an idiot." Ferris made the reply indifferently.

"They make extremely satisfactory husbands. In fact, the very best kind; providing, of course, they come of good family. They are docile, grateful and forgiving; inclined to be tolerant of human frailties which they, of course, share. Intelligent men are always a little overbearing. They do not understand a weakness of the flesh. Never marry a strong man. Bed with him if you must; but avoid the vows as you would blasphemy. They lead to perdition. I never knew a happy marriage where the husband was smarter than the wife."

All of this, Ferris understood, was a diversionary tactic to prevent further discussion of Madame Dessaline's implacable opposition to Ojeda. The absurdity of her naïve plots, hatched with rachitic old friends who lived in a world far removed from reality, simply did not occur to her. The men were so old they could no longer sit a horse or sight a rifle. The women were little more than Dresden figurines. Ferris wondered what it was they dreamed of accomplishing. The men, shouldering ancient muskets. The women, their parasols aflutter, riding upon the capital crying: To the barricades. The idea was grotesque but she couldn't bring herself to state it so brutally.

"I will not be home for lunch."

"The word is luncheon." Madame Dessaline made the correction without glancing up from her correspondence. "I suspect you know better. Lunch is an American vulgarism. God alone knows why they refuse to speak English. George certainly knew what he was doing when he gave them their independence and cut them off."

"I suppose you mean George of England?" Ferris was laughing silently.

"Well!" Madame Dessaline put aside the letter. "I certainly was not referring to George Washington. An upstart. Although," she conceded generously, "he was a gentleman of quality. I suspect he was also tainted by association. You see"—she was pleased by her display of erudition—"I know a great deal more of history than you imagine. I was thought to be quite brilliant as a young woman. That is why your grandfather and I managed so splendidly. He was a dolt. A fine stallion but not too intelligent."

She carefully placed the letters into two sections. One stack would be answered promptly. The others could wait. For a moment Ferris watched her, marveling at her preoccupation and wondering how her cloistered life and a succession of uneventful days could possibly provide material for such widespread correspondence. When she walked the length of the balcony to enter her own rooms Madame Cleo seemed oblivious of her departure.

In a high-backed chair at the head of a long table Ojeda listened carefully to the members of his advisory cabinet as each, in turn, made his report and offered suggestions. This was a necessary part of government and, ordinarily, he gave close attention to what was said. Today he found himself unaccountably bored and his glance frequently strayed to the bright, sunwashed plaza below the windows and the orderly movement of traffic on the broad *avenidas* of the city he had built. In a little over twelve years he had raised it from a commonplace Caribbean port, with only a trickle of commerce and a few tourists who sought something quaint and off the beaten track, to a shining metropolis. He, Jorge Ojeda, had done this.

He lit a cigarette and leaned his head back against the cushion of wine-red velvet. Zamora, his Minister of Agriculture, was reading aloud from typewritten pages. The voice was hypnotic. It would be digested and condensed into understandable specifics later for *el presidente*. Now, however, for the benefit of the others and as a display of industry, Zamora must read it all. Of the report so far Ojeda had caught and understood a few of the figures. The production and export of sugar had fallen alarmingly from what had been refined and sold two years ago. Also, it had been necessary to import rice and this was a condition without precedent.

His eyes studied Zamora's intelligent face. Obvious failure of a plan which he had urged had not slaked his enthusiasm. Zamora was an idealist; perhaps a little of a fanatic. It was possible he had Communistic leanings, or at least was what the Americans called a Pink or fellow traveler. Ojeda had taken him from a chair of economics in the University and brought him into this tight cabinet of advisers. His ardor for reform was boundless.

Ojeda found himself growing impatient. "It does not work." He interrupted rudely. "Fleas do not want to own and care for a dog. They merely want to ride and feed upon one belonging to someone else."

"Excellency?" Zamora looked up from his pages uncomprehendingly. "I do not understand."

"Fleas. The word is a private joke with me." Ojeda lit another cigarette from the butt of the first. "Put away the report, Carlos." He smiled a little to soften the order. He glanced about the table. "All of you are experts in certain things. That is why I have brought you together, why I listen to the things you have to say on finance, commerce, education, agriculture. Not always do I understand your theories but I listen."

There was a soft murmur of appreciation from those who watched him attentively. He flattered them all a little but they knew that in the end the decisions were his alone.

"A long time ago"—Ojeda stared at the ceiling—"I said to myself it was possible to gather the fleas, keep them well fed and comfortable and they would work for you. I still believe that. They will turn the wheels and pull the carts but always you must remember they are only fleas after all. They do not think for themselves. I will tell you now what is wrong with our fleas. We made an experiment and because of it we had a little trouble here, on San Rafael, with the big landowners. I, also, must soothe the worries of the Americans, the investors and the Ambassador, who suggested we were engaged in a creeping form of Communism. I do not take the criticism too seriously. If, and when, the United States loses its big naval base at Guantanamo or its rights in the Panama Canal Zone, they will need us. They know that and so do I. Our experiment is a failure. So, we admit it."

Zamora shuffled his papers unhappily. The others listened comfortably. They had not urged the experiment. They were secure for today, at least.

"I will tell you what is bad," Ojeda continued. "The fleas must be driven to perform. As an experiment we confiscated four great *estancias* and two sugar refineries. You will be paid, the owners were told, in Government bonds. We created the *ejidos*. Each man then held a little piece of the thousands of acres once owned by a few. We said to the fleas: You are now your own masters. This land on which you stand and build your shack is yours. You have property. No one can take it away. The profits from the cane, the indigo and the things you raise with your labor belong to you and not the *patron* who lives in the big house or in a foreign country. Here in this room," he paused for a moment, "we agreed that this land in one piece and ruled by a *patron* or company produced X million tons of sugar. Why will it not do the same with a thousand small owners instead of one? The *falta* was that we did not understand the fleas. They were accustomed to burrowing in the hair of another's dog. So, they no longer raise all the land will yield. One grows only enough to feed his family or take to the market. He has a small patch of beans and chilies, some rows of corn, a pen for a few pigs, a small herd of goats. Why should he work to produce more when he has no use for it? He has a peso in his pocket, a piece of land to squat upon, food for his belly. A man would be insane to labor long hours for what he cannot use or does not need. So thousands of acres which once were in production now choke themselves on weeds. The refineries stand idle. The machines for cultivation of cotton and sugar gather rust. Bananas rot upon the trees and no longer fill the holds of cargo ships, and we must use our dollar reserves to buy the things we once grew in abundance and exported for profit. I am no expert but the situation needs none. We will abolish the *ejidos* and set things right again."

"To take away the land we have given the peon? You cannot mean that, Excellency." The objection came quickly from Dr. Ramon, the Minister of Public Land. "There would be a revolution."

"I am the revolution, *amigo*." Ojeda tapped the ash from his cigarette. He stood up, abruptly terminating the meeting. The cabinet members rose with quick respect. "I will think of the matter and let you know how it is to be done."

Silently, gravely, the half dozen men gathered together their files, brief cases with thick sheaves of statistics. Matters of importance to each had not even had a preliminary discussion.

"*Con su permiso,* Excellency?" There was a small, waspish note in the politeness as it was uttered by Zamora.

The tone did not escape Ojeda and he stared frigidly at the cabinet member until Carlos Zamora experienced an icy coldness in the room and a sudden panic. Men had vanished behind the Presidio walls for less. Ojeda watched him but found no satisfaction in the fear. He merely nodded his permission to leave and they moved in single file toward the huge double doors.

"General." Ojeda spoke the title softly.

Pepito turned. "Yes, Excellency?"

Juan de Cespedes was politely formal. Nothing in his expression betrayed the inner amusement he felt at Ojeda's first public admission of the new rank. The promotion had been made officially, published in the military gazette. Photographs had appeared in the morning newspapers. There had been the expected and extravagantly phrased congratulations. A flag of four stars fluttered from a short staff on his car and they glittered on his shoulders. He waited now until the cabinet members left them alone and the doors had been closed by the two sentries posted outside.

"Sit down, General Pepito." Ojeda dropped into his chair, carelessly draped a leg over the arm. He rubbed at his nose with a knuckle and half smiled. "I have additional honors for you, *compadre.*"

"*A que son?*" Juan voiced a small suspicion.

"The motive?" Ojeda was thoughtful. "It is the same as always. We preserve ourselves. Within the past few minutes I have added a new bureau. The Department of Defense. As of now you are General Juan de Cespedes, Minister of Defense. How does that sound?"

"Fishy."

Ojeda slid the silver cigarette box the length of the polished table and waited until Juan lit one and popped a small ring of smoke toward the ceiling. There was skepticism in the gesture.

"We must prepare ourselves for an attempted invasion of San Rafael by Communist sympathizers. They will come ashore by night and be repulsed with great loss by your loyal and disciplined troops."

"Naturally, *presidente.*" Juan made the agreement dryly.

"This will provide a diversion and distract the fleas who might otherwise be concerned over what is about to be taken from them."

"I don't think so." Juan shrugged. "A man with a piece of land does not give it up easily."

"In a time of national emergency who will deny *el presidente's* wisdom or the necessity to act for the benefit of all? The *ejidos* will be leased back to the former owners. Production! It has a sound of magic. It makes men think of a crisis. One for all. All for one. It is a cry of battle. Eventually, the fleas will again be deep in their small debts to the *patrons*. To free himself of this burden the flea then gives up the right to the land which he does not work anyhow and San Rafael's great plantations again flourish as they should. All sensible men will agree this is a reasonable state of affairs. Besides, I have always promised the people free elections. The idea fascinates them and made a fine impression in the United States."

"That was many years ago, *maestro*." Juan eyed him quizzically.

"They have been years of uncertainty, General. A strong hand has been constantly needed. Even so there are queries now and then as to when elections would be held. A punitive action against the Republic creates unity of thought. The idea of changing leaders at such a time would be madness. Also, and this is of no small importance, *chamaco*"—Ojeda laughed because the notion of calling such a resplendent officer as General Juan de Cespedes "kid" tickled him—"the Government has requested a grant of twenty-five million dollars in foreign aid funds. Our smashing of a Communist plot to seize control of San Rafael will make a most favorable impression in Washington and on the American Ambassador here." He whistled with a soft pensiveness, blowing through a small hole made by curling the index finger within his thumb. "When the attempted invasion occurs I would like a leader of stature killed in the engagement. This would add great significance to the affair."

"This leader of stature." Juan examined the ash at the tip of his cigarette. "He wouldn't be the Minister of Defense by any chance?"

Ojeda swiveled about in his chair, facing the window. A light trade wind curled the pennantlike fronds of the high palms as green banners. Finally he shook his head.

"I won't deny that the plan occurred to me." He turned to gaze at de Cespedes with an honest grin of pleasure. "I even gave thought to a fine marble statue of you in La Plaza de Independencia. Every morning I would salute it. But then I said no. Juan is my *compadre*, I would be unhappy without him. With what other man could I make such honest talk as I do now? My affection triumphed. *A pasar mio*."

"I'm damned if I don't believe you." There was a trace of admiring astonishment in the statement.

"You reject the statue of yourself in the plaza then?"

"Only with a thousand *gracias*, Excellency."

[88]

Ojeda nodded. The subject was closed. He left his chair and went to a cabinet. From it he took a bottle of rum, two glasses and a silver Thermos carafe of iced water. For a moment he studied the label.

"She is a dish, that one. Is she not?" Juan gestured toward the bottle. "The Dessaline one. In the *cajones* she gets you. Like going down a roller coaster. A woman to make a man feel like a *toro*."

"Yes." Ojeda poured the rum for them both. "As you say, it is a thing of feeling, not only beauty. There is an excitement of the mind."

De Cespedes lifted his shoulders with an exaggerated shrug. "You castrate yourself with the reading of books and the learning of words. She is a woman who tickles *los huevos*. Let it go at that. To have a girl like that would be enough even if she had sawdust in her head."

Ojeda drank part of his rum and made no reply. After a moment he walked to one end of the room. Where the wall and ceiling joined there was a long, narrow box. From its center a tasseled cord dangled. Pulling it he unrolled a large map which was flooded by concealed lights. In detail was the island of San Rafael. He studied its contours, the bays, the coves, the *sierras*.

"On this beach, at La Semana." He swallowed the remainder of his drink and spoke without turning. "That is where we made it, Pepito. Do you remember?"

"I damn well should. A son of a bitch with a machine gun in the scrub was shooting the hell out of that piece of beach. I said to myself: Juanito, you go through the Pacific and don't even cut your finger. Now you get it on this lousy strip of sand on an island you never heard of before. I almost made what the bullfighters call *meada de miedo*. The leak of fear."

Ojeda turned and retraced his steps. "I've often wondered about him. How did he go to that exact place? Who told him to do it? There was supposed to be no trouble, no opposition. Just an easy landing on the beach and from there the trip into the mountains and General Quatero's head-quarters." He refilled his small glass with the Dessaline rum and passed the bottle to de Cespedes. Then he again seated himself in the big chair and this time lifted his feet to rest them on the beautifully grained surface of the table. "Do you ever lie awake at night, Pepito, or stop, sometimes, in the middle of something you are doing and wonder about all this? Here we sit, Jorge Ojeda, son of a Tampa cigar maker, and Juan de Cespedes, who took small fish from the sea. We drink rum in the house of Government and the things we say to each other are not the talk between a president and a general of the Army but only of two boys who met on a beach in Florida one afternoon long ago."

"No." Juan brought the bottle with him and placed it within reach be-tween them. "I only tell myself this is what happened. I don't wonder much about it or ask how or why it came about as it has. If I did it would scare the hell out of me."

"I do." Ojeda smiled reflectively. "Often I ask myself: What led my feet to that exact spot on a strip of sand? There were miles in both directions where I could have walked and slept while the sun covered me with a warm blanket. Why was there no grease on the axle of your wagon so the wheel would squeal and complain until it woke me? Why did I pull a net with you that day and later go to your small house where we drank some wine and listened to the Duke of Alba's cousin play an accordion?"

"How do you answer yourself?"

"I say I had no choice. It had all been arranged. Everything that happened had already been placed in sequence. It was as a deck of cards, stacked by the slick fingers of a gambler. Each one came up exactly in the order it should. There was within me a conviction. I knew without knowing what I knew. I did not have to drive myself. It was necessary only to wait."

"That is the talk of a gipsy." Juan turned the glass between his fingers. "Or a drum tapped softly back there in the hills. Of three sticks and a chicken feather laid just so across a path so an evil spirit cannot follow. It is a witch woman's song as she rolls little pellets of mud between her fingers so an unborn child will have *cajones* and be a boy."

"How do you know such things do not work? The child comes out and it is a boy. A man walks a path at night and nothing happens to him because of the sticks and a feather. A drum talks and a strange drum answers because it has been waiting for that sound. I can believe those things."

Juan de Cespedes moved uneasily in his chair. "I know." Impulsively he filled his glass to the brim and pushed the bottle toward Ojeda. "Without saying so, you made me believe them also. Otherwise, why did I go with you as I did? All the way to Jacksonville on the train I kept telling myself: At the next stop I'm going to get off and go back home where I belong. What the hell am I doing with this crazy man who has talked me into joining the Corps because killing is a good trade to learn and at this trade the Marines are the best?"

"We sit here and drink rum together. Do you still think I was wrong?"

Juan did not answer the question. "For ten lousy years I am a machine because I didn't have sense enough to jump off of that train somewhere between New Smyrna and Jacksonville. And at the end, we get the big one. Every stinking, dirty job in the whole god-damned Pacific, and the world is filled with bastards who are trying to kill us. I get shot at, bombed, shelled and starved. I have dysentery, malaria, and you behave like the whole thing from Guadalcanal on is a walk in the park." He lit a cigarette almost angrily. "That was when I began to get scared of you. I say to myself: This is a lunatic who thinks he is an invisible man. No one can see, touch or harm him.

All of the time my guts are sick; knotted and empty with fear. That's the way it is with most of the others. I keep looking at you. I want to see it on your face, in your eyes, but it isn't there. I keep asking myself why? Then I start to believe what I know can't be true. I say he must have a charm; something he wears or carries. I know this is crazy but by now I can't get rid of the idea. Then it gets worse. I say: Maybe he's already dead; killed a long time ago. What walks around now is a zombie without flesh or blood. It only looks, acts and talks like a man. If you tried to run a knife into it nothing would happen. It would be like shoving a bayonet through a column of smoke.

"All sorts of wild things run through my mind. I even think about letting you have it in the back with a knife some night just to see what will happen. I get superstitious, the way my father used to tell me about the people in the old country. They carried stuff called wolfbane to keep vampires away. Or they made a small cross with a couple of twigs and kept it in their pocket to hold up when the devil suddenly appeared on the road. Beach after beach, yard after yard up the Solomons I keep seeing guys all around us get it but we don't. I start telling myself whatever it is that works for you must be working for me and I'll be all right if I can just keep close enough. I want to plaster myself to you like an extra piece of skin." He forced a laugh but it was without sincerity. "I'm afraid to go to the can without you. I want to hang on like a scared puppy to its mother. When I look around and don't see you I almost scream." He swallowed the rum with a single, nervous gulp and shook his head as though to rid it of a memory. Then he looked at Ojeda with a sheepish grin. "That's how it was."

"We were lucky, Pepito." Ojeda made the statement gravely, studying the face of de Cespedes with sympathetic understanding. "Many times I said to myself: If I get through this then everything else will fall into place. Here the decision, the answer to my reason for being, will be made and given. I was afraid, often, as frightened as you and everyone else. I said: If I am killed here I will never know what might have been. Always at my side was the thief I couldn't see, ready to steal my life before I could spend it or even know if it had a value or purpose beyond what was happening. I kept telling myself: This is the moment of truth. I must have luck here. What happens later will not be luck but now I need it." He smiled a little. "Think back, Pepito, and you will see I was right."

Santana. Santa Anna. It is spelled both ways but it is used to designate a wind that boils up without violence from the desert's floor, drifts over the mountains without cooling and then falls upon the coast of Southern California for days at a time. It is the searing breath from a distant furnace; a hot, dry blast that even seems to carry with it the smell of sage, cactus,

bleached rocks in a whitened creek bed, the earth cracked for lack of mois-
ture. It is kin to the sirocco which moves out of the Libyan waste to fall
upon the Italian shore.

On that day the wind held with persistent steadiness upon San Diego.
The city burned beneath it as though caught in the reflection of a dazzling
copper plate. From a window, high in the U. S. Grant Hotel, Jorge Ojeda
stood and looked down upon the leaden shimmer of the bay. The great
machinery of war was shuddering to a halt. The ships began to crowd the
harbor—cruisers, destroyers, carriers, anchored beam to beam in long, silent
rows. On Highway 101 the yellow and green camouflage netting still hung
to hide the aircraft plants from Japanese bombers.

On one of the beds, a towel knotted about his waist, lying in the draft
of an electric fan, Juan de Cespedes leaned back against the damp pillows
and held a glass of iced Scotch and water to his navel. It was one of the
things he had been promising himself for a long time. I will lie on a bed
and do nothing but maybe mix a fresh drink or have a new girl sent to me.
This I will keep doing until I can no longer remember I was a Marine.

In the closets of the suite there were hung new, tropical-weight suits and
slacks. Shoes, black, brown, two-toned, were neatly aligned in trees on
shelves. The drawers of the bureaus were stacked with shirts, socks, shorts
and ties. They had bought everything they could think of. Juan had won
six thousand dollars in the final crap game, which had lasted from Hawaii
to San Diego on the transport.

Discharged from the Corps they had walked the streets in unfamiliar
clothes, feeling alien to the civilians; strangers in a strange land, moving
with the curious sensation of being in a vacuum. They had sat with silent
meditation in the bars and gazed upon the city's lights at night but experi-
encing no kinship with the sights and sounds. In a grill they had picked up
a couple of girls and had taken them to Las Vegas in a secondhand car Juan
had bought for more than it had cost new before Pearl Harbor. Now, after
two weeks, they had temporarily lost their capacity and hunger for food,
liquor and girls. Of the six thousand only a little over a thousand dollars
remained.

Ojeda turned from the window. On a bureau were a dozen or so crinkled
bits of metal. He picked them up and then allowed the small pieces to sift
through his fingers.

"Have you ever wondered, Pepito, why it is that girls always seem to need
fewer hairpins when they leave a room than were necessary to hold their
hair in place when they arrived? This must be so. Otherwise, how could
these be left behind?"

"Maybe they leave with more haste. Whores are always in a hurry even when they have no destination of importance. It is a mark of the profession. They rush by instinct as do the ants."

Ojeda smiled absently. They were making small talk to break a monotony which was becoming unendurable. Neither would confess to the other that an uneasy restlessness possessed him. For so many years their lives had moved within prescribed channels. Outside them now the hours and days seemed without order. Civilian life was a maze of confusion.

Juan fished an ice cube from the glass and rubbed it over a sweaty chest. The piece dissolved quickly and left only a sticky smear on the matted hair. He watched as Ojeda prowled without purpose, back and forth between the two rooms.

"Where do we go now, *compadre?*"

Ojeda halted. "I don't know."

The telephone rang. They both looked at it with surprise but neither reached to pick it up. The sound was repeated with a soft insistence. There was no one they knew in San Diego to call them except the girls and they had left only an hour ago. The bell tinkled again. Ojeda went to the table and picked up the receiver.

"Yes?"

Juan watched and listened with a quiet interest and then finished his drink. Ojeda's face was without expression. The voice at the other end of the line was doing all the talking.

"If you like." Ojeda finally spoke and dropped the cigarette he had been smoking into a tray. "Now will be all right. *Ocho seis quatro.*" He hung up.

"*Quien?*" Juan asked.

"A Señor Francisco."

"Said that way—*Señor?* Not Mister?"

"Said that way and with an accent. I don't know him."

"Sure you do. Old Sam Francisco." Juan laughed, he was pleased with the bad pun. "What does he want?"

"He wants to talk."

"So, we let him talk." Juan swung his legs over the bed and dipped a hand into a bowl for the few remaining pieces of ice. "We need more of this here now *heilo* ice stuff if we're going to drink."

"Let it go for a while." Ojeda was curiously preoccupied. "We'll listen, at first, without drinking."

"He probably has something to sell." Juan collapsed wearily back on the bed.

The knock, when it came, had a sound of timidity, so softly did the knuckles tap the door. Ojeda opened it and stood to one side.

The little man held a small, stiff hat of brown straw in both hands to his chest. He was a clown, made up for a masquerade. The suit he wore hung in limp white folds. The coat was a pinchback model which had been popular somewhere around 1918. He used heavy-lensed glasses and the eyes behind them, magnified, seemed wide and filled with a blue innocence.

"Thank you for seeing me." He spoke in English and bowed with a stiff, unsmiling politeness.

Ojeda closed the door. The visitor glanced from him to the figure of Juan on the bed. His expression of pleased, mild wonder did not change.

"I am Roberto Francisco."

"So you said on the telephone." Ojeda was not curt or impatient. "Sit down."

Francisco bowed again and took the straight chair from within the well of a writing desk. He placed it near the center of the room and seated himself. The hat, still held carefully with both hands, now rested precisely in his lap. Juan had a sudden desire to laugh. This was one of the comedians from the downtown burlesque shows. For some reason the laughter did not come. He wondered why.

"I have an offer of employment to make." Francisco's statement was strangely crisp and in contrast to the almost ludicrous appearance he made. "I hope you will listen."

"What sort of employment?" Ojeda seated himself on the window sill.

"The employment of professional soldiers. Training, at first; fighting, perhaps, later."

"Why us? Who sent you? What makes you think we want a job?" Juan asked the questions.

Francisco acknowledged Juan's presence with a slight inclination of the head. The queries, his manner indicated, were not unreasonable. When he replied, however, the words were directed to Ojeda.

"It has been my mission to find certain men. Here, in San Diego, near the Marine and Naval bases, was a source of supply. Although the selection has been wide the exact qualities I needed were, in most cases, lacking. After careful study I have reached the conclusion you satisfy all of the requirements. About you both I now know a great deal. I am aware, for instance, that you, Sergeant Ojeda, were twice decorated, and Private First Class de Cespedes served with valor. After over ten years in the Corps you have decided not to make a career of the service. I know you have no immediate plans." He glanced at Juan and a tiny smile of embarrassed deprecation was at his mouth. "I know you won six thousand dollars. That you took two young ladies to Las Vegas; where you stayed, how much you lost at the dice tables. The young women left this suite about an hour ago. I also know that of the six thousand dollars there isn't a great amount left. It is my belief you are both becoming bored and this is a most opportune moment for me to make the offer. It is a matter of small coincidence that you both have a background of Spanish parentage and, although you are not fluent in polite, conversational Spanish, you can make yourselves understood."

"*A todo gagnate.*" Juan laughed softly.

Francisco's eyes sparked. "As you say in the idiom, at the top of your lungs."

Juan winked at Ojeda. This was someone's idea of a joke. The amusement faded when he saw the intent speculation with which his friend was regarding the stranger. Ojeda didn't think it was a gag. By some mysterious transmission this Francisco and Jorge were reaching a plane of understanding. It made him uneasy.

"You spoke of training and fighting. You have an army?" Ojeda asked but there was no surprise in his query.

Francisco smiled. "I am pleased, Sergeant Ojeda, that we go so quickly to the matter's heart. We have men. Brave, dedicated men who have suffered dumbly under the tyranny of the present government and those which preceded it. San Rafael is a country rich in natural resources but its wealth has reached only a few, greedy hands. Our history, unfortunately, has been a succession of despots, spoilers and opportunists who have been indifferent to the people." He smiled apologetically. "You will forgive me if my speech is a little extravagant. I am a lawyer by profession. The men are ready. It is your job to transform them into an army."

"How many?" Ojeda asked the question.

"That is difficult to answer. At the moment one or two hundred. More will volunteer; the peons, the intellectuals, the students. The island is ready for a popular uprising." He paused and studied Ojeda. "I am prepared to offer you a captaincy in the revolutionary army of San Rafael at a salary of one thousand dollars, American, a month. For Señor de Cespedes a lieutenant's commission at five hundred a month."

Ojeda could feel the hot core of excitement gather. It began to glow as a coal does when blown upon. He was untouched by this Francisco's fervor. The purpose, the ideals, the goal of revolution left him indifferent. He calculated the opportunity; measured it in terms of what it could mean to Jorge Ojeda. This was the destiny toward which he had moved, possessed by a mystical conviction that his life had been directed to this moment. The years had been stones forming a path to a meeting with this man in a hotel room. He experienced a sense of drama. The stage had been set. He need only to walk out upon it and take his place. Of this he was certain. The plot was a familiar one. Those who were out wanted in. The people would remain captive to a stronger will. The nut to crack would be a small cadre within the present government's military forces. Once that was done the meat was ready for picking.

"Arms, money, equipment?" He asked these questions of Roberto Francisco.

"The money has come from many sources—contributions from exiles and those who cannot longer bear the heavy fist of oppression."

Ojeda's face was without expression but he smiled inwardly. Always men sought to cloak their personal ambitions in nobility.

"Arms and equipment," Francisco continued, "have been smuggled in, brought to San Rafael in small boats from Key West, Miami, New Orleans and Cuba." He paused and there was something close to a surprised wariness in his manner as though he had suddenly sensed a danger. When he continued his features were a mask, his words precise and with a hint of warning. "You must understand your position, Sergeant Ojeda. You are to train and mold an army for the revolutionary *junta*. This and nothing more is expected of you." There was no mistaking the meaning or the monitory tone in which it was spoken. "The *junta* seeks a drill instructor, not a leader. I hope I make myself clear."

Ojeda made no reply. He glanced across the room at Juan, who was listening with a tiny, sardonic smile.

"Well, Lieutenant?"

"*Como no?*" Juan was indifferent. "It pays a damn sight better than the Corps. I have come this far with you." He shrugged.

Francisco took an envelope from the inside pocket of his sagging coat. He tapped it thoughtfully against the palm of one hand as though reluctant, now, to make this final commitment. With what was obviously a small sigh he rose, walked to where Ojeda sat.

"What is it I feel about you, Sergeant?" He was puzzled. "It is as though something was warning me to be careful." He was honest. "I do not like it."

"You came to me, to us." Ojeda remained on the window sill. "The door is unlocked. Leave as you came and our conversation is forgotten."

"No." Roberto Francisco took a deep breath. "It is only that caution has become a second nature." He extended the envelope to Ojeda. "In this you will find transportation, a drawing room to Miami. Also, a cashier's check on the Bank of America for fifteen hundred dollars. A month's salary for you both in advance. In addition there are instructions as to where you will go after reaching Miami. I must trust you. There is no other way." He smiled regretfully. "I do not make an impressive appearance so I must warn you that we engage in no comic opera. Men will suffer and be killed. Your work will be difficult and hazardous and done under conditions far from ideal. You will have only the rawest material with which to shape disciplined units. Should you change your mind, please leave the envelope with the room clerk downstairs." He glanced at Juan and then at Ojeda. "Do you mind if we do not shake hands?"

It was, Ojeda thought, almost a plea for understanding rather than a deliberate insult. He was not offended and merely shook his head.

At the door Roberto Francisco paused and then lifted his empty hands with a comical expression in which were resignation and a wry appreciation for a situation he had freely created.

"*Bien suerte.*"

The latch clicked softly behind him.

VIII.

THEY had lain offshore in the darkness of that night and the small, shallow-draft powerboat had rocked endlessly in a light swell while they waited for a signal from a scrub-crested segment of the beach.

Ojeda, hands locked between his knees, studied the two men who had served as an escort from the time they had landed in Havana, crossed the island to a little fishing village on the southeast coast near Puerto Manati, run down the Old Bahama Channel in a foul and leaky ketch, skirted the Windward Passage, eventually picked up the light at Cap Haitian and moved cautiously toward a rendezvous with this launch off Semana. One of the men held an M-1 across his lap and he fondled the weapon, unconsciously stroking it as he would a woman. His companion was a sullen youngster of eighteen or so who constantly gnawed at his fingernails and regarded Ojeda and Juan de Cespedes with a nervous suspicion.

All of this—an ordinarily simple voyage—was the end result of seemingly endless days of waiting in Miami. They had taken Roberto Francisco's fifteen hundred dollars and the tickets from California to Florida. With the check and tickets was a brief note of instructions. They were to register at the Columbus Hotel but the evening meal was to be taken at a Spanish restaurant, La Ballena. There an agent would make contact with them, identifying himself by mentioning San Diego. Thereafter, they were to place themselves in the agent's care and accept his arrangements without question. Having read this Ojeda passed the note to Juan without comment.

"Someone has been seeing too many bad movies." Juan stretched lazily. "That's a hell of a name for a restaurant."

Beyond this they had not discussed the undertaking. It was a job accepted. Speculation about it would be without point.

In Miami their room at the Columbus overlooked Biscayne Bay and the beach at the other end of the causeway. They loafed around, went to movies, took a charter boat for a day's fishing and found little interest in what they were doing. There was an edge of excitement now; a desire to get on with the adventure.

For three nights they occupied the same corner table at La Ballena. It was a small, authentic Spanish restaurant near the boatyards on the Miami River. The diners seemed mostly Cubans and South Americans. They ate, drank and played dominoes endlessly with a noisy slapping down of the small, dotted pieces. The ceiling was covered with latticework and this, in turn, twined with an imitation arbor of grapes. It was crowded, badly ventilated, but the food was good. They waited, their eyes roving over the tables, wondering about the man who was to meet them here and why he couldn't have come to the hotel.

On the fourth night they had finished dinner and sat with small glasses of heavy brandy. From her seat behind a cash register at a counter near the door the *patrona* moved toward them. She was an enormous woman who invariably wore skin-tight dresses of screaming cerise or purple and her walk was the slow, rolling majesty of an elephant's tread. A faint, dark tracing of a mustache lay upon her lip but her skin was as fair as that of a young girl and her eyes jet ornaments.

"You like La Ballena, eh?"

Juan studied the broad, towering figure and then grinned. "Now I know why they call this place The Whale."

"You real, sharp, good-lookin' fella." She reached down and pinched his cheek with such playful ferocity that he yelped and rubbed at the whitened spot. "You come, sometime, take a ride like Jonah fella on whale's belly." Her great breasts heaved with silent laughter.

"In his belly not on it, *mamacita*." Juan patted the wide, rayon-covered ham with admiration.

She sat down and clapped her hands. When the waiter came quickly she ordered three brandies and took a cigarette from an open package before Ojeda.

"The food is not better in San Diego, eh?"

Ojeda experienced a brief moment of irritation. For three nights she must have been aware of their presence. Why had she waited so long? This was a child's game of intrigue.

She must have seen the impatience in his expression. "The pot does not boil quickly enough, eh?" She glanced up as the waiter put a check in front of Ojeda. The man nodded and left. "This check you do not pay." She spoke quietly. "On it are written words. You should go now." She heaved herself up and left them.

Jorge turned the slip of paper over. On it was penciled an address in Coral Gables. He shook his head wearily at what seemed an unnecessarily involved procedure and shoved the check to Juan, who read it and then put it in his pocket.

"Let's get a cab."

They rode in silence, each settled into a corner of the seat and occupied with his own thoughts. Ojeda was disturbed by what seemed to be a childish delight on the part of the unknown principals for intrigue. Eventually it could become so complicated no one would be sure what someone else had done. It could end in a completely fouled-up tangle.

The address in Coral Gables was a modest stucco house of neo-Spanish architecture set back among oleanders and a few palms. They rang the bell and waited as the two-toned chime echoed softly. After a moment a young maid opened the door.

"Dr. Leras?" Ojeda asked.

"*Si,* señor." She stepped aside and after they had entered, closed the door and led them down a short hall to a room at the rear of the house.

"*Momentito,* señores. *Permiso?*" She made a small bow with a quick smile and left them.

Ojeda looked about the study with interest. It was a pleasant room with bookshelves lining the dark walls. A green-shaded, polished-brass student's lamp dropped a pool of warm light on the polished surface of a large and beautifully carved desk. The furniture was upholstered in soft leather of a subdued red. It was a place in which a man could relax, read or study quietly and would seem to have no place with the violent convulsions of an island revolution in the Carribean.

At the sound of padded footsteps in the hall they both turned.

The man who came toward them and closed the door was slender, almost frail in appearance, but his carriage was erect, his step brisk and his manner quietly confident. From the *pince-nez* a length of narrow black ribbon led to the buttonhole of his lapel. He wore, Ojeda noticed, spats of a dove-gray color and his appearance was anything but that of a revolutionary. But, he quickly revised the estimate, from the pictures he had seen no one would have suspected Trotsky of fomenting a revolt.

Dr. Martin Leras glanced inquiringly from Jorge to Juan and then instinctively spoke to Ojeda.

"Sergeant Ojeda?"

"Captain Ojeda." Jorge made the correction gravely.

"Of course." Dr. Leras seemed pleased. "And you then," he turned to Juan, "must be Lieutenant de Cespedes. You know, of course, a former president of Cuba bore the same name. Are you related?"

"My father was a cousin of the Duke of Alba." Juan made the statement without a flicker of a smile.

For a second Dr. Leras seemed to be a little confused, then he took off his glasses and rubbed them gently with a handkerchief. There was a tap on the door and the young maid re-entered with a tray on which was a coffeepot and cups. She put it on the desk, murmured the politeness of *permiso* and left.

"Will you join me in coffee?" Dr. Leras motioned to chairs and then without waiting for a reply filled the small cups with strong, dark coffee. "There is brandy if you wish."

Both Juan and Ojeda shook their heads and accepted the coffee, took chairs and waited until Dr. Leras settled himself behind the desk.

"You are wondering what place I have in a revolution, are you not, and why what we do must be done with so much secrecy and an air of mystery."

"Something like that, Dr. Leras." Jorge lit a cigarette.

Dr. Leras joined his finger tips in a steeple below his chin and nodded with understanding at the faint note of impatience in Ojeda's voice.

"I am an exile from San Rafael. When General Romero became president I disagreed publicly and violently with many of his policies. Eventually, I became a nuisance no longer to be tolerated. I either had to leave my country or stay and accept an indefinite term as a prisoner. I elected to flee. Here I am a professor of political science at the University of Miami. I am fairly well paid and generally respected but this is not my home. However," he added, "neither is my unhappy country what it was. General Romero has transformed it into a vast prison factory for himself. I, with others who had to leave the country, are determined to oust him."

"A single bullet, assassination, would be simpler than a revolution, Dr. Leras." Ojeda made the comment.

The man shook his head. "Assassination would lead to confusion. There would be an immediate scramble for power. What we might get that way could well be worse than what we have. No. There must be force and order. This can be accomplished only through a complete revolution in which the people take part. It must have popular support and there will have to be a thorough house cleaning from the lowest member of the police force to the *presidente's* palace. Oppression brews the culture for its own destruction as a vaccine is produced from the strains of a once live and deadly virus." He leaned back in his chair and regarded them with a quiet estimation. "You will assist in preparing the syringe. With it we shall inject the cure for the malady which fevers my country."

Ojeda smiled to himself. Always the rhetoric. Invariably the grandiose phrase to shroud a simple fact. The true and selfless patriot, he thought, would go about his task in a quieter fashion. He said nothing and waited for the professor to come to the point of their meeting here.

"We place great confidence in Roberto Francisco. He has assured us you are the men for the task which lies ahead. General Quatero is a man of wisdom, courage and great vision, but he is a statesman and not a military leader. The strategy of violence is yours to shape and plan, although you will consult with the General on everything."

"Why us, outsiders?" Ojeda considered what had been said. "There must be officers in San Rafael's army who are dissatisfied. Why don't you recruit them?"

"There have been furtive volunteers, offers of defection. But"—the lean shoulders raised in a shrug—"I am not sure they are to be trusted. We cannot afford the risk. It is better that such mercenaries as yourselves be relied upon." He smiled quickly. "The word has an offensive sound. I do not mean it to be. The revolution, for you, should be dispassionate and clinical; an operation to be performed, a fee to be collected."

"When we get there, Dr. Leras." Jorge made the suggestion politely but there was a hint of asperity in the tone. "*A todo correr.*"

"Yes, of course," Leras agreed. "As swiftly as possible. Arrangements have had to be made. Now they are complete. You will be taken by car tonight to a small settlement on the Keys, a place called Marathon. From there a boat will take you to Key West and different hands will pass you on to Havana. Each station has been alerted. Everything is in readiness. From Cuba you will be taken to a landing point on San Rafael and a meeting with General Quatero." He paused and regarded Ojeda with sympathetic understanding. "You regard our measures as unnecessarily involved?"

"Yes, Doctor."

"There are things of which you are not aware. First, the existence of a revolutionary *junta* is known to Presidente Romero. The agents of the present government are everywhere, even here in Miami. Our names are known, our movements watched. It is quite possible your presence here tonight has not gone unnoted. You both could easily end with a bullet in your backs and your bodies found in a roadside ditch. You must not think I am being deliberately melodramatic. Several members of our organization have mysteriously disappeared. Believe me, we are not children at play and amusing ourselves with the idea of a revolution. Many of our party are in prison in San Rafael. Others have been executed without trial. They simply vanish. Within the capital city we have men and women who work as did the French underground, in constant danger. And now," he stood up, "at the back of my house is a small orange grove. At the far end is a little-used road. A car is waiting for you. I will walk to it with you. Go with God."

And so, on this night, they waited off the beach of La Semana. Ojeda and Juan both wore the loose dungarees which had been the Marine battledress in the Pacific. From webbed belts at their waists heavy automatics were holstered. Now and then Ojeda's hand unconsciously strayed to the pistol's butt. When this happened the youth abruptly stopped biting his fingernails and stared with an idiotic expression of curiosity, his gaze traveling from Ojeda to Juan while his fingers remained on the lower lip, pulling it into a pout. The man with the M-1 became tautly alert.

Juan took the pistol from the holster and snapped the safety back and forth. He weighed it in his hand reflectively.

"I don't like hitting a strange beach with nothing more than this, *compadre.*"

"Neither do I," Ojeda agreed.

They spoke in English. Although the two guides and the boatman had used only Spanish their attitude, a slight cocking of the head or a too-elaborate assumption of indifference, betrayed the fact they understood.

"I don't like the company, either," Juan continued. "We're gambling with scared money. It never wins."

Ojeda leaned toward the man with the M-1 and he pulled back with sharp alarm.

"*Deme lo!*" Jorge snapped the order.

"No." The guide moved his weapon out of reach with a jealous possessiveness. "No!"

Ojeda's hand swung in a flat arc, the bony edge caught the man just above the bridge of his nose with a paralyzing effect. His body jerked, his eyes glazed and his head began to snap back and forth in a spasm which the helpless nerves and muscles could not control. He started to pitch forward and Jorge shoved him back against the seat, taking the M-1 as it dropped.

With an almost hysterical scream the youth tried to tug a pistol from his waistband. Fear contorted his vapid face. The thing he struggled for was a cheap, nickel-plated gun with an imitation horn butt. It was halfway out, caught in his trousers.

"Uh-uh!" Juan's voice was soothing, gentle, admonishing. The gun was in his palm. "*Cuidado, chico.*"

The boy stared and subsided, collapsing a little as though he had suddenly lost weight. Then, with a stupid fixation he thrust all of the fingers of one hand into his mouth and began to gnaw at their raw ends.

Jorge held the rifle beneath his arm now and watched as the guide struggled back to complete consciousness. The man's eyes were filled with hatred and fury. He coughed, an empty sound, and pressed a fist to his forehead, moaning a little with pain and humiliation. He glared at Ojeda and his body swayed back and forth in a torment of helpless anger. Jorge felt no regret. A man who could be taken so easily could not be trusted with the only real weapon they had. He had made the decision. The first judgment was correct. In the end he might regret not having killed the guide here and now, for the fellow would walk always with the idea of revenge uppermost in his mind. It would possess him completely. At the moment, though, he needed him.

"*Psst.*" The boatman leveled a finger shoreward. "*Aya!*"

From the scraggly line of darkness a light appeared. It winked twice, was gone for an instant, and then blinked again.

"Is that it?" Ojeda demanded.

The guide nodded sullenly, his eyes never leaving the M-1.

"The clips," Ojeda ordered and poked the man in the belly. "Give them to me."

There, for a second, the man seemed ready to spring, so great was his anger. He measured his chances, his shoulders bunched and the muscles gathered there.

"I'll blow your guts out, *hombre.*" Ojeda made the statement with a calm reasonableness. "You know that." He waited and then with the fingers of one hand unfastened his belt with the holster and handed the .45 automatic to the man. Surprise broke through the muddy hatred in the eyes. "Take it. I know this rifle better than you do. That is all."

Not fully comprehending but reassured by the feel of the pistol's weight the guide handed Ojeda the four, flat metal magazine clips in their webbed pockets on a belt. He began to regain some of his stature as a man. They both understood that what had happened between them would not be forgotten; neither expected it should be.

The boat's motor was turning slowly, unevenly, and it edged in toward the shore until its bottom grounded gently in the sand.

"You first." Ojeda motioned to the guides.

With a questioning glance the youth took the hand from his mouth. The other guide nodded assent and followed him over the side and into the water which barely reached their knees.

"Lieutenant, would you like to plant the flag of democracy on this unknown beach?"

"You mean, like the guys at Iwo an' get our pitchers in the papers?" Juan assumed a wide-eyed surprise.

"We'll come back with a PRO and a photographer tomorrow."

Juan grinned and swung a leg over and down. He dropped and waited until Ojeda was beside him. The boat backed off of the shelf and they began to wade through the small ripples toward the shore.

What they were doing now was done as men might move through the sequences of a dream which had reoccurred so often it no longer held a surprise. They were caught, by their imagination, in the shadowy illusion of a battle without sound or fury. In the mind of each there was the memory of the platoons strung out in waist-deep water; the assault boats bringing in fresh waves; the smell and the confused thunder of the attack upon an enemy who had not yet been seen or heard but who waited silently with their fire zeroed in on the beach. So complete was the spell, so vivid the tricks of their fancy, that when it happened neither was actually surprised.

The gun cut loose with a sudden, spasmodic hammering from somewhere on the slight elevation where the scrub was a darker line against the darkness. They threw themselves forward on the dry lip of the beach, instinctively flattening themselves as their eyes sought the position of the gunner as he pounded at them with short, furious bursts.

The fire was without direction, attempting to sweep the entire beach and the water beyond. The heavy slugs tore into the sand, whined into the bay or passed with a silken, ripping sound high above their heads. Wriggling forward, Ojeda caught a glimpse of the younger guide as he rose and started to run with a wild and erratic frenzy of terror. He screamed as that which hit and spun him around tore the life from his guts. Ojeda emptied the M-1 into the concealing scrub and then there was an almost surprised silence and the night was abruptly without sound or movement.

Ojeda slapped a fresh clip into the slot. They lay there for a second and he could hear Juan cursing with a soft monotone. Then they heard the quick whine of a starter, the tinny clatter of a jeep's motor as it was raced with frantic acceleration. The scrub crashed and snapped dryly as the vehicle ploughed against the underbrush. The sound grew fainter and then was gone completely. They waited, eyes straining, ears waiting for a sound, not daring yet to move. There wasn't even the whisper of a wind to rustle through the palms.

"You all right, Pepito?"

"Yeah." There was a pause. "I will be just as soon as I get over being scared. What the hell do you suppose that was all about?" He laughed with soft wonder. "Do you know what I did? I was clawing around, trying to unsnap a grenade as though I had one hooked on me."

They rose slowly, remained in a half crouch for a minute or so and then straightened up. Ojeda started across the beach and Juan followed reluctantly. Above the boy's body they halted. Ojeda stooped and turned him over. He struck a match and Juan slapped it out angrily. Ojeda said nothing but lit another and gazed at the face. Then he blew it out.

"That's a hell of a way to cure yourself of fingernail biting." Juan was deliberately callous. "I'm still a little jumpy. The match." He made the explanation.

A voice, with a faint tremor in it, hailed them from the scrub.

"Señor?" It was a polite, frightened inquiry and it asked for reassurance. "You are all right, señor?"

"Come on out." Ojeda was curt.

The brush parted and the guide stooped out. His head turned from side to side as though he expected the machine gun to start firing again. At their side he stared without emotion at the twisted body of the youth as though the boy had committed an unnecessary offense in public.

"I thought this was supposed to be an easy walk ashore." Now that the moment of immediate danger was past, Ojeda grew angry. "What happened?"

"Who knows?" Absently the guide nudged the body with the toe of his boot. It was a tentative, indifferent exploration to find out if the boy was shamming. "Our own people, perhaps. Someone else who knew you were coming. There is always shooting."

"What do we do now?"

"We wait. A truck will come."

"When?"

"Tonight, perhaps. Tomorrow. Who can tell? Maybe there is no *gasolina*. It happens." He squatted indifferently and lit a cigarette, glancing up from it to Ojeda and then to Juan. "Why do you Americans concern yourselves with something which is not your affair?"

"Go home Yank!" Juan snorted his impatience.

"I suppose," the guide mused, "you are being well paid. We get nothing. Does that make sense?"

"You're a patriot." Ojeda was amused by the man's contention of a great injustice. "That is its own reward; to die gloriously for his country."

"*Cajo!*" He spat his disgust. "I have no wish to die for anyone or anything." He cupped the cigarette and drew upon it. "In San Rafael I killed a man over a woman. The police hunt me. It is safer to hide and live with those who make the revolution. That is all. That is why I am here."

Ojeda looked around. Their position on the open beach was too exposed. The guide seemed indifferent to the possibility that whoever had fired at them would return. He smoked contentedly, balanced easily on his heels, digging in the sand with a finger.

"Let's get up into the scrub. If we have to wait I don't want to do it here. By the way," a thought struck him, "who was the one who made the signal? What became of him?"

"Who knows? Perhaps he ran when the shooting started. Maybe he lies somewhere with his throat cut. It is of no importance, *jefe*." The title was a deliberate sarcasm.

"What do you want to do with your friend?" Ojeda indicated the body.

"He has no friends now nor is he a friend of anyone. Leave him. He does not care. The buzzards will come or the tide will wash him out to sea. It should not concern us."

They moved from the beach, thrusting against the high, tough and thorny scrub until they found a small clearing ringed by brush. The guide dropped to the ground with a weary sigh. Ojeda and Juan settled themselves, their backs resting against the stunted cedars. Nothing the guide had said was reassuring. A truck would come, maybe, perhaps. Whatever happened would be the will of God.

"I don't trust this son of a bitch." Juan spoke clearly, expressing the opinion, knowing the man understood. "The operation is getting all fouled up and we end on a beach without any idea of where we are. What's your name?" He snapped the question.

"Jésus. Jésus Moreno. My mother was a woman of great piety." The guide was slyly amused by their uneasiness. "It has been told to us all that you are soldiers of great valor who have come to teach us how to make the revolution. Have you ever made a revolution before?" He laughed and the sound was unpleasant. "I don't think so. There are women in the camp." He added this irrelevantly. "I wish I had one here now. I am going to sleep." Working with both hands he piled the soft earth into a mound for a pillow. "Women soldiers are no good. They think they grow *huevos* because someone gives them a gun but they are better than no woman at all." He turned to Ojeda. "You should not have hit me in the face as you did. I have not forgotten. I will think upon it for a time and then decide to kill you, maybe."

They watched him as he appeared to fall asleep at once, head resting in the curve of one arm.

"Take some sleep if you want, Pepito. I'll watch and wait. Maybe they will come soon."

"And if they don't?"

"Then we will start walking with our friend there."

The sun had burned through the morning's early hours and began to fill the scrubby waste with a sticky and intolerable heat. Twice during the night Ojeda and Juan had relieved each other at the watch. The guide had slept with bubbling snores, indifferent to the mosquitoes and the swarms of sandflies whose bites were the pricking of red-hot needles. Now they waited with sullen anger and growing impatience. They had no water and the taste of tobacco was foul in their mouths. High in the cloudless sky the buzzards had begun to gather, wheeling cautiously in ever lowering sweeps as they studied the body on the beach.

Over the silence, then, they heard the unmistakable sound of a motor and the metallic rattle of a vehicle as it bounced and slammed along an erratic course in their direction.

"Come." The guide jerked his head. "There is a piece of a road over there."

At the side of the road, which was little more than a couple of deep ruts gouged out of the sandy earth, Ojeda and Juan stared incredulously. What had once, apparently, been a farm truck all but shattered itself as it careened toward them. Two of the fenders were gone and the others were held to the body with pieces of twisted wire and frayed rope. Steam rose in a high plume from the radiator, the neck of which was stuffed with a wad of cloth. Packed on the truck's bed, leaning against the high, slatted sides, fifteen or so men, boys and a few girls raised rifles, shotguns, revolvers and machetes high above their heads in a wild salute as they shouted a noisy greeting.

"These are troops?" Juan turned bewilderedly to Ojeda. "This is the revolution?"

The truck slammed to a halt, sliding at an angle across the ruts, and its passengers tumbled from the open tail gate to form a crescent about Ojeda, Juan and the guide. A few of them wore the loose, Army fatigues which had obviously been purchased through a surplus outlet in the United States. Others had on what seemed to be white pajamas. A couple were clothed in faded blue denim trousers with their shirttails hanging out. Some were barefooted, others were shod with heavy jump boots. The girls covered their feet with sandals fashioned from leather thongs. They were weighted down with bandoliers of ammunition. Save for the arms they bore they gave the appearance of a load of migrant workers; the *braceros* who come across the borders from Mexico at Texas and California for the seasonal crop harvesting.

"Hay-lo, Yonkee!" The greeting, obviously carefully rehearsed, was a chorus. "*Viva* Yonkee. Hay-lo." The scream was ear-splitting.

From the driver's seat within the truck's rusted cab a young man of twenty or so leaped down. He shouted at the crowd for silence, finally overcoming their exuberance by the sheer power of his own voice.

"Is this discipline?" he accused them. "Are these soldiers of the revolution who behave like children?" He eyed them sternly, pretending to be unaware of a few muffled giggles from the bright-eyed girls. "Now, we shall proceed with order."

He wheeled sharply to face Ojeda and Juan and snapped to attention, holding a salute until they returned it gravely.

"Officers, sirs." He articulated slowly, trying his best to disguise his limited English. "I present the compliments of General Quatero who welcomes you to San Rafael. I am Corporal Seta at your orders and services, sirs. I speak the English, as you can see. You may give me your commands and I will translate them."

There was complete and impressed silence from the gathering about them as the corporal spoke to the Americans in their own language. They waited eagerly for the reply.

"I am Captain Jorge Ojeda. This is Lieutenant Juan de Cespedes. Thank you for your welcome. As you hear, I speak and understand Spanish. We do not come among you as foreigners but as soldiers like yourselves."

The boy's face was shadowed with a momentary unhappiness. He was to be robbed of the importance as an interpreter. Then he recovered and his features were animated. He turned and with a magnificent sweep of his hand indicated the crowd.

"These, Officers, sirs"—he insisted on displaying his English—"are the brave soldiers of the revolution."

"God Almighty." Juan breathed the words with awe.

"We have been commissioned," the Corporal continued, "to escort you safely to General Quatero's headquarters. Have you commands to give, Officers, sirs?"

"Yes." Ojeda was sharp. "Address me in Spanish, Corporal. We are thirsty. If you have water."

From as many directions a dozen canteens, stoppered gourds and a goatskin were thrust at them. While they drank deeply every eye was upon them as though they were engaged in some mysterious rite. A collective murmur of astonishment rippled among them as Juan drank from the goatskin, holding it a good twelve inches from his mouth and expertly directing the stream.

Ojeda passed his canteen back. "How far is it to the General's headquarters, Corporal?"

"In kilometers I do not know, Captain. With God's help we shall reach there in the afternoon."

"Let's get going then." He mounted to the truck's seat followed by Juan. "I am in haste to meet the General."

The decrepit vehicle trembled and shook as the guard of honor scrambled back up into the open bed. The starter barely turned the motor over. It finally caught after many backfirings, wheezing and complaining.

"As you say, Corporal, with God's help. I hope he is a good mechanic."

IX.

THE road they had traveled that day many years ago wound steadily upward from sea level toward the dusky blue ridges of the mountains, where the white clouds lay in great cottony bolls upon the peaks.

That the gasping truck kept moving at all was a small miracle. Time after time, as the trail steepened, those who rode in the back would leap to the ground and set their collective strength to the task of pushing it over a particularly difficult stretch. The gears whined and screamed a protest while the banging engine threatened to fly through the flimsy hood. Somehow, though, it kept going without falling apart.

They passed few persons along the way. They were usually old men or young boys who tended small herds of goats as they fed on the grassy slopes. The herders would stand at one side and watch as they labored past and now and then an old one would remove his tattered straw hat with a gesture of respect for the soldiers of the revolution.

Both Ojeda and Juan were aware of the fact that their escort no longer behaved as noisy children in a schoolyard at recess time. They were silent, alert. Now and then when a sharp curve in the road hid what lay beyond, Corporal Seta would stop the car. Without orders four or five of the men or boys dropped off and scouted cautiously with their rifles held ready for a surprise attack. The rest scattered themselves on either side ahead of the truck, taking cover in the woods. Their skilled confidence was not lost on Ojeda or Juan. Despite their scarecrow and ludicrous appearance they deployed themselves as accomplished guerilla fighters.

"What do you watch for, Corporal?" Ojeda asked.

"*La guardia civil*, Captain. This is the only road. It is known we use it. Patrols are sometimes out. They have no real stomach for the fighting. We have killed many. There is a small garrison a few kilometers distant. A place called Los Cumbres."

Ojeda glanced at Juan. Neither was tolerantly amused any longer. This was fighting as they had known it in many places before. The combat of small patrols; the dangerous ground to be covered with caution by men grown experienced in deadly, silent infighting where only a limited number were involved at one time. Without confessing it they felt a familiar tightening within their guts.

Such villages as they passed were scattered. Small settlements which seemed to have no reason for being. On the walls of some of the squat, adobe or stone houses, they saw the paint-splashed words: VIVA QUATERO! Residents who came from the doorways as they rattled through the single main street shouted enthusiastic greetings and sometimes ran out with offerings of fruit and water. Quatero, Ojeda thought, was not entirely without a following no matter how motley it might be. On steep hillsides they caught an occasional glimpse of a cultivated patch of corn or cane and the tiny figures of men and burros as they worked the land high on the seemingly inaccessible foothills. Now and then plumes of smoke would rise out of densely wooded sections. Corporal Seta, noticing their interested attention at what seemed a series of signals, explained that these were the fires of the charcoal burners who brought their fuel down to the communities for sale.

They, also, he explained, served the revolution by keeping them advised of the presence and movements of Government troops who constantly hunted the rebels and their headquarters.

At the edge of one of the villages a small boy came running down the road toward them, waving his arms with a wild excitement. He leaped to the truck's sagging running board and babbled almost incoherently to Seta. The speech was a dialect, Ojeda thought, a combination of Indian and Spanish but in it he caught the words *camione* and *soldados*.

The Corporal braked the vehicle to an abrupt halt and asked the boy a question, also in the dialect. The child replied with vehement affirmation, nodding his head vigorously.

"What is it, Corporal?" Ojeda was caught by the youngster's agitation. "What does he say?"

"He says there is an Army truck just up the road. They have had a flat tire and are halted while it is to be changed. There are four men only. With the Captain's permission I would like to take those men and their fine truck."

"We will go with you, Corporal." Ojeda, noticing how the young man's face grew unhappy, smiled to himself. "As observers, Corporal Seta. As observers only but"—he hefted the M-1—"to assist if necessary with this."

There was a shining gratitude in the youth's eyes. He was not to be outranked and denied this rare opportunity to display courage and resourcefulness before the new Yankee officer. Such a chance, he understood, did not come often to a corporal. The raid would be conducted dramatically; the prize of incalculable value; the demonstration of his ability as a leader impressive. He jumped from the seat and called the names of four men to follow. Then his eyes moved to sweep the girls.

"Tina." He spoke the name and beckoned to one. "You are the small morsel of bait at which the fish will snap. To be a lure is a thing you do well and without effort."

Laughingly the girl passed her rifle to a companion and then unslung the heavy bandolier from a shoulder. Now she was no longer a soldier. With an unconscious gesture of femininity she ran fingers through her short hair, fluffing it out as well as possible. Then, she pulled at the thin cotton dress until it clung tightly to her breasts and hips. Her eyes were polished agates as she dropped down from the truck and stood, posturing seductively before Corporal Seta.

"*Andele, chica.*" He slapped her smartly on the bottom. "You know what to do to take the minds of the soldiers from their truck and the need for caution. The priest will give you absolution should such a thing become necessary. It would be in a good cause."

The girl stuck her tongue out at him and sauntered away up the road. She seemed to walk idly and without purpose, stooping to pick a wild flower and tuck it in her hair. They watched until she had disappeared beyond a bend in the road.

With quick efficiency Seta gave his instructions to the men who moved quickly into the woods paralleling the road. Then he turned to Ojeda and Juan.

"With your permission, Captain and Lieutenant, sirs." He checked the carbine he carried and then walked ahead of them, leading the way into the lightly forested section on the opposite side from the one his patrol had taken.

Ojeda and Juan exchanged a quick smile of understanding. The operation was being complicated beyond all necessity but not alone for their benefit. All of them now—the girl, the men who had gone ahead and even those who remained behind—were part of a theatrical venture. This was a moment of color. They were actors in a drama. To have overwhelmed four soldiers in a truck with their superior numbers would not have furnished the stimulation they felt through this involved maneuver. They were animated by an appeal to natures which were attracted by the flamboyant.

"As you see, Captain, sir," Seta whispered proudly as they slipped with hurried caution through the concealing woods, "the girls of the revolution are not without purpose. Tina is a good girl. She has not lain with the men as have some of the others. She has no lover. But she would go upon the ground for those bastards of the civil guard if such a distraction was necessary to our cause."

They halted at the edge of a slight elevation from where they could look down upon the road. The truck, as the boy had said, was there. It was a heavy GM, shining in its newness, impressive in size and power. Seta drew in a whistling breath of admiration as he stared at it.

Two of the guard were working with a jack at the left front wheel. The other pair had stationed themselves, one at the truck's front. The other was posted at the rear. They watched the road and listened, rifles ready.

Ojeda checked the M-1 he carried and the Corporal, noting the slight movement, shook his head with an almost embarrassed smile.

"It would not be the same, Captain, sir. To do it from here, quickly and with dispatch, as you are thinking. It is a thing difficult for me to put into words. The girl, Tina; the four who are slipping through the woods on the other side; even those who wait in our truck, would all feel cheated. To do it in our own way and by ourselves is the reward. This repays, in a small measure, the loneliness, the discomfort, the hunger and the absence from our families. It is a portion of the debt owed us by those bastards of the civil guard who have raped our women, burned our homes, imprisoned many of our leaders, tortured and killed old men and women and hunted us like animals. In this moment we feel pride in ourselves as fighting men of the revolution." He sucked his breath in with a sharp sound. "There is Tina."

As an actress moves in the spotlight across a stage, aware of the audience but pretending it is not there, the girl halted with simulated surprise a few yards from the disabled truck. The pair at the jack glanced up and whistled a two-note sound of good-humored admiration. Tina ignored them. She strolled to the opposite side of the road and leaned indolently against a slender pine, watching with idle curiosity. She assumed a preoccupation with a bit of ground, digging the toe of her sandal into it but glancing up now and then with a demure provocativeness. The invitation was there. The two men at the wheel dropped the jack and straightened up, passing a word to each other and laughing suggestively. One of the standing guards barked an angry reprimand and after a second's hesitation they went back to the job of changing the wheel.

Absently, Tina scratched at her knee and the flimsy dress was hiked several inches higher than necessary. The guard at the front of the truck said something to her and she tossed her head with affected anger but giggled coyly and made a small shrug of indifferent agreement.

Although nothing of what was being said below on the road was audible to those who watched from the ledge, the pantomime was explicit. The guard had made Tina a proposition which she did not find entirely unwelcome. She was, her attitude indicated, embarrassed only by the presence of the others. The second guard now came from the truck's rear and the pair, carbines slung on their shoulders by the straps, spoke together earnestly for a moment. They glanced up and down the highway as a final security check and then crossed to where Tina waited. They spoke to the girl and one of them reached forward and stroked her breast. She did not pull away but nodded toward the men who changed the tire. They were sullen and angry at being left out of what was about to occur.

With a rude shove one of the guard started Tina back into the woods. She went with a seeming reluctance and then glanced over her shoulder to laugh invitingly.

Now the minutes lengthened. The wheel had been changed, the jack removed. Three men stood by the truck and waited. Finally, the guard with the carbine shouted with impatient anger in the direction of the woods. He waited for a reply and when it did not come, he spoke to the two and strode with an apparent fury into the thicket. One of those remaining stared after him and then spat contemptuously. They lit cigarettes and leaned against a fender.

"Now, Captain and Lieutenant, sirs." The Corporal moved silently down the slope, taking advantage of the cover.

Fifty yards or so from the road's edge they were halted by the unmistakable sound of a car. From behind the brush they watched as a jeep skidded to a halt. The officer beside the driver stood up, surveyed the scene and demanded an explanation. The pair at the truck were at stiff attention.

This unexpected complication momentarily confused Corporal Seta. He hesitated and in that second Ojeda, with the rifle, cut down the two soldiers with fast shots. He then killed the officer—frozen in a standing position by the incredible thing which had happened.

The driver leaped from behind the wheel, spun in a panic of indecision on the road. A rifle cracked from the woods nearest him and seemed to bounce from his heels; he revolved a half turn and fell upon his face. A small, powdery cloud of dust rose from the impact.

For a moment it seemed as though they stood in a world of complete silence. Then the idling motor of the jeep made itself heard. Ojeda glanced up to find the Corporal staring at him. There was disappointment, mortification and a miserable admission of failure in his expression. There was, also, the all-but-imperceptible shadow of anger in his eyes.

"There was no time, Corporal, to wait for you to make up your mind."

"The Captain, sir, is of course right." The words were spoken tonelessly. "It is only that I—" He was unable to finish the sentence and turned away quickly, pushing through the few remaining yards of foliage. "With your permission, *capitan*."

Ojeda lit a cigarette. Juan regarded him with a narrow-eyed speculation.

"You like to earn your money, *compadre*. Eh?" He, also, lit a cigarette but his gaze did not shift from Ojeda's face. "It is a good feeling, *verdad?*"

"It is not a game of tag in the schoolyard, Pepito. I did only what needed to be done."

"*A toda costa?*" The question was softly asked. "At the price of a boy's pride?"

Ojeda was indifferent to the softly voiced criticism. He drew heavily upon the cigarette and studied Juan as though he were a stranger.

"Weigh the Corporal's dignity against that truck and a jeep, Pepito, and see which has the greater value."

"It is possible both could have been saved, Captain"—Juan's employment of the title was faintly derisive—"if you had given him a chance. A few seconds *mas o menos* would have made no difference. They were trapped anyhow." He shrugged. "It is done. We forget it. That M-1 is a woman, is she not; a thing of pleasure? It is difficult not to use her. I have seen that look upon your face before."

"You are a sentimentalist, Pepito. You are, also, my friend. I forget what you have said. Let's go down now and see what we have taken."

As players might move back from the concealing wings to the stage after the curtain has fallen, those who had been engaged in the drama now began to fill the road.

The girl, Tina, trying to fasten an upper section of her dress which had been torn away, walked out of the woods. Her expression was without triumph or interest. She was followed by two members of the patrol. They were loaded with equipment stripped from the bodies of the civil guard and one wiped blood from a knife's blade with a handful of grass.

The old truck, which had been stationed out of sight, labored noisily around a bend. Those who rode upon it leaned eagerly from the sides and shouted with a wild enthusiasm at the spectacle of the truck and jeep so easily and quickly taken. They leaped down and raced forward to surround the prizes, running their hands over the shiny surfaces, examining the heavy-duty tires with exclamations of wonder. The bodies of the civil guard were ignored. They merely stepped over them. Once again they were children, astonished by what they had done. With shining eyes they pressed upon Corporal Seta, demanding that he recount each detail of the ambush and describe, minutely, how each step had been taken; the sudden terror of *la guardia civil* when they found themselves trapped. Sly but laughing questions were directed at Tina as to what had happened to her in the woods.

Because he was embarrassed and unsure of what the Yankee captain might do or say, the Corporal shouted an angry command for order. There was a respectful silence, for the Corporal, by this exploit, had elevated himself to a position which demanded their deference. They waited.

"The Captain . . ." Seta spoke the words slowly.

"The Captain," Ojeda interrupted, "is impressed by what he has seen here today. You are fighting men. The Lieutenant and I are honored to stand at your side. There is little we can hope to teach you when you are already so well led by a man of Corporal Seta's skill."

Seta met Ojeda's gaze steadily. There was no mute gratitude in his expression but some of the smoldering resentment was gone.

"*Mil gracias, capitan.*" He turned and gave the orders which were necessary.

The dead in the road were looted of everything of value; even to the thin, tropical underwear. The girls worked methodically with the men and displayed no interest or false modesty in the nakedness revealed. The bodies were dragged over the highway and tossed into the brush.

Now, the confusion was revived. Everyone wanted to ride in the big, new truck or in the jeep. The old and battered vehicle was an object of scorn and fit only for a peon from the field or the hauling of manure. Diplomatically Corporal Seta established order. Everything had a value to the revolution. Who could tell when the worn truck might be needed? It was decided that places would be exchanged during the remainder of the trip. Everyone would have an opportunity to ride in the big truck. But only the Captain, the Lieutenant and the Corporal should have seats in the jeep. They would lead the way. The old truck would be driven in the middle, between the new one and the jeep. Only those who had actually been engaged in the capture should be permitted places in the new truck when it was driven triumphally into camp.

There was loud discussion and argument over this, but finally it was agreed that Corporal Seta's decision was not without logic. It was accepted.

Listening to the controversy Ojeda and Juan glanced at each other with a quiet appreciation for the ridiculousness of the situation. Juan winked and Ojeda grinned at him. Some of the old accord was re-established.

"I want to live, *companero*," Juan laughed, "long enough to see you at the first drill instruction. After that I shall have looked upon everything. You may fold my arms upon my chest and let me die in peace."

It was late afternoon when they took an almost impassable trail, pitted and boulder strewn, through a high-walled canyon. Once a stuttering of machine-gun fire tore flinty particles from the sheer granite sides. A concealed outpost had fired an exploratory warning. The mustard-colored truck and jeep had been recognized as equipment of the civil guard. The sentries, though, were mystified and made cautious by the familiar presence of their own battered *camione* sandwiched between them.

Corporal Seta stood up on the jeep's seat, waved his arms frantically and shouted their identity. The voice became many as the words echoed back and forth, tossed from peak to peak, bouncing from the stone walls. Figures, holding rifles aloft, appeared to rise out of the earth above the trail as they yelled a greeting, but the sound was lost and they seemed puppet figures against a barren backdrop.

As the vehicles crept forward there were more soldiers of the revolution at strategic corners, from ledges and sheer outcroppings. They yelled their enthusiasm at the capture or stood in silent wonder that such a deed had been accomplished. A magnificent victory and prizes had been snatched from the hated civil guard.

Pitching and rolling on the jeep's seat, Ojeda thought the position of the revolutionary forces was almost impregnable. The Government would have to pry the guerrillas out one by one. Air bombardment would accomplish little. Artillery could never be brought up effectively. It would have to be a campaign of attrition in which small numbers of men would die from time to time as they probed and sought each other. If the revolutionists could sustain their food supply, then they could probably hold out here forever. But this would provide no victory. Sooner or later General Quatero's forces would have to come down and fight this thing out in the streets of San Rafael; village to village, town to town until they could take the capital itself. Unless they did this they would have succeeded in achieving nothing more than a stalemate.

They moved upward, yard by yard, bouncing over unyielding ruts, skirting the huge boulders which blocked the way. Abruptly, the canyon's bottleneck opened unexpectedly on a broad, wooded plateau. Here the grass was lush, the trees tall and murmuring softly in the constant wind as it roamed unhurriedly through the high places. A waterfall dropped as a lacy bridal veil from a rocky shelf.

Ojeda and Juan stared unbelievingly. Within a great, natural amphitheatre, darkly cool and miraculously green, the camp and headquarters of the revolutionary forces appeared as an innocent mountain village. Only the fact that the men who stood about in small knots carried rifles slung on their shoulders denied this first impression. Also, spotting the shelters which were crudely thatched, there was a haphazard collection of pup tents and a few larger canvas awnings stretched between the trees. All activity stopped as the motorcade drew up on the level space, and the soldiers of the revolution pressed in an ever-widening crescent to follow its progress.

Corporal Seta drove the jeep directly to where a large, peaked tent was set upon a board platform. It was tightly stayed with wire and the compound before it swept and unlittered. The two trucks were in file behind the jeep. When the motors were cut the silence was almost breathlessly impressive.

From a hammock swung between two trees a man of thirty or so had watched the approach of the vehicles with a curious indifference. Finally, and with a reluctant effort, he half rolled out of his cradle and stood up. He wore the only complete uniform Ojeda or Juan had seen among the troops. It was smartly tailored in gray serge. The cavalry boots were black, shining and silver spurred. On its shoulders the twin bars of a Captain twinkled softly when they caught the light.

At stiff attention Corporal Seta saluted and after a long moment the officer flipped his hand indifferently and nodded. His eyes, however, never left the figures of Ojeda and de Cespedes.

Subduing his pride in the accomplishment, the Corporal recounted what had happened. Now and then he could not completely control his excitement and his eyes flashed, his voice rose dramatically as he related the ambush, the destruction of *la guardia civil* and the capture of the truck and jeep. During the entire recital the officer's gaze remained with a cold hostility upon Ojeda and Juan. When the Corporal had finished, the Captain merely inclined his head.

"The General will be pleased, Corporal." With this indifferent commendation he turned to Ojeda. "I am Captain Jaime Ortega, aide to General

Quatero." Plainly he was addressing his inferiors. "State your names, if you please."

For a second Ojeda studied Ortega from beneath hooded eyes. There was no excuse for the deliberate insolence. Finally he smiled—not at the officer but to himself.

"I am Captain Jorge Ojeda." He accented the rank. "This is Lieutenant Juan de Cespedes. I'm certain you know who we are and that we were expected. I should like to see General Quatero at once."

Ojeda made his reply in Spanish although Ortega had been almost contemptuously superior in displaying a flawless English. He had done this for the benefit of the camp's soldiers, who were drawn back at a respectful distance but still within hearing of his words.

Ortega yawned. "At this hour the General shoots doves." He glanced boredly at a fine watch worn upon his wrist. "You will have to wait." He started to turn away.

Ojeda controlled the anger which began to seethe within him. This was the behavior of a petulant, spoiled and jealous youth.

"Captain Ortega." The words were pistol shots.

Surprised, Ortega reversed his action. Momentarily he was made uncertain by the hardness of Ojeda's voice.

"It has been a long trip, Captain." Ojeda forced a reasonableness he did not feel. "The Lieutenant and I are hungry, tired and dirty. If you will have someone show us to our quarters and then bring us something to eat and a drink, if you have it."

"General Quatero left no instructions." Ortega had recovered his amused arrogance. "You will have to wait. Anyhow, the revolution has no need for the assistance of Yankee gangsters." This he said in Spanish and in a tone louder than was necessary.

Ojeda and Juan could hear the soft, rippling whisper as it passed through the ranks of the men behind them. Ortega swung away. He walked to the hammock and stretched himself upon it. Arms crossed beneath his head he closed his eyes. He offered a picture of weary disdain.

Ojeda could feel a hundred pairs of eyes upon his back. The silence was so complete it seemed even the wind had stopped its sighing. There was no time to weigh the consequences. What had to be done must be done now and without hesitation or he would never command the respect of a single, ragged *soldado*. They were too innately polite not to be aware of Ortega's deliberate insult. He glanced at Juan.

"*A todo transe, compadre.*" De Cespedes smiled wryly.

Yes, Ojeda thought, by all means the character must be displayed. Without it his presence here would be nothing.

He moved without haste toward the hammock, taking a knife from the sheath on his belt. With a single slash he cut through the rope holding Ortega's sling.

It had happened so quickly that Ortega had no chance to prepare himself. He hit the ground headfirst, sliding in an undignified heap to the ground. His features were a twisted mask of inarticulate fury but before he could move, Ojeda reached down and pulled him upright with both hands. A second passed and Jorge Ojeda spat full into the face before him. Then he cut the backs of his hands across the mouth and nose of Captain Ortega with a cold fury.

Ortega's scream was of rage and terror. He tried to strike back but the shock had robbed him of strength and judgment. Calmly and methodically Ojeda beat him. Fists drove into a belly grown soft with indolence. When the body bent in a helpless agony, Ojeda's heavy knuckles cracked into the face and straightened the man for further punishment. Ortega's face was a bloody smear. He attempted to scream and a crimson froth spewed and bubbled from the tortured lips. Only the eyes had life now and they were pleading for mercy. Ojeda felt none. With a strangled cry Ortega spun about and tried to run. Calmly Juan thrust out a foot and tripped him. He slammed into the ground with the sound of a thrown melon and he lay there, unable to move and barely conscious.

Now the sound from the wide-eyed and incredulous troops was like a single, deep breath drawn and expelled, but there was no movement.

Ojeda wheeled about. "Corporal Seta!"

"Yes, Captain, sir." The Corporal was rod stiff. He came to swift attention.

"You will place Captain Ortega under arrest and post a guard until I have spoken with General Quatero."

The Corporal, as though what had happened was not at all extraordinary, called the names of two men. He directed them as they picked up Captain Ortega and carried him inside the tent. Then he went in and returned with the officer's belt and pistol. He then selected two other soldiers and posted his guard.

At the moment Ojeda was unable to assay the effect upon the men of what he had done. As his eyes swept them, though, he caught an automatic, reflexive action as they drew themselves into a semblance of order and respectful attention. Ojeda turned again to Corporal Seta.

"Where is General Quatero, Corporal?"

"It is, as the Captain said, of the hour when the General shoots doves, sir. They come out of the *barrancas* at this time of day. The General enjoys the sport."

"Do you know where he shoots?"

"Yes, Captain, sir. It is not at a great distance."

"Take me to him."

The Corporal saluted. To hide his bewilderment he shouted an angry command at the soldiers to disperse. They obeyed reluctantly, for it was in their mind to stay and watch this Yankee who could be so terrible in his anger. They broke up slowly, in small groups, moved away and squatted, whispering among themselves, their eyes never leaving Ojeda.

"You have a knack for making friends, Captain Ojeda." Juan made the comment with a sly amusement. "First the guide and his M-1. Now an officer. Some night your back could look like an angry porcupine's from the knives sticking in it."

"Ortega is a fool and gave me no choice. He locked the door upon himself and there was no way out."

"Now you will have to kill him or he you."

"I suppose so."

Beyond the wooded space of the encampment the land rolled gently in dun-colored waves as though an ocean had suddenly dried here and left its crests and valleys in earth. The brown grass was waist high and stunted, scraggly trees and thorn bushes were sparsely scattered.

Corporal Seta drove the jeep with care, jealous of its shiny surface. He nursed it up and down the *barrancas,* halting now and then to listen intently.

"Not always does the General hunt in the same place." He explained, "The doves grow smart and take a new flyway after they have been shot at for a couple of days."

Astride one of the long ridges he stopped the car and shut off its motor. For a while there was no sound at all. The sun had changed from the dusty yellow and was beginning to glow on the western rim of the plain with the color of a ripe persimmon.

They watched as a flight of the big, gray doves came out and up from one of the depressions with incredible swiftness. Their bodies tilted from wing tip to wing tip as tiny fighter planes in evasive action. As they passed overhead they made a small whistling sound and began a long dive to their destination for the night.

Faintly they could hear a double report, as champagne corks being drawn one after the other rapidly. Corporal Seta nodded and smiled. He climbed from the seat.

"That is the General, Captain, sir. We had better walk from here. The jeep would scare away the flights which are just beginning to start. This, undoubtedly, would make the General angry."

They strode unhurriedly, pushing through the yielding grass which had an unfamiliar fragrance, an aromatic perfume it yielded when crushed by their feet. There was upon the land the compelling spell of solitude. Ojeda felt it and was strangely intoxicated by the quiet magic. He, also, knew a curious sensation of excitement and wonder at the succession of events and decisions which had brought him to this place.

A second flight of doves went overhead, veering away sharply and vanishing almost before their path could be marked. From the sound of the shots they had heard, Ojeda thought General Quatero must be using nothing larger than a .410. To bring these flashing birds down with that was a real marksman's job. He was faintly amused by the idea of a revolutionary leader snap-shooting at doves in a glowing twilight. Who drove the rebellion or didn't it really exist beyond the wishful thinking of such men as Roberto Francisco and Dr. Leras? It was, he mused, an oddly unhurried pursuit of liberty. He amended the word—ambition.

For a moment he thought it was a fanciful trick of imagination. He stopped and listened and then turned unbelievingly to Corporal Seta for an explanation. From somewhere, not too far away, came the sound of music. It was the unmistakable beat of a Cuban orchestra playing a samba. He was too astonished to ask the question which was evident in his eyes.

"That would be the General's radio, Captain, sir. He always brings it with him to pass the time until the birds start to fly. He says, also the doves are attracted by the music."

The Corporal made the statement without a trace of emotion or a suggestion that this was at all extraordinary. Ojeda glanced at Juan. Their eyes met and then they shrugged simultaneously because neither could think of a reply. The Corporal made it seem perfectly logical.

Scrambling up the steep side of one of the narrow troughs, they halted. Spread below them in the succeeding depression was something at which they stared but could not quite bring themselves to believe was there.

Drawn beneath one of the thorny trees was a shining English sports car of dazzling yellow. Seated in a canvas chair, just beyond the tree's overhang, was a man of heavy girth. He was booted. Spurs shone at his heels. The uniform he wore was of cream linen and the shoulders bore the four stars of a full General. On his head was a tropical pith helmet. Across his lap he held the small-gauge, double-barreled shotgun. Near, on a folding card table, was a portable, battery-operated radio. Its thin antenna was drawn out in a long, silver wand. Next to the radio was a small cooler and from this protruded the foiled necks of imported beer. The music played steadily. The man drew upon a huge calabash pipe. Two boys, ten or so years of age, were half crouched as waiting sprinters at the General's side.

Against the darkening sky a pair of the birds came up fast. Without moving from his place the General lifted the *escopeta* and fired twice. For a second the birds seemed motionless and then they spun dizzily earthward.

The boys, as trained retrievers, raced forward and almost caught them as they fell. They returned, obedient animals, to hold them up for the General's inspection. The man nodded, reached into the cooler for a bottle of beer, uncapped and drank it with gurgling pleasure. He turned the radio's volume up slightly and drew contentedly upon the pipe. Then he broke the gun and inserted two fresh shells.

"Now, that there," Juan exaggerated a Cracker's drawl, "would make a fine picture for a recruiting poster. Be a General. Shoot doves. Drink beer. Drive a sports car to work. I wonder if they have heard about this in the Corps?"

Corporal Seta led them down the incline. At the crackling sound of their approach through the dry brush General Quatero turned with an expression of mild annoyance. He studied the trio for a moment, puzzled. Then a full smile of recognition lighted his broad face.

"So!" his voice boomed with a hearty good nature. "My Marines have landed." If there was an accent to the words it was British rather than Spanish. "Welcome to San Rafael."

"I am Captain Ojeda, General." Ojeda pursued the informality established by the General. A salute, the observance of military etiquette, under the circumstances would have been ridiculous. "This is Lieutenant de Cespedes."

"General! *Aya!*" One of the boys pointed at a speck in the sky.

The dot grew larger as a single dove came in a long dive toward them. General Quatero threw the gun to his shoulder, fired, and watched the feathered bolt drop with a grunt of satisfaction. The boys raced toward it in contest as eager puppies.

Studying the General, Ojeda thought he gave the appearance of a stolidly contented Boer planter enjoying his beer, his pipe and an hour's sport on the veldt.

The boys returned with the dove and slipped its neck between the double strands of a string already loaded with the plump-breasted trophies. The General nodded his approval. He reached toward the table, counted the remaining bottles of beer and pushed two aside, indicating them for Ojeda and Juan.

"Some beer, my Marines?" He tested the cooler's water. "It is not thoroughly chilled. The boys fill the box at a mountain spring but it is not as good as ice." He suddenly remembered the introduction. "Of course I know who you are. We have everything, even short-wave radio contact with members of the *junta* in Miami. We have everything except that bastard General Romero. But," he beamed, "now that you are here to give me an army we shall have him also." He drew his brows together in a frown. "Let us do things with dispatch from now on, my Marines. I dislike the discomforts of revolution. These doves, for instance. Properly prepared they should be cooked with white wine, stuffed with wild rice and truffles. Where in God's name is my cook to get wild rice, white wine and truffles in these mountains?"

Ojeda uncapped the beer and he drank slowly, his gaze never leaving General Quatero's figure. He had the feeling the man's behavior was deliberate and not that of a good-natured fool. Juan barely controlled a desire to laugh but Ojeda, catching his eye, shook his head in warning. There was a delicate balance to be preserved here. Instinct told him much depended upon this moment. The future of Jorge Ojeda lay in its handling. Of this he was certain. Indolently, matching the General's attitude, he dropped to the ground, lit a cigarette and took a full, deep swallow of the German beer from the bottle's silver-foiled neck.

General Quatero appeared not to notice. He slipped a fresh shell into the place of the one just fired and then examined the bowl of his pipe.

"It was necessary for me to place your aide, Captain Ortega, under arrest, General." Ojeda made the statement casually. "I beat him first."

"You did, eh?" There was not a flicker of surprise in the General's expression. He drew meditatively upon his pipe. "It was necessary for you to do those things?"

"Yes, General." Ojeda kept his tone flat.

"It was not just a Yankee Marine showing how tough he is?"

"No."

Quatero was silent for a moment. Then he broke the gun, unloaded it and stood up. Ojeda followed respectfully. The General passed the firearm to Corporal Seta who had stood at one side, near the tree, at stiff attention throughout all this time.

"Take the gun and the other things with you, Corporal Seta." Quatero was no longer pleasantly, bumblingly vague. The use of Seta's name and rank was an indication of this. "The Captain and I will ride back together."

Seta, with the help of the boys, began dismantling the table, closing the radio and cooler. The General walked away toward his car. In passing, Ojeda glanced at Juan and saw the surprise in his eyes. De Cespedes, also, realized now that Quatero was not what he had suspected.

For a man of his size the General handled himself with a heavy grace. He slid easily into the car's small seat. When Ojeda was beside him he started the motor and let it idle for a minute or so. Then, he dropped it into gear. They drove slowly. There was no road to follow. The wiry grass sprang back into place as the wheels passed over it and left no tracks.

"I draw a certain amount of confidence from your behavior, Captain. It is my habit to permit fools to confuse me with themselves. From this I arrive at conclusions which have invariably served me well."

Ojeda made no comment. His estimation of the man had been correct. Quatero, for his own reasons, liked to play a doltish role. It was, as he had just said, a measuring rod.

Almost uncannily probing into Ojeda's mind, the General smiled faintly. "I am a politician, Captain. And, by the nature of my calling, inclined to a certain deviousness. Because I am tricky I suspect most men of being charlatans. Knowing my own weaknesses I cannot believe it is unique, but endemic in us all. Consequently, I always try to fortify myself against it. You, for instance. I do not believe you are on San Rafael simply because Roberto Francisco offered you a wage of one thousand dollars a month."

"I had no choice." Ojeda made the statement simply.

Quatero nodded. "I sense that in you, also—a certain mystical conviction of destiny. It is a convenient philosophy for it permits a man to indulge himself in all manner of evil without sufferings of conscience." He skirted a deep gully and said nothing more until they were again on level ground. "There is a Christian faith which denies the existence of all disease. However, it happens now and then that one of them acquires syphilis, pneumonia or even a common cold. When the skeptic asks why he blows his nose, goes blind or cannot breathe, he is told it is only because the faith is not strong enough. The spirochete may set his blood on fire and cause him to break out in great sores, but these things are only an illusion. He is a victim of an error of faith and not of the bug. So it is with men of destiny. They say: I do what I do because I cannot help myself. It has been planned for me. As I said, a most convenient philosophy. What I am saying, in this garrulous fashion, Captain, is that I am not unsympathetic to ambition as long as it does not seek to run parallel to my own."

Quatero drew the small car to a halt, reached into a glove compartment and drew out two glass tubes. Sealed in each was a foil-wrapped cigar. He handed one to Ojeda.

"We have an immediate problem, do we not, Captain?"

Ojeda nodded, waiting until Quatero had lit his cigar from a lighter on the dash and then accepted it for his own.

"Your choice is limited." The General tasted the tobacco with quiet pleasure. "Captain Ortega is a man of great vanity and limited intelligence. That is frequently an unmanageable combination. He cannot be permitted to sulk in his tent. Neither can he be bundled off to San Rafael—the city itself, I mean. There he would seek his revenge on you by exposing everything he knows. So, you see, I have been placed in jeopardy by what happened. What do you intend to do about that?"

"Kill Ortega." The statement was without anger. "These are fine cigars." Ojeda sniffed the perfume. "My father made cigars such as these in Tampa, Florida."

Quatero released the car's clutch and they moved forward again. Already the sky was darkening rapidly, for the hour of twilight was brief.

"If Captain Ortega were a man of intelligence," the General mused, "he would be interested in tracing through the convolutions of what you call Fate. He would meditate on the notion that because a Tampa cigar maker had a son he would die without glory in the Sierra Madre. He would be astonished and ask: What made that maker of cigars have a son instead of a daughter? One might have given me pleasure. The other was born to kill me. Why?"

"I could not help it." Ojeda shrugged.

The General nodded an agreement. "Of course not." He smiled. "It is good for a man to believe that." He reflected quietly as he drove. "As I understand you better it is quite possible I shall sometimes lie on my cot and also wonder a little about a Tampa cigar maker's son."

"I will make an Army for you, General. There are many things I need to know beyond the mere formation of men into disciplined units. Men may be clubbed into order. It is something again to make them fight bravely."

"I expect you to give them pride."

Ojeda said nothing. He leaned back and stared at the sky where the first of the stars were making a pale scattering like a handful of mica powder tossed on a strip of dark velvet. For no particular reason he smiled and closed his eyes.

X.

AND so, in the high reaches of the Sierra Madre, the Army of the Revolution was shaped, forged and tempered. It bore with it, as an invisible shield, a fierce pride and a mysterious conviction of invincibility. It became the reflection of one man.

Jorge Ojeda.

No one asked: What is this thing for which we have volunteered to fight? Each man, in his own way, had an answer. It could be the vague hope for a small piece of land; the relief from oppressive taxes. In some it was no more than a personal resentment for an individual member of *la guardia civil* who had been overbearing or taken a man's girl. Others found in the revolution an opportunity for revenge upon a neighbor who had whispered to a tax collector where a few goats, pigs or a couple of cows had been hidden at the time of assessment. There were some who, for a minor offense, had been impressed into labor battalions and rented out to the owners of the great estates until they had worked off the exorbitant fine. All of these things they had endured under a succession of governments. General Quatero now promised them that with the success of the revolution all wrongs would be set right. They only half believed him for he was, they understood, a *politico* given to fine words and a splendid appearance. With this Yankee captain, who had been a Marine, it was different.

Ojeda dangled no carrot on a stick for a stupid burro. He gave them no assurance things would be better. What he said was: You are here because you want to be. What happens after the revolution is for you to decide. First you must win it. To do that you must become fighting men with a heart. I am here to teach you not only how to kill but, perhaps, to stay alive a little longer. Some of you will die. Others will survive because of what they remember.

At first they had no understanding of why they must do certain things. Why they must drill until they could come to a sharp formation upon command. Why they must march long hours under heavy pack and full equipment until they no longer tired quickly. Why there was an hour for going to sleep and another for getting up. Why they were now all clothed in identical garments—the olive-colored, lightweight dungarees which were bought and shipped by agents in Miami, Boston and New Orleans from the vast surplus stocks left over from a war. A man was no longer permitted to wear a bright scarf about his neck because the color pleased him. He was not allowed to wander off down the mountainside to his village to see a wife or a girl because the need for a woman was upon him. Instead of the light sandals, he now put his feet into heavy half boots and into these the trousers must be tucked and laced in a certain way and no other. He was made to take apart and put together, in endless repetition, the few machine guns and the automatic rifles until the operations could be done blindfolded. He was taught to keep himself and his weapons clean. Those who displayed intelligence and aptitude were promoted and a small stripe sewn upon their sleeve. This became a thing of great but unvoiced pride. Now, because they were all clothed exactly alike and did the same things at the same time, they began to think and behave as one. There evolved a uniform way of thinking and acting and the individual identities were submerged. In this there was born a sense of security. Because they had been trained in the same way and for the same things each felt that in a time of crisis he could depend upon the man next to him to behave as he should.

The girls were sent home. They left with tearful protestations or shrill anger. The Captain talked to them quietly, explaining why it was necessary. In different ways they attempted to break down his will but he was firm and, in the end, they left. Now the volunteers were a corps. It was tough and disciplined, no longer a ragpicker's brood who brawled among themselves, fought over the girls, ate when they felt hunger or slept when the desire for sleep was upon them.

For the Lieutenant de Cespedes they felt respect. He was *muy valiente* who carried himself with a dash and knew his job. They admired his courage and on a raid it was noted it was he who moved into the position of danger first. For the Captain, though, they knew something close to awe and he grew daily in stature and authority. In their minds he became the figurehead of the revolution and in time they no longer remembered it was General Alfonso Quatero who was supposed to lead them.

At full strength the corps numbered no more than five hundred men. Their equipment was brought to lonely stretches of the coast and unloaded there from small boats. It came from Cuba, Key West and Miami, and the blockade runners easily slipped past the inadequate patrol of the Government's corvettes. Some of what they received was faulty. Some was good. All was used and brought into the mountains during the hours of the night and early morning.

Even though the capital city of San Rafael was two hundred kilometers away they could sense the Government's growing anxiety. On the General's radio they listened as President Romero assured everyone the rebels would be hunted down and destroyed. The next day, the President appealed for loyalty from the country people and then offered full pardons to those of the rebel troops who would come into the city and surrender. Daily they watched the sorties of the Government planes as they flew aimlessly and dropped their light bombs haphazardly. The explosions blossomed harmlessly on empty hilltops or in the valleys and did no damage save to the wild pigs and a few mountain sheep and cougars. Rural garrisons were reinforced and light-armored cars roamed with futile purpose over the roads. Many of these were captured. Others were destroyed with grenades or torn apart with .50-caliber machine-gun fire.

In small groups the revolutionists struck simultaneously at the rural garrisons. Food supplies to Government troops were cut off or captured. Each time they moved upon a village and drove out the civil guard, volunteers pleaded for an opportunity to join and share in the triumph.

Kilometer by kilometer the perimeter of the revolution was extended. There were wholesale surrenders by Government forces which no longer had the stomach for fighting and were dismayed by the ferocity of the constant attacks. Now the revolutionists had jeeps, trucks, a few light-armored cars and motorcycles.

Wearied by the whole business the pilots of Romero's little air force took their planes and crash-landed most of the obsolete craft on remote beaches or in pastures and sought enlistment in the rebel group.

President Romero sent word to General Quatero. It was suggested a truce be arranged so that two old friends could sit down and discuss a compromise government. Quatero ignored the invitation.

With five hundred men Ojeda took the city of San Rafael on a bright September morning. There was only a token resistance. With the approach of Quatero the forces within the city which had remained underground came out and overwhelmed the police. They took over all communications; the radio stations and telephone systems; the custom house and port facilities. There was rioting in the streets and a looting of shops. Old angers were paid off and screaming bands of irresponsible youths roamed in packs through the city. Into this chaos Ojeda moved quickly and behind him, stretching as far as a man could see, the country people and those from suburban districts formed a procession. The capture of San Rafael became a fiesta. Rockets were fired from housetops, firecrackers thrown in snarling bunches into the streets. Flowers pelted down from windows to make a carpet for the brave soldiers of the revolution. By noontime most of the irresponsible citizens were wildly drunk. In the central plaza two municipal bands pumped away at different tunes at the same time. On street corners there were speeches by professional agitators who had interest only in confusion and not the revolution. Prudent merchants had bolted their doors and drawn the steel shutters over their windows. Most of the decent citizens had remained at home and those who had the means of transportation had fled to resorts in the mountains.

The officers of President Romero's military forces deserted their bewildered troops, destroyed all personnel records and disappeared. General Romero was captured by a roving band of Quatero sympathizers as he attempted to fly out in a private plane from the municipal airport. For a few hours the city was in the hands of irresponsible groups bent on revenge and destruction. Small political factions rioted, shot and clubbed each other in a hysterical effort to achieve a status before a new government could be formed.

Ojeda did not seek General Quatero's advice or aid. With his tightly disciplined troops he ruthlessly stripped the partisans within the city of their arms. He placed Juan at the head of a demoralized police department but the Army of the Revolution, which he had made his own, took over the brunt of the task of restoring order. By nightfall the jails and the Presidio were filled with prisoners and the city was quiet.

General Quatero addressed the people of San Rafael that night over the radio. In a persuasive speech, filled with promises, he appealed now for an orderly transfer of power. Amnesty was offered to all those who had opposed him in good faith. He outlined a program of reform and reorganization. He came to them in good faith. President Romero and his cabinet would be treated with consideration and understanding. To prove this he would meet with President Romero in public before the Capitol at eleven o'clock the following morning. Following his speech General Quatero retired to the Presidential Palace. Ojeda remained at a temporary headquarters in the Capitol Building.

General Quatero did not sleep well that night. He paced up and down his room or sat quietly in a chair trying to decide what he must do. He was a little frightened by the cold efficiency displayed by Ojeda. On this day of triumph he had been little more than a spectator. His army, he well understood now, was not his at all but that of Ojeda. Looking back he wondered what he might have done to retain the authority which had been taken from him so imperceptibly by this Yankee Marine. He tried desperately to think of some means of ridding himself of Captain Jorge Ojeda now that he had served his purpose. Assassination was the logical answer. How? That was the unanswerable question. He must have time to plot this. There was an alternative. Appoint Ojeda to a position in the Government second only to himself. It was upon this idea he finally slept.

By nine o'clock on the following morning the huge plaza before the Capitol Building was packed solidly. By the thousands the people of San Rafael filled the square, the rooftops, the windows. The streets, which ran as the spokes of a wheel to the plaza, were tightly jammed. Almost a quarter of a million persons strained, fought and sometimes trampled each other in an effort to edge closer; to see and hear.

At eleven o'clock promptly a limousine bearing General Quatero inched its way to a position at the bottom of the wide flight of steps leading to the columned entrance of the Capitol. At almost the same moment President Romero, with Captain Jorge Ojeda, appeared on the top step. Behind the President stood the ministers of Romero's cabinet.

Facing the enormous crowd the revolutionary battalion was drawn up in familiar battle dress. The people of San Rafael had never seen such soldiers as these. Pride shone as the sun upon their bayonets. They were crack, well-drilled, seasoned men and bore no relation to the military forces seen on the island before. The Army, save for the officers corps which enjoyed the privileges of authority, had always been a shameful occupation. Criminals were inducted against their will. The ranks were filled with the shiftless, the indifferent, who were badly paid, miserably quartered, fed and clothed. It was a last resort for a man who couldn't make a living any other way. Now, those who could see, stared at the revolutionary battalion with incredulous awe.

At a signal from Ojeda a squad moved out of formation, up the steps. President Romero and his cabinet were taken prisoners. There was a momentary confusion before Romero would accept what was happening. He screamed the words that he had been betrayed into this meeting. He yelled "Assassin" at Quatero and spat his fury as he was marched down the steps and into a waiting car which spun away in the direction of the Presidio.

All of this was astonishing enough. Word of what had occurred ran back through the crowd and into the many streets where the people waited. The news was carried as a swift fire. Romero had been made a prisoner. The words of Quatero on the radio the night before had been without honesty.

At the foot of the steps General Quatero, magnificent in his uniform, could not conceal his surprise. He made a gesture of apology or reconciliation toward Romero as the man passed him. Then in the hush, in which it seemed no sound at all intruded, he turned to stare up at the figure of Jorge Ojeda. Those who were nearby saw in his gaze a question. He was asking permission to mount the steps.

Ojeda offered no sign. General Quatero took a fresh handkerchief of white silk from his sleeve and touched his brow although the morning was cool and a fine breeze came in from the sea. His indecision was a thing to be felt as well as seen and a rippling murmur of amazement was distinctly audible. Those far in the rear who could not see were puzzled and made a little apprehensive by the sound.

The Yankee, Ojeda, who had been an American Marine and about whom incredible stories of daring and resourcefulness during the fighting had been told, remained where he was. Below, General Quatero waited. Now it became apparent to everyone within the plaza that a time of tremendous drama was upon them. A man was being destroyed by silence before their eyes.

Quatero understood. He darted quick, hopeful glances at those nearest him and pleaded with his eyes for one or two among them to join him in taking the first of the steps. No one moved. The attention of all was fixed upon the man, Ojeda. The seconds, as they ticked by, became almost unendurable. The splendid figure of General Quatero, who had spoken the brave words of revolution, stood as an errant schoolboy.

Jorge Ojeda came slowly down the flight of gleaming marble. He did not debase the moment. There was in him no cheap swagger or suggestion of triumph; only an unassailable dignity. On the step above General Quatero he halted and regarded the man with a curious air of detachment. There was no recognition in his eyes, no pity, no interest.

"In the name of the Republic of San Rafael"—the words were clear and carried well in the complete silence—"I place you under arrest."

Four soldiers wheeled about from their positions in the ranks and took the paces necessary to bring them to General Quatero's side. The man ignored their presence. His eyes unflinchingly met those of Ojeda.

"It couldn't have waited until later, Captain?" There was no tremor in the voice.

"Later would have been too late, General."

Because his back was to them the crowd could not see the faintest of smiles upon Quatero's face. They pressed forward, until halted by the bayonets, eager to hear and to pass the word of what was being said to those behind them.

"You do what you do because you have no choice, Captain?"

Ojeda nodded. "It is a thing we once discussed, General."

"Then let us do what must be done, Captain. It is better it be done quickly."

"I promise you that, General. There will be no unnecessary delay. I have no wish to hold you in prison."

The limousine which had carried General Quatero in triumph through San Rafael's streets the day before rolled quietly through the lane which separated the motionless troops from the gaping spectators.

"I should have thought more upon the possible ambitions of a cigar maker's son, Captain. The thing which happened to Captain Ortega in the mountains might have taught me much. Unfortunately, I was too busy with my own dreams to take what I saw in you for what it was. I have no excuse but that of vanity."

"Your car is waiting, General."

"Permit me a question." Again the smile with its suggestion of wry resignation. "What secret shame drives you to such calculated treachery? Ambition I could understand. What is there in Jorge Ojeda which he wants to hide at all cost? The doors of the Presidential Palace are of heavy bronze. Perhaps, you may be able to lock this thing which makes you uneasy behind them. I have recognized upon you, sometimes, the stigmata of a terrible humiliation. Often I have wondered who placed it there and why." Quatero inclined his head in what was unmistakably a sardonic bow. "And now, Captain Ojeda, let us have done with it."

Jorge Ojeda remained where he was until the limousine carrying General Quatero to the Presidio had passed through the tensely curious throng, motorcycled police clearing a path with the high wail of sirens. Beyond this there was no sound, no movement. He understood well that a cry of outrage rested in the throats of the multitude. It would take only a small indication of uncertainty on his part to give it voice. Rebellion was also there but it had no leader. What he faced was a great but indecisive monster. It would remain passive only if he exercised complete control over himself.

Slowly, Jorge Ojeda turned in a quadrant and his gaze swept across the uplifted faces. To those who watched it seemed as though he counted and memorized the features of each man, child and woman. Then the plaza became an arena in which all were sculptured figures. They were waiting for him to speak. Instead, he turned his back upon them and began walking up the steps toward the columned entrance. He did this thing without haste, without fear and without contempt for their presence. It was the supremely confident gesture of a matador who, after a series of brilliant passes, has fixed a brave bull in the exact spot he wished it to be. It was a display of such bravura that the appeal to the crowd was irresistible.

The roar, deep-seated, heavy-throated, rose in a tremendous wave of sound. They screamed, these people of San Rafael, in a frenzy of delight for a superb performance. A nature inherently receptive to the flamboyant was fired. In the thousands of voices raised in delirious acclaim there was an unreasoning fever of appreciation for a great actor. Instead of diminishing in size as he moved upward, he appeared to grow in stature until he dominated the backdrop of the Capitol. In a country of violent colors and emotions this was a dazzling exhibition of histrionics. What man was this who came as a foreigner to prepare an army for revolution, lead it successfully against a Government long entrenched and then depose a *presidente* and calmly arrest his successor? This they had seen and would tell their children and their children's children.

A few muttered protests. Others were gravely silent and thoughtful. They were ignored. Later there would be fights and brawling among the partisans. There would be questions raised and left unanswered. Tomorrow would have to take care of itself. The violence of a new revolution might erupt with consuming ferocity when sober men had time to reflect upon what had happened. Today, though, was one of spectacle. What this Ojeda had done was so incredible, so wildly preposterous, that men and women screamed, laughed and cried with a mass hysteria of adulation. Here was a pirate to dwarf all stories of the buccaneers who once roved these seas and islands. He was a giant, a legend, a mountain, and this September day of his appearance among them would hereafter be marked in numerals of red upon the calendars of San Rafael.

That night, after most of the city's population had exhausted itself with the street dancing, the drinking, the sporadic celebrations and clashes, and the streets were all but empty save for the police and the troops of a new army, Jorge Ojeda broke his cold silence.

He spoke to San Rafael over the radio and what he had to say was relayed by short wave to the neighboring island republics and to the countries of North and South America. His voice carried into the homes of those who could afford receiving sets. It sounded in the Embassies, the Consulates and Legations; in the dingy *cantinas* on dusty roads where a small set was mounted above the bar. It silenced the noise in night clubs and restaurants within the city, came firmly into the tiny cribs of the little whores in dimly lit side streets. It held an audience in the great ballroom of the magnificent hotel built by the former *presidente*, Romero, with public funds for his private profit, and cracked through loud-speakers set in the palms surrounding the plaza. Later, sound trucks with the recordings would travel on the city's outskirts where the thousands of country people who had followed the Revolutionary Army were camped. They, also, would hear the words by the light of their hundreds and hundreds of little fires ringing the capital with flickering light.

Jorge Ojeda indulged in no politician's hyperbole. He spoke no word of liberty, of a better world, of independence and the righting of old wrongs with a better, richer and more equally distributed way of life. For a moment this surprised the people, for they were accustomed to such phrases even while they understood they were empty. As he talked, though, they nodded agreement. Such things must be left for discussion at a later time. Now they wanted only assurance of a firm hand and a feeling of discipline which would give them order.

Captain Jorge Ojeda offered no apology for the execution of Generals Romero and Quatero. He did not even mention their names. He spoke with the clear confidence of a popular leader and without vague promises for the future. After the first few moments of astonished exclamations, those who had spoken became silent. The magic of the voice was such that it occurred to only a few that this man was actually a foreigner, a usurper and, without question, a ruthless executioner of those who opposed him. They began to believe they listened to their own choice of a head of state and identified themselves with him.

As the commander of the Revolutionary Army, he told them, he had taken such measures as seemed necessary and consistent to prevent the riot and bloodshed of an unorganized society. The currents and hatreds of the revolution ran in deep places still and they must not be permitted to erupt to the surface. Until the capital's police force and the *Ruales* were thoroughly reconstituted the Army would remain in control of all civil affairs. For the time being public gatherings of more than a dozen persons were prohibited and a curfew would be enforced. These things only until the city had returned to its normal pursuits. A cabinet would be formed and ministers named as soon as practicable. Such public services as light, water, transportation, sanitation and other departments would operate under their present directors. Those who had given their support to the administration of General Romero need have no fear of reprisals or future discrimination. There were to be no persecutions, but professional agitators or those who sought to disturb the orderly process of reorganization would discover that their efforts would lead them to the Presidio wall. They would oppose the Government. He dropped easily into the idiom: "*A una vuelta de dado.*" At great risk.

These were the words of a strong man and those who listened liked what they heard.

Until such time, he continued, as it seemed advisable to hold a free and general election, he, Jorge Ojeda, would act as the head of State and occupy the chair of *el presidente*. He then said good night as crisply and as impersonally as he would have dismissed the Revolutionary Battalion.

Those who had nothing to lose and, perhaps, something to gain through the astonishing thing which had happened, yelled and applauded the now silent radios and loud-speakers. This was *un jefe maximo;* a man who was not afraid to say how things were to be. He did not come wriggling on his belly as a harmless puppy, which had been the way of previous leaders before they ran off with the steak. Also, he made sense when he said elections would be held when the island was again at peace. In the present ferment who could vote for what, even if given a chance? It was better to wait for tempers to cool.

Those who owned small businesses—the bakeries, markets, tobacco shops, laundries, coffeehouses and bars—glanced at each other in silent agreement. They existed only if order prevailed. A real soldier, such as this Ojeda, was, perhaps, what they had needed all along instead of the fat windbags who called themselves Generals without knowing the right foot from the left. They would reopen their little *tiendas* in the morning with confidence in this man. By a miracle there would be an end to the petty graft, the endless *mordida* taken, by long custom, by minor officials and the police.

There were others: those who represented large foreign investments on the islands—the mines, sugar and oil refineries, plantations and concessions. They, also, listened to Jorge Ojeda. It could happen, they agreed; an honest man, a soldier trained to the habits of order and simplicity. They pondered and discussed the words and then composed long cables with a guarded approval of Jorge Ojeda. In any event the revolution was an accomplished fact and there wasn't a hell of a lot anyone could do about it. This was the word they sent to the boards of directors in London, Paris and New York.

In the American Embassy the Ambassador and his staff also listened to everything Captain Jorge Ojeda said. A verbatim transcript was cabled to the State Department as a matter of form and radio circuit was held open all night between San Rafael and Washington for consultation. No one wanted to commit himself. Was this Ojeda just another in the seemingly endless succession of opportunists or was he the emancipator? Stung repeatedly by criticism that it supported the Francos, the Peróns, the Batistas, the Trujillos, because these dictators served the purpose of Yankee imperialism, the State Department gnawed on its indecision. It had been sweated by President Romero; had privately encouraged Quatero. But Romero and Quatero had been disposed of by a former Marine sergeant, Jorge Ojeda. And if that wasn't a hell of a note, no one in State could think of one to surpass it. The son of a bitch might even be a Communist. No one knew anything about him and his service record was hauled out of the files for careful reading and study. He had been a good Marine. What was he now? For one thing, he was certainly the President of San Rafael. He had the loyalty of his Army and, obviously, the fanatical adulation of the country people and the temporary enthusiasm, at least, of the capital. He couldn't be ignored. The situation in the Caribbean was too sensitive. To pretend he wasn't there was to invite Moscow to make the first friendly overtures. Within twenty-four hours the United States formally recognized the Government of Jorge Ojeda and the Ambassador paid a State call at the palace.

The French and British, not quite so politically naïve, shrugged their shoulders and went along. Ojeda, after all, was the foundling on the doorstep of the United States. If he turned out to be a monster, then Washington would have the responsibility for having taken him in.

And so, because of all these things which had happened many years ago, the son of a Spanish cigar maker and a black Haitian woman sat with his feet on a table of mahogany and sipped the fine rum of La Belle Dessaline in the Cabinet Room of San Rafael's Capitol. Not even the General Juan de Cespedes, who knew him best of all men, suspected why he had done what he had or what drove him to this pinnacle. Juanito would have found it difficult to believe they had traveled this long road because an illiterate Florida Cracker had once yelled the words "nigrah bastard" at a boy made frightened and uncertain for the first time in his life. This, also, was a thing which Jorge Ojeda preferred not to remember. But when it came to him, as it sometimes did in moments of inexplicable loneliness, he experienced the same empty sickness in his guts and felt himself running in panic along the hot pavement of Franklin Street which had no end but stretched across the world itself.

XI.

ONCE each month he appeared on the streets of San Rafael and even those who had known him by sight for a long time always turned to stare after this great, black man who strode the city's pavements as though they were jungle paths.

He walked cat-footed, the bare, splayed toes seeming to reach into the concrete the way an animal sometimes feels its way on alien soil. What he wore varied no more than the route he took. Short in length, reaching only to the oval slab of muscle at the naked calf, were the white trousers of duck. They were thin and bleached now from many washings. The shirt, once blue but faded to an indeterminate color, was worn unbuttoned to the waist. There the tails were gathered into a knot. The tightly kinked hair which never seemed to need trimming was white—not gray nor silvered-gray but the sheer white which is the combination of all the spectrum's rays.

Massau. It was his only name. He could neither read nor write. There was though, in the fingers of his enormous hands, such an untutored skill that with no more of a tool than a sharp knife he produced carvings of such exquisite beauty from the rosewood growing in the steaming valleys that a dealer in the arts from New York had once pleaded to be allowed to arrange an exhibition in his gallery. There were other carvings Massau brought to the city: primitive masks which had their roots somewhere deep within the Congo; curious and deliberately misshapen figures which, after the first shock and a little study, seemed no longer grotesque but moving and sad, as are the silent tears of a woman's sorrow in her loneliness. From the hands and the blade there sometimes came a lightly curving, tightly petaled flower cut from the bone of a shark's jaw. Without knowing why or how he knew these things Massau would sometimes shape the tiny, graceful figure of a girl with the body in the angular, stylized position of a Siamese temple dancer. Massau could not even explain to himself how a mysterious instinct guided the knife to produce a posture and the position of hands and arms of something he had never seen nor even really believed existed beyond his imagination.

Carefully wrapped in a soft leaf freshly cut from a banana tree, he would bring to the city a single mask or one of the carvings. He would take it to the shop of Marchand et Fils, which dealt in native art of value. Massau was no peddler. There were other black men who carved ridiculous faces on coconuts and stuck pieces of shell in gaping slits for teeth. These were offered for sale at the piers, in the markets and at the cigar counters of the hotels along with roughly plaited hats of straw, baskets and colored prints of crude fabric. The American tourists bought these things by the dozens to take back home as souvenirs. If there were customers in the place of Marchand, Massau would wait silently just inside the door until they had left. Then he would place upon a glass showcase the small sack he carried. The elder Marchand, Paul, would take the envelope of green leaf carefully from the little pouch and unwrap it. The figurine or whatever Massau had brought was laid on a square of white velvet. Now and then, for the sheer pleasure it gave him, the merchant would close his eyes and trace his fingers over the carving. He did this tenderly as a man might touch the breast of his love with the softest of pressure because it was something of beauty beyond passion.

They never talked of price or sale. In his dealings with Massau, Paul Marchand experienced an obligation of honor. The artist in him transcended the merchant to a reasonable extent. From what he received from a customer he deducted a third for himself, a third for the establishment of Marchand et Fils. The final third he paid to Massau.

They rarely exchanged a word. If money was due the black man it was ready in an envelope which Massau took, folded and thrust into his pocket without counting. It happened sometimes, during the off-tourist season, that trade had been dull and what Massau had brought in before remained unsold. Only then did they talk and then in the English-Spanish-French-Indian patois of the island.

"Will you need some money?"

"A little. Not much but a few of the American dollars or the pesos with which to buy what I want at the stores."

Marchand would then count out ten dollars or its equivalent in the currency of San Rafael and pass it to Massau. The amount would be noted in a ledger.

Once, after they had finished with their simple transaction, Marchand went to the rear of the store and came back with a large, rough piece of greenish-lemon color. He put it on the counter between them.

"Do you know what this is?"

Massau shook his head and there was a faint light of surprise in his eyes as his fingers traveled over the smooth unfamiliar soapy feel of the stone. He looked up at Marchand with a question.

"It is jade." Marchand answered. *"Piedra. Piedra de ijada."*

"I have never seen it before." Massau held it experimentally in both hands.

"Take it." The Frenchman urged. "Take it with you and make something of beauty from it. Bring it to me when you have finished. I do not care what you decide—a face, a figure, a little animal. Only let it be of beauty for us to contemplate together."

Massau was doubtful. "I have never done a thing of stone before." He ran his hands over the jade. "It has the cool feeling of a young girl; the smoothness of her skin with the warm sun on it when she lies on the beach still wet from the ocean."

"Wait." Marchand was transported by his extravagance. He disappeared behind the curtains again. When he returned he brought a small leather case. "In here are tools you will need. I make you a present of them. You are an artist. I am your patron. Take them as a gift of understanding."

"I will see what happens." The Negro nodded. "For a long time I will only look at it now and then. It happens in that way. I see it first in my mind."

"There is no hurry. I will not speak about it again until you are ready. Time passes but art endures forever. That is a phrase I heard. I am not certain it has any real meaning."

They wrapped the chunk of jade in a heavy cloth and Marchand watched as the Negro turned away. At the doorway he blocked the opening for a moment with his tremendous shoulders and chest and a gigantic shadow, squatly primordial in its foreshortening, was blotted as with ink on the floor. Then it was gone as Massau strode out into the hot sunlight and passed from sight beyond the heavy plate glass of Marchand's display window.

From the art dealer's establishment Massau went to a tobacco shop. There he purchased a bundle of fifty twisted and acridly strong cheroots tied with purple string. At a store dealing in liquors he bought a wicker-covered gallon jug of third-run rum. After this he visited a *tienda de abarrotes*. Here he selected a little coffee, some meal, dried beans, rice and a jar of thick black molasses. From the ceiling there hung withered hams and beef shanks which had the appearance of mummified limbs. Of these he usually selected the beef, so hard it must be cut with a hatchet into small pieces before cooking. Now and then, at a different place of business, he would get a strip of canvas, cord and, perhaps, a new needle for sail patching. One by one he dropped his purchases into a coarse brown sack which, as it grew heavier, he carried slung over his shoulder.

In none of the stores did he engage in conversation beyond a polite request for such things as he wanted, although the proprietors or clerks had been serving him for years. His attitude during the transactions was not hostile or sullen but only detached. It was as though he found himself among a foreign element with whom he had no sympathetic basis for communication. Sometimes he smiled faintly at a child as it played between the counters or a dog lying in a warm doorway. But he never made a move to touch them as a man might place his hand on a youngster's head or bend to scratch the responsive ears of an animal.

No one, not even Massau, had any idea of his real age. There were lines in his face, deep furrows, but they were not the sagging runnels of flesh which grows soft and wrinkled with time. They were sharp and clearly defined as though they had always been there. His carriage was erect, his eyes clear, his muscles solid. Yet there were many old persons in San Rafael who could remember Massau from their childhood and he had been a full-grown man then. They counted their own years and then gave Massau at least one hundred and maybe more. Some said one hundred and twenty-five; even one hundred and fifty. Since this was impossible, those with the dark suspicion strong in their natures whispered he must be a *juju* man who brewed a secret potion to keep him always the same. Tourists who encountered him on the streets halted to stare. Now and then one rudely trotted backwards as Massau walked toward him and frantically tried to focus a camera. At such times the big man halted and regarded the amateur photographer with a puzzled curiosity as though he had come upon a scuttling beetle engaged in incomprehensible antics.

Massau was also an object of quiet concern to Mr. Tedder-Jones Ironsides, chief cashier of El Banco de Londres y San Rafael. As a youth of twenty Mr. Ironsides had come to the island from his native London as a file clerk in the bank. He was seventy years old now and for almost fifty of that number his interest had been titillated by what he considered to be a most remarkable situation. Working his way up from the files to the bookkeeping department of the bank, he came upon what was apparently a dormant account, the holder of which was listed only as Massau. Checking the date of the original deposit, Mr. Ironsides discovered the first money—five pounds sterling—had been entered to the credit of Massau on a January day in 1890. Sometime later, when the dollar succeeded the pound as a standard, the sum of twenty-five dollars had been paid. Still later, when San Rafael began issuing its own currency, the sum of twenty-five pesos had been credited. Going back through the records now with the enthusiasm of a man involved in an intriguing mystery, Mr. Ironsides came upon an additional fact. No matter whether it had been in pounds, dollars or pesos, approximately twenty-five dollars had been deposited to the account of this Massau every month for seventy years. More surprising still was the absence of any withdrawals. The amount simply accumulated year after year until it now totaled some $21,000. This without interest since the account had been opened as a checking one. With interest compounded the total would have made Massau an extremely wealthy man by native standards.

As a sub-cashier Mr. Ironsides nerved himself to ask a question of Hamilton Bates, the bank's manager. Mr. Bates coldly replied it was none of Mr. Ironsides' business and suggested he get back to work. As the sub-cashier was about to leave his office Mr. Bates reconsidered and called him back. It was quite probable, he explained, that the deposits represented a pension for an old and faithful family servant. Such a thing was not at all unusual.

Mr. Ironsides accepted the explanation with a bright nod of agreement which seemed to put an end to his curiosity. Privately, though, he thought it most unusual. In the first place it was highly improbable a family servant would be pensioned off in the full strength of his manhood. Considering the fact that the first deposit had been made seventy years ago this would have been the case. Secondly, a servant thus pensioned by a generous employer would most certainly have used the money and not let it collect as it had. Thirdly, the monthly deposits had always been made in cash by whoever happened to be the institution's manager, the instructions apparently being passed on from one retiring official to his successor. Over the years managers for the branch had come and gone from the parent establishment in London. Mr. Ironsides was exceedingly skeptical of the idea that they had all felt the necessity for making a voluntary contribution to a pension fund for a Negro by the name of Massau.

Armed with these conclusions and the curiosity of a raccoon, Mr. Tedder-Jones Ironsides continued as a loyal and trustworthy employee. As his responsibilities increased he had a greater access to the affairs and inner workings of El Banco de Londres y San Rafael. One day, during a period of comprehensive auditing, he came across a most startling coincidence. At least it startled Mr. Ironsides, for it posed a question and at the same time argued a dark and possibly shameful secret. For seventy years, he found, the exact amount deposited for this Massau had been debited to the account of the Dessaline family. This had started when Emil Dessaline, the father of the present Madame Cleo Dessaline, had been the family's head. Upon Emil's death the sum had been transferred from the account of his widow. When she died and after Madame Cleo, then about twenty-two, married, Massau's pension had come from Madame Cleo's personal account. It was now deducted from the estate held jointly by Madame Cleo and her granddaughter Ferris.

Mr. Tedder-Jones Ironsides thought this all very unusual. It became more curious when he also found out that a piece of property, a small island off the tip of a peninsula on the southwest side of San Rafael, had been deeded outright to Massau as a gift, since the sum of one shilling had been payed for the property by Massau to make the transfer legal. So Massau was not only a man of small wealth but also the sole owner of a valuable island. Nowhere could Mr. Ironsides find a similar case of generosity on the part of any of San Rafael's aristocratic houses whose servants were the descendants of their slaves. Neither did it appear that the Dessalines had ever before concerned themselves with any of their other Negroes or employees to such an extent. Massau, then, Mr. Ironsides concluded, was a special case. The why and not the what was the thing which piqued his curiosity. Because he had no small hobbies, the head cashier decided Massau was a much more interesting pursuit than stamp collecting, orchid raising or butterfly collecting, and the big black man who walked with such a mantle of quiet dignity became something of an obsession. Sometimes, over a pink gin at the club, he would ask seemingly innocent and irrelevant questions about Massau. He was answered either with grunts of indifference from someone behind a newspaper, or an uninterested shrug from a companion at the bar. A big Negro—nothing more, nothing less. Why should anyone care to know more about him?

Since the bank was trustee for many of the old estates, he had access to bills of sale, ancient records of slaves, cattle, properties and business ventures both in San Rafael and abroad. Among these were accounts of the Dessaline holdings and, put together, they comprised what was practically a family history. Nowhere, save in the matter of the regular deposits and the gift of an island to Massau, did he come across anything which illuminated in the slightest what Mr. Ironsides considered to be a most peculiar situation.

As for Massau: If he knew of the bank's existence he ignored it. There had never been a time when he found it necessary to pass through its doors. If he had heard the name Ironsides he would have thought it a strange word by which to be called and never suspected he was baffling its owner to a point of quiet desperation. On the first of each month the bank mailed its depositors' statements. One was always addressed simply: MASSAU. WILL CALL POST. SAN RAFAEL. Since Massau never had a reason for entering the post office the brown envelopes, after a reasonable length of time, were returned to the bank stamped: UNCALLED FOR. Now and then, to vary the monotony, a waggish clerk would send back the statement with a notation, *Identity Unknown.* This, of course, was not true. San Rafael was a city of half a million persons, when its suburban districts were included. Hundreds of persons within the commercial section of the city knew Massau both by sight and name. Beyond that, though, they knew nothing and cared less. He was a part of the local scene as was the historic Presidio—a gigantic figure of a man who excited the curiosity of the tourists. Save for Mr. Ironsides, Massau's visits inspired small interest.

The shining city to which he came held no particular fascination for Massau. Over the long years he had been aware of its change: the fine buildings, the humming sound of its traffic, the ferment which spilled over now and then in revolutions; the broad avenues and towering hotels, the crowded sidewalks; the big ships which rode regularly into the harbor. These things he viewed with detachment. He came to the city only because it held things he needed and could be bought there.

After the trip to Marchand et Fils and then the unvarying rounds of the small stores, Massau carried his sackful of purchases to the public quay. This was a series of concrete piers jutting out from the breakwater south of the Yacht Club. It was a noisy section filled with the rich sound of laughter, of loud bartering and singsong calls of wares for sale. The quay was used by boatmen from the villages up and down San Rafael's coast. In their broad-beamed, clumsy-looking craft, they brought the fresh fruit, chickens, vegetables, fish and other produce to the market. Entire families made the voyages—men, children, girls, women with child at breast. They lived aboard the weathered ketches and sloops during the tie-up at the city docks. They brought with them, for safekeeping from predatory neighbors and animals, their goats, pigs, dogs, cats and an occasional calf. After several trips this livestock became wise in seafaring ways. They learned the danger of a swinging boom which could crack them across the head. As a result, even when the boats were safely moored, they ducked whenever the boom creaked. This constant obeisance created an odd picture. All of the animals seemed to be bobbing their heads in a strange union of silent assent as old men might nod quietly in agreement over a statement made. The native families cooked, ate, slept and made love on the open decks and sometimes spent two or three days along the quay after their produce was sold, just for the purpose of visiting with each other.

Always when Massau came to the docks to stow his sack in the tiny shallop with its sail of softly washed pink he was greeted with good-natured shouts and comment.

"How you reckon big man lak dat gits en smahl boad?" The question would be called innocently from craft to craft as Massau lowered himself into the little sloop. "He ride chip lak man cut wid ax." This was in a simulated amazement. "Ain' yo' heah? Big man swim en tow boad behin'." The explanation would be shouted from another boat. "Hey, you, Massau! Wa'k d' watah lak d' Lor'. Touris' pay to see dat."

By long custom this had become a ritual. The boat people would gather and peer down at Massau, play-acting with a broad burlesque their wonder at his size. Now and then a man would shove a wriggling and laughing girl forward with a bawdy comment on what Massau needed after living for so long a time alone on an island. In all of this there was a gusty friendliness and Massau, in his own way, responded. Sometimes, if the money received from Marchand was sufficient, he would buy an extra demijohn of rum. This he passed around freely, sharing a drink and casual talk with the gathered boatmen. For the child of a family he had known for a long time he might bring a doll fashioned from the fibrous root of scrub palmetto, its face carved into an expression of bright impudence. The son of a friend would be offered a fishing rod of bamboo. They were carefully selected, polished and seasoned with the joints beautifully wrapped for strength. These things he did with an almost shy diffidence as though his size made the small objects seem ridiculous offerings to come from such large hands.

If the mood for talk and company was upon him, he would delay his return to the island and accept one of the many invitations to share a meal. They ate, then, on the open deck in a tight circle about a communal pot simmering on a charcoal brazier. With large clamshells for spoons they dipped into the stew or fish-and-conch chowder and sucked noisily at the small pieces of bone before tossing them over the side. Later, when the darkness was softly heavy along the quay, the strings of an old guitar brushed and fingered gently would fashion a melody to float over the water. A single voice would lift itself and be joined by others in a chant which had been born in the fetid misery of a slave ship hold or the barracoons of the Guinea Coast generations before. These people sang the old laments—not out of unhappiness now, but only because they stirred something primitive within them. They reached back into a time they had never known but could feel without understanding why.

If the hour grew too late or the weather uncertain, Massau would delay his return home. He slept with the others on the deck, head pillowed within the muscled curve on an arm. Early in the morning, when the sky lightened almost imperceptibly into the smoked color of a gray pearl, he would move quietly, stepping over and between the silent figures, and go to his boat. Standing at the stern with a long oar he sculled clear of the docks until a light wind slapped and then tautened the triangular sail and set a small wave curling away from the stubby bow.

With a good breeze the trip to his island took a little over four hours. Sometimes, though, there would be an abrupt shift in the weather. The sail would fall into a shapeless rag and he would lie becalmed until the wind moved into another quarter. If he was impatient he would work at the oar. Usually, though, he simply waited. He would lie, smoking one of his strong cigars, staring at the sea and sky. It always interested him to watch the sharks collect when the boat simply rocked, lifted gently from wave to wave without forward movement. It was as though they scented an unusual situation which might be turned to the satisfaction of their bellies. First one dark fin would appear as the fish cruised just below the surface of the clear water. Then mysteriously it would be joined by others. A word was somehow passed in the subterranean depths. Often Massau wondered about this. How did they know a man, a meal of meat and blood at least, lay in a small shell of wood? Sometimes a larger, bolder shark would slide alongside, scraping the planking as though to test its vulnerability. When the wind came again and the boat was in motion, they disappeared.

Usually, though, Massau returned home late in the afternoon. He completed his customary rounds, starting at Marchand's, and finished his shopping without delay. It was on one of these visits that Ferris Dessaline spoke to him for the first time. She had bought a small hand-carved box as a gift for a friend. Massau waited within the door. In passing him she had looked up, met his eyes and smiled.

Outside, hand on the door of her car, Ferris paused as she realized what an extraordinary thing had just occurred. There had been something about the Negro which had generated a spontaneous warmth, and a smile of recognition as though she were in the habit of seeing and nodding to him daily. Impulsively, not understanding why, she dropped her purchase on the seat, turned and re-entered the shop.

Marchand and the black man were at the counter, a carved figure upright between them on a strip of velvet. The art dealer glanced up and then moved toward her.

"You forgot something, mademoiselle?" He waited.

"No." She was in a ridiculous position of uncertainty for there was no real explanation for her return. "I . . ." Her glance fell upon the statue and it offered a diversion. "What is that?" She indicated the carving.

"Oh!" Marchand beamed proudly. "The work of Massau, mademoiselle." He picked up the figure and gave it into her hands. Then he divided a smile of understanding between Ferris and the Negro, who waited impassively. "We conspire, Massau and I. He brings me these things which we enjoy together for a little while before I part with them reluctantly. But"— the shrug was exaggeratedly Gallic and deliberately comical—"even an artist and a shopkeeper must live."

"You did this?" Ferris turned the slim body of a naked girl in her hands and looked up from it into Massau's face. Her astonishment was obvious. "It is beautiful."

The Negro did not reply but stood watching her with a grave interest.

"I have never seen this wood before," she continued. "What is it?"

"I do not know how it is called, mam'selle." Massau shook his head. "It grows on the island. A single tree, now and then, in the valley jungles."

"It has the appearance of ebony." Marchand voiced a puzzled suggestion. "Yet I do not think that wood is native to these islands. It takes the high polish of a stone, as you can see. It is as hard as flint."

The slender figure was delicately classical in conception; fluid in its line and unlike any native carving Ferris had ever seen. It stood no more than twelve inches high and was perfect in detail. A leg and hip turned provocatively with a sinuous movement. The belly was virginal and flat; the breasts small and proudly high. The face, so minutely executed, had a mystifying, Oriental quality. The eyes were all but closed, the lips half parted as though they waited for a lover's kiss. Just holding it in her hands gave Ferris a curious sensation of sensual excitement.

"I would like to buy it." She spoke to Massau rather than to Marchand.

"It is not for sale, mam'selle." The Negro smiled with his eyes only. "Take it as a gift."

"I can't do that." Her protest was automatic.

"You cannot buy it, mam'selle." What Massau said would have been an inexcusable impertinence from an island Negro. "It is not for sale."

Incredulous, she stared at him and wondered why she was not outraged.

Also, his speech had an unfamiliar inflection. The words came, not in the heavy, liquid tone of the island Negroes. Neither was it accented in the dialect which was part Spanish, part Carib and English. The customary address was: *Ma'm. Mum. Mist'ss. Lady. Señorita. Señora.* Rarely was the word *mademoiselle* employed.

"Why do you call me mademoiselle?" She was astonished, now, by her own casual acceptance of an unprecedented situation. "It is not the custom."

"I am not certain." Massau was undisturbed. "It seems to suit you better, mam'selle."

Marchand was as acutely aware of what was happening as Ferris Dessaline. Only Massau seemed completely at ease. This was an impossible conversation between a San Rafael Negro and a white person. Generations of slave and master, a rigid, time-indented relationship, a system of caste and of color, had fixed the rules of behavior. Servility was not simply demanded; it was taken for granted. In the presence of their superiors the island's black people stood with a patient acquiescence. They shuffled their feet, stared at the ground, mumbled immediate agreement in a period of uncomfortable waiting. Never did they openly meet the eyes of a white person speaking to them. Most certainly they never denied a request or protested a command. Ferris Dessaline recognized the breach of conventional manners but she was not outraged. What did surprise her was the fact she found nothing offensive in what Massau had said. Even when he told her the carving was not for sale but she must take it as a gift or do without she was not irritated or conscious of an insolence. It was only later, when she had time to think over what had transpired, that she realized how unbelievable had been the Negro's dignified assurance.

"I would like to pay you for it." The protest was almost meek.

Massau smiled completely then and the expression illuminated his features. It was a smile of understanding and concern such as one might give a troubled child.

"It is yours, mam'selle, as a gift. Perhaps I carved it for you without knowing I did so. Please take it. If you do not, I will not leave it here for sale."

"Thank you." The words were simply spoken. Further protest would only have made her appear ridiculous. She extended the figure to Marchand. "Would you put it into a box for me? Please."

When Marchand had finished with the wrapping and gave her the package she hesitated, looking up and studying Massau's face. Then she merely nodded, turned and left the shop.

The figure now occupied the center of a large dressing table in her room. Behind it were a series of angled mirrors and the carving was reflected from all sides. It had a mysterious vitality and seemed many small naked girls turning slowly at the same time.

Once, not long after the figure had been placed on the table, Madame Cleo came into her granddaughter's room while Ferris was dressing.

"Where did you get this?" The old lady's tone was almost sharp.

Ferris turned from fastening a garter snap and glanced up in surprise. Madame Cleo was staring at the carving with an expression of puzzled astonishment.

"It was a present." Ferris dropped her skirt and straightened. "I thought I had shown it to you. A Negro. Massau. He wouldn't let me pay him for it."

Madame Cleo lifted the figure carefully. She held it in both hands. The head and shoulders rested in one palm. The legs and feet in the other. She seemed lost in contemplation, oblivious of her granddaughter's presence. Then she replaced the polished girl on the table.

"Yes. Massau." Madame Cleo spoke the two words quietly.

It was the tone rather than the words which aroused Ferris's curiosity. "You know who he is?"

"Of course." Madame Cleo shrugged. "His father and grandfather were Dessaline slaves. He was a young man when your father was born. Now," she was thoughtful, "he must be a very old man as I am an old woman." She turned away and walked to a window and from it looked down upon the sloping valley and the city beyond. "Always," she spoke to herself it seemed, "he had this astonishing talent. It seemed so strange in a Negro. It was difficult then, as it sometimes is now, to think of the blacks as persons. There were so many of them and with no other purpose in life but to serve your wishes. Massau was made an overseer by your grandfather. That in itself was unusual—for one Negro to supervise others. But he did his work well and with dignity. Never did he abuse his office and authority." She returned and again picked up the carving, examined it for a while and put it down with a faintly rueful smile. "The years have given him a great skill. We always wondered that such a big black man should have discovered the gift for beauty in his hands. Anyplace but here he might have been a great artist. That is not really true, is it?" She smiled again. "France, perhaps. Who knows? Dumas was part Negro." She made the statement as though it were known only to her.

"Massau is an artist." Ferris bent to glance into the mirror.

"Yes. I suppose so," Madame Cleo agreed listlessly. "But it doesn't mean quite the same thing on an island such as San Rafael, does it?"

Carelessly, Ferris dismissed the incident and the unfamiliar, almost faintly troubled words her grandmother had spoken. The figure remained on the table, a solitary ornament. Often she caught herself studying it by the soft light of the small side lamps with their shades of yellow silk. It was mysteriously, disturbingly exciting; a demure wanton. Always she marveled at the imperishable beauty which had sprung from Massau's self-taught hands.

What strange thoughts had been in his mind as he fashioned something so wickedly elfin? It had been conceived in imagination—an eternal woman completely unlike anyone he had ever seen or known on this small island.

XII.

SCATTERED in a broken chain along the leeward coast of San Rafael, protected by a long, narrow and palm-crested reef, were a dozen or so small islands. On them a few wealthy Americans, Canadians and self-exiled Europeans had built elaborate havens from the worst of the winter months in their own countries.

Here they lived in a casually magnificent isolation, proprietors of their island provinces. When they wanted company they flew their guests in by private plane from Miami and New York. They fished the sporting waters from especially fitted cruisers; swam, danced, engaged in passing infidelities which no one took too seriously. Deliberately they created a closely knit interisland society in which great wealth was taken for granted. Rarely did they concern themselves with what happened on the mainland save on those occasions when the political seething threatened their title and possession of the marine baronies they had purchased from a prior government. Now and then a fervor of nationalism swept San Rafael. There was agitation against foreign ownership. An incumbent government made vague threats of appropriation. The island society had learned to deal with these political dislocations through flattery and bribes. A succession of *presidentes* were propitiated with blocks of shares in widely diversified corporations which returned gratifying dividends. Their sons and daughters had been launched socially in New York, London and Montreal. Homes and contacts in several countries were made available to them. It was a pleasant and sensible arrangement which maintained a gracious, feudal way of life. It had no counterpart in the Caribbean or, perhaps, anywhere else.

Ferris Dessaline was stretched comfortably on a striped pallet beside a pool. The sun was warm, wrapping her in a soft web of indolent pleasure. From beneath the tall coconut palms which threw small patches of shade upon the lawn came the muted sound of many voices. The guests at a long weekend on the Hollister island sought to cure their hangovers with concoctions of vodka and tomato juice, cold beer, rum collins, gin and tonic. They engaged in conversation more for the purpose of reassuring themselves they could still articulate than because they really had anything to say to each other. A few of the hardier were out somewhere fishing. Others had remained in the darkened comfort and security of their rooms, trying to find relief from the persistent nausea. All, though, and each in his or her own way, were attempting to find an escape from midmorning boredom.

In a deck chair beside Ferris, Jorge Ojeda studied the finely modeled body, smoothly tanned and gracefully animate even in repose.

"I didn't know you ever came to these things." She spoke without looking up at him.

"I came because I saw your name on the guest list."

She did turn her face then, mockingly. "Do the hosts always submit a list of the guests when inviting *el presidente?*"

"It is a courtesy. You are too well bred not to know it." The rebuke was without emphasis; almost indifferently voiced.

"Do you study the list for a possible assassin?"

"Only for well-known bores. They are more difficult to avoid."

She laughed softly, honestly amused. Propping her elbows on the pad, resting chin in cupped hands, she regarded him with bright interest.

"I don't think San Rafael appreciates you. We have never before had a *presidente* with a sense of humor. They all had fat wives and skinny mistresses and took themselves very seriously. Why don't you?"

"Have a fat wife and a skinny mistress?"

"Either or both." She lit a cigarette, waiting for an answer, watching his face.

"The office of *Presidente* is hazardous enough. I don't complicate things deliberately."

"Do you work at it, really?" She was serious. "Do you honestly give a damn about your *niños,* as you persist in calling them, or what happens on or to San Rafael beyond a personal ambition? I have wondered."

"I work at it. You only have to look around to see that. The men in the Cabinet are the best I could find for the jobs to be done. The island is orderly, the Government is well run. Our trade balance has been satisfactory."

"I know that. What I was asking was have these things been done simply to perpetuate Jorge Ojeda in office or because he has a social conscience. You are either a remarkable man or a complete charlatan. I can't decide."

His eyes lighted for a moment. "Couldn't we settle for the combination, a remarkable charlatan?" He paused. "What is good for San Rafael is also good for Jorge Ojeda."

"Secret police? The Presidio wall? A military establishment far larger than the island needs?"

"Only a fool would not take measures to protect himself. I like what I have. I intend to keep it."

She inclined her head in brief agreement. "To that extent, at least, you are honest. But what happened to all those promises of reform which were made?"

"I didn't make them. General Quatero did. The people confused our identities." He paused. "Let me tell you something about social reform. We made a readjustment in the land and the country people wouldn't work it beyond their needs. We cleared some of the city's worst slums and financed a large, low-rent housing project with toilets, bathtubs, running water. Within six months the place was a sty. The toilets were clogged and unused. The bathtubs became catch-alls for old bicycle parts, broken pots, rusty pans, part of a wheelbarrow, anything they couldn't find a place for. Windows were broken and patched with a palm fan or had newspaper tacked over the opening. Now it is a slum again. That is the way they like it. It would take fifty years of patience to change them. No one cares enough to work at it for that long." He was thoughtfully silent and then continued: "When Jorge Ojeda goes it will not be because of a popular uprising. Someone, a man of ambition—one with the 'lean and hungry look' —will come along and want what I have. He will conspire to take it from me. He will manufacture discontent where it really doesn't exist. He will suborn a few key figures within the police and the Army and hit upon a slogan for the country people to chant. Now, the irony of this is that my unidentified traitor will probably end in the Presidio. The intellectuals plot and aspire but in the end one of the shirtless prevails."

"As you did?"

"As I did." He inclined his head in agreement. "The intellectuals are pushed back into their musty corners for meditation. A Lenin prepares a diagram but a peasant, Stalin, consolidates the revolt and usurps the power." He smiled with a faint expression of irony. "I have made a study of revolutions. To be a success in the business you must keep the ants and the fleas believing you are one of them. This need not be so. It is only necessary they think it is."

Listening to the easy flow of words, Ferris was conscious of the magnetic appeal of the voice even when it uttered the obvious. It had the compelling sound of the spellbinder; the quack making a phony pitch; the Bible-whacker sending a congregation into an orgiastic frenzy. It was no wonder the *niños*, the *campesinos*, followed him with an unreasoning enthusiasm.

A shadow fell across the pallet on which she lay. She twisted her head and looked up.

General Juan de Cespedes, in the casual dress of the guests—slacks, light pull-over sweater—stood with drink in hand gazing down at her with undisguised admiration.

[148]

"You know General de Cespedes, of course." Ojeda did not rise from his chair.

"Señorita." Juan bowed.

"I hardly recognize you without the decorations, General." She made the statement deliberately but not maliciously.

"They sag and lump together when pinned to a sweater, señorita." He made the confession cheerfully. "I have tried it." He seated himself on the arm of a deck chair and swallowed the iced rum and lime with pleasure.

"We were talking about you, I believe." She spoke with a musing humor. "Or, at least, it could be you. *Verdad, presidente?*"

"It has crossed my mind." Ojeda agreed solemnly.

"What, Excellency?" Juan was brightly interested.

"That you could be my Brutus, Pepito."

"He thinks I do not know what he is talking about." De Cespedes spoke to Ferris. "My father was a great scholar and I progressed through two years of high school. It amuses me to appear stupid." He turned to Ojeda. "I sharpen no knife for you, Excellency." He smiled then as at an old friend. "When the time comes you will fall upon your own sword. You see, se-ñorita," he grinned to Ferris, "I can also make the classical reference. A little of *el presidente* rubs off on me. It is called osmosis."

"You astonish me, Pepito." There was warm affection in Ojeda's statement.

"You both astonish me." Ferris sat upright and dug for a cigarette in the pocket of her jacket.

Juan left his chair and stooped to light it for her, his eyes deliberately examining the full curve of her breasts beneath the light covering of silk. He did this without the suggestion of a leer but as a man might honestly admire something beautiful.

"You will burn your fingers with that match, General, if you do not blow it out." She reminded him of the tiny flame.

Juan was unembarrassed. He dropped the match to the ground and winked at her.

"What astonishes you?" Ojeda asked the question.

"It is difficult to phrase." Her gaze traveled from Ojeda to de Cespedes. "I just can't reconcile myself to accepting you both for what you are. Some-how, you seem to make a game of treachery, murder, absolutism. There is too much laughter in you. It is a little indecent and," she admitted, "un-nerving. It is outside the pattern of tyranny."

"Are you being oppressed, señorita?" Ojeda lifted a hand to indicate the spread of the Hollister island. "Is a tyrant's heel on the necks of those you see here?"

"That's sophistry and you know it." She was close to being angry. "The

[149]

fact remains you could place the heel there if you wanted to or if it suited a purpose. Let me go back." She was sincere. "What you are is probably no worse than San Rafael is accustomed to having in the Presidential Palace but damn it, your predecessors didn't laugh about it in public. They at least had the decency to affect a certain grimness. They didn't behave as though San Rafael and its people were things they had won in a raffle."

Ojeda interposed almost gently. "Let me ask you. Is San Rafael orderly? Is it well policed? Clean? Industrious? Have schools been built? The incidence of health better? Have medical and dental clinics been established, even mobile units to carry doctors and dentists into the country and mountain villages where a witch woman prevailed only a few years ago? Who is being abused? Who is being ground under?"

"I have to say yes." The admission was not made grudgingly. "But, I wonder if the order is because the Government is wiser or the secret police force larger? I object to having to carry an identity card as the worker must quietly rebel against being told where, when and at what wage he must labor. That is not the function of Government. How can Jorge Ojeda have the effrontery to say who may leave the country and who may not; how much money he can take with him? Homes have been searched, persons seized, property expropriated, public assembly prohibited." She was a little breathless.

"Why do you persist in ignoring the facts?" Ojeda interposed. "For a century such families as yours held the natives in a state of perpetual peonage even though they no longer called them slaves. They were branded on the back as cattle. I give them an identity card. They had no choice of labor but were told where to go and what to do. As for search and seizure, you simply burned an entire village where you suspected revolt to be brewing. A half dozen families decided how the society of the island should be organized. Now you become indignant over such things as freedom of the press and public assembly. What you are saying is that your brand of control was all right while mine is base."

"I think she is mad at you, *presidente*. You as a man." Juan de Cespedes stood up and regarded Ferris unhappily. "I don't think she gives a damn about the *campesino*. No more do you. She is throwing the pots and pans of politics about the kitchen in frustration. I suspect she needs to be made love to. You both depress me. *Adiosita.*"

Ferris stared at de Cespedes incredulously. For a moment she was speechless with anger. He ignored the open fury, bowed with sarcastic formality and walked unconcernedly away. Ojeda watched him go with suppressed amusement.

"You're an idiot," Ferris called after him. Then she turned to Ojeda wonderingly. "He could be right, couldn't he? I hadn't thought about it. That isn't honest." She corrected herself. "There is an attraction. It disturbs me."

"Ever since the day you came to the palace reception I have thought about you." He made the statement quietly, simply. "I haven't known what to do about it."

"Why didn't you call up and say: What about a movie tonight, *chica?*" She made an effort at banter and failed. "Damn it!" The words were self-accusing. "I don't want to get involved with you. The idea of being The Benefactor's mistress doesn't appeal to me."

"I didn't realize it had been suggested." He was undisturbed by her vehemence.

"No. You're right," she admitted wrily. "Just the same it is there and you know it." She rolled onto one elbow and stared at Juan's figure. "It must be obvious to everyone if *he* could see it."

"Pepito has a healthy, animal instinct. I respect it."

She continued to watch de Cespedes, using him as an excuse not to meet Ojeda's eyes. He walked with an easy air of assurance, halting to join Jean Hollister and a group at a small bar within the thatched shade of a *jacalita*.

"Why do you call him Pepito when his name is Juan?"

"I don't know. It was something which came as easily as our friendship."

"How long have you known each other?"

"Since we were boys. A long time. We were fishermen together."

She turned back to him. This was neutral ground, easier footing. She smiled tentatively.

"And," she spoke slowly, "he came with you all the way; never questioning, never doubting?"

Ojeda chuckled. "I don't think so but he doubted himself, not me."

"That's a strange thing to say. I mean, to put it in those terms as though you, also, never questioned or hesitated."

"Once, when I was very young. Then I learned something from an old man who was a thief; not because he wanted to be but only because an unreasoning cupidity possessed him. I didn't work it out in my mind at the time. The years gave it form and substance. Man is in constant danger of being overwhelmed by the overtly innocent things and situations. He must guard himself, not against the obvious threat to his existence but against the seemingly innocuous and helpless things or creatures which outnumber him."

Watching the play of his features, the musing light in his eyes, the curious, meditative smile which hovered about his mouth, Ferris thought his was a strangely beautiful face, disturbing in its mystical serenity.

"I can't say what has always been in Pepito's mind or what is there now.

We attached ourselves and complemented each other without conscious effort."

"You suspect no envy, no resentment? You are *el presidente*. He is a general by your whim and could be nothing tomorrow if you decided it should be that way."

"I don't think he wants more than he has; not, at least, at the moment. In time, who knows? But," he leaned forward, "we make dull conversation."

With an easy, twisting movement she stood up and reached for the jacket on the back of her chair. He arose, took the coat from her and held it.

"Let's take my boat." She glanced back over her shoulder at him with a quick smile. "Your Pepito may be right. All this talk of right and wrong is depressing."

They followed the pebbled ribbon of path down from the graded lawn to the basin where jetties of concrete extended to make a sheltered mooring. A sixty-two-foot cabin cruiser and a couple of heavy-duty skiffs were at their buoys. A mechanic was bent over the motor of one of the small boats and at the sound of their approach glanced up. Recognizing *el presidente,* he dropped a ball of oil-soaked waste and pulled a faded yachting cap from his head.

"*Buenos dias, joven.*" Ojeda nodded, smiled.

Ferris watched the man, saw the wonder of what had happened to him transform his features from awed respect to complete incredulity. *El presidente* had spoken to him as he might a friend, an equal. It would be a thing to tell his wife and children this night and talk about for a long time. She glanced at Ojeda to see if he was aware of the effect of his greeting because this thing, multiplied by thousands, was just short of frightening. Ojeda seemed oblivious of the open adoration.

"It doesn't scare you a little?" she asked quietly. "That a man should look at you as God."

"Only if I believed it. Then it would be dangerous for everyone and for Jorge Ojeda most of all."

Her boat, with an open cockpit protected only by a curving, Plexiglas windshield, nuzzled against the heavy rubber bumpers. She dropped down into it lightly and he followed. A boy from the dockmaster's house trotted down to cast off the lines after the motors were started. She settled behind the wheel on a broad leather seat and turned a switch for the blowers which would clear the engines' housing of fumes.

"I was watching you last night." She spoke above the gentle humming. "You are an adaptable man."

"I had a thorough training in the social graces through the USO."

"I don't mean that." She turned quickly. "So often I say something which sounds patronizing when it isn't at all what I intend. I suspect it is your fault. You put me on the defensive. So many persons here, even though they all have more than they need, would like something from you—concessions, favors, information. You manage to say no without actually saying it and offend no one."

She cut the blower and pressed a starter button which kicked the twin motors into action. They caught with a muffled roar, the exhaust burbling in the water. She nodded to the waiting boy and he unlooped the lines, fore and aft, and dropped the coils into the boat. She touched the throttles and they moved forward, sliding easily out of the marina into open sea. Watching her, noting the assurance, Ojeda caught himself thinking of the days when he and Juan de Cespedes ran their own boat past the Coast Guard patrols to land a load of contraband whisky. He laughed suddenly and she looked at him with curiosity.

"Did you know I was also a bootlegger once?"

"No. But it doesn't surprise me. There is something of the buccaneer in your nature."

Clear of the breakwater she gave the boat full power and it reared on its stern the way a hooked sailfish stands upon its tail. Spray sheeted out on either side of the bow in a sparkling, iridescent curtain.

Leaning back against the cushions he studied her as she stood now, one hand controlling the bucking wheel, her face lifted into the wet rush of wind with an eager pleasure. In this moment she was transformed from a self-possessed, sophisticated young woman into a sprite, a creature of the air and water whose feet must, sometimes, touch the earth reluctantly. There was no sea running and the only wind was created by the rushing boat's speed. The shining hull split the turquoise surface as a sharp blade rips through silken cloth. The wake in its trail lay true and clean.

It was impossible to talk above the motors and he was satisfied to lean back and watch the graceful balance with which she rode the power so deftly controlled. Now and then, as she turned to scan the unruffled sheen of the sea, he could catch her face in profile and marvel at its flawless beauty.

It disturbed him, now, to realize how often since their first meeting she had come to his mind: the way she had smiled; the pride with which she held herself; the oddly compelling, throaty catch in her voice when she laughed suddenly. He wondered how love was defined, for it was a word the meaning of which had, too often, been dulled by repetition and blunted by careless usage. Poets had strung words of shining loveliness as pearls on a platinum strand but they were of little use to a man who would speak them to a girl. The thing which had sometimes caused the world to shudder, toppled empires, sent men into battle or driven them to the frenzy of murder was simply phrased: I love you.

Love waxes in me, rocked in my restless heart, my troubled heart which the cruel brat has taken for his cradle. Your name is like a bell within my heart.

But, those were words for an actor to speak upon a shadowed stage for a Roxane concealed upon her balcony. As such they did not sound absurd for they came from beyond reality and were heard only in a darkened theatre. No, he mused, what men and women said to each other was trite, hackneyed, yet each believed at the moment they were phrases of coin newly minted and exchanged for the first time. Hand reached for hand. Mouth clung to mouth, body to body. There was no real need for words in this moment of complete communion. Yet they were always spoken and had become a part of the ritual of passion. *Tell me you love me.*

As though by some telepathic communication she was aware of his thoughts without fully understanding them beyond the fact they concerned her, she turned and flashed a quick smile. In it there was a new tenderness, something he had not seen in her before. It was gone in an instant as she turned her attention again to the racing craft.

So imperceptibly did the image form, so slowly did it creep from the un-measured depths of his mind, that he was not aware of its existence until it confronted him, fully revealed and ugly. Behind Jorge Ojeda, *el presidente*, stood the son of a Tampa cigar maker and a Negro woman. That boy, now the man, was thinking of Ferris Dessaline as a wife. This fair girl. This white girl. He made himself say the words and writhed beneath the turning of the knife. For the first time in years that which he had thought so securely behind him came from its dark corner. Almost desperately he wondered if it was true. Did the Negro strain run as a deep and hidden current? Could it rise unexpectedly in a child? Was this some ancient super-stition, an old wives' tale, or a genetic truth? Was it possible that in human beings a sport of Nature occurred as a black ewe is born of white sheep? This was a thing he must know. He could feel the revulsion, see the horror in her eyes, when a nurse placed a black infant in her arms and said: This is yours. It was born of you and a mulatto man by the name of Jorge Ojeda.

He stared unseeingly at her straight, proud back and wondered what she would say if he told her: I am part Negro. It is something I have kept secret, even from myself, all these years. I have denied my mother because I was taught to be ashamed of her color by those steeped in prejudice and igno-rance. Once, when I was a boy, a man called me a nigger bastard and I ran in fear, hating myself and the woman who had given me life. Can you understand?

Hands locked between his knees he bowed his head as though he had been struck heavily. Could she be expected to understand that to a boy, at that time, to be all white was something to be desired above all other things? With this armor a man could hide grossness, ignorance, brutality, filth of body and mind. It was enough simply to be white and untainted. That is why I crossed over. I did it because it was forced upon me. There was no other way of life I imagined endurable.

He lifted his head painfully. It was a physical effort. He made himself look at her. She stood safely on the other side of the line; Ferris Dessaline, reared in the tradition of white superiority. She would as soon mate with an ape. She would stare at him with uncomprehending horror if he said: I am part Negro. My mother was a Haitian woman whose black roots go far back into the mysterious darkness of Africa. She was born of slaves. In spite of this I love you. Can it really make any difference to one as intelligent as you that there is in my veins an invisible thread of the color so much of the world finds hateful? Can't it be enough that I love you and sense something in you reaching for me?

He was abruptly aware of the cessation of sound. She had cut the pounding motors to a mere whisper and was staring at him with a puzzled, almost frightened curiosity.

"What is wrong? I felt it—something. It was as though you had touched me. I turned around. Your face. I have never seen that expression before. It was angry, bitter, confused. All of the emotions fixed for a single moment in your eyes." Haltingly, she tried to put into words what she had seen, the transfiguration witnessed. "What were you thinking about? There was something savage, lonely, frightened. I can't explain it." Unconsciously she extended her hand in a gesture of comfort.

He took it. Except for a little while last night when they had danced together on the Hollister terrace he had never touched her before. He turned her hand in his, studying the delicate mechanism, the fine bone structure, as though they were unique. Tanned, the skin was darker than his. This, he thought, was a curious bit of irony, for she had deliberately sought the color over which he had cried as a boy on Tampa's Franklin Street. It was the supreme jest and one which tried all of man's faculties of reason and logic. How did you reconcile this paradox? But even as he asked himself the question he was aware of how superficial the reasoning was. Color, such as he meant, went far below the surface. It was a taint. He rebelled against the word but there was no denying it.

The boat rocked gently; the motors, all but idling, pushed it sluggishly in a wide circle. She did not withdraw her hand but by now she was conscious of the contact. He made the move, released the slight pressure.

"I was a little angry with the world." He made the explanation lightly.

"Yes, I think you were." She was serious. Still facing him, she reached behind her and steadied the boat's wheel with a firm grip. "There was rebellion in your eyes."

He thought, If I am ever to speak of this thing, now is the time. If I don't it will feed upon itself, growing larger and larger, and consume me. How to start? Where to begin? He didn't know. There was no point of beginning other than the one which could be contained in a single sentence. I am a man, part Negro, and in love with you. He couldn't bring himself to shape the words into a sound.

"It isn't something about which you want to talk?" The question arose from a deep concern and was not prompted by an idle curiosity.

"Not now. Sometime. Maybe." He forced himself to be indifferently laconic.

"All right." She didn't press. Turning, her gaze swept the island-spattered sea. "There is a place I would like to go; a man I want to see again. His name is Massau. I found out he lives on The Goat's Neck. He is a great artist. Really. I mean it." She faced him as though expecting laughter.

"Whatever you want to do. I'd rather be here, with you, than at the Hollisters'."

"Yes." She spoke the word slowly, wonderingly. "Yes. That is the way it is and I keep trying to tell myself it isn't. I said before it disturbed me. There is more. I'm a little frightened by something I don't completely understand. I'm not sure I want things this way between us."

"Why?"

"I don't know. It is a feeling, an instinct I can't explain. A sense of apprehension. It shouldn't come this fast and without warning."

"I never thought it could come any other way. I don't believe love walks with a heavy step or pounds upon the door with a hammer fist to say: Let me in."

"Is that what we are talking about? Love?" A frown was in her eyes. "I don't know the word too well or what it demands of a person. Something complete and unequivocal. I have never given that. I'm not sure I could."

"There is no hurry." He didn't force the moment as he might have. "Let it drift for a while as this boat does now. Sooner or later it will find a steadying current. Indecision is a mental vacuum. Nature will fill it. Who is Massau?" He moved them both out of an awkward moment.

"One of your *niños*." She was grateful for his tact and was deliberately mocking again. "Although I am not sure he is aware of you."

"I shall speak to my Minister of Propaganda. One unconverted soul disturbs him as it does the angels."

"Or your tax collector?"

"He prefers to be known as the Minister of Finance."

She whistled with a shrill derision and then turned to stand again at the wheel, shoving up the twin throttles. Under full power the boat swung about and settled on a course where the island of The Goat's Neck lay heavily green and feather-topped in the distance.

The dock straggled crazily out into the cove. Loose boards were laid over a sagging frame fastened to canted, barnacle-encrusted pilings. From its end Massau fished for the small, hand-sized mangrove snapper where they fed along the rocky bottom in clear water.

He baited an empty hook with a pinch of shrimp and dropped it back, holding the hand line of colorless nylon between his fingers. The fish would not take an ordinary line, one of green or gray cuttyhunk. He had tested them many times. They nudged the lure, bouncing the concealed hook playfully, but refused the barb. The all but invisible nylon was their undoing. Either they couldn't see it or the slender thread appeared too innocent to carry their destruction.

He heard the high whine of the motors first. Shading his eyes against the sun's glare on a polished sea, he saw the great shields of spray as they fanned out from the lifted bows in a shimmering spread of beauty filled with streaks of rainbow color.

His attention was momentarily diverted by a hungry fish as it snapped upon the hook. With a single sweep of his arm he snatched it from the water. Gently he disengaged the barb and dropped the catch into a wet feed sack to keep it soft and firmly fresh.

When he looked up again the sound was heavier and the craft easily discernible. Then the beat of the engines diminished and Ferris edged into the cove and parallel to the dock. He stood up and waited. When the boat was alongside, she held it off with a hook and tossed Massau a bowline.

"Mam'selle." He was faintly surprised.

"Hello, Massau." She smiled up at him.

"Tide run out little now." He suggested, "Bes' fix boat at en' of dock an' let it ride at rope."

She nodded and reached up. Massau took her hand and she swung up from the seat as he lifted her without effort. There was a flicker of astonishment as he recognized Jorge Ojeda but he did not speak, only holding the craft until *el presidente* caught a piling's head and pulled himself to the landing. Then he carefully drifted the boat to the pier's head, made the line fast. The tide drew the mooring taut and held the boat away from the punishing abrasiveness of the dock. When he returned to where they waited he studied Jorge Ojeda for a second and then inclined his head.

"Señor *presidente. Bienvenido.*" He turned to Ferris. "I have the honor, mam'selle, you come to my small islan'."

Listening to him, Ferris was aware of a curious change in his speech. In Marchand's he had spoken with only the faintest trace of an accent. Now it was rich with the intonation of the San Rafael native black. It seemed to her to be deliberate and she suspected it was for Ojeda's benefit but could not say why. Also, there was something in the way he had used the possessive pronoun in speaking of The Goat's Neck. *My islan'*. It was more than a careless use of a word.

"Yours, Massau? The whole island?"

"Lak sayin' mine, mam'selle." The smile was self-effacing, as was the shrug which went with it. "Massau live heah so long, say my islan' lak habit." He was inwardly amused. "Once, long 'go, white man come one day. He say, I goin' buy islan', boy. Then he go 'way. Nevah come back. Maybe he fin' out islan' ain' foah sale."

He stooped, picked up the hand line and wound it quickly about a short length of stick. Then he pulled the wet sack from the water and there was a faint clicking sound as the fish inside snapped against each other in their frenzy.

"Got plenty fish now. Only tak what I need."

Listening, watching, Jorge Ojeda was caught in the memory of another day on a Florida beach and an old man, who was the Duke of Alba's cousin, saying: "We take from God only what we need."

By unspoken consent the three of them walked shoreward along the short length of dock. Massau squinted at the sun, marking the time of day.

"Cook fish now wid hoppinjohn, lak beans wid rice an' peppers. I have honor foah you to stay."

Ferris thought Massau was singularly unimpressed by the presence of *el presidente* or that the simple invitation afforded him a sly amusement. She caught Ojeda's eye and saw that he was smiling to himself.

"*Presidente?*" She used the title deliberately and made of it a question.

"I have honor foah to stay, also." Ojeda accepted gravely but the mimicry was unmistakable.

The ear of Massau was acutely tuned. He looked from Ojeda to Ferris Dessaline and then he began to laugh; a sound deep within his throat. It subsided to a chuckle and continued to bubble there as they crossed the remaining few feet of dock to shore. Now and then he darted a quick glance at Ojeda and in it there was a pleased understanding and an appreciation for the ridiculous.

"*Dispenseme, presidente.*" The request for pardon was sincere but not obsequious. "I have made a little joke with you. Why I can't find good reason." It was both an apology and a partial explanation. To Massau it seemed sufficient. "With Mam'selle Dessaline, also."

"How do you know my name?" Ferris was astonished, for at their only other meeting, she was certain Marchand had not spoken it.

"Same way I know *el presidente*, mam'selle."

She didn't believe this. It was too pat. Intuitively she suspected that, for reasons of his own, Massau wanted her to accept this obvious explanation.

"I had forgotten," this was a contrived probe, "you were a Dessaline . . ." She left the sentence unfinished.

"Slave, mam'selle?" Massau prompted.

"Yes. My grandmother told me. She saw the carving you made."

"A long time ago, mam'selle. So long ago, in a different world, an' all of San Rafael maybe four or five big plantations belong to four or five families like Dessalines."

It occurred to her this was probably the most improbable tableau and conversation ever to be held in the entire Caribbean area. The head of an island state, wearing light tan slacks and pull-over sweater, his bare feet in thonged sandals, smoking and listening unconcernedly in the hot sunlight. Ferris Dessaline, in the briefest of swim suits, a jacket over naked shoulders, talking casually with a former slave of imposing dignity and an assurance of manner which, somehow, they took for granted. Glancing at Ojeda she felt that although he seemed indifferent, he had listened to every word spoken; detecting in them an overtone, the existence of which she had somehow missed.

"I'm hungry." She made the statement an incidental interruption. "I'm hungry and I'd like a drink."

"Food I have plenty." Massau took over the duties of a host. "Some rum, not first-run Dessaline rum like you know, mam'selle, but not bad neither with coconut milk an' piece of pineapple."

They moved up the marl path, across the coral ridge and into a clearing surrounded by tall, sleekly gray palms whose slender trunks were inclined gently with the wind, which came always from the same quarter. The area was swept clean and was stubbled by patches of tough wire grass whose roots defied the coral bed.

The house of Massau was no native hovel of crude thatching. It had been built to plan with sawed boards of mahogany, milled and planed. The roof was of hand-cut cedar shingles and the windows, without glass, were held open by oaken staves which could be dropped and the spaces tightly shuttered when the storms and rains whipped across the island. The house was small, compact; no more, really, than one large room. A veranda faced the sea and windward side. A short wing served as a storehouse and cooking space during the bad weather of the equinox. At the rear was a small pen in which chickens pecked and roosted. A goat cropped at the salty, tough grass and lifted its head in a welcoming bleat as they approached. In everything there was an unmistakable feeling of permanency; of care, order and contentment.

At one side of the house where a single, great tree of mahogany had grown for a hundred years or more, its seed brought in the droppings of a bird from the mainland, there was now a low table. Where the forest giant, so oddly out of place here, had been felled to provide lumber for the house, its stump served additional purpose. It had been sawed some three feet above the roots. The surface had been sanded and polished, smoothed and waxed. The grain was deeply ornamental and it reflected a rich, brownish-red tint in the filtered sunlight. Standing beside it Ojeda rubbed his hand appreciatively over the glistening surface.

"Tree mek part of house, *presidente*. Stump mek table." Massau was childishly pleased by the example of his ingenuity. He left them for a moment, going to the porch and bringing back two handcrafted wicker chairs. "You mek comfortable, mam'selle an' *presidente*. I fetch some rum with coconuts to drink."

From her chair beside the table Ferris glanced at Ojeda. He was leaning back, staring reflectively at the sky. His long legs were stretched comfortably before him and he smoked a cigarette with meditative pleasure. She thought, Nothing seems strange to this man, nothing disturbs a latent mysticism and a conviction that everything happens in a predetermined order.

"Massau doesn't seem to surprise you. I wonder if anything does." She was curious.

"Oh, he surprises me all right!" He was thoughtful. "There is an assurance, an assumption of equality. No"—he shook his head—"that is a bad choice of word. He has lived his entire life in these islands where the division between black and white is too sharp. He understands it exists but no longer permits it to affect him. Somehow, he has reached a plane of reconciliation. He has become that rarest of all things—a natural, unaffected man. It could be arrogant but it isn't. There is the small miracle. It may be contrived but I suspect it is unconscious."

"A little of both, I imagine." She was interested in his summation. "His background is too deeply planted in the island tradition for him not to know this is an unusual situation. I keep waiting for him to make the obvious mistake. He hasn't. He doesn't overstep what are simply good manners. You have to wonder how, when and where he learned. He is neither rude nor servile. As you say, he is just Massau."

What followed bore out their opinions. Massau made drinks on the table, lopping off the ends of fresh coconuts with a machete. He mixed the creamy milk with rum, lime and a piece of pineapple. He served but fixed nothing for himself. While they stood, drinks in hand, watching, he built a hot fire, put oil, the *acate de casa*, in a blackened iron pot. He prepared the fish, rolling them in bright yellow cornmeal and frying them quickly as doughnuts. These were served with beans, rice and red chilies and they ate, using clamshells for spoons.

Massau did not make an attempt to sit with them or fix anything for himself. His attitude was that of a well-trained maître d'hôtel who understands the fine distinction between a friendly dignity and familiarity, exercises it and expects the same consideration from his guests. He spoke only when spoken to; busied himself at the fire in order to be unobtrusive. He didn't press food upon them but happily fried additional fish when they were asked for.

When the last of the small, crisp snappers were only a little pile of whitened bones on a section of banana leaf and the rum drinks warm in their stomachs, Ferris leaned back. She sighed contentedly and lifted her arms above her head in an animal stretching of satisfaction.

"You could make a fortune on the mainland, Massau. Open an outdoor restaurant and serve nothing but fish and hoppinjohn."

Massau shrugged with good-natured indifference. "What would I do with it, mam'selle?" He smiled a little. "Am too old for woman to spend it on. My life does not need much money."

"I keep the figure you gave me at Marchand's on my dressing table. What have you done? May we see it? I told *el presidente* about your work."

Massau scratched at the white knots of his hair with a quizzically bemused expression. "I walk aroun' something now, mam'selle." He seemed slightly puzzled by his confession. "M'sieu' Marchand gave to my hands a piece of stone. *Piedra de ijada*. From Mexico, he say. I always am looking at it and cannot decide. In it I keep seeing a girl's face but it has no form yet. I shut my eyes and do not see it very well. So, I let it alone. I have no hurry about things any more."

"Have you ever tried to paint?" Ferris was watching the play of expressions on Massau's face. "With oils or water colors?"

Massau shook his head. "The world is filled with color, mam'selle. All around me God paints better. In the sunrise and at the time of its setting. When the moon is a silver flower on the ocean. The light and the shadows at noontime." He examined his hands. "With these I cut, using a knife to shape the things I feel; the faces, the bodies. God does not do that as well as Massau. He makes too many mistakes, too many ugly people." He spoke regretfully of God as a fellow artist, well intentioned but Whose work was frequently clumsy and imperfect.

"What have you done with the jade?" She stood up, her expression animated. "May I look at it?"

Massau nodded an almost shy assent. He was pleased and tried not to show it.

"It is on a table in my house, mam'selle. There is nothing to see yet; maybe just a feeling. If it would please you."

She smiled her appreciation and left them quickly, walking with her long, free stride toward the house. Ojeda watched her appreciatively. There was an unconscious grace and line in her every movement. He couldn't imagine her making an awkward motion. The need for her was a new emotion and not to be articulated yet. It was something beyond desire. To himself he thought, Give me this woman, this girl, and let me complete my life with her. But first let me have the honesty and courage to tell her what she must know about Jorge Ojeda. Am I, he wondered, man enough to do that? Will I, having come so far and risked so much, take this chance? Is the conviction of my destiny, which I have carried with me all these years, strong enough to bare the truth? He didn't know the answer. Lighting a cigarette, he stared at its smoldering tip.

For a moment he sat in this position and then he became aware of the fact he was being quietly studied. He had the physical sensation of being touched. Glancing up he saw Massau's gaze, somber, penetrating. There was in the big man's eyes a question, a shadowed doubt, as though he did not yet trust a judgment formed even though his instinct had already supplied an answer.

"You Negro man, *presidente*." It was not a question. It was a statement made, not in accusation. There was no charge of deception. What had been said was measured in regret. "Because of that a bad thing happens, does it not?"

Jorge Ojeda met the old man's eyes and waited for his anger to well and overflow. It did not come. A thing which had been concealed and never questioned since that hot summer's day many years ago had been openly spoken. He intuitively understood that the truth now lay between two men and need not be repeated nor would it go beyond them unless he chose to have it that way. Instead of an unreasoning rage, an immediate and furious denial, he felt a curious relief as though a burden had been lifted by sympathetic hands.

"How do you know that?" The tone was expressionless.

"Not sure, *presidente*." There was no alteration in Massau's attitude. "Sometimes black man feels things lak animal. He recognize his own. Don't really know how to say in words. I just know an', back there on the dock when you first come, I had feelin' you knew I knew."

Ojeda bowed his head in assent. There was nothing abject in the gesture. He merely admitted a truth. Instinct. That extrasensory thing which could reach out as an invisible antenna. Massau groped for an explanation which was not necessary. He could remember his mother warning him long ago in a small kitchen on a narrow street in Ybor City. "Now then, lak today." He could recapture the sound of her voice in his memory. "You fin' man who got feelin' lak fox. He know chicken there even though can't see 'im. He goin' to say: I smell nigger." He wondered how many Negroes he had passed on the streets, talked with in the service, handed a bag to in a railroad depot or hotel lobby without thought, had recognized in him a brother. And here, in San Rafael, how many of the thousands of black men had listened to *el presidente* when he spoke on the radio and chuckled quietly to themselves, knowing what the whites did not know and secretly relishing the joke played upon them by a mulatto. With a start he recalled an incident which gave him a kinship with Massau; the animal sensing without question.

The thing had happened in New York, in the days when he and Pepito were running whisky and rum from the Bahamas. With their pockets filled with money they had made a trip North just for the fun of it. In New Jersey they had a connection, a wholesale bootlegger who frequently bought their full load and transported it to New York and New Jersey in a truck. By arrangement they met the man one afternoon in a speak-easy on Fifty-second Street. He had a girl with him; a girl of clear but strangely sensual beauty. He, Jorge Ojeda, had known without realizing at the time he knew, she was part Negro. It was something so immediate he hadn't even questioned the first judgment. Late that night they had all gone to Harlem together and to one of the gaudy clubs patronized exclusively by whites from Downtown Manhattan. The place had been noisy, garish and with a floor show of beautiful, dusky, brownskin girls. It was the first time he had been in such a place and it surprised him a little that, in the heart of New York's colored district, there wasn't a single Negro in the room. He mentioned this. The girl beside him had shrugged tolerantly.

"Hell," she said lightly. "They don't let no jigs in this place."

He had glanced at her sharply and after a moment her coolly contemptuous defiance faded. She had dropped her eyes and studied the glass before her.

Later, they had danced and she was deliberately insinuating within his arms. She laughed softly and whispered mocking obscenities in his ear as her cheek rested against his.

"You're going to make your fellow sore, Spade." He had said it deliberately.

He had felt her tighten, frightened, tense, wary. Then she relaxed and came back again, pressing against his legs.

"How did you know?" The question was a whisper. "No one knows."

He couldn't remember now what he had said. It was indifferent. What did startle him was, that without realizing it, the same instinct which sent Massau to his judgment had also been latent within him.

"Until now," he said to Massau, "I thought I would want to kill a man who said what you did. It is something I have never admitted, even to myself. There was a time when I had to make a choice; be all Negro or all white. I wanted to be all white."

"That not hard to understand, *presidente*." There was respect in the use of the title. No hint of mockery intruded. "You are white man now in mind. Everything you do an' think is like white man. Don't try an' change it for yourself. You live with it. But," he hesitated, "this no real business mine. I think on Mam'selle Dessaline, not on Presidente Jorge Ojeda. All her life she know black men as slave or servant. They ain' people who love, get hungry, unhappy; no more than ox turnin' crusher in cane field. Me she know for nigger an' that all right. You she spit on for black man bein' white. You got to think on that, *presidente*."

Ojeda bowed his head. With simple logic Massau had cut to the bone of the matter. Her feeling of outrage would not spring out of the fact he was a Negro. The dishonesty rested in a mulatto who had passed himself as white. Yet, having come this far he didn't know how to turn back.

A light slap of the screen door closing caused him to turn in the direction of the house. Ferris crossed toward them and now the beauty was magnified because it had become hopelessly unattainable without the sacrifice of all honor. No, he told himself. This, also, is a deception. I am not too concerned with honor. I am only afraid that somehow, sometime, that which is buried beneath the mound of the years will be spaded up as an ugly corpse to confront me. He was faced again, as he had been so many times before, with the calculated risk. Watching her, he decided he had no choice. It must be taken.

XIII.

THE signs, at first, were no more ominous than that of a soft breeze as it winnows through high marsh grass, but in its passing reveals unexpected shades of color and depth. They were only the whispering of a harmless wind and bore no relation to a hurricane of unimaginable fury.

In the villages of the mountains, on the green sides of the high hills, where a few thatched huts formed a community, in the *poblados* of the lush valley, men began to gather in silent groups. They came at no one's call but were moved by a herding instinct as animals will press together against an unseen, common danger. Now and then they talked softly among themselves of what was happening. They argued quietly, discussing things heard or seen, but there was no real anger in them yet. They were only troubled and a little bewildered over what had come about. So, in the indigo twilight or in the hot sun of midday, they rested on their heels, close to the warm earth. With their fingers or little sticks they traced aimless figures in the dirt and disputed endlessly as to the real meaning of things.

Also, in the larger settlements and even in the towns which had a shaded plaza with a bandstand and a circular path where the young men and girls walked separately in the evening, a stranger or two would appear. They came unobtrusively, taking a room above one of the *cantinas*, renting a small, vacant house, or even moving in with a family after mentioning an acquaintanceship with a friend or relative in a distant place. From their speech these newcomers were of the people but their accent was of the city, and they seemed men of learning and with a knowledge of many things. Always, in the beginning, those who played dominoes and drank in the *cantinas*, sat on the plaza benches waiting for the concert to begin, or squatted beside a road in the country were silent and suspicious when these intruders sought to join them in their talk. But after a time, those who had been alien became familiar through the simple thing of daily contact. It then was a polite gesture to accept a cigarette and even the offer of a drink and to listen quietly to what the visitor had to say concerning the matter uppermost in the minds of them all.

This which troubled them was the land given by order of *el presidente* himself. The old ones remembered well the time of Presidente Romero before the revolution. Then there were the enormous *estancias* with the fields of high, green cane; the great plantations of tobacco; the delicate verdance of the first rice shoots as they rose above the sheen of watery *arrozals* which stretched beyond the eye's power to see. Miles of the land and its crops were owned by a single *patron*. For him they worked, on his acres their children were born, grew or died. Sons and daughters followed in the prints made by fathers and mothers. For the *patron* they had done the labor and were never free of debt. For, and it was an incomprehensible thing, the more they worked the more they seemed to have need to buy from the *patron's* store or that owned by *la compañia* and so, at the year's end they always owed more than they had earned.

Then, when it had seemed that this was the eternal way of life, the one who was called The Benefactor came down from the mountains with a small army. He had driven the *patrons* and the foreign owners from the land. For a while it had been a time of terror, confusion and blood. Men had killed each other over who owned what and where. The old families of wealth who had defied the new Government barricaded themselves in their great houses. They hired soldiers of their own from the disgraced *guardia civil* and shot at those who trespassed. Others fled to the capital city and planned their revenge or sent gangs of tough, armed youths into the country to rape, burn and spread fear.

It was the man, Ojeda, who made himself *el presidente* and brought order again to the country. The hired gunmen of the *patrons* were hunted down, captured and shot where everyone could see the justice done. Then there came the soldiers of Presidente Ojeda. They brought with them men who carried instruments for the measuring and marking of boundaries until it was all sectioned off into thousands of tracts. Then Presidente Ojeda had sent other officials of his Government and these called together the heads of the villages, the wisest among those of the towns and little settlements. To them the officials said: This is now the land of all the people. Each man will have so much. What he grows he will be able to sell, use for himself or even give away. No longer will he labor for a *patron* but for himself and his family. Tell us how many there are in this town or village and we will apportion among all what was once owned by a few. That was what had happened.

It had been a good thing, then, for a man to awake in the morning and look over what was his; marked so by a pile of stones at each corner of the section. He could walk upon the land, feel it between his fingers. Here he might grow what he liked and take the produce into the towns to be sold, or barter with a neighbor. The pesos and centavos so earned came into his own pockets and need be shared with no one. There were no longer agents of the *patron* to come among them and say: This you owe and you must work harder to pay off the debt.

So, because in this soft country where it was often pleasant just to lie in the sun and do nothing, a man must be a great fool to grow more than he needs or can use for exchange. Now there were only small patches of cane growing where once the fields were a green, waving sea. Small plots of tobacco were set out and the plants were no more than a man could use for himself. Tobacco is not a thing which simply grows by itself. To raise it breaks the back. It must be nurtured in seedling beds and then transplanted; watched against a sudden rain, the destruction by insects, before it can be cut and placed on the racks for drying. A man would be a burro to go to all this trouble in order to harvest more than he could smoke. Rice, also, is a never-ending task and those who grow it rot their feet in the water and have a swelling of whitened toes and joints. Again, no reasonable man would plant more than could be used in the family pot. These were simple truths and because of them much of the land lay barren. A man raised a few goats, some chickens and pigs, grazed a dozen sheep, planted and harvested only what he needed to eat or trade back and forth for things which a neighbor grew.

Many young people of the country had left the *estancias* and gone to work in the great sugar refineries and the distilleries where the rum was made. They came home now telling how the great stacks of these huge places were stark and smokeless against the sky because there was no longer cane to grind for sugar and molasses. Because of this there was no work. The older people only shrugged. What had they to do with such things? Of what interest was it to them that men no more carried the green stems of bananas into the empty holds of ships or that rice, sugar, tobacco and rum were not exported because the country people did not grow the raw materials? Here they had all they needed. A little cane to be ground when they wanted the sweet juice, a kid, the *cabrito,* to be killed and roasted on a fiesta day, strong tobacco from a tiny patch, beans and corn, were all at hand for the good life. Let those who lived in the cities worry about keeping the mills and factories working.

Then, officials from the Government in the city of San Rafael came among them and said strange things: You must work every acre of the land given to you by *el presidente.* You must plant and grow as before and take the products to the refineries, distilleries and warehouses. If you do not, then these great places where many find work will be closed down and people, not of the country like yourselves but of the cities and towns, will go hungry. They will sicken and even die from the poverty you have created. To this the people of the hills and valleys lifted their shoulders and replied: If this is true then let them all come back to the country where they can plant and grow what they need. What is it to us that a merchant in the city has no rum, sugar, tobacco or bananas to sell?

The Government officials shook their heads and patiently tried to explain. Then they grew angry and shouted. When this bred nothing but indifference, they threatened. Soldiers, at the orders of *el presidente* himself, would come and drive them into the fields with guns and bayonets like prisoners. To this the *campesinos* laughed wisely. *El presidente* would never permit such a thing to happen. He was of the people and one who spoke to them often on the radio as his *niños.* Would such a man turn upon himself? *Andele!*

Now, though, there was the beginning of a change and many who believed in *el presidente* were beginning to wonder. Perhaps he did not know what was happening. Was he aware that more of his officials had come to the countryside? Now they did not talk softly or with a reasonableness. They rode in the small brown cars of the Army which carried four or six soldiers. They visited every town, village, and even the little settlements where only a few houses stood and goats, pigs and dogs slept in the narrow road. These men of authority called everyone together and the soldiers stood with rifles held across their chests. They no longer used the tone of reason or attempted to explain. If the land wasn't used to its full extent then it would be given back to the old *patrons* by the Government itself. And, in time, things would again be as they had been before. When there was defiance or reluctance, the soldiers went about and kicked down the stone markers which separated one man's land from another's until no one could tell what was what.

Some of the older and wiser of the men held meetings and it was decided a few should make the long trip into the bewildering city of San Rafael. There they would request an audience with *el presidente* and lay before him their troubles, explaining how things were and what his officials and soldiers were doing without his knowledge. This was no venture to be undertaken lightly and only the very wisest, with some knowledge of writing even, were selected and the people back home waited anxiously for their return and an assurance that *el presidente* understood.

But the men returned from the capital puzzled and uneasy. They told how, after presenting a petition written for them by a village priest, an officer had taken them into a great room where *el presidente* waited, standing behind a big table. As the spokesman for the group hesitantly elaborated on what had been in the padre's writing, *el presidente* listened gravely. He had nodded now and then as though in sympathetic agreement. But, and this was noted by all, he did not grow angry when the tales of what his soldiers and officials were doing were spoken. He only waited courteously until the headman had finished.

Then, it was recounted, *el presidente* had walked up and down the room for a few moments in thoughtful silence before halting to speak. Life, he told them, was not as simple as they seemed to believe. It was not enough that a family in the country was able to raise what it needed to eat. There were vast complexities. All of the people of San Rafael were but as the small strands which, when twisted tightly together, make a single rope of strength. Unless they were tightly bound, each accepting its share of the strain, they fell apart and there was no longer a rope but a tangle of useless twine. What a man in a hillside village did mysteriously affected another man he had never seen who drove a bus along the city's *avenidas*. The bus driver, in turn, contributed a little something to a shopkeeper, a barber. Because insufficient cane was grown, a distillery or a refinery they had never heard of must close down. Then people like themselves were without wages to feed and clothe themselves. All of these things worked together. So it was not enough for a man to grow a dozen tobacco plants for himself, a patch of beans or a single tree of bananas.

How these things could be, none of them understood but even the spokesman, who was of an education with the ability to read and write, was not bold enough to contradict *el presidente*.

So now they were all back in their villages again and they sat and talked but were without decision. Overshadowing everything they did, said or thought was the fear of a return to the old times when a man owned nothing, not even a burro. If the land once given to them was now to be taken away and returned to the *patrons* then they again would become little more than animals of burden.

Now, also, the strangers who had come among them months before and, because of living with them, were now no longer thought of as outlanders, became bolder in their talk. The men in their small groups listened as they had not before. The strangers who were not strangers told of distant countries where simple people, such as themselves, had rid themselves forever of tyranny. Now, in these places, there were no families of great wealth while others lived in poverty. No *patron* owned the countless miles of land while others could not even claim ownership to a goat. No single man, such as *el presidente*, could say: This will be so because I will it. The people themselves decided these things by nominating *comisarios* to speak in their name. There was no unhappiness, no greed, no envy because a wise Government of the people themselves decreed no one could have more than his neighbor. This, they said, was a way of life called Communism. It meant community, *poblado*; living, owning, working together. Life became a paradise. There were no threats of giving the land back to the *patrons* because the community owned the land and they, the people, were the community.

When such things as these were said there were murmurs and a restless stirring among the groups. Some of the younger men, those who had been away from the villages and worked in the mills, refineries and distilleries, added their voices. They, also, had heard of the *comunista* way of life, and how even such a strong man as *el presidente* had been put aside by the will of the people.

Over such words as these there were frequently loud and angry arguments and, little by little, there evolved a division among the country people. There were those who were strong in their faith that *el presidente* would not allow the land to be stolen from them. They would take a little time of waiting and see. There were others who were impatient and talked of fighting the soldiers if they came again to knock down the stone markers they had replaced on their land. In this *comunista* they would have their strength, and help would come to them from countries beyond San Rafael.

From the depths of a chair upholstered with soft leather, Kent Glastonbury watched Ojeda as he rapidly scrawled his signature on the papers as they were handed to him by a secretary. When they were blotted and collected into a small pile the man gathered them together. He bowed to *el presidente* and the American Chargé d'Affaires. Murmuring the customary politeness he left them alone.

"Now." Ojeda leaned back and regarded his visitor with a pleasant smile in which there was genuine warmth and a little curiosity. "Is this an official call or do we just talk as friends?"

"Unofficially official, Excellency." Glastonbury took a cigarette from the box which Ojeda shoved toward him from across the desk. "The Ambassador preferred it that way. Otherwise he would have formally requested an appointment. I was sent to give things a casual air." He grinned suddenly with a boyish pleasure. "We Americans are becoming devious through necessity. We are learning." He grew serious. "Washington is disturbed, Excellency."

"About what?"

"Jorge Ojeda." Glastonbury was blunt.

Ojeda merely nodded and made no reply. He remained the politely attentive host.

"Washington, as you know, has poured a lot of money into San Rafael. It has provided financial and technical assistance; set up favorable quotas on sugar, tobacco and rum above world market prices or without duty. It has encouraged American investment and native industry whenever and wherever possible."

"Because it needs San Rafael."

Glastonbury accepted this agreeably. "Naturally, it has not been all altruism. There is, in the Caribbean, a situation. No one knows what will eventually happen in Cuba, the Dominican Republic, Panama, or even Puerto Rico. Washington wants and needs stability in this area wherever it can find it. After General Quatero, it supported you because—"

"Because it had no choice." Ojeda's tone had a small edge but the interruption was not rude.

"That is about it." Glastonbury was undisturbed. "It was Ojeda or chaos. Washington wasn't sure about you. Who and what was this man Ojeda? A former American Marine who, by his own decree, made himself the first citizen of San Rafael. Was he simply another in the long line of adventurers which seem endemic in the island? There was no way of knowing, no time to find out. A couple of years ago we turned handsprings in an effort to be the first to recognize Castro. The State Department couldn't wait to pat him on the head with its blessing. Batista had been an embarrassment but at least he wasn't expropriating billions of American investments, screaming Yankee imperialism and providing Russia with a solid foothold in this hemisphere. He made us squirm and apologize, but at least we could consider Cuba safe from outside incursion."

"Now"—the comment was made with an amused curiosity—"under Ojeda you consider San Rafael unsafe?"

"We don't know," Glastonbury admitted.

"What is it you want to hear from me, Kent?" This was the first time Ojeda had used Glastonbury's given name. "Spell it out."

"All right." Glastonbury took a deep breath, partly of relief, for he had half expected an explosion. "First you nationalized some of the most important industries, the banks, the corporate utilities. This had all the appearance of socialism to say the least. Then four years ago you came up with a land reform which broke up the great estates and reapportioned the land among the *campesinos*. Now, little by little, you are reversing yourself. The big landholdings, through a phony system of leasing, are being returned to the hands of the old families and you are flirting with a revolution. Now, not between the American Embassy and the Government of San Rafael but just between Kent Glastonbury and Jorge Ojeda—what in the hell are you up to?"

Ojeda stood. He walked to one of the windows which overlooked the great plaza fronting the Capitol Building. When he turned to face Glastonbury all trace of lightness was absent from his manner.

"A big government can't always afford to admit to mistakes in policy. I can. When the small army I built for General Quatero came down from the hills it was supported by the country people. Quatero had made them all sorts of promises. I made none. But the question of land reform is something I can understand. I have little sympathy for the common man. He is ignorant, selfish, prejudiced, filled with envy and self-pity, he whines and complains. But," there was a faint smile, "he is also the majority. He is the locust. Individually of no consequence but terrifying in swarms. San Rafael was mine. I made it mine by being smarter and tougher than Quatero and I liked what I had. Put any name you want to it. Vanity. The sense of power. Accomplishment. In these things I differ little from many other men. The Harrimans, the Goulds, the Astors and old John D., who stamped out all opposition and made themselves the complete masters of great industrial empires. But, to hold what I had, I finally saw I needed the support of the *campesino*. The old, entrenched families cause me no concern. The peon was my locust, my flea, my ant. To keep him satisfied I gave him the land of which he had always dreamed. But my flea doesn't really want to work for his living. He only wants to find a lazy dog to carry and feed him. He doesn't want to cultivate the land he now owns. He only wants the feeling of ownership; to be able to say: This is mine. A country such as San Rafael, which is eighty per cent agricultural, must work its land. So I have had to say to the *campesino*: Plant and harvest on that which has been given you. If you don't it will be leased to those who will. I don't think that is complicated. Why do you make it so?"

"Because you are inviting a revolution and the United States doesn't want that." The reply was blunt. "Moreover you are embarrassing us. Again we are being placed in the position of supporting the unsupportable. We are wide open to the charge of encouraging the old system of peonage, the enslavement of the people, the few dominating the many and God alone knows what other catch phrases the liberals, the Pinks and the Reds can think of. You are putting us in a damned uncomfortable spot. We have to defend the indefensible. Besides, we must have stability in this area. What will you do if you wake up some morning with a revolution on your hands? Strong as you are, it could happen. What then?"

Ojeda lit a fresh cigarette. "I'll provide a diversion. A circus maximus. A few innocents thrown to the lions. As a matter of fact I have one in mind. But," the smile faded, "that failing, and assuming the impossible, a revolt within my army led by someone who has caught the popular imagination as I did. Then you and your Marines will have to step in and finish the job for me."

Kent Glastonbury stared at the man across the desk. Then his head inclined a fraction of an inch with the resigned acceptance of a stated fact.

"Yes." The admission was made regretfully. "I suppose such a thing could happen, *presidente*."

"It would have to happen." Ojeda was completely relaxed, as though they were engaged in a mildly entertaining, academic discussion. "Suppose you are run out of Guantanamo? Where do you go from there? Puerto Rico? Maybe. I'm not so sure. There is some agitation for complete independence. I know it was offered and refused. But, just suppose a wave of nationalism mounts itself and the Puerto Ricans begin yelling: Yankee Go Home. What will you do? Beat them into submission? Latin-American opinion will force you out. Where will the Navy go for the base it must have in the Caribbean? San Rafael. That is why you need me."

"This possibility hasn't escaped the attention of Washington." Kent made the admission dryly.

"So." Ojeda leaned back and studied the intricate mosaic of the ceiling. "You need me because you may need San Rafael. And if I should need the Corps, you will have to send a battalion or so. They will come, not as Marines but as unidentified *volunteers* who are, somehow, equipped and transported with landing craft, tanks and some jets. That, my friend, is why I do not worry about a revolution."

Glastonbury's smile was twisted and without humor. He pushed back his chair and stood up while Ojeda watched him with a quietly sardonic humor. Then he also rose.

"As I said"—Kent was unhappy—"this visit was unofficially official. Even so I'm not sure I can repeat our conversation to the Ambassador."

They walked toward the doors together. At a touch of Ojeda's fingers on the knob of one they were immediately swung open by two sentries who snapped back to attention. As they were framed within the portal all movement in the long corridor was halted for the barest second. It was, Kent thought, as though a scene from a motion picture was held overly long on the screen. Then, the normal activities of the stenographers, clerks and messengers were resumed as they went in and out of the offices lining the hall.

Glastonbury extended his hand. "Thanks for seeing me. Now, unofficially again, Chris wanted me to ask if you could get away to join us on a picnic Sunday. We thought of driving up into the hills, to Agua Fria. Just folksy stuff with a hamper of fried chicken, potato salad, baked beans, some rum or wine; without bodyguard or protocol or official cars."

"Just the three of us? You and Christina?" Ojeda seemed mildly amused. "My security police wouldn't like it."

"No." For a moment Kent was almost embarrassed. "There is a fourth— Ferris Dessaline. I suspect my wife of conniving. She is a dame of devious mind. I think it would tickle her ribald sense of humor to further an alliance between *el presidente* and such a family as the Dessalines. It is her opinion the existence of one denies the being of the other. She also holds the not too private opinion that such a thing is already under way. It is a situation she muses over aloud in bed at night."

Ojeda released Glastonbury's hand. "I'd like to come. Let me know the time and give my regards to Christina. Also," he winked deliberately, "the Ambassador."

Glastonbury nodded and strode away down the marble passageway. Ojeda stood watching until his visitor had disappeared around the curving staircase. Then he turned and re-entered his office. At the desk he flicked a switch on an intercommunication box and told one of his secretaries to locate General de Cespedes.

The American Ambassador to San Rafael listened in moody silence as Kent Glastonbury repeated his conversation with Jorge Ojeda. Now and then he grunted. It was a noncommittal sound which could have been disapproval, resignation or impatience.

The Ambassador had spent years in the service of his country, most of them in Latin America, and he held to no fast convictions or illusions of stability in any of them. When Kent finished his dispassionate recital the Ambassador sighed wearily.

"The whole trouble is," the senior officer admitted, "Ojeda is probably right. We do need San Rafael and he is part of the package." He rubbed meditatively at his head, scratching strong, thick fingers through silvered hair. Momentarily his face lighted with an acid humor. "Did you know, Kent, I was once offered a chair at Princeton as a professor of international law? I could have walked a serene path. Instead, I elected to remain a career diplomat." He smiled ruefully. "We are being maneuvered, my boy, and by a former sergeant of the U. S. Marine Corps. We shall have to defend him and leave ourselves wide open to the same old charge of supporting a dictator." He packed a worn pipe with shaggy strands of tobacco and lit it. "As a nation we have done a great many foolish things. As individual Americans we have, sometimes, been greedy investors with little regard for the humanities. But I know this—if American, British, Dutch, German and French capital hadn't gone into many Latin-American countries to lay out roads, rails, establish factories, build refineries, probe the mountains for minerals and the earth for oil, most of the population would still be riding burros and living on bananas and coconuts. Capital took the risk, foreign capital, and now they are imperialists." He blew a cloud of smoke ceiling-ward. "You are fairly close to Ojeda. What is your personal opinion of him? Is he a complete scoundrel, a thief without conscience, a man of insatiable vanity and ambition? Does he have a purpose beyond himself? I have never been able to arrive at a satisfactory conclusion. Is his intent no greater than to loot this island as others have done before him?"

"I don't know." Glastonbury was honest. "He is a man of so many contradictions. Unofficially, and somehow we have managed to reach that plane together, he is informal, easy to like, without pretension. He is a guy you would want to be friendly with; play golf with on weekends, poker on Saturday night. Then, damn it, you ask yourself why such a man would fill a city with statues of himself as The Benefactor. My personal conclusion is that he has a grotesque sense of humor and laughs inside every time he sees himself on a pedestal. He is, also, motivated by a curious conviction of fatalism as though everything he has done and does is the result of an influence over which he has no control."

"I don't mind his wrapping himself in a veil of mysticism." The Ambassador flashed a sudden anger. "But I'm damned if I like the idea of forcing the United States into a partnership for the ownership of the lives and minds of San Rafael. You may employ any euphemism which comes to tongue. The truth is San Rafael is a complete dictatorship, a police state. It is a shell game in which the population thinks it gets a glimpse of the pea of paternalism now and then. We are suckered into something which Jorge Ojeda plays according to his own rules." He made a gesture of apology. "Go on. I'm sorry I interrupted."

"As to whether he is a thief." Kent gathered his thoughts carefully. "Time is the only argument against that. He has had the opportunity to steal everything and get out of the country with it. The United States alone has poured millions into San Rafael without asking for an accounting. When he wants an appropriation from the National Treasury for a project, he draws his personal check and there is no one to question how or where it is spent. He has established his own salary which is not large." Glastonbury shook his head. "A man with nothing but robbery on his mind would have cleared out long ago."

The Ambassador pushed a thumb against the gray top ash in his pipe, tamping it down smoothly. Everything his aide had said so far agreed with his private estimate of Ojeda. He was an enigma.

"I suppose," the elder man mused, "we can forget any idea of elections ever being held even though that was a promise made." He was briefly irritated again. "Damn it! If he would only go through the motions then Washington wouldn't continually have to make excuses for him."

"Well," Kent was quizzically frank, "I have asked myself what I would do in his position. Why would I hold an election when the results were predictable? Why would I give a dozen or so dissident factions an opportunity to yap at my heels just to keep Washington happy? Washington has to be happy or take a big chance on someone who might be a lot worse than Jorge Ojeda—a Castro, for instance. He knows we don't want that."

"You like him, don't you?" The Ambassador studied Kent.

"Frankly, yes. I don't understand him. When I listen to him on the radio, talking to his *niños*, I damn near believe what I hear. This is the wise, patient and understanding father telling his children why and how certain things must be done. Later, after I have had time to analyze it—" He shrugged helplessly. "Even then I'm not sure. If he has to be summed up, sir, I don't suppose he is much different from you, me or anyone else who has decided upon a career. He pursues it energetically and according to his conscience. He is human enough to enjoy the sensation of power. Who isn't? He enjoys all the perquisites which come his way as the head of a State. But then," Kent smiled, "who wouldn't if success is a goal? I suspect he has all the normal weakness and vanity, an appreciation for the best things a man can wring from a hostile and competitive world. I can question the methods employed but not the aim."

"You have read our file on him." The Ambassador drew reflectively upon his pipe. "You know his background and that he is part Negro."

"Yes." Kent's face was momentarily shadowed. "It may explain some things. He has been subjected to the most inexcusable of all prejudice. That, simply, of color. But oddly enough, he isn't really a hostile man. He is ruthless but in a strangely detached manner. His parentage, in San Rafael at least, wouldn't be important. Among the country people with the blood strains so confused it would even enhance his prestige and elevate him to a mythical stature. If it has a significance, then it is for Jorge Ojeda alone."

The Ambassador nodded an agreement and then he tapped a cardboard folder on his desk.

"You returned these reports so I suppose you went over them carefully?"

"Yes, sir," Glastonbury answered. "But our agents have uncovered little we didn't already know or suspect. Always there has been intrigue here. It is endemic. Small groups bent upon overthrowing the incumbent. I am pretty sure Ojeda knows the names of everyone involved. The places of meeting. His agents are as efficient as ours and with easier access. He must be aware that the old established families are always encouraging a revolutionary movement. That they are ready to risk their fortunes but probably not their lives to support a revolutionary *junta* acceptable to them. He is also aware the Communists are increasingly active in the country. In these matters he always acts with disarming simplicity. He permits the dissidents to become bolder by his seeming indifference. Then he simply rounds up the leaders and has them shot. In that, at least, he is direct."

"Damn it again." The Ambassador was unhappy. "San Rafael could be a model for the entire Caribbean area if Ojeda would only make a token display of a republican form of government and get us off the hook."

"But," Glastonbury's smile was one of appreciative humor, "he likes us there. You know and he knows you know that Moscow has made offers of support. That they are already in Cuba, were in Guatemala. The area is a breeding ground. He understands we can't permit a vacuum to form in San Rafael. Out of it could spin a whirlwind."

Again the Ambassador sighed. His aide was right, of course.

"Thank you, Kent."

Glastonbury stood up and then nodded pleasantly. He left the Ambassador wreathed in a cloud of smoke as it curled up from his pipe. As for the senior official—he was thinking wistfully of Nassau's cloisters, of its quiet campus and ivy-covered walls. What the situation demanded was a man with the capacity for Machiavellian intrigue. He didn't have it.

General Juan de Cespedes watched with an alertly curious interest as Ojeda ran his glance down the list of typewritten names he had given him.

"Sometimes, Pepito, your department is almost too thorough." Ojeda put the paper to one side.

"I wondered if you would think so, Excellency." There was a bright, tongue-in-cheek attitude about de Cespedes. "Particularly Madame Cleo Dessaline. It would be very embarrassing to have such an old lady shot, would it not, *presidente?*"

"She is a fool." Ojeda shrugged. "As are most of the others. They play at revolution and are no more dangerous than children with wooden swords."

"Besides," Juan was gravely attentive, "she is also the grandmother of the Señorita Ferris Dessaline, is she not? That is awkward."

"I wouldn't let that influence me, Pepito. You know that. If I really thought she was a menace."

"No." Juan was serious. "I don't believe you would. Why I would never understand, but I believe you when you say it. That is a part of you I have come to accept as surely as I believe you would put me against the Presidio wall if a situation came about."

Ojeda smiled. "We have always understood each other, my fisherman."

"Sometimes," Juan sat on a corner of the desk, "I begin to get the feeling we have squeezed the best of the juice from this orange. It would be pleasant to lie on a beach again with a girl in the sun and not have to think about being a General and the Minister of Defense. Or I should like to go to Spain and find out if I am really a cousin to the Duke of Alba."

"Not yet, Pepito." The reply was decisive. Ojeda reached again for the list. With a pen he scratched through a dozen names; those of some of San Rafael's first families. He handed the sheet back to Juan. "Let the ones I have marked-out alone. They are toothless and can only whimper at the moon. The others—those who are going about in the country villages making speeches and stirring up discontent among the *campesinos*—they are dangerous. Get rid of them. Let them be shot or knifed in a brawl. No formal arrests. It is simpler that way." He leaned back in his chair. "We discussed a matter once, some time ago, a diversion."

Juan folded the paper and placed it in the pocket of his blouse, buttoning the flap carefully and smoothing it down with care.

"I have not forgotten it, Excellency." He rubbed the knuckle of a finger against his nose to hide a grin. "You suggested someone of importance—perhaps even the Minister of Defense—be killed repelling an invasion of San Rafael. It was to give the incident significance; impress the United States Ambassador and take the minds of the people off of certain internal dissatisfactions."

"So?" The question was softly put.

"I have someone better in mind than the Minister of Defense. The General San Martin. It is in his heart to be a liberator. He does not care who or what he liberates. These things he has not yet said openly to me but we play along the shore of treachery. He begins to see in me your Judas. Almost, not entirely, he trusts me or suspects I can be used. I have encouraged his ambition to free this island from your tyranny and we have conveniently forgotten what he did in his own country. He burns a little with a resolve to take your place. It needs, now, only a little push from me; a reassurance I am ready to betray you. Then he will not only supply the money to buy off your army but have his agents outside put together an invasion force. The death of General San Martin on a beach of San Rafael as the head of a revolutionary group will cause quite a stir, Excellency. It will reawaken the United States to your position as the strong man of the Caribbean and God knows how much additional money the Congress will vote you for defense."

"Pepito," Ojeda was honestly surprised, "you have a depth and a capacity which I only begin to suspect. It is something I must keep in mind."

De Cespedes ignored the faintly ironic tone. He slid easily from his perch on the desk and lit a cigarette with slow care.

"General San Martin and I have become friendly. He is teaching me chess while talking of revolution but pretending it concerns only the moves of the pieces. When the opportunity presents itself, usually during his time of the siesta, I make love to his mistress."

Ojeda smiled a faint approval. "It is quite possible you are the Duke of Alba's cousin, Pepito. You have a fine Spanish flair for duplicity."

"I am also your friend." Juan regarded Ojeda gravely. "You are making a mistake in this matter of the land. It is one of the few things the peon will fight for. I have been doing some reading myself. Also, you are satisfying no one. The old families resent renting from you, or the Government, that which they consider already belongs to them."

"Then"—Ojeda stood up—"they must all be reminded San Rafael belongs to Jorge Ojeda. It is simple."

Juan de Cespedes rubbed the cigarette's coal out in a tray.

"*Si, presidente.*" There was an almost weary acceptance of a situation in Juan's voice. "It is yours. As my father used to say: *Abriguese usted con ello.* Defend yourself with it."

XIV.

A T precisely ten o'clock each morning General Chivas San Martin walked a restricted course along the flowered paths in a garden of the villa overlooking San Rafael and the sea. He strode with a fierce air of purpose. Head erect, shoulders back, stomach drawn in more than was comfortable, he swung a light cane as though it were a saber.

From a wicker chaise-longue the blond and inexpressibly bored Serafina Lontenon watched him with a veiled contempt. Her protector, which was a convenient word, reminded her of nothing so much as a molting pouter pigeon. Wearying of following the General's strutting, she idly contemplated her tanned legs in the shorts of white sharkskin and thought it a pity they served no better purpose than to be stretched out for the indifferent attention of San Martin.

For two years Serafina had endured this exile with the deposed general and she was weary of a situation from which there seemed no escape. San Martin had fled his country only a few hours ahead of a firing squad and in the face of a popular uprising which had broken an iron-fisted dictatorship of ten years. He ran to no pauper's hut. Millions of dollars had been drained from his nation's treasury and deposited to San Martin's account in Switzerland. When the time came, he left with undignified haste but not entirely without some magnificence. A luxurious private plane had carried him, Serafina, a few trusted members of his staff and a valet to Cuba where they were granted a temporary visa. From there the General explored other possible havens more to his liking. No one wanted him. The United States turned down his request for asylum as did Spain, France, Italy and Portugal; all places where life might have been passably endurable while he conspired to regain what he had lost. Only the Government of San Rafael, which he mentally spat upon, had offered him a haven and this at the price of a thousand dollars a day, his dignity, self-esteem and illusions.

In San Rafael the General was ignored by Presidente Ojeda and most of the island's first families. His movements were restricted, his household filled with spies in the form of servants and, he was convinced, potential assassins in the gardeners and delivery boys. For companions he had only the Generals Morillo and Torralba, also exiles who had misjudged the tempers and patience of their countrymen. They all lived in adjacent villas and played listless croquet on the well-kept grounds. Bored with each other they boasted and reminisced of the power once held and the glory which had vanished. They made a great pretense of each being involved in mysterious, underground intrigues which would eventually lead to their triumphal return to the countries they had ravished.

Now and then the trio, in rare moments of sympathy and accord, spun intricate plots. They would combine their cunning to depose Jorge Ojeda. Drawing upon their wisdom they would evolve a *junta* within San Rafael. From this a mercenary force would be recruited at points outside San Rafael. With their troops they would assault the island beaches, rally the countryside to the call of liberty, march upon the capital, which was in a state of glorious anticipation for their arrival. Each considered himself an expert in such tactical matters and each had plans for getting rid of the others once the revolution succeeded. Thus they maintained the fiction of being *compadres* and in their conversations they always referred to Presidente Ojeda as "that sergeant." Sometimes, after a few brandies and only in the presence of Serafina, General San Martin compared himself to a caged tiger, filled with a fierce and relentless courage who must someday break out and destroy his enemies.

Serafina yawned. Her feeling toward the General now was that of a female cat toward an emasculated male. In it was anger and frustration. She was unimpressed and disillusioned and spent much of her time meditating on the days when her position had been rivaled only by Evita Perón, in neighboring Argentina. She, also, had her organization of screaming girls who called themselves *Las Serafinas*. They paraded in her honor upon every occasion, wearing a modified Girl Scout uniform. They waited in chanting lines outside the opera, theatre or Presidential Palace for a glimpse of their goddess and patron. She had her charities for the shirtless ones and was photographed endlessly showing a skeptical slum mother the proper way to hold and bathe an infant. She had her hospitals, her clinics, her Serafina Fund. It never occurred to the shirtless ones that their taxes provided all of this. There had been statues of Serafina in the parks. Her picture was in every home, in all the shop windows. When she drove through the streets in her open car she was pelted with flowers and her name cheered in an incredible exhibition of hysterical mass adulation. Not even Serafina was sure just why.

All of this she had been forced to leave behind as a result of San Martin's insatiable vanity and greed. The signs of discontent had been plain enough. It was sheer stupidity to ignore them as he had. She had escaped with a small fortune in jewels and the bitter memory of how the crowds had, at last, hooted and jeered her name, thrown her pictures into the gutters and defiled her statues in the parks. Here she brooded. She was nothing and the General an insufferable bore. Only the increasing frequency of General Juan de Cespedes' visits to the villa stimulated her.

At first Serafina had attempted to create an island society of her own. She gave elaborate parties to which only the same dreary group of expatriates accepted invitations. She had tried to charge the air about her with an aura of romance and adventure. Here she was, her manner seemed to say, a heroine who had escaped a mob howling for her innocent blood. She was a woman of history; one with Josephine, Carlotta, Pompadour and Marie Antoinette. No one seemed to take this seriously.

She caught herself thinking of Juan de Cespedes. The man stimulated and angered her to the point of desperation. He laughed at her pretensions, made rudely shocking remarks concerning her past and present, touched her with the casual familiarity he might have extended to a *puta*. She had hoped for something more stable than an affair. Here, in San Rafael, de Cespedes represented the authority which was power. She would have gladly exchanged one General for another but Juan was indifferent to the suggestion. At first she had thought the increasing frequency of General de Cespedes' visits to San Martin were only an oblique approach to her bed. Now, she was no longer certain. He and Chivas played chess and talked endlessly of matters beyond San Rafael. Now and then, when the mood was upon him, he would take her while the General slept through the hour or so of his siesta. In this he displayed as little emotion as he might in going to the bathroom. She was also infuriated by the notion that San Martin was well aware of her infidelity and was content to permit her to be used while furthering his own intimacy with de Cespedes. He was trading her for something he wanted.

Watching San Martin now as he strode up and down, slicing the heads of flowers from their stalks with his cane, she was engulfed in self-pity for her position. San Martin halted abruptly and leveled his stick in her direction, glowering along its length at her.

"I have had better men than this Ojeda, this sergeant, shot." He made the statement without any explanatory preamble.

"So?" She was becoming accustomed to these vagaries and put them down as an indication of senility. "What is that supposed to mean?"

"It means I do not propose to be treated as some penniless refugee by an arrogant upstart."

"You should be grateful he permits you to stay here in safety."

He glared at her. "I was the President of my country, elected by the popular will of the people. He is nothing, a man of no background, an opportunist."

"*Cajo!*" She uttered the obscenity with an angelic smile.

"Your vulgarity does not offend me. I have become accustomed to it as I have to other unpleasant facts of life." He dug a hole in the soft earth with the ferrule of his cane and studied it intently. "However, you have an instinct about men. How does this de Cespedes impress you?"

"He is a man." She yawned with a delicate affectation. "But," the eyes were brightly malicious, "I am in no real position to judge since I am easily pleased these days."

"I am satisfied you find each other companionable. It brings him here oftener than he might otherwise come. I am content to have him as *un amigo del casa*. It does not offend me."

"I spit on you." Her eyes blazed with an amber fury.

"We must all make sacrifices." There was an amused malice in the comment. "I am no man to rot in exile. There are things going on in San Rafael of which you are not aware."

"Coffeehouse revolutionaries. Students behind their horn-rimmed spectacles." She scoffed at him. "They breed in every country like mice. Do you expect to harness them to your ambition?" She was scornful of the idea. "Let me warn you, Chivito—this Ojeda is also an expert at revolution. He is younger, tougher and, perhaps, even smarter." Her voice purred. "He also has had good men shot. I have heard he even does it himself as an example. Leave me out of any intrigue you have in mind."

"I am only asking you to listen carefully to what de Cespedes has to say when you are alone. There are, as you know, those moments between a man and a woman when things are said in relaxation; a time of idle talk, of satisfied musings aloud when one or the other partner is not completely on guard. I want some small hint, some indication of what he really thinks."

"I shall do my best, Chivito. Although Juan is not one given to conversation at such times." She dug at him with sly pleasure. "Besides, he and Presidente Ojeda are *compadres.*"

"Take my word for it. No man is completely loyal," San Martin pontificated. "Always, somewhere, there is that tiny reservation of self-interest."

Serafina was bored. "If you only knew how ridiculous you, Torralba and Morillo sound sometimes. Particularly after you all have had too many drinks. I have listened and understood how it happened you lost your countries. Three old men, tottering about in exile, dreaming impractical dreams." She became sharply impatient. "You might better spend your time by finding a way to get us away from this damned island. De Cespedes will only turn you over to his police and you will end against the Presidio wall."

San Martin shook his head stubbornly. "I have an acute sense of smell for political ferment. It seethes a little now in the city and in the country, bubbling softly beneath the surface. Someone will take advantage of it. Why not San Martin?"

Serafina was unimpressed. Let the fool walk into a firing squad. She examined her lacquered toenails with admiration and wondered if San Martin were shot, how she might put her hands on all the money he had on deposit in Switzerland. She would be without status as a widow or heir. It seemed a shame. Perhaps, in exchange for a pretense of encouraging his foolish dreams, he might be induced to marry her.

"I shall find out what I can from de Cespedes, Chivito." She melted with sympathetic understanding. "Always, I have stood at your side."

San Martin grunted and resumed his military pacing. She was a beautiful but foolish woman and completely without imagination. Throughout the Caribbean there was an uneasiness. It had become the eye of a gathering hurricane. He could sense what was happening. Communist cells probed endlessly for soft spots. The power of the United States, which had once thrown a protective shadow over the entire area, was challenged openly and secretly. The small mistakes in diplomacy that Washington made were expanded and exploited. Outside pressure had forced the United States to drop its support of the strong men, dictators though they may have been. Out of the resulting confusion there had emerged the unmistakable image of Communism. Here, on San Rafael, Ojeda was given the tacit support of Washington because the United States was afraid of what might take his place.

As he walked San Martin sought in his mind for the hinge which would open the door of opportunity. Throughout the city there were small groups of revolutionaries. They had always existed. They met and talked endlessly over their games of dominoes and cups of black coffee. But they were without any real leadership. Discontent could start with the people but successful revolution must depend upon the Army. There the first defectors had to be found and sorted. At the moment de Cespedes was his only contact.

Striding back and forth, it did not occur to San Martin there was something outrageously ludicrous in the spectacle of one deposed and completely discredited dictator plotting against another in his own country. He was of a breed of men who sought constantly for opportunity. He had no political philosophy. If assistance from the Communists was offered he would accept it readily and take the chance on being able to control the situation later. He was convinced that the democracies were on the losing end of a fight. Communism was punitive; democracy defensive. Always the free countries waited patiently to be struck first. This was the dumb steer in the slaughterhouse chute, powerless to ward off the sledge.

Of the three generals who had found refuge on San Rafael San Martin was the only one of intellectual stature. The son of a wealthy landowner, he had been a brilliant student. From his native university he had gone to Harvard and been graduated from its school of law. He was widely read, fluent in four languages and completely without conscience. For Torralba and Morillo he had a condescending contempt. The only bond between them was that of exile. Ojeda commanded his respect and envy. Complete power, he mused, created a tapeworm of appetite which was never fully satisfied. He felt no gratitude toward *el presidente* for permitting him to find a measure of security on San Rafael. It was not so much the outrageous charge of one thousand dollars a day which was imposed upon him for residence. He could well afford the money. What angered him to the point of incoherent fury was the fact he was convinced Ojeda demanded the fee merely to humiliate him. This was a sly and malicious joke which stripped Chivas San Martin of all dignity. They should, he felt, be brothers. The idea of deposing Jorge Ojeda had become an obsession which filled his days and tormented his dreams at night. Because he was an intelligent man he often assayed his position and found it almost hopeless. Here he was without friends or supporters. He was an outcast, a purse-filled beggar. If Ojeda, on a whim, deported him, he would have no place to go except back to his own country where he faced certain assassination or prison. He was in desperate need of such a man as Juan de Cespedes. He paused to study Serafina and thought much more had often been accomplished with less than Serafina had to offer a man of de Cespedes' obvious masculinity. As a woman she was undeniably decorative. There was also in her a good measure of avarice and ambition. She would help him if, in the end, it would serve a purpose of her own. He felt no personal sacrifice was involved. Through Serafina he would have an opportunity to study and evaluate de Cespedes' capacity for treachery and self-interest. These things, he was convinced, were inherent in every man.

"Chivito." Serafina's voice brought him back to the moment.

"Yes?"

"It is time now for an understanding between us. I wish to be married."

"After all this time? For God's sake why?"

"I do not intend to end as a pauper or be forced to sell my jewels one by one in order to live after you are gone."

"It is not in my mind to fail in this." He was made tightly angry by the mere suggestion of defeat.

"Just the same, the calculated risk is yours not mine. I want the status of your widow with all it implies; the bank accounts in Switzerland, for instance. Also," she twinkled, "as your *viuda* it will give me a respectability and permit me to mourn you. I am extremely attractive in black."

"You are a carrion bird." He was furious.

"Just the same, Chivito, you will marry me or I shall continue my affair with de Cespedes and tell you nothing. Do you know"—she leaned back and stared at the sky—"sometimes I think Evita had the best of it after all. She died with drama and elegance and was all but canonized in the minds of her people. At least she didn't have to wander aimlessly down the long hill to obscurity."

"You wallow in a trough of self-pity like a sow." He was beside himself with anger.

"I do not like the comparison, Chivito." The tone was icy. "You want to use me."

"Do not pretend the arrangement with de Cespedes is intolerable to you."

"I enjoy it. Just the same I intend to make a deposit against the future because I think you are, at heart, a stupid man. With a little tact, some understanding of the forces opposed to you, an attempt at reconciliation with the Church, you could have held what you had."

For a moment San Martin's face was drained white with anger. Then he shrugged and sighted down the cane as though it was a rifle.

"It would seem unnecessary for me to remind you that without me you would have been nothing. A second- or third-rate actress with the illusion of a career; passed from hand to hand. In the end you would have had to settle for some second assistant cameraman and a house filled with brats. I carried you to the top. Have you no gratitude?"

"I still have marriage on my mind, Chivito." She behaved as though she had not heard him.

"Very well." His voice rose to a shout. "I will marry you because I have no choice."

"*Mil gracias, mi corazon.*" She was sarcastically tender. "I shall always remember your great generosity and heart. When they stand you against the Presidio wall I shall weep. I shall light a candle to the Bolívar of San Rafael. A lion among men but, unfortunately, dead. *Que lastima!*"

The day had begun so well with the easy banter, the inconsequential talk between persons who liked each other and felt a warm companionship without constraint. In the Glastonbury kitchen there had been a last-minute flurry of repacking the picnic hamper to include a Thermos of coffee and glasses for the wine which had been forgotten. Only the slightly awed attitude of the servants, their shy and averted glances in the presence of *el presidente,* made the excursion seem more than it was.

They—Christina, Ferris, Kent and Ojeda—had crowded into the kitchen to watch and superintend the preparations. Ojeda, now, sat backwards on a chair contentedly chewing on a drumstick. Kent was packing ice around four bottles of wine in a waterproof sack. Ferris dipped into the potato salad, flecked with the bright red of pimento, and Christina ticked off the items in the basket. It was a scene which had its counterpart in a thousand American homes on a Sunday morning.

Chris, catching Ojeda's eye, flicked her glance in the direction of the two maids who stood, almost pressed against the wall, watching with masklike expressions.

"I don't imagine it ever occurred to them the *presidente* could sit as you are and eat a piece of cold fried chicken."

"I could do it to a flourish of trumpets if you think my prestige is suffering." He winked at her.

"As a matter of fact," Christina buckled the hamper's strap, "I think that is the way they expected you to arrive. The place has been in a silent turmoil ever since I told them you were coming. I wasn't sure how I should handle the situation, either. I asked Kent if a diplomatic problem was involved in inviting the Head of State on a picnic."

"What did he say?" Ojeda examined the stripped bone.

"I told her," Kent interrupted, "if the King and Queen of England could eat hot dogs with the Roosevelts at Hyde Park we could be as informal here on San Rafael."

"That's one of the reasons Kent and I took this house instead of living at the Embassy. Now and then we just like to go into the kitchen, poke around the icebox and fix ourselves a sandwich. This horrified the Embassy staff." Christina shrugged. "It hurt their feelings because they thought we weren't satisfied with the way they did things. I think that's everything. Let's go."

Outside, parked in the driveway, were Ojeda's official Cadillac, Ferris's Mercedes and the Glastonbury Buick convertible. Ojeda's chauffeur stood stiffly, holding the limousine's door open. His dignity was plainly offended by the casualness of the whole affair and the manner of their arrival—no motorcycle escort, no siren—just a quiet drive from the Presidential Palace to this unpretentious house.

"Are you going to ride alone?" Ferris lifted her eyebrows.

"I forgot to tell him not to wait." Ojeda turned to the chauffeur and dismissed him. He seemed almost embarrassed by the incident. "Sorry. It's a bad habit and one too easily acquired." He spoke again to the liveried man in Spanish.

"I'll be damned." Christina was genuinely astonished. "You apologized to him."

"Wouldn't you have?" Ojeda asked quietly.

"Yes, but—"

"But you wouldn't expect it of me. Is that it?"

"Now I'll apologize to you." Christina was soberly contrite.

"*De nada.*" Ojeda smiled at her.

"Do you mind if I take my car, also?" Ferris divided the question among them. "It's sort of mad money. I can always get home if I don't like the company. We'll follow you."

"No." Christina was emphatic. "We'll follow you. The idea of *el presidente* helling around in a red sports car excites my imagination."

Twice, on the way down the long *avenida* which was the main artery out of the city, traffic policemen froze at incredulous attention as they recognized Ojeda, and then frantically halted all other traffic while waving the Mercedes through. Once, two motorcycle police pulled alongside until Ojeda with a quick shake of his head caused them to drop away reluctantly.

"You could have taken another route out of the city." Ojeda was aware of the faintest of smiles about Ferris's eyes.

"I know. I just couldn't resist it. I wanted to see what you would do."

"Satisfied?"

"Uh-huh. Would you light a cigarette for me?"

Once out of the city there were no more incidents. The broad, four-lane highway narrowed to a macadam-paved road which climbed steadily into the mountains. Now and then they passed through small villages, but their passing created no particular interest beyond a few double-note whistles of admiration for the blond girl who drove such a fine and magnificently red car. This was a courtesy and not an insolence and Ferris frequently shrilled a sharp whistle in return or flipped a hand in greeting.

Now the time of day had lengthened and the afternoon grown shorter. They had eaten and talked, completely at ease with one another. The wine had warmed and stimulated them. The food had been good and, as Christina had promised, in the best tradition of an American picnic. Once, as Ojeda helped himself to the salad, Christina had admitted to her surprise.

"I keep forgetting you are an American," she confessed. "I thought baked beans and fried chicken would be a novelty."

"They are, but not for the reason you think. I've tried to explain fried chicken and Boston beans to my chef. He just listens politely and assures me it will be as I say. Then the chicken comes to the table sautéed in oil or wine and the beans are in a sauce with *orégano*. I gave up trying. Once," his eyes lighted with amusement, "a long time ago, in Florida, I passed a roadside restaurant. There was a sign out in front. *Real Northern Fried Chicken*."

"In California," Kent chuckled, "the menus list *Eastern Beef*. This means it comes from Kansas City or Chicago. So much for geography."

Once, early in the afternoon, Christina had made a firm effort in the matter of address.

"I'm damned if I'm going to go through the day calling you *presidente*." She appealed to Ojeda. "What should we do about it?"

"My name is Jorge, as you well know. Once, in Tampa, I did odd yard jobs for a woman who called me Georgie."

"No." Christina shook her head. "I don't think I could bring myself to the point of calling the *presidente* Georgie. Not even Mr. Georgie."

So, without effort, they had come to the unfamiliar but easy plane of first names and Jorge was spoken without self-consciousness.

With the sun still warm but beginning to drop through the feathered tips of the high pines on the softly green mountains, they were stretched comfortably on the ground. Kent lay with his head pillowed in Christina's lap. Ferris sat cross-legged on a native mat of woven reed grass. Ojeda rested against a tree nearby. A spring which gave the place its name, Agua Fria, broke from the sheer surface of a cliff, making a miniature waterfall. It coursed off down a stony brook of its own making and burbled with the sound of coffee in a percolator.

The sense of high isolation, of being completely beyond intrusion, had created a magic of quiet intimacy. Somewhere below and beyond lay a familiar city; the everyday problems of existence in a complex society; the small frettings and petty annoyances which were accepted as unavoidable. Here, it seemed, they rested where no one had walked before. Each was aware of this and none wanted to break the spell.

"We ought to be starting back soon." Kent made the statement without conviction.

"*Mmmm,*" Chris agreed but there was no enthusiasm in the sound. She pulled a small, white, star-petaled flower from the ground and twirled it slowly between her fingers. "What would happen"—she spoke to Ojeda—"if you just decided not to go back to the palace, staying out all night without telling anyone? Would soldiers run through the streets with torches and hunt the mountains calling your name?"

"For God's sake," Kent exclaimed, "how does your mind fasten upon such bizarre ideas?"

"I just wondered." Chris shrugged. "It seemed a natural enough question. The life of a *presidente* can't be very private. Someone would have to say: What do you suppose has happened to the old man?"

"What would happen?" Ferris lifted her eyes to meet Ojeda's.

"I'm not sure." Ojeda smiled at her curiosity. "Usually my schedule is rigidly fixed. I don't often get a chance to deviate from it. I don't really know." He addressed Chris with a musing interest as though the notion had caught his fancy. "Suppose I didn't return tonight." He laughed as the idea appealed to his imagination. "At first there would be a mild curiosity on the part of my valet. He would mention my absence to one of the secretaries. Gradually the question would be passed upward until it reached General de Cespedes."

"No one knows where you are?" Ferris was interested.

"If you mean did I furnish the police with an itinerary, your names and probable schedule, no. Eventually, though," his eyes brightened, "one of the police along the *avenida* would remember seeing me with a blonde in a red Mercedes. You should have used a less-conspicuous car and taken to the back streets."

"Isn't this pretty casual behavior for the *presidente?*" Chris reached into her husband's shirt pocket for a cigarette. "I mean, just to walk out of the house on a Sunday morning. What did you say? So long, boys, I'll see you all later?"

"Chris." Kent's protest was sincere.

"Well, I want to know." She pushed his head from her lap. "I never went on a picnic with a President before. Aren't there supposed to be some sort of security measures? All day long I've been suspecting an armed guard lurking in the woods just out of sight."

"Why should there be?" Ojeda was not annoyed by the suggestion. "You are my friends. Anyhow," he continued with a simple confidence, "that isn't the way it will happen."

"What?" Chris disregarded Kent's warning frown.

"What you have not been too subtle in suggesting. A disposition of Presidente Jorge Ojeda. That was what you had in mind, wasn't it?"

"I suppose so." Christina was blithely honest.

"This is a pretty morbid subject for conversation," Ferris interrupted impatiently.

Jorge smiled at her. "Christina has a normal curiosity. Also, I suspect she went to Smith or Radcliffe."

Christina sat upright in surprise. "Smith," she admitted. "How did you know?"

"It was just a guess. Since I have been President of San Rafael I have met the wives of many Americans. Some of them were graduates of Smith College. It always seemed to me they made a fetish of being ingenuously frank. It is like the free, swinging, woodsy stride—a part of the curriculum. It may even be an entrance requirement, for all I know."

Christina laughed, honestly amused. She grinned impudently at Ojeda and relaxed.

"You're right, of course. Not only about Smith. I was being obnoxiously frank which is another way of saying nosy. Kent and I have been stationed in many places. I don't recall any Head of State who came to power as you did, through force, who was ever completely at ease as you seem to be. Or who would dare to do what you have done today." She paused. "I remember Batista, Jimenez, Perón, Trujillo. Their cars were bulletproof. They were surrounded by secret police wherever they went. They lived in constant fear of assassination. I wouldn't be surprised if someone didn't go to the bathroom with them. Why are you different? What makes you so confident?"

"Chris, you are a damned fool!" Kent pulled himself up. He reached for her hand, lifting her almost roughly from the ground. "Now I know it is time we were leaving."

She stood. "Was I too fresh?" Her wide-eyed appeal to Ojeda was disarming. "I didn't mean to be."

"No." Ojeda also rose and offered his hand to Ferris. "People rarely say to me what they really think. General de Cespedes and my valet, Contras. Maybe that is because we were soldiers together. It breeds an understanding. The others only say what they imagine I want to hear."

Together they rolled the grass mats and loaded them with the picnic hamper into the back of Glastonbury's car.

"We'll follow you and Kent." Ferris spoke to Chris. "Thanks for a good day. I'll call you during the week."

Christina divided a quick, knowing glance between Ferris and Ojeda. Then she nodded and slid into the seat of the car.

Kent hesitated for a fraction of a second. "Take it easy going down. It's already dark in the valleys and the road is tricky."

Ferris and Ojeda waited in the Mercedes until the Glastonburys were out of sight around the first short bend of the highway. She made no move to start the motor but sat, arms resting on the wheel, staring off across the peaks.

"Christina is a charming idiot." She made the statement in a small voice.

"She only asked what is probably in the minds of a lot of people." He was indifferent.

Only a slight inclination of her head indicated she had heard. The silence lengthened and the shadows on the high place gathered. His hands took her shoulders and he turned her to face him. She was crying.

"You mustn't do that." His voice was gentle.

"This is a damned thing." It was a fierce protest. "I don't want it to happen but it has and I don't know what to do about it."

"All of my life I have thought there must be a girl like you. One to fill me completely until everything else became unimportant. You are my love. I say it simply because there is no other way."

She bent her head, touching her cheek against his hand and resting there as might a tired child seek comfort.

"Why," her voice was all but inaudible, "do you make me uneasy and uncertain? What is there about you that frightens me? It should be such a simple thing between us. Love. A man and a woman who know they want, perhaps even need, each other. There should be an exultation, an ecstasy. Instead, I am frightened for us both as though we wandered aimlessly down some trackless path that must end in disaster."

He lifted her face and kissed her gently. She clung to him, trembling a little.

"This isn't like me." She drew away and forced a regretful smile. "Always I have been self-contained, sure of myself. The unexpected never happened because I knew exactly what I was doing. Now, without warning, I find myself in love with a man I barely know. That isn't easy to say. Much of what you are offends me. You are an affront to my instinct, my training, my background. If that sounds snobbish it isn't meant to be. I'm trying to be honest because I love you. It is no Bourbon pose. I am not saying I am Ferris Dessaline, who and what are you? Please try and understand me. It is so important for us both that you do. I am what I am because I can't help it. I know you laughed at me once and pointed out that the history of my family was built upon the ruthless exercise of power. I refuse to accept that as an unavoidable heritage. I have a concern for man's dignity. That is the personal opinion of Ferris Dessaline. You strip them naked with a controlled savagery. The end for you will be revolt, exile, assassination or execution. I love you. I don't want that to happen to you, to us."

His expression of meditative concern did not change. "I, also, am what I am because no choice was given me. The mold was cast in such a fashion and no other image was possible." He paused. "Would you marry me?"

She drew a deep breath, sharp in its sound. "Yes." There was a quiet acceptance in the reply. "Oh, I know! The other way would be the easy one. The furtive assignation. The whispers and, eventually, the accepted scandal. Ferris Dessaline. The *presidente's* mistress. That would be too simple. We are not going to be let off that easily, Jorge Ojeda. I'll marry you."

There remained now the thing which should be said between them, and in the second of decision he knew he would not speak the words. He closed his mind to it. In all things, he told himself, I am and have been white. The invisible thread of color within my veins is of no consequence. I will not admit to it. In everything I have thought and done for all these years I have been white. Let it be that way.

"I am going to need a little time with Madame Cleo." For the first time a small laugh sounded in her voice.

"I suppose so." He frowned.

"No one else matters but she is the matriarch. I have been reared in that tradition."

"What happens if she refuses? Do you defy her?"

"Yes. But first I must ask her consent. It is a matter of courtesy." She touched his lips with her fingers. "After all, the *presidente* and Ferris Dessaline can't run off like a couple of high school sophomores and be married by a justice of the peace or some village priest."

"I suppose you know"—he proceeded cautiously—"your grandmother has involved herself in a ridiculous circle of intrigue against the Government with half a dozen of the old families on the island. I do not consider her or them dangerous, but the situation can't be ignored or be permitted to expand."

"I know." She was soberly concerned. "But I wasn't sure you did."

"I make it my business to know. I wish you would tell her that."

"You tell her." The refusal was firm.

"All right." He was serious but then his eyes brightened with an inner amusement. "From what I know of her she is a formidable old lady. In the end I may have to throw her into the Presidio. That would be a hell of a thing for a future grandson-in-law, or whatever I am to be, to do."

"Do you know," Ferris reflected, "she may even refuse to see you. I wouldn't put it past her." She all but giggled. "You may have to send the *julia* for her. Now," the laughter was gone and she came into his arms, "hold me this way for a while. Let's just be Ferris Dessaline and Jorge Ojeda who have discovered it is a wonderful thing to be in love. There are no problems, no complications. Just you and I."

It was a long time before she sighed regretfully and drew away. Far below, in the rapidly gathering darkness, there was the misty aura of the city as it lighted itself against the night.

XV.

THEY had been talking for a long time and although there was a bench at the end of the flowered arbor and an invitation had been given to seat himself there, the man remained standing in an attitude of politely grave attention.

Coming upon them suddenly in the scented and warmly spotted sunlight, Ferris halted in astonishment, staring incredulously. Then, recovering the break in her stride, she continued to walk toward them. Madame Cleo Dessaline was in her favorite, high-backed chair of intricately spun wicker. Facing her, quietly attentive, was the Negro, Massau. At the sound of Ferris's step on the gravel he half turned his head.

"Massau!" There was a question and a surprised greeting in her use of his name. "What in the world?"

"Mam'selle." He inclined his head and the gesture was friendly but respectful.

The old lady, arms resting on the chair's sides, regarded her granddaughter with calm inspection, disregarding her obvious amazement. Her attitude was airily unconcerned. It seemed to imply there was nothing unusual in the presence of the Negro here in the garden. It even managed to suggest a mild annoyance over the fact Ferris seemed to find it so.

"Massau and I have been talking." Madame Cleo made the obvious statement. "It has been many years since I have seen him."

Ferris seated herself on an end of the bench and lit a cigarette. It amused her a little to realize that, despite the old lady's calculated aplomb, she was actually momentarily flustered. This was such a novelty that she decided to say nothing and watch Madame Cleo extricate herself.

"I thought you were playing tennis or whatever physical violence you indulge in at the Country Club." Madame Cleo now spoke as though they were alone. Massau had ceased to exist because she willed it. "You are home early."

Ferris made no comment. She glanced from her grandmother to Massau and then back again to the old lady.

"I mus' go now, madame. If you permit." Massau was aware of the uncomfortable silence. He broke it tactfully. "It be dark 'fore I mek home."

"Yes. Of course." Madame Cleo was gracious.

"Madame. Mam'selle." He bowed shortly to each in turn.

"What have you done with the jade, Massau?" Ferris called as he started across the garden.

He turned and a smile illuminated his face. "I work on it, mam'selle. A little somethin' come now lak I want. Not sure yet. When finish I mek it a presen' to you."

When he had left and they were alone, Ferris continued to smoke her cigarette, eying her grandmother speculatively.

"Why did Massau come here?"

Madame Cleo was serenely undisturbed by the abruptness of the question. She reached for a small silver bell on the taboret.

"I'm going to have some tea. Would you like a cup?"

Ferris shook her head with a determined smile. "I'd like to know how Massau happened to be here."

"He didn't happen. Things don't just happen. You can't imagine he simply walked into the garden without an invitation. I sent for him." This, apparently, disposed of the question.

"Why?" Ferris persisted.

"Why? Because I wanted to see him." The reply seemed an obvious answer to Ferris's curiosity and there was a tiny note of exasperation in the old lady's voice. "It seems to me you are being deliberately dense, if not rude."

"And you are being deliberately evasive. I know you that well." Ferris smiled with affection.

The appearance of a maid and the ordering of tea interrupted the inquisition. After the girl had left, Ferris returned promptly to the question. "You'll have to admit it is odd."

"I admit nothing of the sort. I wanted to see him. I sent for him. He came. We talked. He is gone. Stop heckling me with a vulgar curiosity."

Ferris nodded agreeably. "Sorry." She paused. "I am curious only because I have had a strange feeling about him. Even on that first day, in Marchand's, I felt I had known him for a long time. It is something I can't explain."

Madame Cleo appeared lost in the contemplation of the mountains. Great puffs of white clouds hung over the peaks as a gigantic charlotte russe.

"It is odd you should say that," Madame Cleo reflected, "because you certainly have no way of knowing. Massau once performed a great service for the family. He saved your grandfather's life and made it possible for us to avoid a most unsavory scandal. All of this happened long before your father was born."

Interested, Ferris leaned forward, hands between her knees, the cigarette smoldering. She waited for her grandmother to continue, but the old lady apparently felt what she had said was a complete explanation. The subject had been exhausted; the presence of Massau in the garden accounted for. She picked up a small embroidery hoop and began to pluck at a loose thread.

"Well, don't leave it there! What happened?"

"It is unimportant now." Madame Cleo shrugged. "So long ago in a different age, a different world." She mused on time's passing. "Your grandfather was a vigorous man with a roving eye for a pretty face. It was a thing I accepted. Anyhow, he was lightly involved with a wench of color in the lower town. That was not at all unusual in those days. A lady took these infidelities as a matter of course. They frequently spared her the constant burden of childbearing. This was no house serving-girl, no common *puta*, but a mulatto of some education and great beauty. She had been maintained by several gentlemen in considerable style and had her own carriage. Apparently, she was a lusty girl. In addition to her white lovers she also gave her favors to a great buck of a Negro, a Dessaline slave by the name of Samuel. It was, I suppose, some sort of a primitive urge for mating with her own kind. One day your grandfather was on horse in the fields looking over some drainage work being done there. Samuel had grown sullen and intractable. It had been necessary to have him beaten several times. On this day, inflamed by jealousy and probably some stolen rum, he suddenly attacked your grandfather, rushing at him with a machete, pulling him from horse. Massau killed Samuel there in the field. They say he broke the man's neck between his hands as he might snap a branch. He was terribly cut, though, by Samuel's blade. It left a hideous scar, so I was told. In any event, he prevented your grandfather's murder. The whole affair was hushed up as simply a quarrel between two Negro men. The girl was sent away from the island, to San Salvador, I believe."

The maid brought the tea, placing the tray on the small table. Madame Cleo put aside the embroidery. Ferris was lost in the hot picture of this sudden, carnal fury in a cane field years ago and wondered at her grandmother's calm recital. There was a portrait of Emil Dessaline in the drawing room. He had been a handsome man and a bright-eyed vitality and arrogance made itself felt through the artist's brush strokes. She had studied it many times, wondering what sort of a man he had been. Now for the first time, because of what her grandmother had told her, he became a person. She tried to imagine how he had conducted himself on that blazing day within the high, green banners of the cane when a maddened Negro had struck at his life with a flashing blade.

Madame Cleo poured tea for both of them, adding small slices of crystallized ginger to the brew. Ferris left her place on the bench to take the cup.

"What about Massau?" she prompted.

"I have already told you, child." The old lady was obviously disturbed by her recollection of what had occurred. The subject had become distasteful and she wanted done with it. "In return for what he had done your grandfather released him with a pension for life. He was also given title to one of the offshore islands we owned. He has lived there ever since."

"That's what he meant!" Ferris exclaimed. "The Goat's Neck. He said 'My islan'' as though he really owned it."

"It is a curious thing." Madame Cleo sipped her tea. "He has never touched the money. Mr. Tedder-Ironsides once wrote me about it. By now it must be a considerable sum. He always had a great pride, Massau. When he was young he was a magnificent animal. We had one pregnant house servant after another. The good God alone knows how many children he sired among the field hands. Your grandfather was quite delighted with this display of vigor. He parted with Massau as reluctantly as he would have given away a fine stallion. However, we felt an obligation."

Listening, watching the play of expression on her grandmother's face, Ferris marveled at the primitive violence, the hot savagery this exquisitely dainty and fragile-appearing woman must have known as a young girl. The brutality of slavery, the volcanic turbulence of island life where a half-dozen families dominated the uncounted blacks and native shadings. These things must have been an accepted way of life, taken for granted by those who had made themselves masters of the majority. How had she survived to this gentle charm and wisdom of old age? What innate serenity of character had lifted her above the narrow insularity of her existence on San Rafael? She had never expressed a desire for travel and had little interest in things which did not directly concern her and the small circle of remaining friends. From things said now and then, Ferris knew Madame Cleo hadn't been off the island for at least a quarter of a century. She reached for one of the small spice cakes which had been brought with the tea.

"I am trying to picture you as a young girl."

Madame Cleo smiled a little wistfully. "I have all but forgotten, myself. Everything was so different—conduct, outlook—it was a way of thinking as much as living. It is impossible to recapture the time in memory."

With a grudging admiration Ferris realized her grandmother had adroitly managed to avoid answering the original question concerning the presence of Massau in the garden. The conversational gambit had been deft. The old lady said no more than she had intended to say in the beginning. She understood it would be futile to press the question.

The arbor had grown completely silent. Even the *macayo* which had been walking stiff-legged up and over the rim of Madame Cleo's chair, shrieking petulantly now and then, was quiet.

"I am going to marry Presidente Ojeda." Ferris made the statement without emphasis. It was a casual irrelevancy.

"That, of course, is ridiculous." Madame Cleo made her reply in the same tone. She spooned out the sliver of ginger at the cup's bottom and fed it to the *macayo*. "This silly bird has always liked ginger root."

"Very well." Ferris was patient. "If that is the way you want to leave it."

"It is not a matter to be taken or left. One simply ignores an absurdity."

"It is something we must talk about."

"I would be equally interested in discussing whether the moon is made of Roquefort cheese. Both ideas are preposterous. I know, of course, you have been in his company several times. It has disturbed me."

"How did you know?"

"I have my sources of information. Matters of importance are brought to my attention. I suppose, being a Dessaline, you will be headstrong about this. Such a marriage is out of the question. Distasteful as it is to me, I suggest a compromise. Have a discreet affair with this Yankee adventurer and let it go at that. Talk of a sanctioned union, a marriage, is utter and complete nonsense."

Ferris put aside her cup. "Just the same I intend to marry him." She was quietly defiant.

"I shall have Bishop Mendoza forbid it." Madame Cleo made the statement as though it created an irrevocable decision. "You will not find a priest on the island who will marry you after the Bishop issues an edict against such a ceremony."

"A little while ago," Ferris refused to become impatient, "you said something about a different way of thinking, of living. I deny you the privilege of forbidding me to do what I will." She drew a deep breath.

"One does not mate a fine, blooded animal with a mongrel. It is eugenically unsound."

"You know nothing of the man," Ferris protested.

"In His wisdom God has spared me many unpleasant things. An acquaintance with this Ojeda is one of them." For the first time she dignified the President with a name. She studied the young girl before her. "It is time, of course, you considered marrying someone. There are several men of good family from which to choose. I suggest we discuss the possibility of a union with the Bishop. He is a very sound thinker; a little too liberal, perhaps, but a sound thinker."

"You are not going to lead me down that path, my darling." Ferris shook her head with a smile. "I don't give a damn what the Bishop thinks or how he thinks it. I still intend to marry Jorge Ojeda."

"How?" Madame Cleo was complacent. "Like some runaway servant girl, skittering down the back steps at night with her belongings wrapped in a 'kerchief.'"

"No. As Ferris Dessaline. In the church. With or without your consent. Won't you at least meet him?"

"I would as willingly share my broth with a leper."

"I have never known you to be unreasonable; prejudiced, perhaps. I love this man. I can't attempt to explain why. Love isn't something to be put on a slide beneath a miscroscope. I only know that being with him completes me. My life is richer. Let me have it that way, full and satisfying. You and I have been so close. There is love and respect between us. Don't destroy it."

Madame Cleo leaned back in the chair, resting her head against the wicker. Always, she thought, women had been attracted by the pirate, the adventurer. A latent savagery in the female responded.

"Bring the man to me." She was tired. "I will receive him."

Beside the blue-tiled pool in which fresh gardenias and crimson camellias were floated each morning Serafina turned her all but naked body to the sun. Now and then she rolled on a hip to regard the Generals San Martin and Juan de Cespedes through sulky eyes. It was long past the time for Chivito's siesta and she grew impatient.

At a table within the shade of a coconut palm, San Martin and Juan sat with a chessboard between them. Save for the opening move the pieces were untouched, for chess was not the purpose of these meetings which had grown increasingly frequent and intimate. The game served only as an excuse for talk; oblique at first but now with more purpose and frankness.

San Martin reached for a tall, iced glass of rum, lime and soda. The rim was frosted with crystallized sugar which glinted as snow in the light. He drank slowly and with pleasure, leaning back to regard Juan de Cespedes with an interested smile.

"I think, General," he said, "we begin to approach a plane of understanding."

"*Como no?*" Juan shrugged.

"You will forgive me," San Martin continued, "if I employ a word which is generally regarded as offensive. But I have never encountered a rogue who did not have some personal interest to serve through his treachery. You have intimated your willingness to betray Presidente Ojeda and link your fortunes with mine. To what purpose do you do this?"

"That's a fair enough question." Juan nodded agreeably. "I am no longer satisfied to be a General."

"Then why do you throw your lot in with mine? Because"—the voice hardened—"let us have no misunderstanding. With a successful revolution I shall be the *presidente,* not you."

"I have no wish to be President." Juan lit one of the General's cigars. "The casualties run high in that office. I only want a chance to make myself rich and get away from this island which has become a prison. I want a pocketful of money, women, cars, yachts, Paris, the Riviera, New York. I want to get some fun out of all this. There are a lot of fat geese to be plucked on San Rafael. So far I have only seen the feathers."

"But surely as the close friend of the *presidente* . . ." San Martin allowed the question to remain unfinished.

"This you will probably not believe. Jorge is an honest man." He made the statement with half-humorous resignation. "It is in his hand but he will not close his fingers about it. Even I, who know him best of all, have never understood. He only wants to live well, as he does, and be *presidente.* A man who was a thief at heart would have cleaned this place out years ago and skipped. Don't misunderstand what I am saying. For the people he does not give a damn. He believes they get what they deserve. In his own words, they are only his trained fleas. He uses them but he does not mistreat the dog on which they feed. He keeps it fed, clean and contented."

"You mean there is no private fortune to which he can turn? That he has been stupid enough to allow this opportunity to escape him? I find it hard to believe, my friend." Incredulity was stamped upon San Martin's expression.

Juan shook his head. "He would have told me. I am his *compadre.* If he were stealing we would be in it together. He would say: This is mine. This is yours. We would have divided it as children sometimes do with candy. No, something in Jorge years ago made him want to climb the peak and put himself beyond reach. To be sure, San Rafael is a small mountain but he stands at the top. He likes what he has—the feeling of power, the prestige, the luxury of the palace, the sentry outside his door at night. This is the fulfillment of his ambition: to be untouchable. You should have seen San Rafael as it was when we came out of the mountains with the army of General Quatero. Then you would believe what I say. The taxes, the duties, the capital and income from the properties which he confiscated, the funds granted by the United States, have gone into the building of a modern city, roads, schools, public buildings, transportation, public health services, rural improvement. He has imposed his will but he has not stolen. I would know."

"It is difficult to believe," San Martin admitted. He mused upon this for a moment and then took a long swallow of his rum drink before returning to what was uppermost in his mind. "If we succeed, and we must, what do you expect from me? I warn you." The voice was suddenly harsh again.

"I am no stupid Quatero to be used and then duped. I shall take advance precautions to protect myself from your ambition—assuming you have one."

"My ambition is to be rich." De Cespedes was bored. "I have already told you. When it is over I expect us to sit down together and cut up the goose. There is plenty for us both. I am a simple man with extravagant tastes."

For the first time San Martin began to believe what he so desperately wanted to believe: that Juan de Cespedes was a completely dishonest man who would admit to this without embarrassment or qualification. An honest thief could be handled. It was the altruist, the man of noble purpose, the bleeding heart, who failed in a pinch and had to be watched.

"If you can make me *presidente*"—San Martin could not conceal his eagerness—"then you can make yourself rich beyond what you can imagine."

"I have a big imagination, General." Juan was amused. "Now, since you have warned me"—the voice was cold—"let me caution you. I will control the revolutionary army. As surely as I sit here I will use it to destroy you along with Jorge if you try to double-cross me. I say this so there can be no misunderstanding of wills in the matter."

"I have no need for the money to be picked up here." San Martin accepted the threat without resentment. "If that is all you want it is yours. After I am *presidente* you shall have access to the Treasury. I give you my hand on it."

Juan laughed without restraint. The sound caused Serafina to roll over and regard him with interested surprise.

"What," she called, "is so funny, Juanito? The General has no sense of humor."

"You are mistaken," he continued to chuckle, "he has just offered me his hand as proof of sincerity."

"Take it." She stood up and stretched. "But keep your eye out for a knife in the other one. I would like to go to the beach. Will you take me?"

"Why not? In a few minutes." He turned his attention from her to San Martin. "How much are you prepared to invest in your ambition, General?"

"As much as is necessary. As things stand my private fortune is without value, since I am unable to enjoy it in my present position. I am virtually a prisoner here. What good is money to me?"

"We will need outside contacts," Juan suggested.

"I have them. There are refugees from my own country in Cuba, Guatemala, San Salvador, the Dominican Republic and even in the United States, which are still loyal to me. The contacts will be made."

"Two or three hundred men, well equipped, will do it. There will be no real opposition from the Army of San Rafael. I will see to that. I have Ojeda's own pattern to follow. I saw it done once before. But you will leave Jorge to me."

[199]

"The place for opposition is against the Presidio wall."

"That too, but in my own time and in my own way," Juan agreed. "I leave it to you to make the outside contacts we need. You have been through revolutions before and know what it takes to make them. Work carefully and only with those you can trust to recruit and equip. San Rafael will be my problem. Already, in the country where the strength of revolution lies, there is unrest and dissatisfaction. Jorge has shut his mind to it. Also, there is assistance, in money at least, to be found among most of the old families." He laughed quietly. "As Minister of Defense I have that information. Castro threw Batista out with less. It does not take quantity but only determination."

San Martin nodded his agreement. "There is one thing more we must consider." He frowned a little. "Do you think the United States would dare intervene here on behalf of Ojeda?"

"It will be over, an accomplished fact, before the Embassy here knows what is happening. That is, if you work outside with intelligence. Word will leak of what is going on. You cannot recruit mercenaries without the news getting around. I suggest you buy the assistance of a Cuban of stature, one of the original Fidel officers who have defected and fled to Miami or Mexico. Let him be the figurehead of the movement with an open declaration of intention to overthrow Castro. No eye will be turned toward San Rafael. The United States will look the other way because it wishes to believe this. By the time it turns around it will be too late."

"I am beginning to have great confidence in you, General." San Martin made no effort to conceal his excitement. "We will work well together."

"It had better be that way, General." Juan arose. "Because if we don't, one or both of us will be standing in the Presidio's courtyard without our shirts on." He turned to regard Serafina. "Do you still want to go to the beach?"

"Yes." She strolled toward them.

"In that?" He indicated the wisp of silk at hip and breast.

"Why not?" She was indifferent. "It is for swimming we go, is it not?"

"You have no objection, General?" Juan addressed San Martin and the question was almost contemptuous.

"Serafina is of an athletic disposition." San Martin all but yawned.

"You are a pig, Chivito." She made the statement as merely a conversational observation.

"And you, my beautiful Serafina, are what is known as a *quid pro quo*. Since your education was limited I translate it for you as a something for something. It is pleasant to know we all understand each other. By all means go to the beach. I shall take my siesta."

Through half-closed eyes San Martin watched as Serafina and Juan de

Cespedes walked from the garden. They were fine animals, both of them. And, at the moment, valuable and serving a purpose. Later, perhaps, it might be pleasantly interesting to have Serafina beaten and exiled. As for General de Cespedes . . . San Martin did not conclude the thought. He was weary and it was time for his siesta.

He lay back in the chair, enjoying the sensation of the sun flooding over him like a warm bath. Always in an undertaking of an adventure of this magnitude there were the imponderables and the unexpected to be weighed and considered. Drowsily he mused on the character of Juan de Cespedes, for this was the key which must turn in the lock. If he was what he so readily and cheerfully admitted—a man whose only ambition was to make himself wealthy and get out—he could be trusted within certain bounds. If, on the other hand, he wanted to create an incident which in the end would strengthen his and Ojeda's position, projecting themselves as the true defenders of San Rafael against foreign intrigue . . . Ay! San Martin sighed. That was the unknown quantity and he knew of no way to make an infallible analysis.

Resting, eyes closed, mind sorting, retaining and discarding the pieces of his ambition, it did not occur to San Martin that what he was engaged upon was outrageously preposterous. He, an alien refugee on San Rafael, planned boldly to seize its Government, making the land and its population his own. Was it more than Ojeda had done or, for that matter, many of his predecessors?

The mechanics of the operation were not complex providing de Cespedes was what he acknowledged himself to be. He was the front, the shield, the façade. In the memory of the people he was one with The Benefactor who had delivered them from the tyranny of Romero. He had been a soldier, exposing himself boldly with the guerrilla forces. Now, because of what Ojeda was doing with the land reforms, there was growing a resentment and a distrust, a slow-burning anger and a sense of betrayal. What more natural, then, that General de Cespedes free them again from oppression with an army of liberation? And since the General had once been a common soldier, it would seem natural he appoint as temporary *presidente* such a one as San Martin, who had knowledge in the ways of administration. The rationalization came effortlessly.

People, San Martin ruminated, desired order above all other things. Order and a small opportunity for profit. The relief from turmoil which disturbed the norm of their small, unimaginative lives. They would want a quick end to a revolution, placing a childlike faith in promises made. He would make them and avoid, at all costs, the dangerous expediency of martial law and military control to enforce his position. San Martin distrusted an army. It could not be relied upon. Batista had learned this as had Perón, Jimenez and others. The list was endless through history's pages. From the Army of San Rafael he wanted only indifference. How strong, he wondered, was its loyalty to Ojeda? Less, probably, than he suspected. Troops stagnated in barracks. Allegiance was mercurial. Small pockets of discontent developed. His own army had defected in a time of crisis and left him a helpless fugitive. The ordinary soldier did not die willingly for a cause. He fought because he was placed or driven into a position where he must fight or die. He doubted Ojeda's army had the spirit for resistance. The troops and others like them had exchanged one *presidente* for another many times. The island had a history of revolution. Even the most stupid private in the ranks must have discovered by now that the leaders of these upheavals were not worth dying for. In any event it would be the job of de Cespedes to subvert, to buy off the officers and sergeants. The enlisted men, abandoned by command, would be passive. This was an axiom. He had never seen it disproved.

Having arrived at certain satisfactory conclusions, San Martin allowed his mind to wander in fancy. Behind closed lids his eyes could see the map of the Caribbean area. Beyond this lay the fringe countries of Guatemala, Honduras, Nicaragua, Costa Rica; all held in a precarious, political balance. There lay the opportunity for subversion in the grand manner. It was a conception of Caesarean magnitude. To infiltrate them one by one, putting class against class, sowing dissatisfaction, appealing to the young intellectuals in the colleges, the poor in their slums; playing upon the fears of the wealthy until they all began to fight as dogs sometimes do in a senseless, snarling tangle, no longer knowing why they sought to tear each other apart. Then to step in with force and order, gathering them together beneath one strong hand. The idea fascinated him. What would the Organization of American States do? Nothing, probably. Each of the countries was possessed by a fierce spirit of nationalism. Each would claim the disturbance was an internal matter and reject outside assistance. There was the soft spot to be dug at—the conception of individual sovereignty to be protected at all costs. It was the weakness to be exploited. He was cynically amused by the grandiose concept. It could be done. First San Rafael and then, perhaps, an arrangement with that undisciplined, fanatical visionary Castro in Cuba. He had only to nod in the proper direction for all the material aid needed. The Communists were as eager as rug peddlers to find a lucrative corner on which to stand. He sighed. If only he were younger, possessing the drive of ambition. What an opportunity lay at hand.

It was upon this thought that he finally dozed off and slept peacefully in his garden while Serafina and Juan de Cespedes made love without love on an isolated section of the beach.

XVI.

WHERE before in the villages and scattered settlements there had been only a sullen bewilderment, a talking of things not understood, violence flared with anger as the country people rebelled against the restoration of an old and hateful order.

It was in the minds of most of them now that *el presidente* had betrayed them. No longer was it possible to say he did not know or understand what was happening. The land which had been given to them was being taken away.

First, the agents of the *patrons* had come among them offering employment as before. These many thousands of acres would be in cane. There the rice fields would be flooded. Here tobacco was to be grown once more. They had shrugged. A man with a piece of land of his own had no need to work for someone else. Although this had been reasonably stated, the agents grew angry. They raised their voices, displaying papers which certified that the land had been leased from the Government. This, also, had been met with polite skepticism. How could the Government rent what it no longer possessed? In a fury at their stupidity the agents made threats. Soldiers would come and drive them away. Labor would be brought in from another province of San Rafael, or even from some distant island. The *campesino* lifted his shoulders and said he would wait and see.

Then had come the first of the machines, the tractors and earth-ripping contrivances. They advanced upon the land as devouring monsters, tearing and uprooting. The small boundaries were swept away. The little plots of corn, tomatoes, beans, chilies and other things a man needed to feed his family were ground beneath the metal treads. The soil was churned into tumbling furrows by the blades of cultivators until where there once had been some small order was now a channeled sea. No one could say what was his or a neighbor's. The machines did not stop with the land itself. They rode over the pens for a pig or two. Where a family refused to move, a bulldozer thundered upon its mud-walled, thatched-roof *casita*, flattening it into rubble. Finally, the thing which was inevitable happened. A man, watching as a Caterpillar tractor smashed through a low wall of stones he had built with his own hands to separate his plot from another's, leaped upon the machine. With his machete he killed the driver. In an insane fury he cut the operator into a bloody pulp while his wife and four children stood and watched with silent terror. On that day other men, hearing of what had been done, came to see for themselves. They made a quiet circle about the tractor. Then, without command or suggestion, they put their strength against the machine and turned it over, burying the dead man beneath it. From the tank they drained the gasoline, pouring it upon the Caterpillar and watching it explode in the flame of a match.

The word of what had occurred spread. It was talked about in the *cantina* of a village or at a place on the road where there were small platforms for a bus stop. Someone told how he had been told, heard on the radio or even read how, in a foreign country, machines bigger than the tractors had been destroyed. A bottle was filled with gasoline. A wick of cloth inserted in the neck. When this was lit and the bottle thrown against a machine, it exploded and burned everything into uselessness.

Armed with these things, their knives and machetes, the men and even some of their women attacked the tractors, the bulldozers, the graders and cultivators wherever they appeared. They destroyed and killed until the *patrons* could no longer induce a driver to operate one unless he was accompanied by a soldier guard of the *Ruales*. An appeal from the lessees of the land to the Government was made. The people waited to see what would happen. Since, for the most part, the enlisted men and noncommissioned officers of the *Ruales* were country boys themselves who had enlisted in more peaceful times for the sake of a regular wage, the uniform, the status of carrying a gun, they were reluctant to move upon their own people. They were indifferent guards at best, disappearing from the fields when needed. Then they began to desert from the widely scattered garrisons. When they slipped away they took with them their rifles and such ammunition as they could carry, and collected in small groups in the hills and hidden valleys where they had been born. In idleness they passed the days and nights, for they were without any plan or even an idea of revolt against the Government. There was no anger in their behavior. They simply did not want to use their guns against those they had known all their lives. So, they made their camps. When food ran short they began to forage. They expended their ammunition on the small deer, the wild hogs and stray goats for meat.

As always, there were girls who were attracted by the excitement of this undisciplined gipsy life. They ran away from home to become the women of the men. This caused jealousies, quarrels which erupted violently into brawls and the quick knifings for the possession of a girl. They remained hidden in the all but inaccessible semijungles and cliffsides, festering slowly in their idleness, afraid to return to their barracks and the punishment awaiting them for desertion. As the time accumulated they became a terror to the villages which they began to raid for food supplies. By their own doing now they had become outcasts even from their own people. Doors of relatives and friends were bolted against them and they became shabby, furtive pariahs. Then out of boredom or because of some fancied insult they began to attack each other in their hideouts. There would be swift, vicious and deadly forays made by one camp upon another and the senseless fury spread.

In the capital city of San Rafael, Ojeda was being pressured on all sides to bring a halt to what amounted to almost open anarchy in the rural districts. For the first time there was criticism of The Benefactor in the newspapers. Save for the first few weeks after the revolution against Presidente Romero, the press had been uncensored. The Leftist paper which had hailed Ojeda as a deliverer after his land reforms now attacked him as a capitalistic tool. The conservative papers cautiously pointed out that governmental policies were without purpose or direction. The American Embassy and the Consulates of European countries requested an audience. There were large investments of their nationals in the mines, mills, urban businesses and ranches. They wanted reassurance that order would be restored and the island not torn apart by a full-scale revolution. Capital began to be drained off and San Rafael's reserves were dangerously low.

Each morning one of Ojeda's secretaries placed a seemingly endless list of appointments on his desk. To the presidential offices came a delegation of the island's oldest families. These were the men whose landholdings had been measured in miles and their mines in mountains. Their roots were generations deep in San Rafael and they had never spoken the name of Ojeda save with contempt and hatred. Now they came, not with their hats in their hands as had the *campesinos*. They approached with a tight-lipped pride and anger. They still considered the land as their own. It had been taken from them by an autocratic decree and distributed among the people. Then, because they had no choice, they had leased back their property from the Government. A workable contract had been made for the *ejidos*. They demanded that the Government restore a measure of security and use the Army if necessary.

Ojeda listened to them all. He heard the complaints of the bankers, the Association of Merchants, representatives of the bondholders, operators of the great hotels. The Tourist Bureau reported alarming statistics. Several steamship lines had threatened to eliminate San Rafael as a port of call for their winter cruise ships. He met daily with his Cabinet, listening to the advice and protestations of the men he had placed in high office and could dismiss tomorrow if he so decided. Still, he had done nothing. For the first time he displayed an indecisiveness. He was reluctant to send the Army against the people even though it was obvious the *Ruales* who remained in obedience were unable to control the situation.

Juan de Cespedes, at his place at the long table where the Cabinet members took their seats, studied Jorge Ojeda while the Ministers suggested, pleaded and advised for a course of action. It was impossible, Juan thought, to read anything in Ojeda's expression or to guess at his thoughts behind the screen of words. The session ended as they always did. Ojeda stood up abruptly. It was the signal. The Ministers gathered their papers, their notes, their portfolios of statistics and recommendations. They left reluctantly, with solemn and unhappy expressions. Again no decision had been reached; no word of reassurance offered by *el presidente*.

Juan remained in his chair, ignoring the quick glance of impatient irritation from Ojeda. He sat at the table, tapping it soundlessly with the eraser end of a pencil. Ojeda walked to a window and stood there, back to the room.

"*La huera.* That blonde. She is too much on your mind, *presidente*." The opinion was softly voiced.

Ojeda whirled with quick anger. He turned upon de Cespedes, who lounged comfortably in his chair eying him with a quizzical interest.

"Is that what you think?" Ojeda's question was harsh.

"I don't know what to think," Juan confessed easily. "Always before there was no hesitation. You made up your mind. Then together we did what your mind told us to do. Now, it seems to say nothing and so, we do nothing. *Que pasa?*"

"What happens is that I am confronted by fools." Ojeda made a gesture of weary assent. "Stupid *guajiros* who want only to squat on their land and say it is mine. Fifty or a hundred boys from the *Ruales* who have deserted and now live in desperation. Can I shoot them all?"

"A few years ago you would have done what was necessary." Juan watched him. "More, you would have done it yourself at the head of your own troops. Now you grow a little soft. There is too much heart and not enough head. The Army could clean this situation up in a couple of weeks."

"For that I have a Minister of Defense." Ojeda's gaze of implied criticism was cold.

"Is that what you want, *presidente?*" Juan's tone was finely edged with sarcasm. "Do you want me to do the job for you? Would you trust me to issue a general mobilization order, with the Army at my back, *presidente?* Think what might happen to you."

"Stop calling me *presidente*." Ojeda had difficulty in controlling his voice. "I have never demanded that of you. I don't want a revolution, Pepito."

"You have one already." Juan lit a cigarette and leaned back in the chair. "It is a small thing and one to be controlled by a strong man. But," he gazed at the ceiling, "you can't have it both ways, *compadre*. It must be either with your *niños* or those of the old families such as the Dessalines."

"Stop bringing up her name," Ojeda snapped.

"Is she a secret between us?" Juan was undisturbed. "I am smart enough to know you can't run in the middle between two packs. You move with the old families or the *gente baja*. Only you can decide how it is to be. You stand by the leases of the *ejidos* to those like the Morales, the De Landas, the Dessalines and the others. You send out the Army to enforce them. Or, you side with the little ones; let them have their land and do nothing but pee on it." Juan paused. "I said once before," he continued thoughtfully, "we have had the best of this. Let us take what we can get now and quit. I would not mind too much being a fisherman again. It is better than the Presidio."

"No!" Ojeda's fist slammed upon the table. "I did not come this far to run like a rabbit because a few dogs bark."

Juan shook his head. A faint smile of understanding and sympathy touched his lips. "Always," he spoke slowly, "we must come back to the same thing. La Dessaline. As *presidente* you may have her. But does she go with Jorge Ojeda, son of a Tampa cigar maker? I don't think so. Neither do you." He closed his eyes and scratched his head against the chair's back.

For a moment Ojeda stared at the half-reclining figure. There was anger in him for a moment and then it drained away, for there was too much truth in what Juan had said. He understood how close they all stood to revolution. It always started with the poor in the slums of a city, and in the country among the peons and the laborers. It ran as a small brush fire now because there was no leader to order the piling of fuel upon it. Before this happened it must be stamped out. He would not deny what de Cespedes had said about Ferris Dessaline. Without what he had he was nothing. He had no trade but that of fighting and revolution. What was he to offer such a girl if he lost now what he had fought for? Hand in his pocket, his fingers closed upon the crisp bonded paper of a note. It had been delivered by messenger. On it she had written:

Madame Cleo will see the President. What do you do now?

F

He half smiled and wondered. Did the President call upon anyone? It had never happened before. The smile vanished. He must first find a solution to the trouble without provoking more. But there had to be order in the country before any real decision or program could be reached. One step at a time. The deserters from the *Ruales*—a disorganized rabble with no purpose but to spread terror. They must be brought in for trial or destroyed in their pockets of abscess.

"I will do it myself, Pepito." He spoke his thoughts aloud.

"*Que?*"

"Take a mobile unit, a couple of platoons, and put an end to this business with the *Ruales* who went over the hill. You may be right. I grow soft in this chair. But it isn't as you think—in the head."

"I'll keep an eye on the chair while you're gone." Juan stretched lazily and affected a yawn. His eyes, though, were brightly inquisitive. "I might even sit in it and try it on for size."

Ojeda shook his head. "It wouldn't fit you, Pepito."

"Maybe you're right." Juan accepted the implied warning indifferently. "You know. With enough trouble in the country we may have no need of San Martin after all. It is too bad. He is so eager and has so much money to spend. He burns with the ambition to be a *presidente* again. It doesn't make any difference to him of what. Why don't we make a deal and sell him San Rafael? Then, you could take it back with a counterrevolution. The people would rally behind you as the deliverer from a foreign oppressor. Once again you could be the true champion. I can almost hear them screaming in the plaza now. *Viva! Ojeda! Viva! El Bienhechor!* We might even get another statue of you in the park. You haven't had one for a long time. That is a bad sign." De Cespedes examined his fingernails with an exaggerated casualness.

Ojeda studied his companion without expression. "You have developed an unsuspected capacity for cynical intrigue, Pepito."

"I only begin to think of my old age and a little something put by with which to enjoy it. I wonder," his thoughts rambled, "if the Duke of Alba's cousin is still alive. He would be over a hundred by now. It is possible. He was as tough as a hickory nut. He always said he would live as long as it pleased him. When he no longer found pleasure in life he would die. He could still be there on the beach with his accordion, a jug and, maybe now and then a woman." He swung booted feet to the table, regarding their high polish with pleasure. "What a chance we have missed here. By now we could be men of wealth and in comfortable exile someplace. Instead, I begin to feel a prickle of fear along my spine. It scratches like a nettle beneath my shirt."

"When it is over for us here, Pepito"—Ojeda was gravely amused—"we shall have no need for money. So why worry about it?"

"I know." There was a note of weariness in the voice of de Cespedes. "You hear the voices." He turned this subject. "This business in the *campo*? When will you go?"

"Day after tomorrow. I have an engagement first."

"More important than bringing what could be a revolution to an end? I tell you these people are not going to give up their land. You shouldn't have given them a taste of it. A few deserters from the *Ruales* are the smallest part."

"I will keep my engagement first, Pepito." The decision was final.

Juan shrugged and dropped his feet to the floor. "Then you will do it as you have always done and I will go along with what you decide because it has become a habit." He grinned companionably. "Maybe, on that very first day on the beach, I should have run like hell and never looked back."

Ojeda shook his head with a smile. "What we have had between us, Pepito, is a rare thing among men. Truth. Confidence. Trust. Respect. Love. If you do not object to the word."

De Cespedes spread his hands, palms up. "I only object to ending with you against the Presidio wall. When you see that in your tea leaves, let me know. Now." He stood and made a short, mocking bow. "*Con su permiso, presidente?* I have things to do. A full-dress inspection at Fort San Felipe this afternoon. Presentations of citations to the motorcycle corps of the city police. A banquet at El Mirador this evening. It is no small thing being Minister of Defense. I still think I would rather be a sergeant." At the door he turned. "Give my regards to La Dessaline. I still don't think you will get her entirely or that any blonde is worth what you may have to pay. And," he laughed with acid amusement, "it is possible I may be included in the cost. *Que pricio!*"

Ferris was waiting just within the door as the servant held it open. She came to him quickly, lifting her face with a shining smile.

He touched his finger tips to her cheek gently but did not bend to kiss her as she so obviously expected. For a moment her eyes clouded with a question.

"Is it that official, *presidente?*"

He waited until the maid had vanished on sandaled feet and then took Ferris's hands. She drew away and made a mocking curtsy.

"Our house is honored, *presidente*." The words were murmured demurely.

"It is only that I can't always believe what I see in your face or feel when I'm near you."

"Don't be stuffy. Just a man and a girl. That's the way a Marine would describe it." She took his arm. "Now! I'll take you to our Leader."

The drawing room was softly lighted with candles set within hurricane glass fixed to silver wall brackets. Because upon the hills at nighttime a chill settled on the air, a small fire burned in a gracefully fluted fireplace. The old lady in her chair studied her granddaughter and Jorge Ojeda as they came through the double doorway and crossed toward her. It was impossible to say what she was thinking. Her expression was masked.

"Madame Dessaline. Presidente Ojeda." Ferris made the simple presentation.

"Madame." Ojeda bowed politely, regarding her as she considered him.

"Of course. You had to look as you do." Madame Cleo made the statement unemphatically. "Otherwise," she continued, "there would be no explanation for my granddaughter's extraordinary behavior and state of mind. Rogues, at least the ones I have known, are invariably handsome. Rogues and villains." She catalogued her summary. "Usurpers and tyrants." She completed the description in a gentle voice. "They always seem to bear classical profiles. I suppose that is because they are forever having medals bearing their likenesses struck off for distribution and sale. It is a source of income not to be ignored."

If Ojeda thought the old lady's words extraordinary, he concealed the impression. He met her gaze as impersonally as she evaluated him. He was aware of a small pressure from Ferris's hand within his arm. It was a touch of silent laughter.

"I am being deliberately offensive." Madame Cleo made the statement with quiet satisfaction.

"I frequently use the same method, madame." He nodded understandingly. "Make a man angry and you have him at a disadvantage."

She ignored the comment. "At least," her glance flicked over him, "you keep yourself well. Most of our Presidents, after a few years in office, begin to run to fat around the belly. Please sit down."

He took a winged chair facing her. Ferris sat in a corner of a small divan where she could watch them both.

"There are cigars in that box on the table." Madame Cleo indicated the humidor with a small lifting and turning of her hand. "May we offer you something? What do pirates drink these days?"

Ojeda took one of the panatelas. "I don't imagine their tastes have changed much, madame, since your husband's great-grandfather sailed the waters off the Main, preying upon the ships there."

A sudden brightening of her eyes betrayed Madame Cleo's amused interest. She lifted a small bell and rang for a servant.

"So, you know about Pierre?"

"I have made a point of studying the history of your family, madame. We have some things in common. As a matter of fact I know a great deal about you."

A maid came to Madame Cleo and waited.

"We have some rum, put down many years ago, which is as rare as fine brandy?" The old lady made a question of the words.

"Thank you." Ojeda nodded.

Madame Cleo gave the order and waited until the girl had left the room. Ojeda examined the cigar between his fingers and then lit it carefully.

"You were saying?" Madame Cleo prompted.

"I was saying," Ojeda continued, "my interest has not been limited to the Dessalines' family history. It includes your current activities."

"Yes?" She invited him to continue.

"I know, for instance, that you together with half a dozen of the old families are constantly plotting and encouraging a counterrevolution. This has been going on for years. Lately you have stepped up your efforts. I could give you names if you want them."

"I am aware of the names of my friends." The retort was sharp.

"I know, also"—he pursued the subject calmly—"you have even gone so far as to plan a staging depot to stockpile arms and, later, gather men on an offshore island called The Goat's Neck from where, when the time came, you hoped to launch an invasion of San Rafael."

"Massau!" Ferris's exclamation was surprised and involuntary.

"Naturally." Madame Cleo spoke to her granddaughter with a complacent air. "You don't imagine I summoned him here that day for a social visit!" She directed her attention again to Ojeda. "If you had this information why did you permit the situation to exist and possibly expand?"

"Because you are beating at the air." He smiled, not with amusement but with understanding. "It would be as sensible to arrest a troop of children who paraded across the plaza with wooden guns."

"That is insolent." Madame Cleo's anger betrayed itself.

He shook his head. "You, madame, display the insolence and arrogance. I consider your activities and intent an irritation, perhaps, but not a real threat. Otherwise," he spoke with complete impersonality, "I should have had you all arrested long ago."

The old lady eyed him coldly. He met her stare. Then she relaxed. Filling a small glass with the amber rum she turned it in her fingers, admiring the color before touching it to her lips.

"A real danger can be dealt with in the Presidio." The statement was amiably phrased. "A nuisance must sometimes be endured."

"I find you stimulating," Madame Cleo admitted. "Detestable but stimulating. The fact, however, that you excite my interest in no way affects my opposition to you or your relationship with Ferris. I'll admit you are not without a certain primitive attraction. You also have an agile mind, which was rare in your predecessors." She sipped the rum. "They were, for the most part, men of little imagination." She paused thoughtfully. "Am I to assume you have come here this evening to ask my permission to marry my granddaughter?"

"No, Madame Dessaline."

"I thought not." She turned to Ferris. "Is it your intention to disregard my wishes in the matter?"

"Yes, grandmother." Ferris matched the even tone of the question.

"Then there is nothing I can really do about it, is there?" She was thoughtful. "In another era"—a faint, rueful smile accompanied the words —"I could have threatened you with the convent or sent you packing off to Europe. That was the way things were handled then. I don't suppose such measures or threats of them would have the slightest effect upon you?"

"No," Ferris admitted. "But I should be happier with your consent."

"I refuse that." The reply was coldly adamant. Having disposed of the subject, she turned again to Ojeda. "You have maneuvered yourself into considerable trouble, haven't you?" There was no mistaking the malicious satisfaction in the question.

"There is nothing in the situation which I can't handle, Madame Dessaline."

"Your land reform program was an outrageous and extravagant gesture. Why did you make it? It was unnecessary and created nothing but trouble. By the way, while you were expropriating so willfully how did you happen to overlook the Dessaline estates and distilleries? They were ripe plums for the picking."

Ojeda refused to be nettled. "They were included in a list prepared for me by my Minister of the Interior. After I read the report I decided they were being run better than the Government could do the job. I confiscated only where real abuses existed. As to the redistribution of the land, it was a mistake. I made it. I will correct it."

"I could have told you it wouldn't work." There was nothing smug in the statement.

"Unfortunately," he smiled at her, "I didn't ask your advice."

"The congenitally indolent and irresponsible do not become industrious simply because they are given a few acres of land." There was impatience in her tone. "They remain what they were. But"—there was no doubt of the spite in her voice—"they will fight you now to hold what they have. Eventually, you will be confronted by a complete revolution with the paradox of the old families and the peon standing against you. When that happens, you will go the way of the other adventurers who have occupied San Rafael's Presidential Palace. You will have to run for your life as did those generals, Morillo, San Martin, Torralba, Batista, Perón, Jimenez. The list is endless. What will you do then? Where will you go? Do you imagine I would subject Ferris to that willingly; give my consent to her exile? No. What you offer is shabby, furtive and completely unacceptable." Madame Dessaline placed her empty glass on the table. "Now, if you will excuse me. I am tired and in danger of losing my temper."

Both Ferris and Ojeda stood up. The girl came to the old lady's side as she rose and touched the pale cheek with a light kiss. For a moment grandmother and granddaughter gazed at each other. Finally, Madame Dessaline relented. She touched her finger tips to the girl's chin with a gesture of affection.

"Unfortunately you will go where the blood calls, where the heart cries. I have also known love. Don't think me a stranger to it or insensible. I do not say I know what is best." She included Ojeda in her words now. "I am agreeably surprised by you. I can understand the attraction. Yet you remain what you are and your end will be no different than those who have practiced the same tyrannical methods. You will die at the hands of an assassin or be deposed by a stronger, shrewder man. They will hang you by your heels as they did Mussolini or shoot you in the Presidio as you have had men executed there. Is it true," her eyes searched his, "as I have heard, that you personally executed Raúl Valdez and the others? You actually held the gun?"

"Yes." He met the accusation calmly.

"Why?" She was curious.

"Valdez and his *junta* were a threat to me, to Jorge Ojeda. He wanted what was mine and was willing to pay for it with my life. Also, he had pretended to be my friend and so the punishment was a personal thing between us. I took no real pleasure in the executions. But I felt better for carrying them out myself. Raúl Valdez was a soldier, an officer in the army I had made. He understood what he was risking. You cannot fail at treachery more than once. Does that answer your question?"

Madame Cleo eyed him steadily for a moment and then nodded. She hesitated as though about to reply and then changed her mind. Without a word to either of them she turned and walked with a quiet, proud dignity from the room.

Ferris watched her go and then shrugged and smiled regretfully at Ojeda. "I'm sorry. That is the way she is. I really didn't expect anything more. Simply talking with you was a concession." She took his arm. "At least we tried."

His hand covered hers with a warm reassurance. "I've never met anyone quite like her. Anger without spite. Resentment without fury. The serene conviction that her judgment is unassailable. I don't imagine she ever questioned her right to do exactly as she pleased."

"Have you?" Ferris asked innocently.

"It's not the same thing." He was honest. "Hers comes from generations of breeding. I have had to build my confidence block by block. It's not the same as being born with it. I would like to know how that feels." His glance covered the simple perfection of the drawing room. "This"—a lifted hand indicated the walls—"this room and the house are what I mean. How is it to be reared here and take it all for granted?"

They took places on a low settee in front of the fireplace. Her arm was still linked with his and she leaned slightly to rest her head against his shoulder.

"I know so little about you." The statement was made, not as a question but with a certain wondering regret. "Sometimes I ask myself, How can you really be in love with a man you don't know? It should be important, but somehow it isn't."

The burning logs of cedar flaked away in golden scales and blackened quickly as they cooled. He watched them, his eyes bleak. She had, without pressing, made it possible to say what should be said. He turned away from the answer.

"I'm going into the provinces tomorrow. Maguey. Serrita. Tulare. I don't know how long it will take until I can put an end to the trouble there."

Her concern was immediate. She straightened up and faced him with obvious surprise.

"Why you? Is it something the President has to do himself? You're not a sergeant in the Marines any more. You know the stubborn temper of the country people. Haven't you officers in the *Ruales* or the Army you can trust? Are things that bad?"

"If this isn't the President's job it isn't anyone's. I can't afford to turn it over to someone else. There is too much at stake. Force will not do what must be done. Not," his smile was wintry, "if I want to remain *presidente* of San Rafael."

"And, of course, you do?"

"Is there an alternative?" He was genuinely surprised by her question. "I have no profession but that of arms. I was and am good at that. It brought me where I am from nothing. So, I hold this or my hands are empty. What road leads from the Presidential Palace? There is none, not for Jorge Ojeda. I knew that when I walked through the doors for the first time. It was the calculated risk. I took it."

"When will you be back?"

"When what I have to do is done. Some frightened, young *Ruales* to be brought in, punished and disciplined. The people in the country persuaded to do what they will not want to do; some of the old landowners made to understand this thing cannot be done as they once did it, with whip and gun."

She stared at the flames as they leaped and twisted within the fireplace. Her lips were softly parted, turned in a barely discernible smile of resignation.

"This is a damnable thing." She spoke quietly. "For the first time in my life I feel helpless; a captive to something I don't quite understand. I don't think I want to be in love with you, Jorge Ojeda. But I can't help myself. It is a hell of a damned thing." Her voice rose in protest. "What is noble, beautiful or sacred about love if it leaves you naked and vulnerable, at the mercy of your emotions? I don't want to be frightened or concerned over what may happen to you. It strips me of all self-confidence. I am as—as helpless as a soft-shelled crab." She finished with a burst of anger and then laughed but without amusement. "That's a fine comparison, isn't it? But you must know what I mean. I'm not made for the role of a passive woman sitting in a corner by the fire, waiting for her man to come home. It isn't decent. I was all right before you came along."

He turned her to face him. "Were you?"

For a moment she seemed ready to pull away from him, resenting his touch. Then she shook her head and came into his arms.

"No." The voice was muffled. "I was only part of a woman. I suppose this is the female's destiny no matter how she may rebel against it. I don't suppose you can go through life without loving anyone or anything simply because it may leave you open to being hurt."

He kissed her with infinite tenderness, his lips brushing the corner of her mouth, touching her cheek, her hair. She sighed with a troubled contentment.

"This is as new for me as it is for you." He held her. "I have no defense against it; no preparations made."

"Then I guess we're stuck with it and all the complications, *presidente.*" She made an attempt to smile.

He stood up, lifting her by her elbows to stand close beside him.

"I have to go now. There is an emergency meeting with Sebastian, the Commandant of the *Ruales,* Juan and some others. San Rafael isn't a capital city the President can leave, even for a little while, and be sure he will still be President when he returns; not lately, at least."

"I wouldn't mind. Your not being *presidente,* I mean. Honestly." She stared up at him. "It is the least of your attraction for me."

He shook his head. "It isn't that simple. What would I do? What would you say? 'This is my husband, Jorge. He used to be *presidente.* Just now he is out of work and looking for a job. Maybe you know of something?' " He thought for a moment. "I'm not even sure I could go back to the United States and if I could, to what?"

They walked together through the long hall toward the entrance. A maid sat with quiet patience in a chair. She stood quickly to open the doors for them, glancing shyly at Ojeda. He smiled at her and nodded.

In the driveway the black official limousine waited. At the sight of them the chauffeur straightened, quickly dropped the cigarette he had been smoking and covered the butt with his heel.

"I always wanted to ask." She posed the question with an assumed lightness. "Is the glass in your car bulletproof?"

"No."

"Do you mean it?" She was surprised. "I was only joking."

"It won't happen that way." He spoke with a quiet conviction.

For a second or two she stared at him and then turned away unhappily. The chauffeur was at stiff attention, holding the door.

"I'm not sure what one says at a time like this, *presidente*." Some of the old mockery, but gentle now, was in the statement. "So long. Have a good trip. Give me a ring when you get back." She paused. "I don't give a damn if your man is watching." She strained to her tiptoes with a quick eagerness. "Kiss me good-by."

For a moment they were sculptured into a single figure. Then he reluctantly let her go. His fingers touched her cheek and chin as though to memorize the features.

"I'll be back." He was reassuring.

"You damn well better be back," she whispered fiercely, "or I'll sue you for breach of promise. I'll scandalize your name."

She stood at the edge of the broad walk ending at the driveway's edge until he had entered the car. The chauffeur closed the door and, turning, saluted her respectfully before sliding into the front compartment. Then she turned away and walked toward the house without looking back.

Ojeda stared straight ahead, past the chauffeur's shoulder. The car descended rapidly, tires hissing on the bluestone gravel. Waiting behind the turn below the house, a motorcycle escort of four policemen moved at the first sign of the headlights. They fell into position, two in front, two at the rear, to pace the car's swift progress. Ojeda appeared not to notice them.

Below lay the city, spread in a twinkling pattern, and a faint aurora was a gauzy curtain against the sky. He had given it light where once only smoky kerosene lamps had burned. Light and order. Swamps had been drained. The fetid *barrios* which had once crowded the water front, noisome and disease-ridden in their wretched confusion, were gone. Narrow, unlighted streets had been paved. Fine roads spanned the island. There were schools, hospitals, free clinics, a central employment office for urban and rural districts. The old, time-honored system of petty graft, the *mordida,* the bite by police and minor officials, had been abolished. These things he had done—not out of love or compassion but on the theory that what was good for San Rafael was good for Jorge Ojeda. He had given the country discipline. It had been drilled to a cadence by which the people marched, each man knowing what steps he should and could take. The people had a security they had never known before. Those in opposition had talked of a police state. Their alternative had been the slovenly confusion of generations. Ojeda had allowed them to talk. His methods had been as thorough, as uncompromising, as those of a Marine drill instructor shaping a contingent of raw recruits. Now, though, he was being confronted by a restless muttering and an uneasiness in the city. He would deal with both in turn. What he had made he would hold. It was a simple conviction, arrived at by a boy in a pine flat years ago. You crawled with the fleas or you trained them.

From the last, sweeping elevation of the road he could see the white marble dome of the Capitol. It loomed above the low buildings surrounding the central plaza. In the night it was a smooth, Junoesque breast picked out by the floodlights concealed within its base. There, in an office, Colonel Sebastian of the *Ruales,* the Minister of the Interior, Juan de Cespedes and half a dozen ranking officers of the Army waited. Each, Ojeda thought, was in his own way wondering what personal advantage might be snatched from the troubled situation. Each, he qualified the opinion, each save, perhaps, Juan. A faint light of humor rested in his eyes for a moment. Even Juan. Who knew?

He spoke softly to the chauffeur. *"Al capitolio. A todo correr."*

"Si, presidente."

The chauffeur touched the siren's button, and at its wail the leading motorcycles leaped ahead with a quick acceleration as they swung into the long *avenida* at the end of which was the Capitol Building.

XVII.

THEY came. The angry. The frightened. The confused. They were set down at Miami's International Airport by regularly scheduled flights or in planes commandeered in mid-air by gun point. They came ashore furtively from small boats at scattered places along the ragged coastline of the Keys and made their slow, uncertain way to the city, to be absorbed by the swollen Cuban population.

Miami, magnificently shining and proud on its fine bay and the long, white beach of the ocean peninsula, didn't know what to do with them. There were doctors, teachers, lawyers, engineers, dentists, students and shopkeepers. Some had friends and relatives to whom they could turn. Some had nothing at all. Few spoke English. None of them wanted charity. They sought work and refuge from the hysterical oppression of their homeland. They filled the streets of the Cuban section, milling in a restless discontent. They listened to the radio, watched television and read the Spanish-language newspaper. Behind them they had left their homes, their professions, their businesses and their studies. They talked hopefully of a counterrevolution against Castro. Some even drilled without arms in the parks, preparing for the day. Some had a little money. Others arrived with no more than the five dollars the Castro Government permitted them to take from the country. Lawyers offered to wash cars. A surgeon became a headwaiter in a nightclub. Wives who had once employed their servants now sought a cleaning woman's work. The young and the eager filled the cafés and coffeehouses. They argued with each other and fought with the pro-Castro element. Washington appropriated a million dollars to assist the city in caring for the refugees. It was a temporary measure and no answer to the problem. Everyone knew this.

Each morning, when the doors opened at ten o'clock, a man appeared at a café, La Casita Blanca. With him he brought money and a smiling air of confidence. Word of his presence and mission spread from ear to ear. He took a table at the rear of the room, ordered coffee and waited. They came, singly at first and then in pairs or groups of three and four. Some the man at the table rejected at once after the most casual inspection. They were too old, too young, too frightened or bewildered and had no real heart for the job being offered. Those he selected, strong, young enough and with a deep anger in them, he talked with in a low, compelling voice. Some who came to him had been officers in Batista's army. Others had been the original revolutionaries with Castro in the mountains when the bearded ones had numbered no more than one hundred determined men. Now, these were disillusioned. They were in exile with little aptitude for anything save soldiering. To these the man at the table offered immediate employment, but the thing to be done was stated in vague terms. Desperately needed money was passed from his hand to theirs. To all was promised the hope of a liberated Cuba.

First, though, there was another job to be done. He would not say what or where but only that an island republic in the Caribbean was to be set free. After that had been accomplished, with additional forces at their command and the island serving as a steppingstone, an invasion would be launched against the pro-Communist government of Castro. Cuba would be unchained and they could return in safety to their homeland. The "volunteers" would be supplied with the best of everything in arms and equipment. Experienced officers would lead them. The way for a successful assault was even now being laid within the unidentified country. Already there was revolt steaming in the rural districts. The Army could be counted on to offer no more than a show of resistance; shots fired in the air. There would be nothing to block a triumphal march into the capital. No names were mentioned, no island area indicated, but those who gave the offer serious consideration suspected the identity of the target.

Other men came to La Casita Blanca. They answered the call of General Chivas San Martin from Guatemala, Mexico and the Gulf ports of Texas. These the man at the table welcomed with effusive *abrazos* as old companions in arms and intrigue. They talked animatedly as conspirators in a familiar cause. Little by little the nucellus of revolution was formed and about it the mercenary army was gathered. No attempt was made to hide what was going on. A section in the pine flats northwest of the city was leased and on it a small community of tents sprouted. Word was openly spread that the men who lived and drilled there had as their objective the overthrow of the Fidelistas. The authorities were embarrassed but decided to look the other way. In Havana the Castro press screamed that the United States was encouraging and supporting an invasion of Cuba. Washington pretended it didn't know what was happening and the city of Miami was secretly glad to be relieved of a few of the refugees who were pouring into the city by the hundreds each week.

There began to arrive in San Rafael, by scheduled air flights, couriers in the guise of tourists, and the liaison between San Martin and the agents in Miami was established. The F.B.I. reported these tourists to the American Embassy in San Rafael and Ojeda's secret police followed their movements in the capital and prepared a daily memorandum for the President and General de Cespedes. No attempt was made to obstruct their movements.

In the seclusion of his villa General San Martin fretted impatiently. Things were going well. An army was being whipped together but nothing was happening fast enough. To purchase the arms and equipment, to pay the "volunteers" in Florida, and to keep pace with Juan de Cespedes' constant demand for more and more money with which to subvert key officers in San Rafael's Army, he had drawn heavily on his accounts in Switzerland. He was risking everything—his fortune, his life—on the word of one man. Juan de Cespedes. The timing, he understood, must be exact. What drove him into a frenzy was the fact that the most opportune moment of all was at hand and he was not ready. Ojeda was in the country chasing deserters from the *Ruales* and lending the stature of his office to quelling the discontent among the *campesinos* over the problem of the land. De Cespedes was in virtual control of the city. Never would such an opportunity present itself. He pleaded with Juan.

"It could be done now." They sat over coffee and brandy in the dining room of the villa. "Even without the volunteers in Florida. With Ojeda away, you command the Army. What have you done with all the money I have given you if it has not been used to buy the loyalty of the garrisons?"

Juan was indifferent to the protests. "Some of it I have spent where it will do the most good. Some of it I have kept for myself." He winked at Serafina.

"Then," San Martin's tone changed to one of pleading, "intercede with the American Embassy and get me a visa so I can go to Florida and see for myself what is going on. I do not fully trust those who have reported to me."

"Take my advice and don't trust anyone." Juan was bored. "I don't. Anyhow, there is no need for you in Miami. If you identify yourself with the recruiting there then its real purpose becomes known."

"I am spending hundreds of thousands of dollars." San Martin almost wailed his protest. "I would like to see for myself where it goes."

"You would like to lead a parade down the Avenida de Independencia here, in San Rafael." Juan was contemptuous. "This you would like to do in full uniform and in safety after the shooting has stopped. Well, you must wait for that time. Let your agents in Miami handle things there. When the time is ready we will move."

"But now, with Ojeda out of the city." San Martin made the suggestion eagerly. "Never, if you have done your part, such a chance as this."

"The *presidente* is not too far away and," Juan's eyes lighted with amusement, "don't underestimate his hold on the Army. He made it and he is a tough man in a fight. I should know. I have stood beside him. He is in daily touch with his Ministries here and with me. It would not take much to bring him back."

"How do I know you are not playing me for a fool?" San Martin pleaded for reassurance.

"You don't."

San Martin stared at him for a moment and then wearily drooped his head in assent. How could he know? At this time some things must be taken on faith. The hope on which he leaned was propped on the conviction that a man's greed superseded all other emotions. He had to believe this was true of Juan de Cespedes.

"As you say," San Martin stood up, "I will believe what I want to believe." He walked to a cabinet and took from it a map of San Rafael. He spread it on the table, weighing it down with glasses at each corner. "Show me where you plan a landing when the time comes and how we go from there. I am not completely without experience in military problems. Let us consult together. This much, at least, I am entitled to know."

"If you insist," Juan humored him. He took a pen and marked a section of the coastline. "Here the beach is easy. Small boats can get within a man's wading depth of the shore. It is flat, sparsely settled country with only a few villages to the town of San Sebastian here." He drew a circle. "There is a motor vehicle pool in Sebastian. Also, it is a junction point for the railroad and two main highways. We take that and the garrison there by assault. That may be the only real fighting. With San Sebastian we get transportation—trucks, weapons carriers. The railway we cut. I will have arranged things so the troops stationed at Fort San Felipe, here in San Rafael, are on maneuvers. Ojeda will have nothing but the police force and a small, frightened militia to cover the capital. We walk into the city and it is over." He tossed the pen indifferently aside.

San Martin studied the map with growing excitement. This was a thing he could see with his eyes, understand with his mind. The seemingly impossible was not impossible for a man of resources and determination. He even began to feel a little easier over de Cespedes' part in the venture. The man was no fool. He had his own neck to protect in this affair. He would not stretch it out too far.

"It seems feasible." San Martin rolled the map and put it away. "Simple. Direct. I like that." He stood thoughtfully for a moment and then glanced at Serafina. "I am retiring now to read a little and think for a while. Perhaps you will be good enough to entertain General de Cespedes." He seemed to take a sardonic pleasure in his own cuckoldry.

"I will do my best, Chivito." She turned a flawless and indifferent cheek for a perfunctory good-night kiss.

"I am certain you will."

He bowed with a formal dignity to Juan and left the room. Juan looked after him and then at Serfina. He filled his small glass with brandy and lit one of the General's cigars.

"God, but I am bored with this place!" Serafina rested the back of her head against the chair and stared blankly at the ceiling. "Pour me some brandy, Juanito. Will you take me with you when you leave here?"

"I don't think so." He made the statement without a note of regret. "Besides," he was cheerfully casual, "think of the future. You will be the wife of President San Martin. That is, of course, if you can get him to marry you."

She lit a cigarette and eyed him over its tip. "I think Chivas is a fool to trust you."

"He has no choice."

"I suspect you intend only to get as much money out of him as you can and then turn him over to the police to be thrown into the Presidio as a political prisoner. It would serve him right. He should be satisfied with what he has. But, no. He is a man who, like a dog, is forever trying to run off with another's bone. All men are stupid. Unfortunately, for a woman, life is unendurable without them. Perhaps," she yawned, "the Lesbians have the only sane approach to life after all. Tell me," her thoughts wandered, "is there anything to the gossip I have heard concerning Ojeda and this Dessaline girl? It is a comical situation. I hear the old families are outraged."

"I don't think Jorge or Ferris Dessaline give a damn what anyone thinks." He finished his brandy. "I have to go now."

"Chivas asked me to entertain you." She pouted a little.

"Some other time."

She shrugged and rose from the chair. "You see how clever he is? By accepting our little intrigue he reduces it to nothing. Already we both are becoming bored with the situation. It has no spice. *Que lastima.*"

She did not see him to the door but rang for a maid, who brought his uniform cap. Serafina nodded an indifferent reply to his word of good night.

In the car which was waiting to take him back to the Presidential Palace Juan leaned in a corner of the seat. His eyes brightened with amusement as he thought of San Martin. He understood well enough the General was already wondering frantically how he could rid himself of Juan de Cespedes once the revolution succeeded. There must, also, be a flaming hatred within him for the man who had so casually appropriated his mistress. Juan chuckled softly. If the old man only understood how simple were the desires of Juan de Cespedes he would sleep easier at night.

He leaned forward, opened a compartment in the back of the front seat and took out a cigar. The taste of San Martin's brandy was still pleasantly fragrant in his mouth. He lit the tobacco and drew upon it with pleasure. He marveled a little at the curious, almost dreamy sensation of complete peace which enveloped him. Once certain things had been decided, a course of action accepted, he found himself without doubts or hesitation. Now what he planned seemed right; almost inevitable. He was plagued by no nagging conscience or division of loyalties. One step followed another, as a man might set his feet to walk upon a line.

The heavy upholstery cushioned him as he rested upon it. The car moved with a silent swiftness, taking the wide curves with perfect balance. He caught himself thinking of the old man and the beach at Coronado. The memory came to him often these days, almost as though something dreamed. The Duke of Alba's cousin and his accordion and how he had talked to a son with quiet authority and a wide range of knowledge. There had been between them a great affection and the pleasure in sharing a life which now seemed incredibly simple. Then Jorge Ojeda had come to them and this, also, seemed as it should be for there had never been the feeling he was a stranger. Closing his eyes he could feel the hot sun on the clean, white dunes; the faint, indefinable perfume of scrub palmetto when it glistened with the damp pearls of early morning; the way the racks of mullet, smoking over the smoldering bay wood, had glistened as they cured and the flaky, white meat falling apart in his fingers. He smiled a little, recalling how he and Jorge had brought the old man a case of fine Burgundy, a pale Montrachet, from the Bahamas. He had tasted it with critical approval and then reached for the wine he made himself from the wild scuppernong grape. So much, he seemed to say, for France's Côte d'Or and its vintages. He smiled, remembering the old man's quiet stubbornness. How then, he wondered, had he been spun out of this placid orbit and whirled effortlessly to this pinnacle? Jorge, of course, was the answer, and he, Juan de Cespedes, had followed without questioning the path or where it led. Because of this the son of a fisherman rode now to the President's Palace; held the title of General and Minister of Defense; was the *compañero*, the *compadre* of the man who had taken this island as his own.

He studied the fine, white ash on the cigar's tip and mused on the thing which had happened. The years had not dulled the wonder. But, he confessed, he was no longer exhilarated by the dangerous heights upon which he stood. There was in him an uneasiness; a conviction that the icing had been eaten from the cake. He could not deny the satisfaction which his position gave him. It was something to command respect, obedience; even fear. To know that by speaking a word or scrawling his name he could give or take away a career, or even a life. Yet he could not rid himself of the notion that this was the summit. From this peak there was no safe and easy road down.

He called the chauffeur. At the moment he had no wish to return to the empty cavern of the palace. The car swung into the Avenida de Septiembre Cinco, renamed to commemorate the liberation of the city by the forces of General Quatero under the command of Captain Jorge Ojeda. It was gaudily bright with neon signs; the haunt of tourists on the prowl for night life; noisy with the cries of street vendors, lottery ticket sellers and the music which spilled from the clubs and bars. At another time, he thought, Juan de Cespedes could have strolled into one of the bars or the sidewalk cafés, picked up a girl and spent the night, drinking a little and later making love. This, and he grinned ruefully, was forbidden to the Minister of Defense. Everything he did was tightly ringed by a tiresome importance. Even such a simple, elementary thing as making love to a girl was all but surrounded by invisible attendants and protocol. Even with ladies of position and good birth he must always wonder what they sought in return—a favor, a promotion for a husband, father or brother, a word in the ear of the *presidente*, information on the matter of a Government policy. He sighed with a mocking grin. When a woman made love with a fisherman it was because she liked the fisherman.

The Avenida de Septiembre Cinco ended at the great crescent drive along the water front. Here the hotels were jeweled towers. Lights spread in rippling waves from the yachts anchored in the bay and the night was filled with a soft murmur and the faint sound of music. Aboard any of the shining craft the Minister of Defense would be a welcome guest. He had only to halt the car and call for a tender or water taxi. More than that, if he wished he could send word to the management of any of the night clubs and have it cleared of all patrons save such girls as he might desire. The doors would be locked, the orchestra and staff placed exclusively at his disposal, and no one would question his authority or even right to do this. He shook his head. There was a somber mood upon him and a night of such carousing would be as tasteless as flat champagne.

He spoke an order to the driver to return to the palace. After they had left the city's central section and started the long climb he caught himself wondering where Jorge was this night. Somewhere in the mountains or camped in a valley, prying out a few scared *Ruales*. He would be sleeping in the open as a common *soldado*. He would do this, not as an affectation but because he was at heart a soldier. He liked the cold feel of a gun in his hand; the order and discipline with which he was surrounded. But, Juan thought, nothing of what he was doing approached the heart of the trouble. He must reach some terms with the country people. There the pot boiled. He must kick it over or put out the fire. Logic, argument, explanations, would not do.

As the car passed through the gates with the sentries at attention he absently replied to the salute. He was puzzled by Jorge's indifference in the matter of San Martin. It was one thing to set up a cardboard counterrevolutionary movement with someone with the stature of San Martin as a scapegoat. This was common enough practice in an uneasy, internal situation when the President's position required strengthening. It was something else again when the farce began to grow out of its designed proportions and become a real threat. It needed but the resolution of Juan de Cespedes to make it so and he wondered if Jorge didn't realize this.

For the first time Juan realized completely what it was he held in his hands. It was only by his choice that a mock revolution did not become real. In Miami there were already men who waited for guns to be put at their disposal. Other men, wise and experienced in the ways of revolution, were eager to lead them. Money and equipment was at Juan de Cespedes' command. He could, if he wished, force the decision. Mulling over these things, he discovered the notion of complete duplicity fascinated him. Also, he began to understand the almost irresistible appeal of total power coupled with danger. These were the things which drove men to the heights from where they could hurl the lightning. The idea of possessing sovereign authority, exercising it upon the minds and lives of others, had the fascination of a beautiful and thoroughly corrupt woman. It became almost irresistible. Yet—and as he pondered on this he came to an astonishing conclusion—it must be coupled with the element of personal risk. He remembered a gambler he had known in Florida and recalled the man once saying if you didn't bet more than you could afford there was no real excitement in the turn of a card, a throw of the dice. Unless it could hurt it meant nothing. The hazard must be there, for it generated the all but unendurable stimulation. Now he placed the situation upon the scales. At what peril did or could Juan de Cespedes use Chivas San Martin and Jorge Ojeda against each other? What pit of oblivion lay on the dangerous path between them? He laughed softly to himself, feeling his pulse quicken as his imagination explored such a situation. The car was eased to a smooth halt before the imposing entrance to the palace. Sentries posted at both sides of the wide flight of steps presented arms with the crisp slapping of hands on their rifles, and a guard moved quickly to open and hold the door for him.

Inside he went first to his own rooms and poured a drink of brandy, swallowing it in a single gulp. Then, on a sudden impulse, he walked down the long corridor to the wing which held the President's suite. Actually, the rooms differed little from his own. He did not turn on the lights but stood in the silent gloom. It was, he thought, a strange thing. Four or five silent, empty rooms, and yet, they were filled with a mysterious and disturbing current as though charged by the personality of Jorge Ojeda. He could all but feel Jorge's presence. The walls, the furniture, the thick carpet on which he stood, were impregnated with the man's quiet force. He turned a little uneasily and with the sensation of being watched. Then, almost too hastily, he moved to the hall and closed the door hurriedly behind him, feeling a quick relief in the barely audible snapping of the latch.

In the blackness of the mountains there was a bone-reaching chill. Stars were hard, diamond points in the sky and a wind riffled and played through the treetops. About a central fire the men of the patrol were ringed. Two jeeps and three canopied troop carriers were drawn up to form a sheltering wall. Standing against the vehicles, staring blankly at the whipping flames, were the prisoners. What they wore now were only the dirty, often ragged, remnants of uniforms of the *Ruales*. They were all young, none over twenty. Fear and shame were stamped upon their faces. They pulled nervously at the short butts of cigarettes cupped within their hands, pinching them until the live coal seared their fingers. Now and then one would dart an apprehensive glance toward the awesome figure of *el presidente* as he stood apart, eating from a common mess kit. When the flames ran along a vein of pitch in the logs of pine the sudden flaring of light illuminated his features. In them none of the captured could read a sign of thought or intent. The time would have been more easily endured if they could only know what was in his mind. Were they to be punished; shot now, in an hour, in the morning? Would the trucks carry them to prison or to years of labor in a camp? Speculation became an agony. Perhaps, at this very moment, he was forming the order which would call upon a firing squad and so all life for them would end on this night which already held the bitter chill of death. Yet, and a few snatched eagerly at this hope, there seemed no real anger, no fury, in the eyes. They were almost sad.

Pressing against each other for warmth, the prisoners considered the incredible thing which had happened to them. Pursuit they had expected. Squads from the *Ruales* garrisons would scratch and comb through the hills searching for them but there would be no real heart in the chase. Hunted and hunter were all boys of the country and none would look too diligently for an old friend or neighbor. What had filled them with a superstitious terror was the word that *el presidente* himself had come after them. It was as though God had come down to point an accusing and identifying finger in the direction of their hiding places. How was a man to escape this awful vengeance?

Ojeda wiped at the bottom of his pan with the end of a tortilla and finished the hot, black coffee in the aluminum cup with its folding handle. An orderly came to take the utensils and washed them carefully in a separate kettle of steaming water. Although they pretended a hungry absorption in their own food, the men of the patrol were acutely aware of every move *el presidente* made. When he lit a cigarette the soft scratching of the match and the sudden, flaring cone of light lifted their heads as though jerked up by a single cord. They also could not fully believe what they had witnessed this past week. It was impossible *el presidente* had undertaken this tiresome mission himself. It was a thing to be handled in a leisurely fashion by a few squads of men led by a lieutenant or even a captain; an excursion and a relief from the boredom of garrison duty. Why had *el presidente* given it this importance? More than that, he had conducted the search with the true, sure instinct of a fighting man. Now they could believe the stories of their parents how he had created an army out of almost nothing and led it down from the mountains to take a city and the country with a few hundred men.

He was, in truth, a *jefe maximo*. Now he stood smoking after eating as any soldier would. The uniform he wore was little different from their own; of finer cloth, perhaps, but without the mark of rank; no gold braid, no stars upon the shoulder. When they slept upon the ground he had slept with them. The food they ate was also the food which the orderly brought to him in the issue kit. The jeep in which he rode, leading the motorized column through the hills, the valleys, the mountain villages, bore no flag of *el presidente* or identifying insignia. Instinctively they sensed there was honesty in this. He was not playing at being a soldier nor did he seek their favor by pretending a common touch. It was only when he spoke or gave a command to be relayed to them that they were aware of the complete authority. There was no mistaking who *el presidente* was then. The even confidence in the voice told them. They had talked among themselves, each adding some small detail of how this had been done there or something said here. Piece by piece they built a mosaic of a man into legendary proportions. He had hunted with the sure instinct of a ferret. The word that *el presidente* himself had come was spread quickly, and hearing this the deserters from the *Ruales* had broken their slovenly camps, their shabby collection of palm-thatched shelters, and scattered; singly or in pairs they ran as animals to find a secret cave or a covering in the heavy woods and jungles, hoping to gain a place of safety until the danger had passed.

Methodically Ojeda had followed. He took a scrap of information from a man in a village, another shred from a farmer, a word from an angry woman or girl who had been molested or abandoned by one of the deserters. From these he created a map in his mind, an area to be searched. Where there had been no roads and not even a trail for the burros of the charcoal burners to follow from the hills they had gone on foot. He strode at the column's head, an automatic rifle slung over one shoulder, taking the miles at an effortless pace as though the march were a daily, routine thing. Each man had marked how *el presidente* did certain things, and in his own way sought to imitate his bearing. There had been a dark cave in which half a dozen of the deserters had crouched. They had long ago expended their ammunition but their knives, bayonets and machetes were formidable. Ojeda had walked in alone while the patrol waited apprehensively outside. He came out, herding the refugees ahead of him, and the rifle still hung at his shoulder untouched. From the caves, the miserable hiding places in the jungle and the rocky retreats in the mountains they had taken the terrified deserters. Almost one hundred had been returned to the garrisons of the *Ruales*. Only once had shots been fired and then by *el presidente* himself. He loosed a burst over the heads of three panic-stricken men who had bounded from a hiding place to race through a savanna of waist-high grass. They ran in unreasoning desperation as wild things. At the rifle's cracking they halted, frozen and unable to move, waiting dumbly to be taken and punished. They had expected fury. Instead there was a cold indifference, a contempt. Now, those who waited in a miserable line by the trucks and jeeps were the last of the hunted. They had no knowledge of what had happened to the others and so, this time of silence was made more terrible.

Ojeda finished his cigarette, dropping the butt to the ground and pressing it into the earth with his heel. He crossed the path of light from the fire and then walked the length of the dejected file, his eyes studying each of the men as he passed. At the end of the listless, shabby column he turned and retraced his steps until he halted at a point near its center.

Surveying these young men—these boys whose faces had grown old and gray with fear—he was uncomfortably aware of a compassion, an understanding. It was an emotion with which he was unfamiliar, for it violated everything by which he had lived. He fought against it but it would not yield. For what they had done, the punishment should be swift and not subject to sympathy. Yet in his heart he understood why these boys had left their garrisons, the duty which had set them against their own people. They came from the small towns and villages and in them there was a kinship with the land. It was the one changeless substance in an uncertain world and a man might strive all of his life to gain possession of one small piece. They had been unwilling to use their arms to enforce the decree which would take it from their own people and return it to the big estates. Because of this they had deserted, and from this one act the terror and lawlessness had spread as an epidemic among them. He, Jorge Ojeda, *el presidente,* could not dismiss his share of the responsibility for the situation created, for he had signed the order dissolving the *ejidos.* Where, then, lay the real blame?

His eyes traveled from one face to another. In them he could catch a glimmer of hope, desperation, uncertainty, dull submissiveness. Some of these things, also, wrestled for the mind of Jorge Ojeda. There had been a time when he would not have hesitated. The duty, the obligation, would have been clear, for he had held an unshakable faith in order and discipline. Without it there was chaos. Now he wavered and thought a little wearily that as he grew older the self-evident truths were no longer so clear and inflexible. He asked himself, What do I do with these boys and the hundred or more already captured? Do I shoot them because this is the traditional punishment for deserters? Do I do this because it is something I really believe or do I want to make of them an example and create the fear which is sometimes necessary to maintain order? I don't know. He made the admission wearily. To order the executions would inspire the fear but not the comprehension of duty.

He began to speak to the prisoners slowly and in the idiom of the country people. "You know there should be a punishment. You ran away from your garrisons, stole Government property; the rifles and equipment. The orders of your officers were disobeyed. Each mistake you made led to another. A pattern was created as surely as a roof is thatched by laying one palm within another. Because you violated order, disorder grew. You have raped and stolen from your own people until they, in anger and fear, have turned against you. All of this grew from a simple root. You were ordered to do certain things; to protect property, enforce a law. If I try to explain to you why these orders were necessary you will not understand, for they concern things of which you have no knowledge." They were listening attentively now. Unconsciously they had drawn themselves up to attention. "A soldier," Ojeda continued, "has but one duty and that is to obey orders. This you did not do and we come now to what is to be done with you. Do I have you shot? Do I send you to prison where you will rot away until you become old men? Do I simply release you? I don't know." He acknowledged his perplexity. Here and there his gaze was met with something close to a shy smile as though he had, somehow, become a partner in a grimly humorous game. "Do I return you to your barracks, have you scrubbed, deloused and with new uniforms and equipment issued to replace what you have lost or ruined? Surely you must have thought of what might happen to you. Tell me, *niños.* I am listening."

He stood waiting, knowing there would be no reply. His glance traveled up and down the line. The eyes were flinty now and beneath them the prisoners were uneasy again. They shuffled their feet, pretending an intense preoccupation with the ground. They sensed a decision and were unwilling to meet it.

"Go home." Ojeda made the statement with a flat indifference. "You are no longer men of the *Ruales.* Return to your homes and villages and tell those who ask that *el presidente* sent you away because he was ashamed of you as soldiers. Go now before I change my mind." The final command was harshly impatient.

He turned his back on them and walked away to where he had stood on the opposite side of the fire. For a moment or two there was no movement. Then one by one they detached themselves from the abject file. A few, starting away, even turned to glance back at the figure of *el presidente* as though they struggled for words of explanation or, perhaps, even gratitude. There was a silent plea in their eyes for understanding. Ojeda ignored them. They slid off into the night, disappearing quickly; carrying with them their humiliation.

A corporal among those ringing the fire rose and pulled a fresh log onto the glowing heap. The light flared brightly and the troops stared at it as though hypnotized. Ojeda was lost in a contemplation of the night into which the prisoners had vanished. He was oblivious of everything else. Finally, he spoke with a weary indifference to a young lieutenant.

"We'll go back to San Rafael in the morning. There is no need for a guard. Call the men at daybreak." He gave the order absently and as though it were of no consequence.

"*Si, presidente.*" The officer was at attention immediately and Ojeda dismissed him with a casual wave of the hand.

For a time Ojeda stood where he was, then he dropped to the ground and rested his back against a tree, feeling the fire's warmth as it flooded out to reach him. He had an uneasy feeling he had acted unwisely. The heart inexplicably ruled the head in a situation where there should have been no place for emotion. Having turned these few deserters loose without punishment he must now extend the same clemency to those who were confined to the rural garrisons. He was disturbed by the over-all effect this would have on the *Ruales* and, for that matter, the regular Army. I grow older, he thought moodily, and no longer hungry. My guts do not cry out for the meat of this job.

He lit a cigarette and the tobacco was flavorless. Save for the rounding up of the deserters, the mission had been a failure. In the villages and towns where the column had halted there had been no excitement over the unexpected appearance of *el presidente.* There had been a ceremonious welcome by the local officials; a gathering of the curious when the detachment halted. But, and it was impossible not to sense this, the speeches, the words of welcome, had been stiffly formal. The people of the country had stared with a masked politeness which was unmistakably sullen. The man who had given them the land had taken it away. Beyond this simple fact they did not inquire. There was suspicion now where once there had been a wild, unquestioning enthusiasm. Yet he would not, could not bring himself to talk to them as the simple people they were.

The Department of Information, in San Rafael, had broadcast the facts of production and why crops must be grown to feed the mills and factories. A corps of lecturers had traveled from town to town, city to city, village to village throughout the island, and at public meetings had attempted to make the position of the Government understandable. Mobile units, with projectors and generators, were sent into the most remote of the rural districts. On a screen, strung many times between a couple of palm trees, the people were shown the progress of the cane from the time it was cut in the fields until it spilled from the refineries and distilleries as sugar or rum. A sound track explained each step. Similar films were run showing the picking of cotton to the finished bolt of cloth. Rice from the paddies to the box on a grocer's shelf. Cattle from the ranges to meat, fresh in the butcher's shop or tinned on a counter. Through all of these things an attempt was made to show the people their interdependence; how one supported and made possible the livelihood of another. The *campesinos,* most of whom had never seen a motion picture, squatted cross-legged on the ground and watched with loud murmurings of astonishment over what they looked upon. But, the Ministry of Information conceded unhappily, they regarded the showings as a form of entertainment which had no connection with their everyday lives. Nothing moved them from the stubborn determination and will to own their small pieces of land and work them as they pleased.

Ojeda finished his cigarette. The orderly was making his bed, laid upon branches of pine heaped upon the earth and no different from those made by the men themselves. Ojeda nodded and rose, stretching the weariness from his limbs as he stood up and then walked to where the blankets were spread.

"*Buenas noches, hombres.*"

"Buenas noches, presidente." The words of reply came with soft respect.

Wrapped in the warmth, eyelids drawn against the light's flickering, he sought for the oblivion of sleep but it would not come. The mind kept shifting from one thing to another with a maddening persistency. Never did it remain on one problem long enough to reach even a partial solution. He was fully aware of the pressures and their danger. With a keen instinct for the temper of the country people the Communists were growing bolder daily with their propaganda. The hard core of radicals had always existed but a succession of dictators had kept them underground. Now, sensing a wavering on the part of the Government, encouraged by what had occurred in Cuba and bolstered by the cautious offers of assistance from Russian and Chinese agents outside the country, they were growing increasingly militant. The soil had been fertilized for their sowing. The wealthy, the privileged of centuries, who had regarded San Rafael as their own, were angry and dissatisfied with the Government's half measures which had produced nothing but further disorder. The *campesino* was a stubborn burro, refusing to be led or driven. So, he mused ironically, do I shoot them all? Do I fill the prisons with the malcontents? Or do I permit Juan to continue; allow more than a token revolution to erupt and then by crushing it unify the country behind Jorge Ojeda against a common enemy from the outside? There was, he knew, real danger in this.

In the semidarkness he wondered a little about Juan and General San Martin. Do I trust you, my fisherman? he asked the question of himself. Have we finally come to the time when you would like to be *el presidente?*

Juan had briefed him fully on what was transpiring between him and San Martin; the recruiting going on in Miami; San Martin's growing impatience. But, the question repeated itself in his mind, what of Juan himself? In the devious folds of a man's mind strange things hatched themselves; ambitions ovulated, power became attractive. It was something to remember.

He was startled into full wakefulness by the abrupt realization that part of him was completely indifferent to the extent of Juan's or San Martin's ambition. This dollop of coral and granite, of plains and forests, jungles and mountains, rising above a jasper sea. It had been contested and fought over for centuries and he was but one more of the men who had wrenched the power from another. What, in all truth, was it to him? He felt no real love of country for it. Always, in his heart, he had been the alien usurper. In the conquest there had been excitement; the keen edge of knowing the stakes were no less than his life; the sensation of standing on the peak from which lesser men continually sought to dislodge him. As though there were a complete division of mind one part of his brain supplied these answers. The other half reasoned coldly. He must hold what he had, for there was no other place for him to go. If he was not *el presidente* then he was nothing.

Jorge Ojeda, ex-Marine sergeant with no trade, no occupation but that of soldiering. Was this all he had to offer Ferris Dessaline? You are my love, my life. He spoke the words to himself. A girl beyond anyone or anything I have ever imagined. I have nothing to offer you but a gipsy's existence wrapped in the bright kerchief of my love. Share it with me. It would not do and he knew it. So, he must fight if necessary to keep what he had even though the coins now held a counterfeit ring and could buy nothing but time and too little of that. He wondered desperately whether he and Ferris Dessaline could endure the truth. More frightening than this was the question: Could they survive the lie?

Sleep would not come and he lay awake throughout the long, silent night until the eastern sky broke apart with the smoky color of an oyster, and the men began to shift restlessly with reluctant awakening on the cold ground.

XVIII.

OUTWARDLY there was no change within the capital city of San Rafael. On this morning it lay as if newly washed and burnished beneath a bright sun. The first of the early traffic began to flow into the main arteries and in the business district there was the familiar, gonglike clanging of the iron shutters as porters cranked them up over the display windows of stores and shops. As the tempo of the day increased, the shrilling of traffic officers' whistles grew louder and more frequent. Air brakes on the buses hissed as the vehicles halted to load and unload. Cries of the news-boys became louder and the pulse of the city quickened.

In the markets the cooks moved with sedate dignity from stall to stall, their baskets carried by trotting boys. They fingered the mounds of fresh fruit and vegetables with an assumed critical disapproval. The produce still held the smooth chill of the hills and country fields. Fishing boats, their sails rippling limply as the wind spilled from them, eased into the quay. From their places on the docks the buyers shouted the prices they were pre-pared to pay for the catch. In the parks the boys with their shoeshine boxes took their stands before the green benches and waited for the first customers. Men halted to study the lottery listings posted on bulletin boards or sat at a sidewalk table drinking small cups of black coffee as they read their pa-pers. Heavy black type across eight columns announced the triumphal re-turn of *el presidente* to the city. Broadcasters had been on the air earlier with the news. The expedition was extravagantly proclaimed as a triumph of wisdom and justice in which The Benefactor had displayed courage, determination, tempered by mercy. Order had been restored. The renegades, the deserters from the *Ruales* who had terrorized the country, had been captured. Correspondents who accompanied the patrol gave eyewitness reports of how *el presidente* had led the operation; what he ate, where he slept, how he had done this or that and with what understanding he had handled a difficult situation. The editorial writers, skilled in the craft of saying nothing while indulging in hyperbole, performed the adroit exercise of expressing no opinion while seeming to state one. Men read and were pleased, angered or puzzled according to their tempers and understanding. The more thoughtful followed the columns of print, stared at the photographs and realized that, save for the captured deserters, the heart of the situation remained untouched. And so, as they talked of this later, a strange undercurrent of uneasy tension began to run below the surface. Nothing, save a semblance of stability, had been achieved.

At midmorning the most liberal of the newspapers, *Hoy!* appeared on the streets. For years it had been published almost furtively, existing only through Ojeda's tolerance. Its radical opinions were cautiously expressed and then, usually, in the typical Latin-American form of a question such as: IS THE GOVERNMENT TYRANNICAL? or DOES THE GOVERNMENT ENCOURAGE PEONAGE? It rarely mentioned *el presidente* but made all comment as though no individual existed as head of state and the Government was an amorphous thing without form, body or identity. This day though, made unaccountably bold, *Hoy!* denounced the expedition as the use of overwhelming force against a few ignorant country boys who had refused to harass or fire upon their families and friends, who had resisted Ojeda's plan to return the people's land to the great *estancias*. Ojeda's part in the operation was characterized as a cheap theatrical trick designed only to give him stature in the eyes of the privileged and ignorant.

After one glance at the screaming headline the news vendors kept *Hoy!* out of sight beneath their counters, and the street peddlers inserted their copies between the issues of the pro-Ojeda papers and sold them only upon request and then with hesitation and fear. In the offices of *Hoy!* the editor waited for the arresting police while in the *cantinas*, the larger bars, the restaurants and coffeeshops there was violent discussion as to what action the Government would take. Nothing happened and this only served to increase the uncertainty in the minds of the people.

In the American Embassy the Ambassador discussed the intemperate and challenging tone of *Hoy!* with Kent Glastonbury and a coded cable was sent to the State Department in Washington. No one was quite sure what had suddenly emboldened the openly but heretofore cautiously proCommunist newspaper. From what unknown source had sprung this courage and what, if anything, did it mean? Either San Rafael was perilously close to revolution in the country or the editor and publisher of *Hoy!* was a reckless fool who deliberately walked to a wall in the Presidio. The latter seemed most unlikely; the former unthinkable. At the Ambassador's request Kent telephoned the Capitol and was told *el presidente* was unavailable at the moment. It was impossible, unfortunately, to arrange an appointment. The voice of the secretary was courteous, regretful, but Kent thought he detected a nervous uncertainty as though things were, somehow, mysteriously out of place. Then, ignoring the diplomatic niceties of the situation, Kent made a personal call to the Presidential Palace. Carlos Ponti, Ojeda's secretary, explained that *el presidente* had slept late this morning; the return to the Capital had been made hours after midnight. When he awakened he would be informed of Señor Glastonbury's inquiry.

On the east terrace of the palace Jorge Ojeda sat at his breakfast. He drank the first cup of coffee black and then the servant brought fresh china and a pot of coffee with hot milk. Ojeda squeezed half a lime over the golden meat of a halved papaya. On a chair beside him were the morning newspapers and atop the pile the edition of *Hoy!* As he ate, Ojeda glanced down and sideways at the paper.

He looked up as Ponti came across the terrace. The young man carried an envelope in his hand.

"This was just delivered, *presidente*. I thought you would want it now."

Ojeda took the square of heavy, gray-blue paper across which was scrawled the bold handwriting of Ferris Dessaline.

"Sit down, Carlos. Have some coffee." He slit the envelope open with a knife. "There are the morning papers." He indicated the stack. "If you haven't already seen them."

"It is an outrage, *presidente*." Ponti's voice quivered with emotion. He took a chair on the opposite side of the table and sat stiffly. "Such a thing is beyond journalistic license. The man should be arrested; publication of the paper suspended."

"Have some coffee. It is good for the digestion." Ojeda smiled. "Ramos would like to be arrested. He would not like to be shot, of course, but merely imprisoned for a while. He courts martyrdom within safe limits."

"The American Chargé d'Affaires telephoned, Excellency. He said it was personal and unofficial."

Ojeda nodded. "Later, Carlos." He gave his attention to the letter, his eyes lighting at the salutation. *Presidente!* He understood that this form of address amused her and appealed to an impish sense of humor. "We will talk of everything later." He began to read.

It is a relief to have you home although Madame Cleo does not entirely share my sentiments. It was her pleasant notion one of the campesinos would cut your throat, disposing of you for all time. To say I have missed you would be an understatement. To write more than that would embarrass me. Also, I have been a little angry with you over what seemed to me to be a dangerous and most unnecessary gesture. To that extent I share the sentiments of Hoy! On what strange meat does this Ramos feed these days that he has grown so reckless? Anyhow, it has been a new and disturbing experience for me to worry as I have over a man. If this is love then a fig for it; whatever that may mean. In the hope that I will see you this evening I shall put perfume behind my ears and a light in the window.

F

He smiled and carefully refolded the single sheet before replacing it in the envelope. Then he put the letter in his pocket and lit a cigarette. He leaned back and regarded Ponti with an indulgent smile.

"Now, Carlos." He nodded his readiness to discuss the secretary's immediate problems. "What is on your mind other than indignation?"

Ponti flushed lightly. *El presidente* was being almost paternally indulgent. More than that, he appeared to be completely indifferent to the implications of *Hoyl's* personal attack, refusing to take it seriously. However, he was too well schooled in his job to press the matter.

"There are no appointments, Excellency." He was formally correct again. "Nothing was scheduled since we had no way of knowing when you would return. Tomorrow is the regular Cabinet meeting with your Ministers. Do you wish to see Señor Glastonbury?"

"Not particularly." Ojeda leaned back and stared at the high, cumulous fleece of clouds as they gathered above the distant mountains. "I suppose, though, I will have to. Call him back later with my apologies and an appointment at his convenience. Here. Has General de Cespedes left the Palace?"

"General de Cespedes has been away for the past four days, Excellency. I have not seen him."

Ojeda dropped his gaze from the sky, caught the disapproving look in Ponti's eyes. Actually, there was no reason why Juan should have been waiting at the palace for his return. Yet he was mildly puzzled by his absence.

"Very well, Carlos. There is nothing more."

Ponti nodded, rose and with a short inclination of his head left him alone. Ojeda folded the knuckles of one hand into the palm of the other and blew with a soft, whistling sound between the finger openings. What are you up to, Pepito? The question was in his mind. He wondered why. A feral instinct for danger? He shrugged off the notion; not because Juan de Cespedes or any man, for that matter, was above suspicion but only because he felt he knew and understood this one so well. Pepito had what he wanted—splendid uniforms, a position of authority, money as he needed it. His ambitions were at the level of a beautiful woman's bed. So, Jorge decided, he had a new girl and was shacked up someplace. He would return when he had wearied of her, filled with the cock's strutting of conquest. Having answered this question his mind turned to the Cabinet meeting tomorrow. There was no problem here. The men appointed were the best he could find but the ultimate decision on all matters rested with the *presidente*. He would, as before, listen to the reports, the recommendations and then pronounce his conclusions. Out of its creation by force the Government was, of necessity, that of one man. To this San Rafael was acclimated.

He lit a fresh cigarette from the stub of the old, his thoughts roving over the solemn charade which would take place in the Cabinet Room tomorrow. It occurred to him he might remain here in the palace for months and the affairs of San Rafael would move in an uninterrupted flow. Men would perform their duties out of long, disciplined habit and because life was simpler if they remained within the prescribed grooves. Taxes would be collected, salaries paid. The street sweeper would go to the familiar closet for his cart and broom; the Ministers of the various departments to their desks. Trains would run, mail be collected and delivered, power generated, streets and districts policed, classrooms filled and emptied. He wondered how long the momentum generated by years of unvarying practice would carry the civil and military affairs of the country on course. At what precise moment would the guiding touch of Presidential authority be needed to correct a deviation? No, he mused, order was preserved because of the physical presence of authority. It must be seen as well as felt. It was not entirely true that a thing set in motion tended to continue on its course. It was subject to too many unequitable influences. That, he thought with a quick grin, is why I shall sit at the head of the Cabinet table tomorrow so men will pause before they think of throwing a rock beneath the wheels of the carriage of State.

Although his mind had been idly pursuing an abstraction there had been a tiny gnawing uneasiness. On an impulse he left the terrace and went into the small library which served him as an office within the palace. There were four telephones of different color on the desk. All had direct lines to key departments. He picked up one. This flashed a light at the headquarters of the Federal Police and would be answered by no one but the Commandant himself. For a moment he hesitated, curious as to his motive. The

Federal Police was actually San Rafael's Central Intelligence Bureau. Through it pulsed every activity of the island's life. From the arrival of the most casual tourist aboard a cruise ship down to the coffeehouse *juntas* of revolution and discontent, all were minutely noted. It was as sensitive as a cardiograph to every murmur, each flutter of the country's heart. Those who despised the dictatorship referred to the department and its officers as the Secret Police, the Gestapo. Yet it had been no creation of Jorge Ojeda's. In one form or another each *presidente* had employed it as a matter of self-preservation.

"Si, *presidente!*"

The response to the lifting of the receiver was immediate. Throughout all these years, Ojeda thought, he had never touched this particular instrument without finding Colonel Pio at his desk. He wondered, and was on the point of asking, whether the Commandant took an extension of the telephone with him when he went to the toilet.

"General de Cespedes?" He made of Juan's name an unmistakable question.

There was an all but imperceptible hesitation at the other end of the line. Ojeda could feel it. Then Colonel Pio's reply came deliberately; without surprise, without insinuation or implication.

"In Miami, Florida, *presidente*. Since Tuesday of this week." This was the information requested. This was the information given. Colonel Pio waited.

"Yes, Colonel . . ." Ojeda prompted but betrayed no interest.

Pio, in a flat tone as though reading from a report waiting on his desk for this moment, continued.

"On Sunday evening General de Cespedes had dinner at the home of General Chivas San Martin. On Monday he held a review of troops at San Sebastian. Tuesday morning, at five thirty-seven he was flown in an Army plane from Carrantas Field. The flight plan was for San Isidro. Instead, at General de Cespedes' direction the course was changed. An emergency request for a landing was made of the authorities at Santiago, Cuba. From there General de Cespedes was driven to a dock and boarded a cabin cruiser, *La Golandrina*, owned by General Raúl Cortez, former aide to General San Martin. The craft was presumably on a fishing trip but the information has come to us that General de Cespedes was put ashore somewhere on the Florida Keys. He is at present in Miami."

"Thank you, Colonel." Ojeda hung up.

He stood by the desk, his hand pressing the receiver into its cradle. A soundless whistle puckered his lips and then he spoke the question in his mind aloud.

"*Que pasa, Pepito?* Do you play seriously at this business of revolution?"

A lizard, its gun-metal sheen striped with vertical markings of red and yellow, raced as a brilliant streak up the table's leg. With a stiff wariness it halted an inch or so from the heavy, clasped hands of Massau.

There was an understanding of sorts between the black man and the little reptile. It came often this way to poise itself with ornamental stiffness when Massau sat or worked here. The reward was a half-dead fly or a crippled ant which the man held captive beneath a downturned water glass in anticipation of the visit. The lizard never saw beyond the fingers or a portion of the hand which lifted the glass and pushed the offering of food toward it. When this happened a gland within the sleek throat grew swollen with greedy hunger. The head darted forward and the insect vanished. Then the lizard, expecting no more, disappeared as flashingly as it had come. For his part Massau was delighted by the grace and coloring of the lizard and the fact it displayed an intelligence beyond caution. He had come to expect the visit.

Today there was no fly, no ant. The hands and fingers did not move. Massau ignored the jewel-like creature. He was staring at the finished carving before him. It was the jade given months ago by Marchand. Now that it was completed he wondered how and why. In a strange way he was a little frightened by what had evolved. It had not been a thing done consciously. At least, he could not remember at what moment it had started to shape itself beneath his fingers and he became aware of what was happening. The figure had flowed from the carving tools until now it seemed he had no part in its creation but it was mysteriously done for him.

His hand reached out and at the unexpected movement the lizard fled. Gently, Massau's finger tips traced themselves over the curiously warm, almost fleshlike texture of the jade. What he had carved was a native girl, bare of foot, one hip thrown out as though to hold a basket. It was the face though which held him, for the features, to his eyes, were those of Ferris Dessaline. Yet, and he almost pulled away fearfully, there was an unmistakable Negroid quality about the mouth and the nostrils. What he had captured was such a subtle blending he could not be sure it existed beyond his imagination. How would other eyes see this? He pushed it to the far edge of the table for better study. Still he was not certain. He bowed his head. This was a lie. It was there. A wave of superstitious terror swept upon him. In a moment of desperation he reached over, picked up the figure and was on the point of smashing it against the heavy table. He could not bring himself to the destruction. Carefully, regretfully, he replaced it. Then he covered what he had made with a piece of cloth. He would keep it here and no one should see it. If Marchand asked what he had done with the jade he would show him nothing nor speak of what carving upon it had been made. If, and this was possible, the art dealer became insistent then he would find some way to repay him for the stone. Marchand himself had said it was not of great value, being of Mexican origin and not of the fine quality with which the Oriental artists worked. So he would pay for it by bringing the dealer other carvings in wood which he could sell and Massau would take nothing for his work.

Impulsively, he swept the cloth from the figure. He could not deny himself the artist's pleasure in what he had fashioned. There was great beauty in this thing, terrible though it might be. Examining it he could almost hear a black girl's husky, insinuating laughter, smell the musky odor of her body, hear a chanting song within the throat as she swung with a careless grace down a dusty road on her way to market. He even began to understand why he had done this piece in just this way; knowing the dark blood of *el presidente* sought to blend itself with that of Ferris Dessaline and so color her shape and existence. Only a black man, he thought, would know and recognize what he, Massau, had done. He looked about the room for a place to put the carving. It wanted light, the warm rods of the sun as they came through the window. He would build a small shelf high on the wall where the flaming colors of the afternoon's late sun would bathe it. Here it would be safe from curious eyes and only he would know its secret radiance.

Juan, his legs stretched comfortably beneath a table in the little café, La Casita Blanca, sat with three men who regarded him with anxious hopefulness. Before them were the small cups of black coffee and between them a half-filled bottle of the brandy of Pedro Domecq.

Listening to their whispered talk, Juan's thoughts slid back easily through the years to another time and night when he and Jorge Ojeda had waited at just such a table and in just such a small café. He sought in his memory for its name and then it came to him. La Ballena. He laughed suddenly and his companions looked up quickly, surprised. They were respectfully curious.

"It is nothing," he explained. "A thing came to my mind. That is all." He wiped one hand across the table as though to erase a memory.

"You have seen all of what we are doing and have done," one of the men said with a quiet intensity. "Tell us now what you think, General. Is it good enough? Can we hope to succeed with what we have?"

Juan shrugged and thought to himself, There is no real dedication in these men. They are *politicos* seeking an advantage for themselves.

For the past two days he had lived in harassing discomfort, sleeping on a cot in a faded tent, washing and shaving in a pan filled with swamp water, eating soggy, greasy, tasteless food. Within a section of the vast tract of scrub- and pine-forested flatland a few miles north of the Tamiami Trail a camp had been established. Here the recruits for Chivas San Martin's army of the revolution struggled against boredom, inefficient planning, inadequate supplies and an absence of real purpose. Through the careless ranks ran the small stench of petty bickering between those who sought to establish for themselves positions of authority. No over-all command had been achieved, no discipline forged. There was a surface appearance of military order. Tents had been pegged down in two rows. Between them the trucks which brought in the supplies from the distant city had churned deep ruts, slashing out what passed for a company street. A bugle recording blasted reveille through a loud-speaker and the men turned out reluctantly to stand at indifferent attention for an unnecessary roll call. They had no place to go. A uniformity of dress had been made possible through a purchase of khaki trousers and shirts, army surplus shoes, socks, underwear. There the resemblance to troops ended. They were without arms, inspiration or leadership. Their mission, if any, was a matter of individual translation and each man worded it according to his own desire, hope or fear.

Most of the recruits were Cuban refugees. They were, or had been in their country, a segment of the disillusioned middle class—clerks, professional men, students, operators of small businesses, barbers and taxi drivers. All, for one reason or another, had fled Cuba. In Miami, at first, they had found a sympathetic welcome and the first few were eagerly greeted as propaganda instruments against Castro's communism. Refugee centers were established. Clinics and a central employment office opened. Gifts of money and clothing were freely made. But as the numbers increased, the problem created could no longer be denied. Despite the aid and a million-dollar grant from Washington—the efforts to weld the refugees into a Freedom For Cuba movement and give them a status—a stark fact emerged. Miami simply could not absorb them. There were not enough jobs for these people. Relatives who had embraced and cried over cousins and aunts arriving daily by plane and boat found themselves all but crowded out of their apartments and small homes. The city's economy was seasonal, depending to a large extent upon winter tourists. There was a pool of unemployment, and when the refugees entered into competition for work hostility developed. The water of charity grew turbid. Violence flared, resentment festered, when the dispossessed offered to take any job at any wage.

Because of these things the agents of San Martin had found recruitment a simple matter of selection. They took the strong, the young, the discontented. Shelter, food and a small wage were the inducements. The local and federal authorities were well aware of what was happening but they pretended this camp in the flatlands was an innocent expedient, financed by a nebulous charity, to relieve the congestion within Miami and ease the tension. There were rumors, of course, that the camp was training anti-Castro Cubans who would eventually overthrow the bearded fanatic. Washington declared it had no knowledge of such preparations.

Among the volunteers were a few professional soldiers. Some had fought for and with San Martin in his own country. A few were adventurous mercenaries. Others had served in the army of Batista. San Martin's agents snatched eagerly at these and gave them the job of whipping the recruits into shape. With a contemptuous impatience those with training attempted to drill and mold the raw material which, for the moment at least, must use sticks for rifles and vocal noises for the sound of shots. Their disgust over the ineptitude of the material was in every command, each gesture. Only the fact that they were generously paid kept them at their posts. This and a hope of eventually finding places of authority and prestige with the success of San Martin's chimerical revolution were the spurs which made them try to do the job. There were, though, Cuban men of sincere will who believed, or wanted to believe, San Martin's agents who had assured them the army, once formed and triumphant on San Rafael, would then be turned against Castro. These patriots attempted to keep the sharp edge of fervor honed and ready. For the most part, though, there was apathy and a listless attitude toward an unidentifiable goal.

This was what Juan had seen. It had been the reason for his sudden trip—the flight from San Rafael to Cuba, the secret landing from a boat. The craft had taken him in and through one of the many cuts leading from the sea to Key Largo. There he had been met by a car and San Martin's men and shuttled to this camp. He had made the voyage because he wanted to see for himself what San Martin's agents had accomplished. Also, he had grown weary of listening to the General's fretful complaints about the money being spent, the absence of any real information. He had urged the inspection tour on Juan as one of necessity and self-protection.

"Tell us, General de Cespedes," the man opposite Juan at the table repeated his question, "is it enough what we do?"

"It is nothing." Juan was blunt. "It will continue to be nothing but a free flophouse and soup kitchen unless you get those men out of that camp, put real guns in their hands with ammunition in the chambers. There is something about a loaded rifle that lights a man's desire to use it."

He poured himself another brandy and studied the grave expressions of the trio. In them, he thought, there was no fire beyond that of personal ambition no matter how earnestly they protested their devotion to San Martin. Already there was graft in the purchasing of supplies and equipment. Each was trying to cut himself a slice of the cake San Martin was so hopefully attempting to bake. They struggled among themselves with a silent ferocity to get control of the funds which San Martin was releasing to them for the formation of this revolutionary army.

"Right now"—Juan swallowed the brandy—"your volunteers couldn't take a water pistol away from a child."

"What do you suggest, General de Cespedes?"

This was the one man, Juan thought, who might be trusted. Benevades. He had been the Minister of Labor under San Martin in the old days. From this post he had formed a hard militia from among the workers and they had fanatically resisted the trained troops sent against them.

"I would put them in the mountains of San Rafael." Juan made the statement promptly. "I would move them from that camp, out of reach and touch of their wives, women, children and relatives in Miami. There they will have to learn to fight to survive. It is simple."

Benevades nodded agreement. "I think you are right. But," he smiled uncertainly, "will they go or is it as you say—a convenient flophouse and soup kitchen we maintain with General San Martin's money?"

"Tell them they are going to Cuba. How the hell will they know the difference? Even when you put them ashore, the country of the two islands looks much the same. When they find out it is San Rafael and not Havana they are to march against it will be too late. What about equipment?"

"We have the arms, General," Benevades assured him. "More are on their way. It is being stockpiled in the lower Florida Keys, near Boca Chica. There are Czech rifles, Russian machine guns, ammunition, grenades, mortars, even flame throwers. You see," he added with faint humor, "the Communists are eager to sell anyone anything as long as the purpose is to create trouble in this area. We have had no difficulty in arranging for equipment or its transport and secret delivery. In that department we have been efficient. After all, San Rafael is not such a large country. Presidente Ojeda took it with less."

"It is big enough, my friend." Juan was grave. "And a big man straddles it. Forget everything else but remember Jorge Ojeda. He is tougher and smarter than any of you. And that," he concluded with a quick grin, "includes me. He isn't going to run the way the others did."

"You come directly from General San Martin." Benevades pressed the question. "What are his orders?"

"I give the orders." The reply cracked. "It is my back, also, which might end against the Presidio wall if we fail in San Rafael. General San Martin wants only to head the parade of victory and mount the Capitol's steps." He pushed the brandy glass away with a gesture of weariness. "I am tired and itch from the sand and the mosquito bites. My belly rumbles unhappily from the food I have eaten these past two days. Tonight I will sleep in a real bed and tomorrow we will meet again. I will tell you how and where the men can be landed, how they are to be moved into the mountains for training. Until we can take part of the country and live off it supplies may have to be airlifted and dropped. There are problems you have to work out. Anyhow, all of this is something I have done before."

He stood up, not bothering to conceal a yawn. The three rose politely and shook hands with courteous and solemn gravity. Then with a brisk nod Juan left them to find a taxi at a stand near the café.

In the hotel room whose windows overlooked the dark shimmer of Biscayne Bay he lay for a long time in a hot bath. Here, in this same hotel, he and Jorge Ojeda had waited those long years past for the instructions which eventually had taken them to San Rafael. He was filled with a disturbing sense of loneliness, as though he walked alone through an empty world in which there was no sound save that of his own footsteps.

Out of the bath, he wrapped himself in a light robe and poured himself a drink. For a long time he stood with the glass in his hand, looking out over the water. On the beach side the glow of lights lay on the sky as a shimmering, gauzy scarf. Beacons winked where they marked the channel to the sea. The wind as it came through the open windows was salty and damply fresh.

He swallowed part of the whisky. It had no taste. He thought, I feel like crying and that is a strange thing for a man.

He was puzzled. At what exact moment, he wondered, had his mind turned away from the pretense of revolution and begun to plot in earnest? He was not aware of a time. He could not say, on that day, at such and such an hour, I made the decision to do this thing. Maybe the intent had been there all the time, waiting to be recognized. He could still turn away from it.

He finished the whisky and lit a cigarette. There was in his eyes a small, sad smile.

"*Compadre.*" He spoke aloud without realizing it. "You would not understand why I am doing this."

XIX.

NOW the small cells of discontent began to link themselves and multiply as a malignant cancer which spread with a flash-fire swiftness, eating away at the body of the island. That which had once seemed healthy was in a state of soft rottenness beneath the surface.

In the country the *campesinos* began a methodical campaign of destruction, willing, if necessary, to perish in the ruin they sought. Where there had been some order on the large estates and productivity, the fields erupted into flames from half a dozen scattered places. A crop waiting for the harvest was destroyed. Warehouses with their sacked grain and tobacco mysteriously burst into fire in the middle of the night. Pens at cattle-loading depots were opened and the animals stampeded. Trains were derailed, power lines cut, bridges dynamited. The fleets of fishing boats rocked at their moorings on the slick water of tiny bays and coves, and the once busy market at the municipal quay in San Rafael was deserted. The drivers of the interurban buses, long accustomed to the queues of docile, patient passengers at rural stops, now brought their vehicles reluctantly to a halt. Time after time, without warning, men armed with rifles and machetes, shotguns and knives had swept out from both sides of the road. Drivers had been hauled from their seats, beaten and sometimes killed if they resisted. With the thrusting and straining of a hundred backs and pairs of arms the buses were overturned, the gasoline tanks hacked open and fired. Instead of a few desertions among the *Ruales,* entire garrisons fled after murdering the officers. The barracks were stripped of everything and then turned into huge pyres.

Those of the country people who did not actively aid in the sabotage adopted an attitude of passive resistance. They sat on the land once given to them and would not move. Only the barest trickle of the food necessary to sustain an urban population reached the city of San Rafael. This was a revolt of dumb rage, of idiotic fury, which could not be reached with logic and reason. The families of the great *estancias* fled to the Capitol for sanctuary, leaving behind them their fine homes and most of their possessions. They traveled in a panic in automobiles which streaked through the night carrying extra gasoline in cans to avoid the necessity of stopping at a filling station where they might be ambushed, as had others before them.

Made bold by the Government's indecision, professional agitators moved openly from town and village. All opposition to Ojeda which had festered for years broke as a long-putrid boil. In the small plazas of rural villages and towns Communists harangued and inflamed the people. Militant groups of young men and girls were formed into *cazatorpederos*—the Destroyers. They began a systematic wrecking of all radio sets. They ripped the instruments from the shelves of stores, *cantinas* and cafés. They invaded private dwellings and smashed the radios with axes. No longer would the gullible be swayed by the voice and words of The Benefactor. Obscenities, coupled with Ojeda's name, were streaked in black paint on stone walls and the sides of buildings.

Because unrest is endemic in youth and the idea of revolt is exciting, its fever spread to the schools in the island's half-dozen cities and to the University at the capital itself. Students, arm in arm, marched in chanting lines which spread from sidewalk to sidewalk and brought all traffic to a halt. They gathered in the plaza before the Capitol and shouted: *Tierra o muerte!* Mounted police and the Fire Department broke up the assemblies with clubs and hose. The students screamed their defiance, melted away and scattered only to re-form at another place. Although most of them were city bred and drawn from the island's middle class, without knowledge of agrarian problems or kinship with the soil, they were loud in their demands that the Government reinstate the *ejidos* and return the land to the people.

Small planes appeared over the city at night and showered it with inflammatory leaflets calling for the resignation of Ojeda and a free election of his successor.

The hotels were quickly emptied of their tourists and Caribbean cruise ships struck San Rafael from their itineraries.

Dozens of rumors raced through the city. Ojeda had fled. Ojeda had declared martial law. A revolutionary force was concentrating in the mountains. United States Marines would land at the request of *el presidente* to restore order. Cuba was preparing an expeditionary force. China and Russia were sending "volunteers."

The conservative newspapers pleaded for sanity among the country people and hopefully suggested that the Government take the steps necessary to put an end to the anarchy. The publication *Hoy!* grew hysterically defiant. Its headlines brazenly called for a general strike by all workers in support of the *campesinos*. The Government took no measures to suppress what had become an avowedly Communistic propaganda instrument.

At an emergency meeting of the Cabinet, Ojeda listened gravely to his Ministers. There was, first, the matter of increasing food imports to supplement the meager supplies trickling into the urban centers. This was quickly agreed upon. Then came the plea that the Army be ordered out on a punitive expedition to smash the rebellion in the country. As he considered what was being said, Ojeda glanced thoughtfully now and then across the table at Juan de Cespedes. The Minister of Defense lounged carelessly in his chair, smoking a cigarette and staring at the ceiling. He appeared completely indifferent to the proceedings.

When each man at the long table had spoken of what was on his mind, Ojeda answered them.

"If the Army moves against the people"—he chose each word carefully—"it must destroy them. Is that what you want? Is that the solution you suggest? We shoot down five, ten, maybe fifteen thousand peons?" He shook his head. "That is no answer. I have never hesitated to use force. You are aware of that. It has its purpose but in this case no. This is a revolt without plan. It is a fire which must eventually burn itself out. You cannot send the Army against a state of mind. Also, this Government can only be destroyed by a man or men of determination who have something to offer to take the present Government's place. Purpose alone supplies the fuel of revolution. There is no purpose here, no leadership." He paused, his gaze on Juan. Then he added the question. "Or is there, General de Cespedes?"

Juan's shoulders lifted with a small gesture conveying ignorance of the whole matter. "There are rumors, Excellency." His eyes met Ojeda's. "You know what I know. I am certain"—then an amused smile crinkled his expression—"Colonel Pio has already supplied you with all available information and Colonel Pio is a thorough man. So far, and in your own words, this is a revolt of the ants. They swarm blindly and without direction. When I was a boy we used to pour kerosene on the anthills and set them on fire. We destroyed thousands but there were always more to build another nest. Nothing was accomplished."

At the end of the table the Commandant of the State Police, Colonel Pio, studied Juan as he spoke. If, he thought to himself, this de Cespedes plots revolution, then he manages a singularly innocent face. He had been wondering about Juan de Cespedes for a long time now.

"On your trip to Miami, General?" Pio was respectful and courteous but there was no mistaking his intent of the questioning accent. "What did you learn?"

The faces of the dozen men at the table swung as a unit to focus complete attention in Juan's direction. Everyone in the room was aware that, with or without the knowledge of Ojeda, the Minister, in the *presidente's* absence, had made an almost furtive trip to Florida. Small pieces of information dropped here and there had been put together. No one quite knew why he had left the island at a critical time and while Ojeda was out of the city, but they were unmistakably suspicious. All were concerned about their positions and safety. This man de Cespedes, close to Ojeda though he might be, could prove a great danger.

Juan was undisturbed. "I reported in full to President Ojeda, Colonel Pio." He pressed his cigarette out in a tray, locked hands behind his head and gazed upward again at the ceiling. "There are no secrets between his Excellency and me. What you have been told is something else again. Should I continue, *presidente?*" He dropped his eyes to look at Jorge.

Ojeda nodded and resting an elbow on the arm of his chair propped chin in upturned palm. Juan, he thought, had come a long way from a fisherman's hut. He had developed a fine sense of the theatrical.

"General Chivas San Martin," Juan continued meditatively, "is financing the formation of a revolutionary force. This has been done with the knowledge of his Excellency and my encouragement."

There was a soft, almost whistling murmur of astonishment from the attentive members of the Cabinet. They leaned forward at their places as though a word or inflection might escape them.

"I went to Florida secretly because I am not certain of my status there as a citizen now; also, I did not want to answer a lot of questions. I needed to know that San Martin's preparations have not grown too big for us to control them. As for the danger, San Martin is in San Rafael where we can keep track of him. His supporters and what passes for an army are in Florida. They will remain apart until the *presidente* gives the word to use them. San Martin cannot get off of San Rafael. His army cannot land without my, our, help."

Complete bewilderment was stamped on the expression of every man in the room with the exception of Ojeda and Juan. The Ministers glanced worriedly at each other. It seemed to them that Ojeda and his Minister of Defense had lit a fuse. Now they were calmly sitting on top of the powder keg waiting for it to explode.

"*Presidente*," Colonel Pio spoke the word, "with your permission may I speak of what is in the minds of us all?"

"*Como no,* Colonel?" Ojeda nodded.

"I, we, have much at stake here—our homes, our careers—possibly our lives." He paused, momentarily embarrassed by what he was going to say. "Also, our country is on the table and you gamble with it. For some of us this has an importance beyond ourselves. San Rafael has been our home, our native land, for generations. We do not want to see it destroyed or torn apart again by revolution. If you will permit the suggestion—you maneuver dangerously and at great risk. You are," he continued without a hint of obsequiousness, "a man of great personal courage and resourcefulness. We all saw that in the Revolution of September Five. You placed a firm, strong hand on San Rafael. I think it has been good."

"A minority opinion, Colonel Pio." Ojeda half smiled. "At this moment, anyhow."

Colonel Pio shook his head. "It is true everyone in this room has had a personal advantage from the power you took so boldly. Perhaps, in one way or another, most of us have been loyal because this loyalty furthered our fortunes. There are some who have followed you unquestioningly because, astonishingly enough, you have never been anything but honest in your ambitions. Those who held the office of *presidente* before you were mainly thieves on a greater or lesser scale. Now, out of respect to this loyalty, whatever its inspiration, would you explain your encouragement of General San Martin's plotting? I would like to understand."

Before he answered, Ojeda thought how strange it was he should know so little about this man. There was no mistaking his sincerity. Usually taciturn, he had become briefly eloquent. Through the words a patriotic fervor, a genuine love of country and concern for its future, shone brightly. Pio, a graduate of the University, had made police work his career. He had been a lieutenant under President Romero. Ojeda had advanced him and multiplied his responsibilities. Through the network of his department he could, if he wished, exercise a great and dangerous power. Without this man, Ojeda reflected, I might never have been able to hold the island government so completely. He took a cigarette from a box before him and lit it.

"Let's put it simply, Colonel Pio." His reply was friendly. "Two brothers squabble and eventually fight. A third party intervenes, taking one side or the other. The brothers forget their differences and fall upon the stranger. His intrusion unites them. We have on San Rafael a family torn apart by conflicting interests. It is my intention to use General San Martin and his ambition to take over the Government to unite this family against a common enemy. He, an alien, lands a revolutionary force on a beach. He becomes a threat and an intruder. San Rafael unites against him. The root of our domestic trouble remains but it gives us time to solve the problem. At least, so it seems to me. I do not evade the responsibility for San Rafael's disunity. I made a mistake. With the mistake I created a situation. Now I must find ways and means to remedy it."

"The risk is great, *presidente*," Colonel Pio objected. "It assumes the complete loyalty of the Army. Even," he smiled candidly, "my own department." He paused. "The *Ruales* have been made impotent by wholesale desertions. What of the Army, General de Cespedes?" He shifted his attention to Juan.

"I can control the Army." Juan was deliberately short.

"That isn't quite what I asked, is it, General?" Colonel Pio looked at him sharply.

"Are you asking if I can be trusted?" Juan's voice had a silky whisper.

"That is enough." Ojeda displayed an edge of impatience. Then he relaxed. "Let's not carry the analogy of a family quarrel too far." He addressed Colonel Pio. "I trust the Army. I made it. I gave it steel and guts, pride. When the time comes I will command it as I brought the small battalion down from the mountains on that day in September." He paused and his eyes swept over the men around him. Then his words were quiet and filled with an understanding for their apprehensions. "I have not grown complacent in this chair nor do I propose to allow anyone to pull it from under me. I am in sympathy for your concern. It has been my habit to decide all things for and by myself. In this case you will be kept advised of what is happening. For the time being we will let it go at that."

The dismissal was obvious. The Cabinet members rose and made their respectful, if perfunctory, bows.

"Colonel Pio," Ojeda spoke, "if you and General de Cespedes will remain."

When the doors had closed and only the three of them remained in the room, Juan glanced from Pio to Ojeda and then one eyelid dropped in a quick, humorous wink.

"I think the time has come to pull the cork on this one, *presidente*."

Ojeda nodded. "Each move we make now must have a significance. First, I think, Colonel Pio, you will have the Generals Morillo and Torralba arrested on suspicion of counterrevolutionary activities. The Department of Public Information will make an announcement to the press and I will hold a conference with the correspondents. With this we alert the country to possible dangers from without. Since Torralba and Morillo are guilty only of failure, make them as comfortable in the Presidio as possible. We use them only to point a danger. Of course," he mused on this with a trace of grim humor, "the facilities of the City Prison are better but the Presidio has a historical significance which they will appreciate. We give them a certain status there."

"At once, *presidente*." Pio displayed no surprise or appreciation of the jest. "We leave General San Martin alone?"

"Completely." Ojeda nodded emphatically. "When the time comes, I want him waving a sword, figuratively of course, and leading his revolutionary forces in an assault. Now we come to the ultimate phase." He gave his attention to Juan. "If you pass the word to General San Martin that your plans for betrayal here are complete, General de Cespedes, how soon can the landing be attempted?"

"The men sweat in a camp with nothing to do. It is only necessary to transport them. A week or ten days should be enough."

"Good. We are being pressed for time. Now, Pepito"—he smiled at the unconscious lapse in the formality they employed before others—"General de Cespedes. It isn't going to be enough simply to put two or three hundred invasion troops ashore and destroy them there. It is too easy and the affair will be over before it achieves our purpose. I want to alarm the country. The landing must be successful. They will have to move inland and take a small town or two. It will be well if they behave in a completely un-disciplined manner with rape, murder and burning of a few villages. I want them to inspire terror. If this doesn't happen, the people will regard the whole thing as of no importance. I want them awakened to a fearful danger."

"Innocent people are going to be killed, *presidente*. You understand that," Colonel Pio objected sincerely.

"Sacrifices must be expected." Ojeda dismissed Pio's remonstrance without hypocrisy. "More will be killed if the present situation isn't controlled."

"As you say, *presidente*," Colonel Pio agreed reluctantly.

"Where," Ojeda addressed Juan again, "do you suggest a landing?"

"The beach at La Semana." Juan chuckled. "It is a good piece of sand. We should know. That bastard with a machine gun—I have never forgotten him."

Ojeda traced a pencil's point carelessly across a paper pad. For a moment he was lost in the memory of a night long ago. La Semana. There it had started. They had come ashore in soiled dungarees with little but his confidence as a shield. Glancing up, his eyes lighted as he considered Juan's resplendent figure in its immaculate tailored uniform and the row of self-bestowed decorations.

"All right." He gave his approval. "La Semana will do. The nearest town of any importance is La Questa. You will occupy it."

"You?" The personal pronoun exploded with Juan's immediate surprise. "I?"

Ojeda made the correction gravely. "I confuse you with the revolution, General. I do not mean you, of course. General San Martin."

Listening, watching the play of expressions, Colonel Pio wondered if his imagination was tricking him. Had there been the faintest overtone of sarcasm in Ojeda's voice and words? His glance passed rapidly between the two men. He decided he must have been mistaken. Juan de Cespedes, certainly, was oblivious of anything more than a faulty choice of phrasing. These two knew and understood each other well. If a threat or suspicion had been implied in Ojeda's words, de Cespedes would have recognized it.

It was Juan, surprisingly enough, who voiced the question which had flashed through Pio's mind. He left the table, strode to a cabinet, opened one of the doors and selected a bottle of rum. With his back to Ojeda and Pio he poured himself a drink and swallowed it. He stood for a long moment, glass in hand. Then he turned and eyed Jorge Ojeda quizzically.

"Let us not have any confusion of identities when the shooting starts. Eh, *presidente*? I have no wish to serve San Rafael that well. If a figure of importance is needed to point up the seriousness of the revolution, then let it be San Martin. It can be arranged that he die most gloriously. The foreign correspondents will be delighted with the drama. One dictator attempting to depose another. It will make fine headlines everywhere. Your *niños* will be thrown into a patriotic frenzy."

Ojeda suppressed a smile. He touched a switch and a voice replied at once on the intercommunication system.

"*Si, presidente? A sus ordenes.*"

In rapid Spanish, Ojeda spoke to the press officer who had answered. "Colonel Pio will have an announcement of importance to make"—he looked at his watch and then at Pio—"within an hour."

Pio nodded an agreement. Ojeda continued with his instructions.

"You will make arrangements for an immediate broadcast of the report both locally and on short wave. A complete text is to be furnished to the correspondents of the American and Reuter's wire services. There will undoubtedly be a request for a conference with me. I shall be available. Arrange it. Also, call the newspapers and tell them to hold their early editions from the presses until the material is in their hands. Colonel Pio will be in touch with you." He closed the circuit with a flicking of the switch. Then he turned to Colonel Pio. "Offer my sympathy to the lovely young women who share the exile with the Generals Morillo and Torralba. See to it that measures are taken to protect them from any demonstrations after the news of the arrests have been made public. Now, if you will excuse me."

For a long time after Juan and Colonel Pio had left he sat alone in the great, high-ceilinged room. As the minutes lengthened he had the curious sensation that he was shrinking physically until he was perched, dwarflike, within the cushion's center of the massive carved chair. He thought, if I sit here long enough I will vanish and there will be nothing in this place to show it was once occupied by Jorge Ojeda. No one will care or even remember. It occurred to him that the thrust which forces a baby from the womb remains forever with it. That once released from this security it is driven by the urge for movement—to crawl, to walk, to climb, straining for a place beyond the reach of other men. Then, having come to the high plateau, he looked about him and found it empty and frightening. Power alone was no companion on this eremitic plain. There is no one. Nothing grows here but the seed of loneliness. In my entire life I have known but one man and one woman to love. Now I have begun to distrust one and am afraid to speak the truth to the other. To this barren place have I brought myself.

In her favorite chair within the garden where the sunlight was sifted through the trees as a fine golden dust, Madame Cleo Dessaline held the morning's edition of *Hoy!* between her finger tips. The attitude was one of fastidious distaste as though contact with the paper might produce a particularly loathsome disease.

"The man is a fool." The remark was made generally and not to Ferris, who was stretched on a wicker chaise longue, her face to the sun. "A complete fool." She added this with emphatic satisfaction.

"I never thought I'd live to see you reading *Hoy!*" Ferris was amused by her grandmother's reluctant handling of the paper. "Aren't you afraid of contamination?"

"Certain unpleasant things must be endured for the ultimate satisfaction they give. I accept *Hoy!* with the same stoicism I would submit to a high-colonic irrigation. This," she rattled the pages, "prints such titillating vilifications of your lover."

"He is not my lover. Yet." Ferris added the qualification with deliberate malice.

The old lady ignored the comment. "I can't imagine why he permits it to continue publication. God knows he has never before hesitated to exercise his authority on this island. Perhaps," she looked up, "like Delilah you have shorn him of his strength. Love makes him weak. In time your contribution to liberty may be celebrated in folk song and legend—a female Saint Patrick driving the serpent into the sea."

"You are a delightful, if slightly insane, old woman." The description was made with affection. "By the way, how is your private revolution coming along? Are you all armed with staves, ready to storm the palace?"

"I told him"—Madame Cleo was indifferent to the gibe—"I warned him, God alone knows why, that one day he would be confronted by an alliance of the first families and the peon. Now the bell tolls. The hour is approaching. At the end he will be buried in the ashes of a tyrant's ambition as was that German, Hitler. My friends and I await the Götterdämmerung with equanimity." She was brightly smug. "You may say what you like about Wagner—he is noisy but thorough." She considered this irrelevancy for a moment and then added, "I hope you noticed I remained in discreet seclusion when he called last night. However, I heard him leave. It was very late. I was reading. What is it you do together when you are alone? I would suspect fornication save for the fact that you are too well bred to permit yourself to be tumbled in the garden as a milkmaid or a peasant wench."

Ferris was convulsed by the absurdity and the archaic phrasing of her grandmother's speech. It was, she understood, an affectation the old lady enjoyed. She laughed until tears were heavy in her eyes. Then she swung up from her place, moved to Madame Cleo's side and bent to kiss her cheek.

"My darling," she choked again with laughter, "there is no one in the world just like you. You talk as those French porcelain figurines on your mantel would speak if they could. Tumbled indeed. The image is preposterous. A flying tangle of skirts and legs. Layed. Perhaps. Gently layed but certainly not tumbled. If you must know we sat and talked. He held my hands and later kissed me good night. He was serious and concerned and not the ardent lover you suspect."

Madame Cleo glanced sharply at her granddaughter. "Do I detect a note of uncertainty in your voice? Is the hot broth of passion being cooled by the breath of reason and common sense? I never thought there was anything more to this than an infatuation; a fascination, as when one is mesmerized by something completely evil. I was quite certain you would never marry this person. That is why I permitted you to receive him here."

Ferris was silent. She stood in deep thought. Out of all of Madame Cleo's words one struck her. Fascination. It had a disturbing impact with a validity which could not be honestly denied. To be with him was a new and exciting experience and he seemed many men in one. There was humor and gentleness; strength and courage. Yet she was aware that he was a man of ruthless determination, a predatory creature of elementary impulses; the lone stalker; the jungle cat. All women, she mused, are susceptible to these things, for there is in them an unadmitted, latent atavism. The mink stole is centuries removed from the cave, yet the desire on the part of the female to wrap herself in fur had not changed since the dawn of mankind. Despite all the surface glossing, woman remained a barbarian at heart and such men as Jorge Ojeda appealed to the feral instinct. They followed the conquerors willingly and without question, wanting to be possessed and made captive. Even, she thought with a wry inward smile, Ferris Dessaline.

"You are perturbed by what I said, are you not?" There was no mistaking the small, triumphant note in Madame Cleo's question.

"Not really. One word, maybe."

"He is new, an unfamiliar species. Believe me, I can understand the attraction. But when that wears away, eroded by time and intimate association, what will you share with each other? You may try to deny family and friends; the background which generations of Dessalines have given you. But this is your home, these your people. This Ojeda is an alien. I do not mean that in the literal sense. With him, you move to a completely unfamiliar plane. When he is stripped of the power, thrown naked from the office which he seized by violence, treachery and murder, what will you have? An adventurer. A penniless soldier of fortune. Another in the long list of opportunists who have come and gone. You will be Mrs. Jorge Ojeda." She pronounced the name reluctantly. "Your friends . . . my friends . . . the families from which you have drawn companions, playmates and associates since childhood, will turn their backs on you. What a lonely path you set your feet upon." She gazed unhappily at Ferris. "I cannot, and see no reason why I should, deny my prejudices. I do not subscribe to the ridiculous notion of a completely classless society any more than I would accept the theory that a mongrel cur is as good as a blooded animal with its selective breeding. So, my child, if you marry this Ojeda you must be prepared to renounce those things which you have taken for granted since infancy. You can't honestly believe the two of you could remain on San Rafael! You, who have known nothing but security, become the wife of Ishmael?" She shook her head. "I am not a vindictive, meddlesome woman who has outlived her time. What I want for you is a full, rich and happy life. I cannot believe Ojeda will give it to you."

Listening, watching the expressions of concern and affection as they passed over her grandmother's features like small shadows, Ferris was miserably aware of the fact that the old lady's words were not without some foundation of truth. Beyond the heart, which could not always be trusted, there were all but insuperable difficulties. They could not be overcome by saying: I love this man. He loves me.

"Think what you will of me," Madame Cleo continued sadly, "but do not doubt my sincerity. When I spoke of Ojeda as a penniless adventurer I was indulging myself in the pleasure of words. A succession of Dessaline men built a great fortune. All or any part of it is yours. So, of all the things which you might be deprived of through a union with this man, money would not be one of them. But his purse will be empty of the coin by which he has lived—authority and the subjugation of man's life and thought. You will not be able to refill it for him."

More disturbed by her grandmother's words than she wanted to admit even to herself, Ferris stood irresolutely for a moment, her eyes upon the ground. She felt ridiculously young and childishly defensive as though, clad in a pinafore, she endured in a silence of embarrassment the reprimand of an elder. This, she told herself, is outrageous. I am no wayward youngster to scuff my feet, stand toe upon toe while being scolded like a naughty child. I am twenty-two years old and capable of making my own judgments. It shocked her a little to realize she did not fully believe the things which she was telling herself. That was the intolerable advantage of age. You might deny it wisdom but you could not contest against the armor of experience. It was too formidable.

"I'm going out for a while." She touched her hand to Madame Cleo's cheek with a parting gesture of affection. "Maybe I'll take my boat and spend the rest of the day around the islands. Don't worry about me. It is only that I think I would like to be alone for a few hours."

"Be careful—not with the boat but with your thoughts." Madame Cleo smiled with a gentle understanding. "I can't honestly say I am sorry if I have distressed you a little. We have been very close, you and I. It is my only excuse for what you may resent as an intrusion."

The red Mercedes flashed as a bright bird on the wing down the sloping, tree-bordered road toward the city. Ferris drove with a mechanical perfection. The way she traveled was so familiar she was all but unaware of the long, sweeping curves. The car took them with the sure guidance which required no conscious thought or effort. Only a small part of her mind occupied itself with handling the power which responded to her lightest touch.

She was thinking of her grandmother and of Ojeda. The two, now, were irrevocably linked. Although it had been quietly drawn, the steel of the old lady's opposition was unmistakably bared. Cleo Dessaline was not given to flighty conclusions. Once made they remained unalterable. So, there was the choice to be decided.

With Ojeda last night she had sensed a man different from the one she had known or come to expect. He had been drawn within himself and there had been long periods of silence. For the first time she felt his concern for what was happening on the island and understood it was a thing apart from the man Jorge Ojeda, his personal fortunes and ambitions. He had talked not as a lover but as one who reached for the hand of a friend; someone with whom he could share an uncertainty. He was deeply troubled by the events which were shaping themselves so swiftly on San Rafael.

"I have not been bad for this country." He made the statement abruptly as though in answer to a charge.

She remembered now how the words had startled her. They had been sitting beside the pool where the moon floated motionlessly. The night air was almost cloyingly sweet with the scent of magnolia and the jasmine which flowered and gave off its perfume only in the darkness.

In the lounge chair beside him she had turned with surprise. "Why did you say that in just that way as though you must answer a charge?" She reached over to place her hand on his.

"A mood, I suppose." His hand turned until their fingers were interlocked. He held them tightly and the hard grip was painful but she said nothing. "I defend myself against myself." For a moment she detected an all-but-embarrassed smile behind his eyes. "There is no one to do it for me."

It was, she understood, a strange thing for him to say; as close as he had ever come in her presence to a confession of self-doubt. Yet in the tone there was no hint of yielding to a situation; no retreat from or concession to the forces on the island which were gathering in opposition.

She had leaned over to rest her cheek against his arm, feeling the knots of muscle beneath the lightly nubbed jacket of white silk. It had been meant as a gesture of tender solicitude, of understanding. This and nothing more. But as always, she experienced the electric shock which physical contact with him produced. Such a simple thing as the warm, firm clasp of his hand as they strolled a path earlier made a small catch in her breathing. She had felt the desire, the need to rub against him; a feline movement of invitation and desire.

At the far end of the garden an ancient and enormous banyan tree spread its branches as a dark canopy. Its central trunk was hidden and it seemed to stand upon the great roots. These curved out and downward into the earth and created a rounded, woven hut of igloo design. As a child she had used it as a playhouse. One of the Negro boys had cut away a couple of the fibrous tentacles to make an entrance through which she might stoop. It was her place of secret heart and she had never invited her most intimate friends to share its mysterious and wonderful seclusion. Standing before it she had told him how she had covered the ground within with mats of plaited grass, the *patates* of the island's natives. How she had sat there cross-legged for hours at a time with only a doll for a companion and pretended no one could ever find her. She and the doll would peer out through the slitted openings of the roots and watch the gardeners and the house servants, the carriages and cars of visitors as they came to the house.

"It was mine alone and I was certain no one could ever find me. I was beyond all reach. I could be whatever I liked—a native girl, a runaway slave, a princess hiding from the witch, a serving wench in a pirate's den. Never," she concluded with a reminiscent smile, "was I Ferris Dessaline. That would have spoiled the game."

She had thought he might share with her a certain wistful amusement. Instead, he had stared at her with a strange wonder.

"You, also." He had spoken the words so softly they were barely audible. "You."

He took her in his arms with a deliberate roughness and kissed her with fierce possessiveness. Try as she had she could not control the quick gasp which was close to one of pain and his hands moved over her breasts and body until she writhed in an agony of desire and erotic hunger. Here. Now. Beneath this tree. I don't care how it is done. Take me as some wild and rutting animal. Those were the things she had thought but had not said.

Then, he had released her almost angrily. She could sense the closing of a door between them. She was aware of the barrier but had no explanation for its presence. Many times, but under different circumstances, she had felt this inexplicable withdrawal on his part. It was as though a veil—transparent but, somehow, impenetrable—dropped to separate them. Last night she had been angry and frustrated, made uneasy by what she could not understand. He had taken her hand, not as a lover but as an adult might guide a child away from a place of danger, and they had returned to the chairs beside the pool.

The winding road at the base of the rolling hills led into a four-lane highway and this, in turn, made an intersection with the long, straight Avenida de Flores which led to the water front. Within her memory this had been a nondescript street of middle-class homes, small *tiendas,* boarding houses and a couple of frame hotels of English Victorian design. In the replanning which had been done under Ojeda it had become a gracious thoroughfare. Dividing it was a broad strip of flowering shrubs, the graceful sago palms and medallions of scarlet and yellow blossoms. Fine new apartment houses and modern hotels lined the *avenida.* It was an accepted fact that those close to *el presidente* and, perhaps, Ojeda himself had made fortunes here by purchasing for almost nothing the property before the plans for its reconstruction had been made public.

As she drove, lacing in and out of the slower-moving cars, Ferris was well aware of a completely new attitude on the part of the traffic control officers at busy intersections farther downtown. She knew most of them by sight, many by name. It had always been her habit to lift a hand in casual greeting or flash a smile of recognition. These friendly gestures had been replied to in kind. Now, though, the police on duty came to obvious attention. They saluted with a crisp, military correctness and their faces were graven and almost sternly polite. This, she thought with amusement, is because they have heard I am *la huera*, the blond girl of *el presidente*. The woman of Ojeda. When her car had been observed far enough in advance, all opposing traffic was brought to a screeching halt and the Mercedes waved through without hesitation. A couple of times Ferris grinned to herself and thought, I ought to be a little self-conscious and embarrassed by the obviousness of this but I'm not. I get a boot out of it.

At the Yacht Club she stopped for a moment at the dockmaster's cubicle and left instructions to have her boat made ready. Then she walked into the club, through the lounge with its discreetly cased trophies: the cups, the plaques, the photographs of racing yachts under taut, ballooning jibs and sail. The servants, clerks and stewards were ancient in service here. It was, she thought with amusement, the last stand of the old families. There was a newer club, built with American capital, which was open to visiting yachtsmen. But here only those whose names were deeply carved in San Rafael's history were members. There were no open guest privileges or reciprocal arrangements with foreign clubs.

Beyond the lounge and overlooking the bay was the dining terrace. As the steward led her to a table near the railing she halted now and then to speak to old friends. These were young men and women she had known since childhood and their families were all interlocked by marriage and business ties. As she chatted briefly, refusing half a dozen invitations to join a group, she was well aware she had become an object of bright, inquisitive interest. She could read the questions in the minds of the politely standing men and the upturned faces of the women. Was she or was she not the President's mistress? If she was, how should the situation be handled? A snub might be dangerous; a too-friendly attitude obvious. Most of those with whom she talked for a minute or so were honestly fond of Ferris Dessaline and found it difficult to share the outraged indignation voiced by their families at the many rumors which had attached her name with that of Ojeda. The girls secretly wondered what sort of a lover *el presidente* was. The men, behind the casually friendly façades, were envious and puzzled by their failure to trip Ferris Dessaline into an amatory escapade. What persuasion had this Ojeda used?

At a small table she had a couple of sour Daiquiris and then an un-hurried luncheon of salad and the small, iced crayfish which were served pinkly whole and had to be peeled first then dipped into a sauce of herbs, melted butter and tarragon vinegar. She forced herself to eat slowly and deliberately, aware of the pressure of a hundred eyes. She was amused at first and then mildly irritated. Pressing a cigarette out with an impatient gesture she left the corner of terrace, with the faintest nods of good-by to those at the tables she passed, and walked outside.

In the slip where her boat was moored one of the boys had stripped away the canvas covering from the open cockpit. It had been months, almost, since she had used the craft; that weekend on the Hollister island when she and Jorge Ojeda had first become fully aware of each other. This made her think of The Goat's Neck and of Massau. She wondered what he had done with the jade. She had no destination, only a desire to get away for a while. A run up to the Negro's island would serve as well as anything. More, there was a serenity about this big, black man. She needed that.

The motors were turning over evenly. Hull and brasswork caught the sun and reflected it with a soft brilliance. She dropped down from the land-ing float with an easy grace and the waiting boy cast off the lines. The boat drifted away from the dock and she gave it just a touch of power to hold its bow through the passageway between the boats at their numbered buoys. The shoreline of San Rafael was a scimitarlike curve ending with a coral spit atop which was the channel light. She had sailed these waters since she was a child of twelve or so. First in a sluggish but safe catboat. Later in sharper and more delicately balanced sloops. Now, sail had all but dis-appeared; gasoline and diesel-fueled cruisers and yachts had taken its place.

Outside the light she was in the open sea for a few minutes and was forced to ride a heavy swell. The lean beam of the boat was not built for this and it slammed with dangerous impact into the narrow troughs. Then she was in the lee of the long island which was the ridge of a marine range and extended for thirty miles up San Rafael's coast. Here the water was barely rippled. It was a place to open the craft's full power but she was content to cruise at a quarter speed, feeling the warm sun on her cheeks and the salty freshness of the air. The weight of uncertainty which Madame Cleo's words had laid upon her lifted. She even caught herself smiling a little, remembering the old lady's attitude as she had held the morning's copy of *Hoy!*; a thing of repellent attraction because it so viciously at-tacked Jorge Ojeda.

And what of Jorge Ojeda? How did he meet this hour or look upon this fair day? She tried to imagine what he was doing. There was, she supposed, an endless routine of administrative problems which any president, good or bad, must meet and decide. Yet she had never been able to picture him in this sedentary role. It was impossible to visualize him signing papers, dictating letters, decreeing legislation, concerning himself with the myriad of problems which must range from a rural sewage to the balance of trade; the negotiation of a foreign loan or the revaluation of local currency. Yet he must have done these things. Where did a sergeant of the Marines find the understanding, the patience and, in some cases, the wisdom for this task? Not in her time but well within the memory of many, the office of *presidente* had been briefly held by men who could not even sign their names. Once, in a native uprising, an illiterate Negro of tremendous voice and a spellbinding hold upon the superstitious fears and hopes of the credulous hill people occupied the palace. He called himself The King. Stories were told of how he was carried into the city on a gaudy, gold-incrusted litter with purple drapings. Stores had been looted, private homes ransacked. The owners were murdered by their own servants in a frenzy of jubilation. When he went to the Capitol, The King had been followed by a long, shouting, prancing procession of his courtiers. Men and women of many shadings decked themselves in stolen finery. Most of them danced exultantly in the dusty road, bare of foot but clad in morning coats, top hats and evening gowns. The legislative chambers had been filled with drunken roistering and primitive orgies. There were bloody fights and endless brawls within the corridors and The King, from his litter, presided over public executions on the Capitol's steps. Only the intervention of the United States had restored order and sanity to the island. San Rafael, she thought, had survived all of these things. More important to her now, though, was the troubled question: could Jorge Ojeda survive San Rafael?

From its tip the mainland of San Rafael rose steadily at a few hundred feet above sea level to the high, blue mountains. Great fleecings of clouds lay upon their tops and filled the valleys. It was almost impossible to believe that the essence of violence and political upheaval was being distilled within the towns and villages of this innocently peaceful scene.

A heavy, interisland supply boat passed her. The deck was loaded with drums of gasoline and merchandise for sale and trade. Below, in a freezing compartment, were hundreds of pounds of ice cream, Popsicles and Eskimo Pies. Having no refrigeration of their own the people on the small islands waited eagerly for the bimonthly arrival of this craft. They swarmed aboard at the docking places, snatching greedily at the frozen sweets and going, she thought with a grin, on a Popsicle debauch. She lifted her hand in response to the boat's whistled greeting but her thoughts returned again to Ojeda and San Rafael.

She had been a child when Ojeda had come down from the mountains at the head of the army which General Quatero foolishly thought of as his own. The change-over in government, she knew now, had been quickly made because Presidente Romero had been a weak and indecisive man and General Quatero without understanding of Jorge Ojeda's driving ambition and icy calculations. This time it would not be so easily accomplished. Revolution, if it came, would not be met by the halting actions of a politician. Her eyes lighted as she recalled her first meeting with Ojeda at the palace reception. It had not seemed at all unusual at the time that he should leave his guests and the two of them walk the shaded paths together as a natural thing to do. She remembered her curiosity about him and asking: You were an American Marine sergeant, weren't you? This had amused him. She remembered the reply in idiomatic Spanish: *Acaso es borra?* You think that is nothing? No, Jorge Ojeda would fight with every trick and resource at his command. There would be no easy way out for him; no submissive abdication, no ignominious flight, no trade or capitulation. In this role of determined and savage action she could see him well, but not as a man occupied with the signing of papers and the making of speeches. But—and the question frightened her—what if he failed to hold what he had so boldly taken? What then of Jorge Ojeda and Ferris Dessaline? She had no answer beyond the ominous prediction of Madame Cleo.

From her low seat in the cockpit The Goat's Neck appeared to float upon the sea. Its sandy beach seemed without substance. Only where the massed vegetation offered color did the land itself become distinguishable from the clear water and seem to hang above it.

Her gaze searched for Massau's weathered ketch with its faded pink sail. It was not moored nor was the small dinghy drawn up on the beach. He was probably fishing or visiting at another island. For a moment she hesitated, for she had no real excuse to come here or to intrude upon Massau's home in his absence. But she knew, somehow, he would not mind. Also, and this caused her to smile to herself a little, he would be completely unimpressed by what the average San Rafael Negro would consider an embarrassing honor. He had lived so long with the security of just being Massau that the distinctions of color did not exist. She doubted if he ever thought of a person as brown, tan, black or white. For a moment she felt a little ashamed because what she was doing was, or had been, an unconscious assumption of privilege.

A gull rested atop one of the pilings. Its head turned slowly and without alarm as she drifted in. Standing, she held the boat off with a hook until a line could be made fast. Then she stepped from the cockpit's seat to the dock's loose boarding. When the hitch in the line was secure she watched as the boat lay motionless upon the slack water.

Walking up toward the house she was caught by the simple beauty and peace of this scene where the house stood, ringed by the tall coconut palms with their smooth, silky hoared trunks. She was aware, also, of a complete cessation of all sound. A moment before, the air had been alive with the calls of birds, their trebled whistles and the seemingly aimless flights of the small yellow and gray canaries. A hawk which had been cruising in search of a lizard or small snake suddenly hung motionless upon its wings, held there by the light wind current. The wild things recognized an alien presence and became alertly cautious.

With an instinctive feeling for what created a natural beauty Massau had allowed the heavy massed ferns, palm scrub and brush to grow in a protective ring about the house. But where they seemed in place and unobtrusively decorative he had laid out small beds and circular patches ringed with polished conch shells. Here multicolored phlox, zinnia and marigold blossomed in colorful plaques and borders. She stood, admiring his skill and the care with which he kept his home. The yard seemed freshly swept of each stray leaf or fallen twig.

On the porch, before the door, she paused again and then rapped lightly although she was certain there was no one in the house. The knob, which Massau had carved from a piece of heavy, gnarled root, turned easily beneath her hand. She stood on the threshold, feeling a little guilty and wondering why the personality of Massau had made an ineradicable impression. He excited her imagination and curiosity. Leaving the door open she moved to stand in the center of the room. Her gaze traveled over the woven mats with their barbaric streaks of color, the hand-carved chairs and tables, the bed of polished bamboo. Then she saw the jade.

It had been placed upon a shelf a little above her eye level. A rod of sunlight thrusting through a window seemed to fill the carving with an inner fire as though a bright flame burned there. Carefully she took it in both hands. It was the body first which held her attention, for it struck an abandoned, almost lascivious pose of what the natives called a "bright girl," the *mestiza* of dusky coloring. Then she studied the face and a small frown gathered about her eyes. There was something familiar here. She thought, This is someone I have known or seen but that is impossible. Cradling the figure she almost absently sought a chair and sank into it, still holding the carving and bent forward now, looking down upon it. There was first the slight upward tilting of the head and then the delicate structure of the cheekbones, the chin. Unconsciously she released one hand and her fingers moved over her face. Then her eyes widened, for there was no mistaking now what she saw. It was no trick of the imagination.

"This is my face." She spoke aloud. "This is Ferris Dessaline with somewhere in her the strain of Negro blood."

For a moment there was anger, a sudden fury over the insolence of the black man who had dared to superimpose the undeniable Negroid features upon her own. This was no illusion, no fancy. The artist's skill had created a cameolike fidelity, an exquisite miniature, and then overlaid it with this mystifying quality so the nose, at its base, was just a shade broader; the lips all but imperceptibly fuller. Then indignation drained from her and curiosity took its place. Why had he done this? More, what had he seen which was not there? How, out of the deep recess of his mind, had he come upon this strange and frightening blending? It was not, she understood, a thing done without conscious thought. This had not shaped itself. A hand had guided the tool; the brain instructed the hand and so it was no accident of creation. Why? Why? Why? The question pounded at her and she felt a curious terror as one might in a dream when pursued by an unimaginable phantom. For a moment she had a desire to smash the piece into unrecognizable bits, but the impulse leaped from an uncertainty rather than outrage. She thought, I will come here again and he will tell me why this was done. I will make him tell me. For one wildly fantastic second she wondered if somewhere in the Dessaline line there had been an intermingling of blood. Was it something Massau knew and with a black man's sardonic humor had revitalized the strain in Ferris Dessaline? She dismissed this; not because it was impossible or improbable but because her mind refused to accept it. It could not be. Therefore it was not.

She stood up and replaced the figure on its shelf. Then she turned, walked to the door and closed it. For a while she stood in the bright sunlight, the sudden, hot silence. Only her footsteps on the crushed marle of the path winding to the dock made a sound. She wanted to run in blind haste from the house and what it held. The question she did not want answered.

XX.

THE spectacular arrests of the Generals Morillo and Torralba with their confinement in the Presidio, the widespread coverage of the incident by San Rafael's press and broadcasting facilities, stunned the city and sent waves of excited speculation out over the country.

There was alarm in some quarters, incredulity in others, open cynicism in the American Embassy and some of the foreign Consulates. Those who believed what they read or were told were shocked by the idea of an intrigue of such magnitude—a plot extending far beyond the perpetually dissident groups, the coffeehouse and *cantina juntas*. Morillo and Torralba were figures with an international stature. If they were involved in fomenting a revolution then such a thing went far beyond the intramural scrambles to which San Rafael had inured itself over the centuries. The press and radio stations were fed hourly bulletins by the Department of Public Information. Powerful interests abroad had given their support to Morillo and Torralba. There was still the possibility of an invasion. Jet fighters without identifying markings had appeared over remote sections of the island. Landing craft were cruising just beyond the territorial waters. A bomb had been discovered in the Capitol. A general mobilization had been ordered for San Rafael's Army. Men were to be recruited into a militia for a constant patrol of the coast. Sensation was piled atop of excitement. In the streets people halted to stare at a speckless sky for the first sight of hostile aircraft. As a precautionary measure all schools were closed. A large portion of the business section was empty of employees and customers, the windows shuttered, doors locked. In the plaza before the Capitol crowds gathered waiting for *el presidente*, who would speak to them. So it was rumored. Here was a common danger to be met only through unity.

Even *Hoy!* was unhappily aligned on the side of Ojeda. The paper had ceaselessly protested against the residence of Morillo and Torralba in San Rafael. It had accused the Government of harboring criminals, providing sanctuary to the "Fascist murderers." With their arrest *Hoy!* was in the embarrassing position of being forced to applaud the action of *el presidente*. Editorially it adopted a "we told you so" policy and screamed for the arrest of San Martin as part of the unholy trio. Why are two Fascist dogs chained while another runs free?

At his villa San Martin waited fearfully behind the locked doors. Was this a complete betrayal by de Cespedes? Had the fortune he had spent only filled the pockets of a Yankee Judas? He paced up and down the living room carrying a revolver while Serafina languidly pricked at him for being a credulous fool. He would end, as she had predicted, against a wall in the Presidio.

In the old homes within the folds of the green hills the families of ancient privilege gathered to discuss in hushed tones the startling turn of events. Those who had secretly and ineffectually encouraged opposition to Ojeda were in a small panic. The American Embassy had call after call requesting visas. From the Ministry of Defense came an order prohibiting anyone from leaving the country.

Over the luncheon table in the garden with Madame Cleo, Ferris kept a small radio tuned to the news reports. The old lady imperturbably squeezed half a lime over a cup of jellied consommé and appeared unaware of the announcer's half-hysterical comments.

"Do you," Ferris asked, "hear the rumble of the tumbrel? The thunk of the guillotine? The dropping of heads in the basket?"

"There is no such word," Madame Cleo tasted the consommé, "as *thunk*. It does, however, have an expressive sound. I believe nothing of this fantastic gibberish. I will admit the man has cunning. He has achieved a momentary distraction with this pumpkin head on a stick draped in a white sheet. It only delays the inevitable."

Ferris made no immediate reply. She didn't know what to believe. Then her eyes kindled with amusement. One of Madame Cleo's oldest and closest friends had telephoned her an hour or so earlier. The lady, whose family had been on San Rafael for almost as long as the Dessalines and who had been tight-lipped but unmistakably disapproving of Ferris's public association with Jorge Ojeda, had delicately hinted at a favor.

"Doña Ramos called." She made the comment now absently, pretending to be completely occupied with her luncheon. "It was quite a surprise."

"Tina?" Madame Cleo was betrayed into astonishment. "Why wasn't I told?"

"She didn't want to speak with you." Ferris looked up innocently. "It seems that just today the entire family decided to visit friends in New York. She suggested that since I was such an intimate companion of the *presidente* I could use my influence to have them granted permission to leave the country for a while. I told her," the tone and expression were demure, "it was the duty of all patriotic citizens to remain on San Rafael in this time of crisis. She was quite provoked."

"Good!" The old lady was emphatic. "Although I share Tina's loathing for the man I consider the request impertinent, intolerably presumptuous. She was always a scuttling little bitch, even as a young girl." The word leaped as a toad from Madame Cleo's mouth. "Let her stand by her principles, if she has any. When the day of mass arrests and executions under that man's bloody hand arrives, I shall take great satisfaction in seeing Tina Ramos precede me to the gallows."

"I shall request Jorge to have the lethal procession arranged in that order. First Doña Ramos and then you."

Madame Cleo ignored her. "Fancy Tina attempting to use you as some soldier's strumpet. The miserable little coward. I shall strike her name from my guest list. The idea!" The old lady thrust her spoon into the jellied soup as though she were digging at the vitals of Tina Ramos.

Ferris leaned back in her chair, half closing her eyes. Several times during the past couple of days she had been on the point of telling her grandmother of the jade figure Massau had made. The mysterious implication in the carving disturbed her. Try as she might she could not dismiss it from her mind. Still, she was unwilling to risk the blunt question. She could not ask her grandmother: Is there Negro blood somewhere in the Dessaline family? It was impossible even to imagine the reaction. She had decided to say nothing. If there was an explanation, then it lay buried in the mind of Massau.

"I think I'll call Christina Glastonbury." She dropped her napkin on the table.

"I would like to know what the American Embassy thinks of this." Madame Cleo was interested.

"I thought maybe she'd like to go to the club and play some tennis. However," Ferris rose, "I'll see if I can find out when the Marines are expected to land." She blew a smiling kiss in the direction of her grandmother. "Be steadfast and unflinching."

Madame Cleo watched as Ferris crossed the garden, and wondered a little unhappily at the blithe confidence of her carriage and the secret power which was contained in a young girl's heart. No misfortune or, at least, conception of it, could penetrate the armor.

Colonel Pio had followed the directions of the President and kept the murmurings of conscience to himself. All measures for the security of the households of Morillo and Torralba had been taken. Demonstrators had been roughly handled. The Generals were being held incommunicado within the Presidio; their not-too-distressed mistresses had been provided with a detail of police. Now, Colonel Pio had begun to wonder about Jorge Ojeda. The President was either completely sure of himself, confident he was not leading himself into a labyrinth from which there was no exit, or he was secretly uneasy. An insecure and frightened Ojeda was an unstable and dangerous quantity and a threat to everyone in high position within the Government. For this reason the Colonel had requested an audience.

When the doors had closed upon him and only he and Ojeda were in the President's office, Colonel Pio came directly to the point.

"I hesitate to ask, *presidente*." Reluctantly he had accepted Ojeda's invitation to sit down. What he had in mind demanded an impersonal formality between them. "But," he leaned forward earnestly, "the question must be put. It concerns General de Cespedes. Can you, do you, trust him fully in this matter?"

"I am not certain." Ojeda reflected. "That is an honest answer."

"Then the risk you are taking is inexcusable." Colonel Pio was well aware that a public official did not speak in this manner to the President. He indicated an envelope on Ojeda's desk. It bore the seal of the Federal Police. "I sent that in advance of my appointment in the hope you would read and study it before I arrived. The information it contains is vitally important."

"I have read it, Colonel." Ojeda reached for a cigarette. "I have always been aware of your efficiency, Colonel. You are, also, one who does not give loyalty as a trinket. Sometimes I have wondered why a man of your ability was satisfied with the position you hold."

"I am a policeman," Colonel Pio replied stiffly. "To be a good one is no small thing. I have been content to do my job well. If you permit"—he declined the offer of a cigarette from the box—"may we come to the subject of that report?" He waited and, when Ojeda assented with a nod of agreement, continued. "My—*our* agents are among the volunteers which San Martin's *junta* has recruited in Miami. Their reports are accurate. The arms which have been purchased are as modern and effective as our own."

"But, Colonel," Ojeda interrupted, "they are without the will to use them. All soldiers are heroes in the barracks. It is a latrine courage and drains from them swiftly."

"Of that I am not so certain," Colonel Pio objected. "There is a courage of terror when a man will fight to save himself. These volunteers of General San Martin find themselves on an unfamiliar beach. They move inland without opposition, because that is the way you have planned it. They take a town or two without effort. They loot and rape and suddenly the feeling of being conquerors is good. They become giants." He paused, gathering his thoughts. "You are well aware there is the spirit, if not yet the deed, of complete revolution among the *campesinos*. San Martin is shrewd and a man who can make the most extravagant promises. These things sound good to the peon. So, they flock to the new liberator. What you have set in motion may easily spread beyond control. It is a danger you, above all men, should recognize, for you used the same means with General Quatero's army. Your political 'diversion' could get out of hand."

"I have considered these things." Even as he spoke Ojeda was aware of an inward weariness; a real absence of determination for this project. He did not really care and yet, he must. "I have weighed the dangers. The situation is not quite the same as it was with Quatero. The General was a man of San Rafael. San Martin is the foreign invader. That is how the people will regard him. I think he will find small support among them."

Colonel Pio shook his head. The *presidente* would not or could not bring himself to place his finger on the spot of danger. He wondered how far he should intrude with the obvious, for it concerned a delicate relationship. His deep drawing of a breath was almost a reluctant sigh.

"*Presidente.*" He spoke the word slowly. "Within the privacy of this office let us speak honestly. Suppose General de Cespedes does not seal off the mock invasion at La Questa and Punta Gorda as you have directed? In this matter you can trust no one but yourself."

"That has been in my mind. I have prepared orders for the Army myself. When the times comes I will take it and destroy San Martin."

Colonel Pio frowned. "In that report I have brought to your attention, the condition of the Army, *presidente*—it has grown soft at the core. There are half a dozen high-ranking officers who have listened treasonously to the offers of the Communists; have met with and conspired with some of the old families who have always opposed you. There are ties of blood, friendship and ambition between them. It is not the army you brought out of the mountains. You are or were," the qualification was delicately made but unmistakable, "a professional soldier. You know what happens to troops when they are not commanded by authority. The best of machinery grows rusty through disuse and a lack of care. San Rafael's Army is sluggish, fat with doing nothing."

"The officers noted in your report, Colonel Pio, were taken into custody half an hour ago." Ojeda glanced at the watch on his wrist. "By now they have been stripped of uniform and rank and sit behind bars in the Presidio. They are no longer a threat to anyone."

"This is not public information!" Colonel Pio was astonished.

"No." Ojeda understood the officer's consternation. "I'm not so out of touch with my army that I do not know of the cadres within cadres. We walk a narrow path on which there is no room for a military revolt. The officers in the Presidio are on detached duty. By my instructions the orders were cut that way. There is a general inspection of all military forces on San Rafael. That is why the officers are absent from the city. This is the information which will be published in tomorrow's papers."

Pio was relieved. Better than anyone he knew how delicate was the balance of power within the armed forces. The public arrest of ranking officers would split the Army into a dozen undisciplined factions.

"I must, in honesty, return to General de Cespedes," Pio persisted reluctantly.

Ojeda blew softly against the knuckle of a hand. His eyes studied the concerned expression of the man on the opposite side of the table. Pio was a man of brain and courage. He was risking the *presidente's* anger. It was, Ojeda thought, a determination and a sense of duty to be admired and, also, to be remembered.

"When you asked me about General de Cespedes earlier, Colonel, I said I was not certain. Unhappily, this office breeds suspicion. Without it I would not have survived the first year in this chair. Juan. Pepito—" he spoke the name reflectively—"he is my *compadre*. With him I made the revolution. I must trust him because there has been a great wealth of understanding between us. A man cannot wander alone through this world. There must be something to love. That is why, even though a natural caution at the moment makes me suspicious of almost everyone, I must trust Juan de Cespedes. I have no choice."

"Very well, *presidente*." Pio spread his hands with a gesture of reluctant acceptance. "You will forgive what must seem to you an obvious impertinence."

Ojeda stood up. He walked around the desk and offered his hand to Pio, who had risen automatically with him. For a moment there was a warm pressure of understanding in the clasp.

"I must trust you, also, Colonel, although I am suspicious of dedicated men. Where there is fervor there is danger. It can lead a man on a reckless course. Fortunately, our interests at the moment run parallel." He laughed with a sudden amusement. "Do you know, that, almost, was what General Quatero once said to me in the Sierra Madre! I must keep in mind what happened to him."

San Martin watched with a gnawing terror as the black limousine swept up the long driveway and halted before the low terrace at the villa's entrance. The chauffeur and the man beside him were in the uniform of San Rafael's army. One of his own servants opened the door of the car and bowed respectfully as General de Cespedes stepped out and down. That Juan had come alone without a detail of Federal Police was, in a measure, reassuring.

"He is here." San Martin spoke to Serafina without turning. He still held the revolver which he had carried about with him all day. "Now we shall know." He struck a dramatic pose. "We have come to the moment of truth. It may be that our lives end here but I will kill him first."

"You are an idiot, Chivito." Serafina was unimpressed by the posturing. "For God's sake put away that gun before you shoot yourself in the foot with it."

"We are at a turning in the path of history." San Martin ignored her. He watched Juan as he crossed the terrace to the front door. "Do not debase it with your misplaced sense of comedy."

"Oh, my God!" Serafina intoned the words as a weary prayer.

Juan, within the open doors of the drawing room, regarded San Martin with an amused curiosity. The General had drawn himself into a stiff, commanding position. The revolver rested flat against his chest where the arm holding it was crooked.

"*Que pasa?*" Juan cocked his head slightly, his eyes bright. "What's with the *pistola*, General?"

[268]

"I will defend myself to the death." San Martin spoke with a hollow echo in his voice. "Make no mistake about that, my friend."

"This has been going on ever since he heard about the arrest of Morillo and Torralba." From her chair Serafina made the explanation. "Do you realize, Juanito, we stand at the crossroads of history?"

"Have you betrayed me?" San Martin demanded sternly. "I warn you, I am a man of steel. I will not go obediently to the Presidio. I am no sacrificial goat to be tethered with Morillo and Torralba."

"What the hell are you talking about, General?" Juan tossed his cap to a table.

"Don't you understand?" Serafina rose, walked to Juan's side and linked both arms with one of his, pressing against him intimately. "Chivito would honestly like to be a martyr. Only he is afraid it will hurt a little. He even winces when the manicurist cuts his cuticle."

"Put the gun away, General." Juan dropped into a chair and pulled Serafina to his lap. "*Como estas*, my little slut?"

Serafina bit his ear.

Watching them, San Martin grunted disgustedly. He carefully placed the revolver on a small stand within reach. He eyed Juan's familiar handling of Serafina with a thin-lipped disapproval but without jealousy.

"I demand to know what is going on." He spoke without any real force.

"*Como no?*" Juan agreed indifferently. "It is simple. Tonight you disappear."

"I knew it." San Martin snatched at the revolver, waving it recklessly. "Now you die."

"He saw that in a movie once." Serafina nuzzled her face against Juan's neck. "Always he has wanted to speak those lines."

"I'm going to take that away from you in a minute, General." Juan was bored and mildly irritated. He placed a hand against Serafina's back and pushed her from his knees.

"You are both idiots." Serafina pouted and then admired herself in a mirror.

"I demand an explanation." San Martin was indecisive.

"I said tonight you vanish." Juan lit a cigarette. "Poof! A cloud of smoke. You are gone." He watched the perplexity gather on San Martin's face. "There is a town called La Questa. A car will take you there tonight. You will go in civilian clothes. No uniform, please." He made the request in a reasonable tone but as though he expected a petulant argument. "You are a tourist, nothing more. You will take a room in a *posada* called La Ancira. Two, three rooms if you like. After all, you are to be the next *presidente* and we shouldn't stint on the details. There you will await the day. The hour of glorious liberation for San Rafael."

"How do I know this is no assassin's den to which you send me? It could be a trick." San Martin was skeptical.

"Why should I want to trick you?" Juan leaned back, thrust out his legs and admired the high sheen of his boots. "You want to be *presidente*. I want the *dinero*. First, I make you *presidente*. Then you make me rich. We wash each other's hands in a little dirty water."

San Martin relaxed, but warily. Then he made a magnanimous gesture. He replaced the revolver on the stand and walked to Juan, both arms extended.

"Forgive my suspicions, my good friend. I trust you again."

Juan turned away from the offered *abrazo* and watched critically as Serafina pressed the heels of her hands against her hips, smoothing down the sheath of blue Chinese silk.

"What about me?" Serafina addressed Juan's reflection in the mirror.

"You stay here, in the villa. You will be in protective custody. I'll send a young lieutenant to keep you company."

"What of you, my friend?" San Martin drew a chair close to Juan's.

"I have things to do here. At the proper time I will join you at La Questa. Information has already been sent to Miami. As you say, we are at the crossroads of history." He slapped Serafina on the bottom.

She stuck her tongue out at him.

"What of Ojeda? He suspects nothing?" San Martin's voice dropped to a conspiratorial whisper.

"Now"—Juan thought this was funny—"I haven't asked him. He might think it was pretty odd if I went to him and said: *Compadre*, are you suspicious of me?"

"Yes. Of course." San Martin appeared satisfied.

"I have decided on another thing." Juan snapped the cigarette butt into an empty fireplace. "We will make no one landing on the beach at La Semana. I like it better if they come ashore at several different places. Fifteen, twenty men at a time with full equipment. Then we make a rendezvous with them all under one command. Mine. We take La Questa and with it the motor pool and the small garrison. I have already arranged for its surrender. I need ten thousand dollars more to spread around where it will do the most good. There will be no resistance."

"There is no end to your demands for money. You spend it like it was your own." San Martin shook his head unhappily.

"No, I spend it like it was yours, *presidente*." Juan eyed him coldly. "You do not buy a revolution for centavos."

San Martin thought this over and then nodded a weary agreement. A tiny suspicion still nagged at him.

"Why were Morillo and Torralba arrested?"

"I ordered it," Juan lied placidly. "It was to divert any suspicion from you. After all, the San Martin genius for revolution is well known. In this time of unrest the light of doubt could fall upon you."

"Yes, of course." San Martin agreed. "It was a shrewd move, my friend. You will go far with me."

"Only as far as the vault in the National Treasury."

"It is agreed." San Martin was emphatic. A sly, complacent smile touched his lips. "I should like to see that sergeant, Ojeda, when he realizes how easily he has been trapped."

"Unfortunately, General," Juan rose, "you will be at the head of your victorious troops." He qualified the statement. "Or, at least you will be with them."

San Martin was oblivious of the sarcasm. His expression was rapt as he contemplated the future and the downfall of Ojeda.

"Ojeda," Juan continued firmly, "*el presidente* you will leave to me. This must be completely understood between us. I want him in the Presidio and quickly, once our move is made. I will take the city of San Rafael. It will receive you with a great welcome. You will be pelted with flowers. Pretty girls will dance in the roads before your troops."

"Chivito." Serafina's voice was sharp. "You are a fool to trust Juanito. My instinct tells me he is a great liar. He will betray you. I know him better than you do. He is making fun of you. Can't you hear the mockery in his words?"

"I am wounded, señorita." Juan affected a wide-eyed injury. "You stab me in the heart."

"Aaah!" She turned away impatiently. "You are both fools. If I had any sense I would go to Ojeda and ask for his protection."

"This occurred to me." Juan grinned at her. "That is why I have arranged protective custody for you. However, the guard, the lieutenant, is a handsome goat of a boy. The time of waiting will not be unendurable."

San Martin was in an unhappy moment of indecision. He chewed at his lower lip, eyes flicking between Juan and Serafina. He had always admired her uncanny ability to make a sharp, accurate estimate of a man. In the past her predictions had served him well. Finally, his shoulders drooped slightly with an indication of assent.

"I have no choice," he admitted, "but to go with you all the way. It is part of the risk calculated in advance. At what time do I go?"

"The car will be here for you at eight o'clock. The driver is a boy I can trust. He will take you to La Questa, a nine, or so, hours' drive. Your name— Let it be Garcia. Señor Jaime Garcia. I will be in touch with you by telephone. Take a camera. Be a tourist. Amuse yourself. Believe nothing of what you hear unless it comes from me."

"I am in your hands." San Martin made the admission without enthusiasm.

Juan stood, took his cap from the table. Then he winked at Serafina. "The lieutenant will console you, *chica*, in your hours of anxiety. I have given the orders."

"I spit twice on you, Juanito." She made the declaration with a limpid tenderness. "And twice more for your mother and father."

"*Adios, presidente!*" He snapped a crisp salute to San Martin. "When we meet again it will be at the hour of our destiny. It is a phrase I learned from Ojeda."

XXI.

A T exactly eight o'clock in the evening, in widely separated districts in the city, four things happened simultaneously and without seeming relation.

Jorge Ojeda stood before the mirror of his dressing room and pulled the two ends of a black tie into alignment. Across his shoulder, in the reflection of the glass, he could see his valet waiting as he held a white dinner jacket.

A dark blue sedan, nondescript in appearance, waited before San Martin's villa. The driver smoked indifferently and made no effort to assist with the stowing of the General's luggage in the trunk. The servant closed the lid with a crash and hurried to hold the car's door open for San Martin as the man descended the terrace steps and ducked quickly into the dim interior.

Colonel Pio, who disliked the ostentation, took the salutes of his motorcycle escort and uniformed chauffeur at the side porch of his home. Then he stood in the hedge-bordered driveway, finishing his cigarette in the black-crepe softness of the night before mounting the steps. The car and cycle officers disappeared with red twinkling of taillights. He watched them blink out at a turning of the avenue. There was an uneasiness within him to which he could give no name. He studied the house, the gentle feeling of the small plot of ground with its shrubs and flowers. Behind the drawn curtains of nubby, yellow material, the light from inside was amber. With a smile Pio thought how pleasantly he would spend the evening. A drink first and then out of uniform and into a warm bath. After that, comfortable slacks, an easy jacket, slippers, a second drink before dinner with his young wife, Marta, sitting on the arm of his chair. As his feet reached the porch and a hand extended to touch the bell a grenade, expertly timed and hurled, thudded with an ugly sound within inches of where he stood. It blew the life from Colonel Pio, shattered the windows and scarred the thick stucco with its steel fragments beyond where it had ripped a gaping hole in the wall.

At the Officers Club, General Juan de Cespedes shook the dice in their heavy, leather cup and rolled them out to lose a second round of drinks to a colonel, a major and two captains of San Rafael's Army who stood with him at the bar.

Ojeda slid his arms into the jacket and nodded to the valet who, after a quick inspection, turned away to pour the *presidente* a glass of sherry and turn up the lid on the humidor of cigars.

"You make a long face tonight." Ojeda took the wine. *"Que pasa?"*

"One hears things." The valet straightened the silver-backed brushes on the bureau. "Things to make a man wonder and think."

"Que son?" Ojeda took a swallow of the pale liquid.

"They are but things." The valet kept himself busy and in movement, avoiding Ojeda's questioning glance. "How *el presidente* has lost all touch with the people and no longer tries to understand them. How, where a strong hand is needed, one is not extended. It is said he does not think, now, as a soldier; the one who came down from the mountains on a day long past. How the Army he made now falls apart a little here and there and high officers in it disappear behind the Presidio because *el presidente* can no longer trust anyone."

"Does one also hear how a valet who talks too much can be quickly replaced?" The query was softly, speculatively voiced.

"One knows of such a thing." The valet was not alarmed. "But sometimes one who has fought at the side of another, even though he is only a valet now, can speak without fear. I learned many things from you but not that. Besides," his gaze met Ojeda's, "you asked the question. I only obeyed the command and answered."

Often Ojeda had wondered at the mysterious transmission of information, rumor and fact, as it was spread on an invisible network throughout the island. The officers on Pio's list had been taken by surprise; individually and without confusion, the arrests quietly made. Yet this was already known to his manservant and was, probably, furtive but common gossip within the city. There had not been, nor would there be, anything in the press or on the radio until the information was officially released.

"Do you believe what you have heard?" He placed the empty glass on a tray. "In your eyes am I different from the one with whom you fought for San Rafael?"

The man shrugged. "I see you every day. So. It is like looking at one's self in a mirror each morning for a lifetime. One does not notice a change but sees only the same face. Even an old man peers at himself in this way through the eyes of his youth and sees the boy he was. So it could be with us."

There was a sharp knock on the door which communicated an excitement. It was repeated before the valet could reach for the knob.

Carlos Farnese, one of the secretaries, stood on the threshold. His expression was drawn and alarmed.

"There is a call, Excellency. On the private line. The red one." He made an unnecessary gesture toward the bank of three instruments and his hand trembled a little. "I took it downstairs."

Ojeda picked up the telephone with its direct connection to the Headquarters of the Federal Police.

"Yes?"

He listened without expression and then his eyes hardened as the excited words of Colonel Pio's aide cracked through the transmitter. When the man at the other end had concluded his report, Ojeda stood thoughtfully, the instrument away from his ear. Then he raised it again and spoke calmly.

"Thank you, Captain. Convey my deep sympathy to Señora Pio. I will make a personal call in the morning. I suppose there was no trace of the one who did this thing?" He took the reply unemotionally, nodded. "I'm certain you are." He hung up.

"There are no instructions, Excellency?" The secretary waited.

"No."

The man bowed and backed out, closing the door behind him. Ojeda took his glass and refilled it from the decanter.

"Colonel Pio has been assassinated. A grenade."

"I could have told you that, Excellency." The valet spoke without emphasis.

Ojeda's head snapped up with a startled, unasked question.

"Oh, not that it had been done! Only that it must sooner or later happen. But this you know as did Colonel Pio. He was a shield as are all of us who are close to you. He was an officer of much loyalty and courage. It was necessary to remove him. There are those who would like to have you naked in the plaza. First, such men as Pio must be taken care of."

Ojeda walked to the closed French doors and drew them open to the night. He stepped onto the narrow balcony and stood there, glass in hand. As the valet had said, Pio was a shield and with him the large, efficient and disciplined Federal Police. In this corps he had instilled the obligation of duty and devotion to service without question. Always there had been those in the Army who had been jealous of Pio's authority, broad powers and system of espionage. They were afraid of him. If, as the valet had said, the Army cracked a little in places, those who might have ambition to lead a defection must first contend with Pio. This had been done.

"Have Farnese locate General de Cespedes." He spoke to the valet without turning.

He heard the door close. The wine in the glass was abruptly flavorless and he placed it on the railing. He glanced at his watch. It was only a few minutes after eight. He considered canceling the small dinner party arranged for tonight. Among the guests was Ferris Dessaline. To call it off, though, would be a gesture without real meaning. He had admired and trusted Pio but he felt no sorrow. It was a loss but an impersonal one. His immediate concern was for a replacement. Who could be trusted with the broad power of the office; the information in the voluminous files built up over the years by the Federal Police? Juan? By long habit the name came first to his mind. Then he smiled at the idea. Juan would have no patience for the job, which demanded the capacity for absorbing infinite detail. Even if he had . . . Ojeda's speculation ended there. He was unwilling to pursue what, of late, lurked continuously in the back of his mind; the small, unadmitted suspicion. The decision could be postponed for a few days, at least.

In a private room at the Officers Club, Juan de Cespedes and the four officers who had been at the bar now sat at a circular card table. On the green baize the chips were stacked at each place. A new deck of cards lay in the center. In an adjoining room two uniformed stewards moved quietly to set the places for supper.

Juan broke the seal on the deck, tossed out the jokers, and began running the slick oblongs through his fingers with a whispering sound. As he put them before the man on his right for a cut there was a short knock on the door, which was opened before one of the stewards could reach it. A page boy brought a folded slip of paper to Juan on a silver tray.

The quartet at the table watched as General de Cespedes read the note and then crumpled it into a crisp wad. He nodded to the messenger and shook his head to indicate there was no answer. When the door was closed again, Juan arose, went to a small radio and turned it on. Almost immediately there sounded the voice of the announcer. Even though he was repeating what had been broadcast continually for the past fifteen minutes, there was still a note of almost breathless excitement in his voice as it relayed the information of Colonel Pio's assassination. The men at the table were as fixed as statues in their attention. Juan closed the door to the dining room and the heads of the officers swiveled to watch each movement he made and the return to his seat. No one spoke.

Juan dealt the first two cards of stud poker swiftly. As the last card was turned up before him he held the deck in the palm of his left hand while his eyes studied the tense expressions on the faces. As an afterthought he left his chair again, went to a telephone and spoke to the switchboard officer.

"This is General de Cespedes. I am not in the club. I have not been in tonight. No," he answered a question, "not to anyone." He hung up and returned to his seat.

The cards before the officers were untouched. Juan's gaze traveled, holding for a moment on each face. In them he saw fear and uncertainty. A small smile of ironic contempt brushed his lips.

"It scares you all a little now that it is done?"

There was a scraping of chairs as the officers shifted uncomfortably, twisting unhappily beneath the mocking accusation. Each of them, willingly, had set his feet upon this dangerous path of intrigue with Juan de Cespedes. They had conspired in whispers and secret plans, each measuring the opportunity for himself. They had taken money supplied by Chivas San Martin; listened attentively and without objection as Juan had outlined each step as it must be taken in a swift coup which would overthrow the Government of Jorge Ojeda. In this each saw himself as a selfless patriot, eager to sacrifice honor for love of country. With the arrest earlier in the day by the Federal Police of the officers now in the Presidio they had all suddenly experienced the icy touch of fear at their throats. Although de Cespedes was as committed as they, his involvement deeper, not one at the table fully trusted him. This was not a thing they said to each other but kept hidden away even from themselves. But the suspicion escaped at night to haunt their dreams. Suppose this de Cespedes, *compadre* of the *presidente,* was the instrument which Ojeda used to lay bare the Army's soft belly? He could be using them to destroy themselves and seat Ojeda more firmly than ever in the palace. Because of greed, ambition, they gambled desperately on this not being so and tried to reassure themselves that Juan de Cespedes was too thoroughly mired himself to be other than what he professed to be. Now, they understood, the first, irrevocable step had been taken.

"What was necessary to do has been done." Juan's voice was a velvet whisper. "Why are you frightened?"

No one was willing to reply. The colonel got up abruptly with an inarticulate sound and went hurriedly to the buffet. He poured himself a drink of straight whisky and gulped it nervously. Seeing in this a temporary diversion, a relief, the others followed each other to the bar. They filled their glasses, emptied them and then stared fixedly as though to find a small pearl of resolution at the bottom. Finally, reluctantly—because there was no other place to go—they returned to their chairs. Juan watched them with open scorn.

"Did you think it was going to be easy? A simple thing in which there was no danger, no problem? Did you imagine you could go to sleep one night and awake in the morning to find the revolution accomplished? That it could be done with a little blood as might come from pricking your finger? If that were the case I would have no need of you."

"Ojeda will not take this simply as the murder of a police officer by someone who had cause to hate him." Unconsciously, the major lowered his voice to a whisper as he spoke the *presidente's* name. "Pio is something else again. Ojeda will think about it and understand what is beneath."

"So." Juan lifted his hands, palms up. "Where do his suspicions lead him? To the Presidio cells where Cavarina, Guise, Tremoille and Larvadin shake with cold in their sweat."

"I hope you are right." The colonel sighed, voicing what was in the minds of the others.

Juan was not disturbed. "Listen," he was emphatic, "the one who took care of Pio is himself already lying in an alley, a knife in his back. And," he lit a cigarette and inhaled deeply, "the one who did that is at this moment on his way back to Cuba. He was a tourist who arrived yesterday by plane and had only a few hours to spend in San Rafael. There are no loose threads to make a rope for anyone's neck. Besides," he met their worried glances with a grin, "remember you are all patriots. This should put the iron in your guts. In a case like this, patriotism can be a rewarding profession. Think of the rank vacated by those in the Presidio and how it must be filled by such dedicated men as yourselves. What would the Army be without you?" He put the cigarette on the edge of a tray and picked up the deck. "Let's play some cards for more than any of us can afford to lose. That is how *el presidente* goes at a game."

The small dinner party at the palace had been a strained affair. This was not as it should have been since the dozen persons at the table were without motive other than to enjoy themselves. They had an acquaintanceship of long standing as members of San Rafael's foreign colony—the directors and field representatives of American and European capital investments on the island. There was, though, an undeniable tension. Over the table hung the shadow of Colonel Pio's assassination. They were all aware of its implications. Even Christina Glastonbury's bright and frequently amusing chatter failed to break the uneasy constraint. No one mentioned Pio but there was such an obvious skirting of the news which had been repeatedly broadcast since shortly after eight o'clock that it might have been better if it had been brought to a frank discussion.

The party broke up early and Ojeda made no effort to hold his guests. The relationship between Ferris Dessaline and the President was so generally accepted now that no one found it strange when she remained behind with Ojeda as the last car disappeared down the driveway.

Standing on the broad steps Ferris put her hand through the crook of Ojeda's arm. "You should have called the dinner off. Everyone wanted to talk about Pio and what it means."

"It means he is dead." Ojeda was unemotional.

"No." She half smiled. "Not with me you don't get away with that. Beneath this beautiful, empty head may be a beautiful empty head but I know better and so do you. The hand that did it, or planned it, reaches for Jorge Ojeda."

"Let's walk for a while." He led her down the steps and to one of the many shadowed paths.

She went reluctantly. "Do you think he couldn't be out there someplace" —her head indicated the dark hedges, the ordered groves of cedar, the many places of concealment—"waiting?"

"I can have the floodlights turned on if it would make you feel easier." He humored her.

"No." She half smiled. "We'll walk the dark road together. Have you," she hesitated, "any idea who gave the order?"

Ojeda shook his head. "Not yet. A picture begins to develop though in my mind, the way a photographer's print takes shape in its bath. Not yet can I see this man clearly. The one who wants me. Give him time. Give me time. We will know each other."

She shivered a little, pressing fingers into his arm. As always this gipsy conviction of fatalism disturbed her. It was a frightening concept. How did one live with the mystical acceptance of all things being ordained to happen in a predetermined sequence? How, she wondered helplessly, was it possible to reconcile one's self to the conviction that no twisting, turning or dodging could mislead the stalker? The idea filled her with a small panic.

"I would feel easier inside, Jorge—" She made the statement an appeal.

"All right." He indulged the apprehension, turning her to face him. He kissed her with a quiet tenderness and she clung to him, pressing her face against his cheek. "The only way into the grounds," he was reassuring, "is through the main gates. The fence is always patrolled by guards and their dogs. Not even a rabbit can get through undetected." He dropped his hands from her shoulders. "I suppose a really determined man could make it with a parachute drop. I don't think he has appeared yet—this man of resolution. I would recognize the invisible strength of authority and determination."

"And when you do?" She pulled away to stare up at him. "What then?"

"Then"—they began to walk again—"we will find out who has the greater purpose. He or I."

They ascended the broad flight of steps, past the two expressionless sentries flanking the entrance. Inside they skirted the formal reception rooms where the huge crystal chandeliers blazed with many-faceted color on an empty scene. He took her to a small study. Here the walls were softly paneled in rosewood and the furniture was heavy, masculine and upholstered in rich leather. In was the first time she had been here and she regarded the book-lined shelves with interest, glancing at him over her shoulder.

"General Romero." He laughed at her quizzical gaze. "Romero or one of his predecessors had the shelves filled with dummy backings. Just the book spines, strips upon strips of titles pasted on the wall. There was even a phony set of Zane Grey, which always seemed to me to be the ultimate in useless deception. Would you like a drink?"

"No." She changed her mind almost immediately. "Yes, I would. Some brandy. Let's tie one on just for the hell of it. Or," her expression sobered, "because booze has a way of making reality seem improbable. I don't want to think about Colonel Pio or what it means."

He poured brandy for them both and brought it to a couch. Settling himself in a corner, he warmed the glass between his hands. Ferris swung her legs up and then leaned back against him with a quiet sigh of contentment. She sipped the liquor and then stretched to place the glass on a low table.

"When you goin' mek marriage wit me, *presidente?*" The accent was soft, darkly rich and fluid. She laughed a little at the mimicry of an island girl. "Tell me dat, now."

When he didn't reply, she twisted about to stare uncomprehendingly at him. His face was grave, unhappily shadowed.

"You t'ink on *mis*-take, *presidente?* Lak sayin' t'ing to girl ain' meanin'. You mek play wit me? Ain' no marriage en min'?"

He drew her back against him, holding her firmly within the curve of his arm.

"Tell me true, now?" she insisted.

"Don't talk that way." His words were harsh, commanding.

The tone surprised her a little. "Only foolin' 'roun', *presidente.*" She was deliberately meek and there was laughter behind the words. "Light me *cig*-rette, please, man."

He put the one he was smoking between her lips. She inhaled deeply and then burrowed her shoulder against him as though to make a pocket in which to rest. His hands touched with a reflectively tender gesture through the bright blond softness of her hair.

"You remember Massau?" She was comfortable, wanting to talk.

"Yes, of course."

"One day last week I took my boat out. I went over to The Goat's Neck. Massau wasn't at home. I wanted to see what he had done with the jade

Marchand had given him. I went in, looked around and found it. It is something I wanted to tell you about."

"You said he wasn't at home?"

"Yes." She was unaware of the deceptively innocent question. "He was out in his boat somewhere."

"But you went in anyhow?"

"Well . . . yes." She was mildly impatient and made an effort to turn about to read what was in his expression. He held her where she was. "You're hurting my shoulder," she protested. The pressure relaxed slightly but she was still captive. "All right"—she was resigned—"if you want to show your muscles."

"Why did you do that?" He spoke so mutedly she could barely hear. "Would you have walked into a white person's home the same way, alone and uninvited?"

"No-o-o." She made the admission slowly, aware of the question's inescapable implication. "I suppose not. But, that's a curious thing to ask. It just never occurred to me I shouldn't walk in if that's what I wanted to do."

"Why? Because Massau is a Negro?"

"Well . . . yes. I guess so." Her voice was slightly edged with uncomprehending impatience. "But I didn't think of it in just that term; not consciously, anyhow." Then, intuitively realizing they were fencing dangerously with words, she made a determined effort to relax. She drew upon the cigarette and the seconds lengthened uncomfortably. She was aware of his resentment but could find no logical reason for it. "You're angry, aren't you?"

"No." His tone was normal again. "Curiosity."

"But you were angry. For just a moment back there. Why?"

"I guess it was just your assumption of an ancient privilege that surprised me. The notion that a black man's house has no door, no latch. He squats without privacy in the open."

"Why are you talking this way to me, Jorge?" She didn't want to turn now and see his face. "I'm certain Massau doesn't or wouldn't mind."

"Are you?"

"Yes, I am." She jerked away, half turning to stare at him. "You're reprimanding me. I don't like it. You're talking to me as though I were a willful child. It—" She halted abruptly, as though realizing she was leading herself into an untenable position. Then she made an apologetic concession. "It is something I have simply taken for granted all of my life. I'm not prepared to defend it. Perhaps it is even indefensible. I don't know." She smiled suddenly, illuminatingly, and touched a finger tip to his lips. "We're quarreling, aren't we? Our very first fight." She sighed with a mock rapture, reached for her brandy and finished it. Then she resumed her former position, leaning comfortably against him. "Now, I guess it's for real, *presidente*."

He said nothing. Her hands covered one of his. He could feel the slow, even rise and fall of her diaphragm. The resentment against his censure had been short lived and was now forgotten. She had explained. *It is something I have taken for granted all of my life.* It was an attitude, a philosophy; the unquestioning acceptance of things as they were. One did not debate the obvious or dispute the incontestable. What she had said and felt was so inherent she could not regard the spontaneous reflex as a prejudice.

"I still don't know why he did it." She mused, unaware of the tangent flight of her thoughts.

"Who?"

"Massau, of course. The jade. I told you I saw it. At first I was furious. It seemed an obscene caricature. Then I was disturbed. What at first appeared to be grotesque became frightening. Yet," she confessed, "it has a wonderful, exciting beauty." When he made no reply she tilted back her head in an ineffectual attempt to study his face. "Are you listening, *presidente?*"

"Yes." He humored her. "But you're difficult to follow. I haven't any idea what you're talking about."

"The jade, of course. Massau carved it in the figure of a girl, fifteen, sixteen inches or so high; a native girl. But," again the puzzled wonder, "the features are mine. You would have to see it for yourself to understand. It is as though, by a subtle magic—transubstantiation, I guess that is the word— he had superimposed a *mestiza* on Ferris Dessaline. It is an incredible thing. I held it in my hands and said: It is I. This is Ferris, how she would look and hold herself if somewhere in the Dessalines there was Negro blood. How you lak dat, *presidente?*" The words were husky. "Git bright girl fo' woman who slap through palace en bare foot wit bas*kit* en head?" She laughed, amused by the outrageous fancy and the sound of the words in San Rafaelian dialect. "I was going to tell Madame Cleo about it and then decided I'd better not. She would be furious with Massau. I suspect she would order him beaten for the insolence."

"Why not?" The question was mild enough. "As you suggest, it is an unforgivable insolence."

She was silent for a moment, wondering if her imagination was shading his words with sarcasm. Then, deciding she had imagined the inflection, she pressed against him with a soft murmur of happiness.

"You know"—curiosity still nagged at her—"I keep wondering why. It wasn't an accident. The artist's hand didn't slip or falter. It was done deliberately but without malice. That is the riddle. Why did he see me as a *mestiza?*"

"Massau is an old man. His parents were your family's slaves. Suppose," he moved cautiously, "suppose he knew things you couldn't even suspect. Could it honestly make any difference at this far date in what you are or how you feel? Suppose you found out that somewhere in the Dessaline line there had been this black transfusion? It is so faint now in its dilution that it really doesn't exist beyond your mind. Just the same, how would you feel?"

"I don't know." Her fingers traced absently over the knuckles of his hand. "I suppose I would be incredulously shocked. I guess some shame would go with it. I'm not sure. It would be something one could learn to live with." She hesitated. The doubt and question were there. "Other persons have. There are old, highly respected families on the island. We all know and they know we know. Yet it has never been spoken of openly. It is something buried long ago, covered with the mound of time. No one wants to dig it up. I have always thought, though, they must walk a little in shame and fear."

"Why? Because they are afraid someone might say nigger?"

She was startled by the unexpected vehemence in his voice. There was a bleak anger in the tone; a suppressed fury in the question. For a moment she did not reply.

"I guess so." She spoke slowly. "I wouldn't have tagged it with just that word. In the end, I suppose, that is what it amounts to."

He closed his eyes to shut out the pain and hold back the empty sickness in his guts. Perversely he drew upon the rack and tightened the screw, thinking, Let me do it myself. Let my own hand turn the knife.

"They, the families you spoke of, have learned to live with the knowledge. Could you?"

"Why . . ." She was uncertain, sensing an urgency in the question. "I guess so, Jorge. I'm not certain. It would upset everything I have been taught to believe. Taught isn't exactly the word. Prejudice isn't passed on to a child as a piece of knowledge the way it learns the multiplication tables."

"How does a white child come to know he or she is better than a nigger?" he interrupted.

"I don't like that word, Jorge." She sat up abruptly and faced him. "You're trying to make me say something. Why?"

He wanted to answer. He almost said: I am a man born of a black woman and I love you. Instead he drew her back so he would not see the young, bewildered hurt in her eyes as though he were goading her into a shameful confession.

"I want to know what you feel. How you feel. Where do you draw the line of demarcation? Is it color alone? That wouldn't make any sense."

"No-o." She was uncertain. "Color by itself certainly isn't offensive. I've —I've never tried to explain it before. It is almost as though I suddenly began to wonder why the sun comes up in the east instead of the west. And it isn't that I honestly feel superior but only that the Negro is a race apart, an alien and mysterious grouping. You know San Rafael well enough to understand the barrier between black and white. Here, as a child, you first begin to notice things. The people who wait on you; who, when you say bring me that or take this away, they are black. The Negro never says to the white fetch me this, tote that. So an inescapable conclusion is formed. You are somehow different. You grow older and learn that in other parts of the world servants are not necessarily black. But here, on your island, they are. Also, you sense something primitive; a way of behaving. A black man takes a girl in the bush as an animal. And instead of feeling humiliated she pulls at her skirt, saunters off down the road with her hips swinging, a flower tucked behind her ear, laughing softly to herself. Oh I know"—she hurried the words, sensing he was about to interrupt—"the old cant about being warmed by the same sun, chilled by the same cold, feeling the same pain and nourished by the same foods. That proves nothing. It is true of all animals. The fact remains. The cat does not mate with the owl. The things which move a Negro to laughter would, often, not provoke a smile from a white person. And that which causes a white to lament would stir no emotion in the black. I have seen our own Negroes hunkered down by their fires at night. They chatter in words which have no meaning to us, dip their fingers into a common pot of food, scratch at their bellies. Watching, listening, it is hard not to believe they have just come down from the trees, swinging by their tails. The inescapable gulf is there. I don't say I am necessarily better simply because I am white, because I'm not sure what that means. I do say I am different."

Each word she spoke widened the dark pit in which he stood. Unknowingly she had told him there was a line over which neither of them could cross. Good-by, my love. The words formed themselves in silent anguish. Farewell, my bright and shining girl. There is no need to tell you now what I thought might be said between us. To speak in honesty would only destroy something in us both. I am the black ram and you the fair Desdemona. Cry for me a little sometimes as I will call your name to fill my empty heart.

"I read a joke somewhere." Unaware of the torture, she was laughing softly to herself. "Two Negro men in Georgia were talking about integration. One said to the other, 'You think this integration is a good thing? Let me tell you something. How would you like to have your boy marry one of those white New Orleans women? Tell me that.'" When he said nothing, she straightened up and regarded him with surprise. "Don't you think it's funny?"

He managed a smile. "It's pretty funny all right." Rising, he reached for her hands. "It's late. I'll drive home with you."

She was puzzled. "Is that a Presidential order? I thought, maybe, we were going to smooch around in the parlor some. Did I say anything to offend you?"

"No." He shook his head.

"I only tried to explain what and how I felt. You asked, remember?"

"Yes, I remember." He took her face in both hands, gently as he might have held a flower. She waited for his kiss, lips half parted. When he made no move to bend toward her, she studied his eyes, a question in her own. "I'll have my car follow us." He released her with a tender regret.

"All of a sudden," she spoke slowly, "something has gone wrong. You have walked away from me. What happened, Jorge?" She groped for the words. "I feel as though I were alone or with a stranger." She paused. "It frightens me."

He kissed her then, but as he might a bewildered child. She sensed the mood.

"That was a parental kiss if I ever felt one." Her smile was forced. "Now I know I have stayed too long. I'd better go home before you say you'd like to be a brother to me."

They walked together down the long, formal hall toward the main entrance. There was a tomblike quality about the passageway with its marble and bronze busts of the *presidentes* who had occupied the palace. Their feet made an echoing sound on the uncarpeted mosaic. In this place, he thought, I have buried my love. This is how I will walk from now on; down an endless, empty corridor of time.

"When you get this way, one of the moods," she reached for his hand at her side; "where is the secret place you go? I have felt it with you before."

He didn't answer, understanding she expected no reply, but his hand tightened with a spasm of loneliness on hers. This is the way the heart breaks; quietly, without sound. The tears come later. It dies as the flame in a gutted candle. When it goes there is no feeling, only an empty sickness of the soul.

A waiting servant opened the wide doors of bronze for them. There was the slapping sound of hands on wood and leather as the sentries came to attention. Neither of them noticed.

The red Mercedes was in the driveway. Hand in hand they descended the steps.

"Don't bother to go home with me." Her fingers were linked tightly with his. "I'll be all right. No one is going to take a shot at *la huera*."

He made no protest but closed the door as she slid behind the wheel.

"I wish you would tell me what is wrong. I'm not going to sleep very well if you don't." She looked appealingly at him.

"It is, as you said, a mood."

"Well," she was resigned, "when you come back from wherever you are, *presidente,* let me know."

He stood watching until the car dipped below the first terrace. Then he turned, mounted the steps.

When he had passed again through the doors the two sentries relaxed and glanced wonderingly at each other. It was not a thing to be put into words but each thought he had never seen such an expression of anguished torment on a face before. It was the look of a man who walks slowly and deliberately to his destruction.

XXII.

WITH a dead stick the small training plane came down a path of moonlight on the beach at La Semana as silently as a moth. It ran for a few hundred yards along the hard-packed sand and came to a fluttering halt of silvered wings.

Juan de Cespedes lifted himself from the front cockpit and dropped down. The pilot, a young captain in San Rafael's Air Force, followed. They stood without speaking, listening intently. Both men wore the loose tropical dungarees tucked into paratroopers' jump boots. On a sling over one shoulder Juan carried a semi-automatic carbine. The captain had a .45-caliber automatic on a webbed belt at his waist. They waited, seeming to sniff with suspicion at the air. Then the double-noted call of a night bird sounded. It was eerily plaintive. Juan replied, and he and the captain moved from the solid beach toward a dark line of scrub. Two shadowy figures appeared against the blackness and waited there. Juan and the captain plodded through the soft sand now toward them.

They spoke no word of greeting but ducked quickly through the underbrush, pushing aside the clinging branches with their arms until they reached a clearing. There a staff car, of San Rafael's Army, and a jeep packed with radio equipment waited. A squad of soldiers lounged against the fenders of the car. At Juan's appearance they came to attention but he waved a silent word for them to stand at ease again. From the jeep the operator looked up from the dials of the short-wave set and pushed the headpiece from his ears.

"We have a contact, General." He spoke softly. "With Puerto Manati, on Cuba. They are waiting for instructions."

"Good." Juan lit a cigarette. He studied the group about him with a half-smile. "Tell them I have changed my mind. Forget the original plans for separate landings. It will all be done here. Tomorrow night."

"*Todo*, General?" The soldier was surprised.

"All of them." Juan nodded. "It is better that way. The other is bad. Too many points of dispersal. There would be confusion. Some would get lost. Others would straggle away and disappear. Give them instructions for an exchange of signal lights. Tell Major Oruna I will be waiting for him and *bien suerte*."

The operator spoke in soft, rapid Spanish, his lips close to the transmitter. Juan listened for a moment, was satisfied with what was being said. Then he turned and walked away. The captain and the two officers followed.

Away from the vehicles and the curious, sidelong glances of the soldiers who had listened intently to every word while pretending an indifference, Juan squatted down on his heels in the sand and scratched aimlessly in the dirt with a twig. Then he looked up at his companions with a crooked grin.

"You know, *chamacos*, that by tomorrow we will all be wanted men. *El presidente* will figure this one out when I don't show up for breakfast."

There was a murmur of agreement. Then the three settled themselves about him and waited for Juan to speak. He continued to prod at the earth with his stick.

"This Major Oruna is a good man." He sensed the question in their minds. "He was with San Martin during the revolution in their own country. I have talked with him in Miami. San Martin has made some fine promises to him so he is eager for the job. He will get them here."

"It is a big risk. All at one time. Here, General," one of the officers suggested.

"Maybe. Maybe not. I have thought about it. The President and I agreed the landing would be made here, at La Semana, and the revolution contained around La Questa. Now, tomorrow, when he finds I am not where I should be he will begin to think. He will say to himself, I hope, 'Suppose this son of a bitch Juan de Cespedes is making this revolution for real? What would he do? Where would he go? Not surely where I would expect to find him.'" He pulled reflectively at his nose with an expression of wry humor. "He will say to himself, 'If I were Juan and had told the *presidente* I was going to make this phony invasion, which is no longer phony, at La Semana, then I wouldn't make it there but somewhere else. I would put them ashore at Le Marin, St. Joseph, Puerto Plata or anywhere except the place agreed upon.' Of course," Juan whistled speculatively, "he could think as I am thinking now and figure for it to happen here. It is a chance we have to take. If I guess wrong"—he stopped speaking and made the stuttering sound of a machine gun, snapping tongue against palate—"then we could get it here. He will have planes all up and down the coast looking for us. He will even come in one of them himself. Believe me, it is not a good thing to be hunted by Jorge Ojeda."

Silently, each in his own way, they were measuring the anger and stature of Jorge Ojeda. One did not play at revolution. The two officers, one from the Quartermaster's Depot at El Centro, the other from the garrison at San Sebastian, had been easily suborned by Juan with San Martin's money and promises of promotion in their careers after the overthrow of Ojeda. Juan put no real faith in them for they would blow this way or that as the situation dictated. Once they were committed to action, though, he could count on them to save their own skins. They would remain steadfast as long as things went well.

"How good are the men we are getting with Major Oruna, General?" one of the officers asked. "Can they be trusted to fight? To do as they are told?"

"As well as any troops for hire and without a real cause." Juan shrugged. "They will fight to protect their lives, so we expose them. I may have to shoot a couple of them first before the others are convinced." He looked at each of them in turn. "I don't expect any real opposition from the Army. San Martin's money has had its effect. The junior officers are already uneasy over what happened to their superiors, those now in the Presidio. The *presidente* will call up the militia but they are of the people and will have no more heart for it than the *Ruales*. We could do this, maybe, with only some token shots." He glanced at the pilot captain. "We had better get that ship off the beach." He stood up and looked around, trying to orient himself. "There is a road over there. I remember it. Maybe we can pull the plane through the scrub and cover it with brush. Put the soldiers on it."

The pilot nodded. He left them and walked toward the car and jeep. Juan watched as the squad listened to his instructions and then followed the airman back down to the beach.

"You know," he dropped his cigarette butt and pressed a heel over it, "all of you do what you do at great risk. There are rewards, though, to be picked up in a business like this." He laughed softly. "I should know. It made me a full General and Jorge *el presidente*. Keep it in mind."

"What of the city, General? San Rafael itself." One of the officers spoke the question in all of their minds. "In the end, to be successful, we must take the Capitol."

"There is one hard nut to crack there. The Federal Police. Even with Pio taken care of I have the feeling they will stand with Ojeda. But, they are policemen and not troops. Anyhow, I have something in mind for the march on San Rafael. I learned it from reading about Castro. It is a real good trick if it works. We shall see when the time comes to use it." He looked up at the star-filled sky. "I was going into La Questa to see San Martin but it is late. Let's get some sleep here and see what happens in the morning."

In a sleeping bag, which had been made ready for him from a pile in the back of the staff car, Juan lay apart from the others. He marveled a little at his own cunning in this matter. The mechanics of duplicity meshed perfectly when they were once set in order and lubricated by San Martin's money. Tomorrow night unmarked planes from Cuba would crisscross San Rafael, showering propaganda leaflets on the island. The country people and those in the towns, cities and villages would be told the purpose of the revolution. The dictatorship of Ojeda would be replaced by a government of benevolence. The people would be able to keep their land; taxes on small businesses and urban enterprises were to be reduced or done away with entirely. Something for nothing was offered to everyone. People, being what they were, would believe what they wanted to believe. He was not underestimating Ojeda. Brought to full anger Jorge would be relentless, shrewd and without mercy. There was, though, in Juan's mind the suspicion that Ojeda no longer had the drive, the will for the job. Something, someone; perhaps *la huera*—Juan considered this with humor—had sapped at the quiet determination and icy detachment which had carried him so far. It could be that *el presidente* now secretly yearned for respectability and the quiet twilight of middle age with a wife and children and a home among the green hills. But, Juan knew, he would be brought to a fury of resistance by the treachery with which he was confronted. In his resentment he would forget how lonely was the pinnacle to which he had climbed. This was the high sanctuary from a secret fear. From it there was no path down but that of oblivion. Juan had always vaguely sensed this. What drove Ojeda was not simply ambition and a lust for power. These were the cheap coins in which such men as San Martin traded.

It occurred to Juan he had no full spirit for what must be done. He was obsessed by doubt. Who was Juan de Cespedes to make the decision for another man's life? He thought, Now, when there should be resolution, I waver because this man is my friend, my brother in blood. We have walked together where others faltered. I would like to tell you why I do this, *compadre*, but there is no time. For this I am truly sorry. But I, Juan de Cespedes the fisherman, am also a part of the destiny in which you believe. This cannot be changed. It is better the hand reaching for you be mine than a stranger's. At least, his thoughts concluded, I must believe this. Without this confidence there are only echoes in the empty caverns of a man's heart where there should be a steadfast voice.

There was no fire and the early hours before dawn were filled with a chill, damp wind from the sea. Juan twisted uncomfortably within the lined bag, drawing upon himself for warmth. He worked around, freeing his arms and lighting a cigarette. Propped on one elbow he smoked thoughtfully as his mind moved over the pieces on the board of this game.

Tomorrow the radio station, the telegraph and telephone systems from La Questa must be taken over and all communication with San Rafael cut. This before Oruna and his volunteers attempted a landing. Roads and the railway line must be blocked. He studied the sleeping figures. The two officers were first and second in command of La Questa's garrison and supply depot. If they could be believed, then there would be no trouble with the troops. They were ready to take San Martin's pay as had their officers. With Major Oruna safely ashore they would have an army of about five hundred men. This was enough to start with. Ojeda would have to come after them. If he didn't they would take one town after another, broadening the base of operations. From the La Questa radio station San Martin and his skilled propagandists could carry the message of LIBERTAD Y TIERRA to the country people. Let the slogan be empty of meaning if San Martin wished. The appeal to the *campesino*, the backbone of any revolution, would be irresistible.

If, Juan pursued his thoughts, San Martin's money had been well spent, there would be wholesale defections in the Army posted at the Capitol. Already the junior officers were uncertain and frightened by what had happened to their seniors now in the Presidio by Ojeda's order. When the time came The Benefactor might well find himself standing alone on the Capitol's gleaming marble steps. He would face an empty plaza. The enraged bull with no enemy to charge.

Juan found no satisfaction in this thought. It filled him with a sudden melancholy. His eyes smarted a little and he brushed at them impatiently. There was a burning sensation within his nostrils. He told himself it was the acrid smoke from a cheap cigarette.

Throughout the morning Ojeda had been in seemingly endless conferences with his Cabinet heads. He received them one by one, masking his impatience, listening wearily to the overtones of uncertainty and fear in their voices. These sometimes rose to the raw edge of panic. Each officer was certain revolution was about to break over his head but none could say from what direction. Before their eyes loomed the bleak image of the scarred Presidio wall where others who had been unfortunate to be on the wrong side of a revolt had ended. What they felt but could not put into words was the unbearable pressure of a political vacuum. They had difficulty in breathing and were restless, as are animals caught in the deadly pall of air which precedes a hurricane. Entering or leaving the President's office they had an inclination to walk on tiptoe.

Outwardly the busy city beyond the Capitol plaza moved normally. Traffic was brisk and noisy. A warm and reassuring sun flooded the streets. But the people there, also, were aware of things they could not name happening about them. Groups of strangers would halt compulsively at a corner and glance self-consciously at each other as though herded by a common instinct. They bought copies of newspapers they had already read and scanned the front pages to see if what they felt could be identified in the print. They stopped before radio and appliance stores to listen to music blaring from loudspeakers. Others abruptly forgot about their business or shopping plans and hurried to catch a bus or taxi which would take them to the comparative security of their homes. No one mentioned the word revolution but it was in everyone's mind.

At the urging of Dr. Serrana, his Minister of Public Information, Ojeda had signed an order of censorship. The newspapers and radio commentators were not to be permitted any editorial speculation on the assassination of Colonel Pio. *Hoy!* defied the order and was promptly closed down; its editor was arrested and the staff dismissed indefinitely. It would be foolhardy, Serrana had pointed out to Ojeda, to permit this radical paper to play upon public uncertainties with inflammatory articles.

The Minister of Finance reported a great uneasiness in the capital's banking circles. There was a threatened flight of foreign capital and a run to exchange San Rafaelian pesos for dollars or pounds. Ojeda closed the banks for the balance of the week.

The men who went in and out of Ojeda's office made no mention of General de Cespedes' conspicuous absence from any of the meetings. But the question was in their eyes. Ojeda left it unanswered. A glacial anger froze his emotions when he thought of Juan.

On the President's desk was a stack of memoranda placed there by the corps of secretaries. There were requests from American and British press services for a statement on the rumors which flitted darkly about the city. Was Colonel Pio's assassination regarded as a link in the invisible chain of whispered revolution? Did the Government have bona fide information on revolutionary activities within or outside the island? Was a general mobilization of the Army being considered? There were also requests from foreign Consulates for an audience and one from Kent Glastonbury in the name of the American Ambassador, who was absent and in Washington. On these requests Ojeda had made no decision, but as the evidence accumulated on the tension outside a hot anger began to assert itself.

He sat now with Captain Raúl Betancourt, who had been Colonel Pio's most trusted officer within the Federal Police. Like Pio, Betancourt was a career man. Unlike Pio he was a member of one of San Rafael's oldest families and among its members spoken of as a renegade. He had associated himself with the Federal Police in the early days because he believed Ojeda was the strong man San Rafael needed.

"You will succeed Colonel Pio as Director of the Federal Police and with his rank." Ojeda made the declaration without emphasis.

"Thank you, *presidente*." Betancourt was not humbly grateful.

"I want General de Cespedes arrested." The order was sharp. "Also, General Chivas San Martin."

"General de Cespedes left the city last night in a light training plane. He was accompanied by a Captain Huerta. That much I have already determined on my own. The whereabouts of General San Martin is unknown. Colonel Pio had given no instructions to keep him under surveillance. Only that his residence be protected against demonstrations after the arrest of the Generals Morillo and Torralba. The servants say he left the residence last night shortly after eight o'clock. The Señorita Serafina Lontenon is indisposed and will see no one."

Ojeda made no comment. He rose and walked to the cased wall map, pulling it down on its roller. Without being asked, Betancourt joined him.

"I was in Colonel Pio's confidence, *presidente*." The young officer spoke earnestly. "It was never in his mind to trust General de Cespedes completely in this matter. It is necessary for me to know now what you think." He paused. "Does he go all the way with this now against you or do we still regard it as a planned diversion as originally outlined?"

"I have ordered him arrested, haven't I?" Ojeda's words were harsh. "That should answer your question." He relented a little. "It is hard for me to accept. My head tells me one thing; my heart the other. Of the many things I might have expected of Juan, ambition was not one of them. Some foolishness. A boy's delight in medals, uniforms, women . . . but, not this." He kept his face turned from Betancourt. Eyes on the map, his finger traced the outline of San Rafael and then moved inland, halting at the principal cities and towns. "We came this way once before. He and I."

Betancourt lit a cigarette and blew at the flame. "It would be simpler to have de Cespedes killed, *presidente*. The Federal Police has many agents who work in plain clothes in the mills, *cantinas, posadas* and in the fields. They have been well placed for years in the villages and towns. Arrest is a cumbersome thing. The other can be done quickly and without confusion. My men will find him. Be sure of that. Before the day is over I will, also, have a report on San Martin. When you cut off the snake's head the rest of it can only twist and thresh wildly but without harm."

"No." Ojeda turned away from the map. "I want Juan before me. Alive."

Betancourt shrugged. He had made the practical suggestion. Ojeda's reply intruded sentiment and emotion into the affair. They were incompatible.

"I will issue orders for an air patrol alert of the coast." Ojeda mulled this over. "*La guardia costa* will do what it can." He smiled a little. "There are advantages in authoritarian form of government in a case like this. No debates. No questions. We pursue our end. However, the Coast Guard will not be much help."

They both understood San Rafael's marine forces were inadequate for the job. They consisted of two destroyers, gifts from the United States, and half a dozen high-speed cutters used in the Customs Patrol. There would be no real problem involved in landing an invasion force along the hundreds of miles of coastline. The air patrol would be all but ineffective at night.

"Also, I will order a mobilization of the militia. To avoid a suggestion of panic, the announcement will be made that this is simply for training purposes. I do not put much confidence in militia. It has no real heart for killing; only parades."

"I would not put too much confidence in the regular Army, either, *presidente*," Betancourt added. "It is worm-ridden. Many things have conspired to demoralize it."

Ojeda nodded. He gazed out of the window as though he searched for the past. "An army stagnates as water in a quiet pond. Yet, Colonel," he used the title unconsciously, "once it was *muy valentie*. It had the lean, hard belly of the fighting man. I made it so. I could do it again. If," he added softly, "there was time and a purpose in my heart."

"*Gestapo!*" Madame Cleo savored the word as though it added flavor to her breakfast melon. She put aside the morning's newspaper and glanced across the table at Ferris. "Violence feeds upon itself."

Ferris lifted her eyes from her own newspaper. "I suppose you are talking about the assassination of Colonel Pio?"

"Is anyone talking about anything else today?" The old lady was smug. "This, you may be sure, is the beginning of the end. *Sic semper tyrannis!* Like that Hitler, he will end in the ashes of his defeat."

"Please." Ferris was weary. "No dramatic pronouncements this morning." Her eyes were dark with concern.

For a moment Madame Cleo peered angrily at her granddaughter. Then compassion and understanding softened her expression. She reached across the table and placed a delicate hand over the firm, brown one of the girl.

"I am truly sorry." The apology was surprisingly gentle. "I am an old woman and inclined to be vindictively waspish in my satisfaction over what is happening. You must forgive me, if you can."

Ferris nodded absently. Carefully, she folded the paper and laid it beside her plate. Without a word she turned and walked down a path leading to the far end of the sun-mottled garden. The heaviness in her heart reflected itself in her step. She moved slowly, with a feeling of weariness, and found no pleasure in the heady, tropical beauty which lay open about her. She was bewildered by the conviction that something irrevocable had passed between her and Jorge Ojeda last night. It was as though they had been standing together and a great cleft suddenly split the earth, separating them by a chasm which could not be spanned. She strained to reach for his hand. He was there but she could no longer touch him.

There was within her a dull ache; a desire to cry silently as though the hot tears would assuage the pain. I have lost you, somewhere, somehow. Now I am also lost and wander on this lonely plain. Painfully, hearing his voice in her mind, she retraced the time and the words spoken. Empty of conviction, she told herself nothing had really happened. There had been an honest difference of opinion, candidly stated. Beyond that there should have been nothing irreconcilable between them. Yet it was there—a thing of ugly formlessness. A quarrel, an angry outburst of words, could be quickly forgotten; a difference of opinion understood. But there had been no temper. Simplified, it was only whether she should have entered Massau's, or any Negro's house without an invitation and in his absence. What had magnified it out of all reasonable proportion? What, in this simple act—performed not furtively, but with an unconscious assumption of right—had moved him to such quick resentment? They had regarded each other as strangers. A mysterious barrier had dropped silently between them; an impenetrable gate. Why?

Head bowed, she walked slowly. Desperately she asked and reasked the question of herself. What had stirred this acid bitterness in him? He had lived on San Rafael long enough to know this was a thing a white person did. It was as incomprehensible to her as it would have been to Madame Cleo if someone questioned her right to inspect the servants' quarters without notice. This was an accepted pattern of behavior. To argue whether it was right or wrong was pointless. Yet, her easy admission of what she had done had filled him with a dark, inexplicable indignation. He had tried to make her feel she had done something disgracefully brutal and shameful. As though by opening the unlatched door of Massau's house she had engaged in an act of degradation, stripping the Negro of all human dignity and making of him the word so bitterly spoken: nigger!

Why? Why? She tortured herself with the question. Why had he made something done thoughtlessly, perhaps, but with an innocent acceptance of a way of life, so intensely personal? Jorge Ojeda spoke the resentment of all men of color. It was almost as though he stood in their place. It was as if . . . Her eyes widened unconsciously with something close to fear and horror. But she dismissed the fantastic notion as abruptly as it had come. It was unimaginable. A preposterous idea without credible foundation. She instinctively shrank away from it.

A half dozen times during the long and sleepless night which had stretched out its hours interminably she had gone to the small desk at the windows of her room. She had taken paper and pen, thinking that the written word might more readily explain how and what she felt. The words would not come. The pen made aimless tracings on sheet after sheet of paper and she crumpled them into an untidy pile. What could she in honesty write? *I am sorry.* She was mystified but not sorry for anything done. *This is a ridiculous situation, a foolish misunderstanding, the importance of which is being magnified.* Was it only that or were there deep and basic differences between them? *Forgive me.* For what? For doing something which I would do again and never question my right to do it?

Suddenly she was angry with him. He was presumptuous, scolding her as if she were a delinquent child, trying to make her feel ashamed where shame was not involved. The anger receded and was replaced by a feeling of helplessness. It was a torment and brought with it an inexplicable nausea. Something irreplaceable had been lost. She thought, I have never loved before. If I had I would know how to cope with the empty sensation of having lost my love. Without it I am frightened, hurt and inexpressibly lonely in this place.

Halting now within the lacy shade of a spreading magnolia tree she stretched upward, breaking off one of the tightly conical blooms. It lay within a nest of waxy green leaves. She held it carefully, cupped within her hands. Miserably she thought of how Jorge Ojeda had put his hands to her face in just this way and there had been a sadness in his eyes. Deliberately, she pressed a finger to the blossom, knowing how the pressure would cause the spot to turn brown and ugly. So, she thought wistfully, is love destroyed by a careless or indifferent touch. It is much too fragile to be handled by man. She dropped the bloom and it fell to the ground with a soft thud. The corrosive imprint of her finger tip was already showing on its moon-pale surface. Why she was not certain. But she knew with a desperate sensation of finality that what had been between her and Jorge Ojeda died passively now as did the magnolia. It was gone beyond reach and hope and for no reason she could name. Alone, she cried a little, head bowed as Niobe might have wept, in despair and stony silence.

XXIII.

THE rusted freighter, its bottom fouled with barnacles and weed, rolled on the easy swell with the heavy, sluggish movement of a sleeping turtle. Against the darkness it was hotly limed by the searchlight's beam from a patrol boat of *la guardia costa*.

From a shadowed companionway Juan de Cespedes watched as the craft maneuvered alongside, armed seamen on her deck and the forward gun swiveled to cover the freighter's crew who hung at the rail in attitudes of passive indifference. Crowding the way with Juan were half a dozen men with automatic rifles. Forward, concealed beneath a tarpaulin draped over a winch, others waited. The cutter's captain spoke again to the freighter's officer over a loud-speaker.

"We're boarding with a search party. Stand by."

The Panamanian skipper of the freighter lifted his shoulders with a weary shrug of assent.

"*Hay nada, capitan. Venga.*"

Juan heard the rasping squeal of the corded bumpers as the patrol craft lay along the scabby side. Then he glanced over his shoulder at the tensely waiting men.

"Not until they are all on deck." He whispered the caution. A familiar stricture tightened his guts and for a moment he was carried back through the years to a night, long ago, when he and Jorge Ojeda had been spotted just so by a hijacker's boat on the way back from Bimini. "We take them all at once."

He had picked up the Panamanian freighter off a headland point in the late afternoon, going out to meet her in a chartered fisherman's ketch. All day Ojeda's aircraft had been sweeping up and down the coast. He had watched them from the beach. When the darkness fell with tropical suddenness, they had left the skies. The freighter carrying San Martin's volunteers had moved unmolested from some twelve miles out toward La Semana until it was abruptly halted by *la guardia costa*.

The head and shoulders of the Guard's officer appeared at the deck level as he came up the ladder. He was followed by four seamen. They stood for a moment in a tight grouping, and in that second Juan stepped forward and swept them with a light machine gun. It was over in less than two minutes. Forward, the men under the canvas turned their guns on the cutter's deck, raking the guard there and smashing the light. Then a beam from the freighter's bridge spotted the cutter. Two men in greasy dungarees emerged from the patrol boat's engine compartment, terror on their faces, their hands lifted high in surrender and supplication. One of the volunteers stared dazedly at the gun in his hands and then hung his head, sobbing and retching on his vomit. The others who, for the first time in their lives, had used guns against other men fingered their weapons with a twitching nervousness and licked with dry tongues at drier lips.

"This is going to make *el presidente* one real mad man." Juan spoke in a level tone to Major Oruna. "He has a great pride in these boats and their crews. He won't like what has happened this night."

Major Oruna was unconcerned. He called to a couple of men, one of them wearing the stripes of a sergeant on the sleeve of his splotched, green and yellow tropical dungarees. The sergeant saluted self-consciously and then quickly shouted the names for a squad from the timorous volunteers. Almost timidly they began disposing of the bodies crumpled on the deck. Other troops went over the side to the cutter and callously shoved the dead men into the water. The two engineers were eagerly helpful.

When this was done, the vessel's cargo booms lifted two flat-bottomed landing craft from the forward well deck and swung them out and in the lee of the cargo ship.

"What do we do with the patrol boat, General?" Major Oruna watched the operation.

Juan blew into a circle of his fist thoughtfully. "I'll take her into a cove up the shore. There's deep water there. In time I may have need for just such a boat. Repainted she will make a fine private cruiser."

"As you wish," Major Oruna agreed. "Where is General San Martin?"

"At La Questa. He awaits the army of liberation impatiently."

"Do we succeed in this, General?" Oruna was sharply annoyed by Juan's levity. "I have made revolutions before. They are not games to be played lightly."

"We will succeed, Major. My neck tells me we must."

Oruna studied him for a moment and then nodded. He called an order for the disembarking to a captain. The men shuffled into a semblance of formation, peering unhappily over at the dark water where the landing boats floated as chips.

Throughout the early hours of the night the volunteer force, their weapons and ammunition cases were put ashore on the beach at La Semana. The men went down the nets at the freighter's side with an agility born of long practice at the camp outside Miami. After everything was ashore the freighter picked up the landing craft and moved out beyond San Rafael's coastal waters. San Martin's troops made their way back from the shore and into the deep woods which would hide them. An incoming tide washed away the furrowed sand where the invasion force had landed. Only once during the night was there a moment of tense waiting. Out of the darkness, a searchlight from a patrol boat stabbed and probed at the beach. It swept up and down along the scrub and finding nothing, snapped off.

Near daybreak Juan and Major Oruna sat apart from the huddled troops. There was a container of hot black coffee and a bottle of rum between them. With the light from a pencil-sized flash Juan indicated their position on the map. He looked at his watch.

"In an hour there should be troop carriers here. We will take La Questa, the motor pool, the arsenal, the supply depot, the radio station and the telephone exchange. There will be no resistance. The garrison there has already been bought off. After La Questa"—he lifted his shoulders—"who knows? It all depends on how much stomach *el presidente* has for resistance."

"I have heard how it is you are the President's close friend. The *compadre* of Jorge Ojeda." Major Oruna peered at Juan. There was a shade of contempt in the words for the open treachery. "If that is so, how do you do this against him?"

Juan tilted the bottle and allowed the dark rum to trickle and swirl in the black coffee. "It is something I have asked myself. The answer is in my mind but it doesn't sound well when I say it aloud."

"You know," Oruna spoke thoughtfully, "San Martin will not be good for this little island of a country. He will put his foot on its neck. I have been with him before on such a venture. This doesn't concern you?"

Juan shook his head. "No more than it does you, *compañero*. If it is not San Martin today it will be another man tomorrow. If I do not betray Ojeda now, someone will come later to do it for me." He smiled, amused by his fancy. "There is a little of the gipsy in me, also. From Ojeda I have come to believe certain things will happen." He swallowed part of the coffee and lit a cigarette. "From these things there is no place for a man to hide. He stands and does not know from which direction the wind will blow. He can be sure only that it will come and against it he can only bow his head." His glance moved away and roved over the men. Some slept. Others turned restlessly. Many sat, knees drawn to chin, arms clasped around them, staring blankly at nothing. "The men will do, Major. They behave better than I expected. It is only necessary they watch a little bloodletting. It is too bad they do not serve a better cause than the ambitions of Chivas San Martin and Juan de Cespedes."

Oruna considered this statement moodily. He was suspicious of such open cynicism. "How deep will opposition be here, General? After all, no real, patriotic fervor stirs the men I have brought with me. This must always be kept in mind. Mercenaries, in a pinch, will always look to their own skins first. You cannot buy the will to fight."

Juan blew on the coal of his cigarette and watched it brighten. This was a question to which he had given much thought. "A few years ago," he made the answer gravely, "the entire country would have risen with Ojeda and stood against us. He had the people in his hand with the exception of a small, hard core of the old families who oppose everything. At that time I would have said what we are doing could not be done. Today it is different. Ojeda is different. He was a man of great *cojones* with the simple belief of a priest in his God, which was himself. He made mistakes. One of them was in the matter of the land. He gave it to the peon and then had to take it back. This was the great *yerro,* for the countryman wants nothing so much as a small piece of earth to stand upon and call his own. The good things Ojeda has done for this island have been forgotten by his *niños.* They don't give a damn about the roads, the clinics, the public baths, the security of jobs, the schools, railroads and hospitals. They want that piece of dirt even though they plant no more than a patch of beans on it. It is in my mind to make of these country people our shield."

"You think they will not resent a foreigner, a San Martin, and fight against him?" Oruna was doubtful.

"They will remember me, Juan de Cespedes, who fought for them once before. I will be the voice of the revolution even though San Martin speaks the words. Tomorrow, from La Questa, San Martin and I will make a radio broadcast. In it we will talk only to the *campesino.* I will say: I have come again to right a bad wrong as I did once before with the man who is now your *presidente* but who has betrayed you. The land and all it means will be returned to you once Ojeda is deposed. This, I promise."

"You will feel nothing in speaking those words against the man who has been your friend?" Oruna's eyes lighted with an expression of sarcastic amusement.

"What I feel is not important. Later, San Martin can talk to the city people and the old aristocrats. He is one of them, holding a divine right by a matter of birth. He will make promises to them, also. And," Juan knuckled his nose to hide a grin, "he will make an offer of amnesty to Ojeda for surrender. This, Ojeda being Ojeda, *el presidente* will refuse. It remains to be seen how deep his anger is against me, how firm his will to hold what he has. If he decides to fight, then we must do this as he and I once did it before, village by village, town by town; gathering the men of the country into our ranks, until we blast an opening to the Capitol itself and the road is clear. Much depends on how Ojeda feels. This we will know soon enough. That," he yawned, "is all I can tell you, *comandante.* Now, let us get a little sleep before the trucks come."

Oruna nodded but he knew sleep was not for him. He sat for a moment and then rose. He walked away, moving quietly between the sleeping men, halting now and then to speak to one or a group who were wide-awake and in whispered conference as to where they were and what the daylight would bring. To them all he appeared as a quietly reassuring figure. The General was as yet too tough for their consciences.

Juan drew a blanket over his shoulders and settled his back against a tree. The coffee and rum made a small, hot pool within his stomach. It is too bad we do not do this together, *compadre*. He spoke as though Ojeda were beside him. There was great excitement in it for us once. It was a big road on which you set our feet. Now it comes to an end. I must do what I do because, as you have said, I have no choice. Much of you, Jorge Ojeda, is in my heart this morning. I would cry a little if I could.

Framed on the balcony with the light from his rooms behind him, Ojeda looked out upon the first indications of daybreak. A mist steamed up from the terraced gardens, enveloping them all in a whirling, drifting obscurity as though the hilltop was suspended in the sky.

He stood and thought, Now, at a time when my life and what I have made of it are at stake, I think only of a woman, a girl. Everything else is without meaning for me, even the treachery of a man I have loved as a brother. What am I to tell this girl who must have asked herself: What did I do? Can I say: You did nothing but be yourself and that I would not change. But, I am what I am and the day would come when you would know. Contempt and even horror would be in your eyes and mind for having given yourself to a man of Negro blood. No words can change this. It is in your blood as the Haitian woman is in mine. He shook his head and passed a hand over his eyes as though in a spasm of pain. The world outside has changed much but not the world of Ferris Dessaline.

He turned and went back inside. He rang for coffee and lit a cigarette which tasted foul. There had been no rest for him during the night. Throughout the hours he had received reports from Colonel Betancourt, whose police maintained the only real discipline in the capital. By radio and telephone the intelligence had been gathered. There were wholesale desertions from rural garrisons. Where the few loyal officers had tried to hold the men against their will, they had been seized, imprisoned and, in some cases, murdered. Colonel Betancourt had pleaded with him to take offensive action.

"You are the only man who can do it." The officer was earnestly persuasive. "Ojeda is a name which still carries a magic to your Army. They want you to tell them to make a stand."

"Even those who have run away and are now hiding in the hills or joining San Martin?" Ojeda was coldly contemptuous of the deserters. "My officers who have betrayed my confidence?"

"There is still a core of loyalty. It needs to be fired by you. What is the alternative, *presidente*? Surrender? Abdication? I need not remind you where *ex-presidentes* usually stand in the Presidio."

"I will have to think about it. When my mind is made up I will let you know. I will not run as did the others. My life, at the moment, means little to me. I am not certain I want to endure it longer."

Betancourt stared at him for a moment and then inclined his head. There was a great sadness in the eyes of the man across the table from him. He turned again to a map spread between them.

From scattered rumors, gathered into a report, they had pinpointed the landing of some two hundred or two hundred and fifty men around the beach at La Semana.

"I did not think Pepito would do it there." Ojeda spoke aloud but to himself. "He begins to conspire too well."

Out of all the conflicting rumors one thing had been established. The *comandante* of *la guardia costa* had come to the palace with definite information. One of the Guard's cutters had made contact with a suspicious-appearing freighter. A brief radio conversation had been held between the cutter and headquarters. The craft's captain said he was boarding the ship. After this brief intelligence there had been complete silence. All efforts to raise the boat by the coast patrol had failed. It was assumed, now, the cutter's crew had been ambushed, the boat captured and, perhaps, fired or sunk. A second craft had been dispatched to the scene and one destroyer was working along the coast.

This much they knew. After a conference with the Ministry of Information, Ojeda had officially released this announcement to the newspapers, radio stations and the clamoring foreign correspondents. The news would create a sensation within the city. Absence of any definite information would breed the panic of doubt and speculation.

Ojeda picked up one of the smudged leaflets Betancourt had brought with him. During the early darkness a plane had sounded briefly, high above the city. These papers had fluttered down by the thousands. They were smeared and badly printed. The text was in English on one side and in Spanish on the reverse:

THE HOUR OF LIBERTY IS AT HAND
A Force of True Patriots Has Landed.
San Rafael's Exiles Return.
The Tyranny of Dictator Ojeda Now Comes to an End.
Be Calm and Understanding in the Cities.

ARISE IN THE COUNTRY!
LIBERTY AND LAND!
LIBERTY OR DEATH.
INSTRUCTIONS WILL BE BROADCAST.
Signed: THE CENTRAL COMMITTEE
GENERAL CHIVAS SAN MARTIN
GENERAL JUAN DE CESPEDES

Ojeda tossed the handbill away. "They must be very sure of themselves, those two."

"The time to stop them is now, *presidente*." Betancourt made no effort to hide his concern. "The longer you wait the stronger their position becomes. Will you order out the militia?"

"I will let you know in the morning, Colonel."

Betancourt had left the palace reluctantly and throughout the night Ojeda had fought his indecision. He had no faith in the militia in the guerrilla warfare he knew Juan would fight in the country. They might hold the capital from strong positions, but Juan would destroy them with the savage, slashing attacks in the valleys and hills. Juan would cut them to pieces.

There was a knock on the door and the valet entered carrying a tray with coffee, some fruit and a couple of sweet rolls.

"*Nada mas, presidente?*" The man put the breakfast on a table.

"Just coffee." Ojeda pressed out the cigarette.

The valet poured the coffee. "Some brandy in it, *presidente?* You have not slept well this night."

"How do you know that?" Ojeda took the cup.

"I have heard you walking up and down, back and forth across the rooms. Many times I waited outside the door in case you wanted something." His glance flicked at the half-filled cigarette box. "*Permiso?*"

"Why not? We have smoked together before." Ojeda pushed the box toward him with a wan smile. "I would like to talk for a little while I have my coffee. You know what is happening. Tell me what you think."

"Only that it will not be solved by you in this room."

Ojeda drank some of the bittersweet coffee. "Do you think, then, I should walk with the troops as I did once before?"

"If it is still in your mind to be *presidente*." The valet lit his cigarette. "Men of purpose oppose you. They cannot be destroyed with words."

Ojeda dropped into a deep chair and stretched his legs before him. He stared at the floor for a moment. There, in what his man had said, was the nub of it all.

"It is in my thoughts"—the valet held the cigarette upright between thumb and forefinger—"you no longer care what happens to you. If this is so then there is nothing to do but sit and wait. Without real hunger in the stomach the guts are empty for fighting." He paused. "I have always spoken with honesty to you, *presidente*. You will not be permitted to retire with honor. There is no safe place to which you can go from this palace."

Ojeda nodded wearily. His eyes lifted to watch the dawn as it crept upon the island. Over the sea the morning broke in crimson streaks. The light picked up the soft tones of the tiled roofs and illuminated the scarred and worn battlements of the Presidio. In a couple of hours the capital would be awake and its people anxiously scanning the newspapers and listening to the radio for what these things could tell them of the revolution. The time of his decision could not long be delayed.

"And if I have no heart to be *presidente?*" He closed his eyes, leaning his head against the rest. "What would you think of that?"

"Then you go as the others have gone." The valet refilled the cup. "The General de Cespedes, being your friend, will see that it is done with dignity."

Ojeda glanced up at the man, amused by the faint irony. There was no trace of humor in the valet's expression.

"Make a bath for me, my honest man." He rose and loosened his tie. "If I do what you suggest it would only be to save Jorge Ojeda and that, now, seems a small thing for which to ask men to fight."

Juan had moved rapidly to take La Questa and San Sebastian while the people of the cities were still asleep. With only scattered resistance Major Oruna's men occupied the police departments, the radio stations, the telephone exchanges. With daylight both strategic points were under firm military control. The first boys, going for their newspapers, saw only soldiers at the corners, before the banks and in the streets. In the outlying districts those who drove their goats to the pastures found troops at the crossroads and machine-gun posts set up in the square, thick-walled schools which The Benefactor had built to command the broad central highways. As the warm sun began to flood the country the news of what had occurred during the night began to spread as the light itself. Men did not go to their fields or their herds as usual. They gathered to talk while their women dressed themselves and the children for a trip into La Questa. There, it was said, those who made this revolution—those in whose hands it was to return the land to the people—were gathered. The people wanted to see with their own eyes and hear with their own ears if this was true. By midmorning the dusty roads began to choke themselves on the stream of men, women and children on their way to the town.

In La Questa, the larger and more important of the two towns taken, the local newspaper editors and the string correspondents of San Rafael's metropolitan press had been called to a conference in the Mayor's office.

Seated on a dais of the chief magistrate's bench General San Martin was flanked by Major Oruna and Juan de Cespedes. San Martin was eager to make a speech but he had been rudely and abruptly silenced by Juan.

"It is better that the announcement come from me, as Minister of Defense of San Rafael, General." Juan was quietly firm. "You are, after all, a foreigner. The scales here could be too easily tipped. After all these years the people think of me as one of them."

San Martin had been suspicious, belligerent, then sulky. What Juan told the reporters was what they could see with their own eyes. La Questa and the neighboring San Sebastian were fully invested. There had been no opposition; a moment of misunderstanding, perhaps, at San Sebastian. This was a popular, a people's revolution. In their name he, General Juan de Cespedes, called upon the *presidente* to capitulate and resign. Unless this was done the irresistible Army of the Revolution would take the capital whatever the cost in blood and lives.

The correspondents were given permission to use all telephone and telegraph facilities to get the news to San Rafael. General San Martin, they were told, would make a broadcast at noon to the people in the name of the revolution and with an understanding of the Ministry of Defense.

Now, in the central dining room of the inn at La Questa, San Martin, Juan, Oruna, two officers from the local garrison and the city's Chief of Police were gathered at a buffet breakfast.

General San Martin had recovered from his petulance. It was, he agreed, better that he remain in the background for the moment. Mentally he had reservations. This de Cespedes would take watching. He disguised his suspicion beneath a genial expansiveness and clapped his hands to the shoulders of Juan and Major Oruna.

"I shall decorate you both on the steps of the Capitol. The highest decoration of the country. If it isn't high enough we shall create a new one and have the design destroyed so it cannot be duplicated."

"We have not yet succeeded, General," Juan cautioned. "There is still *el presidente* to be remembered. If he decides to fight, the road to San Rafael may be a long one. He still has the militia if he wants to use it."

"Militia. Civilians." General San Martin was contemptuous of the corps.

Juan shrugged and did not reply. There was in Ojeda, he well knew, the spark to fire men if he wanted to use it. The initial success of the operation, though, could not be denied. The revolutionary forces now held all communications and the one important bridge across Los Rios de Piños. Ojeda could not get at them save by air and the Army had never trained a paratroop battalion. The motor pool at San Sebastian had yielded lightly armored vehicles, trucks, weapons carriers and jeeps. The garrisoned forces in both towns had, for the most part, either volunteered to join in the rebellion with their officers or had simply disappeared into the surrounding hills. If, though, Ojeda could not get at the rebels, the rebels could also not get at him without moving directly upon the Capitol. It could become a long campaign of attrition if Ojeda chose to make it so.

Juan walked to the windows and gazed at the palm-fringed plaza. From the four central avenues the people were gathering. Already they stood shoulder to shoulder in a packed mass, their faces turned questioningly toward the blank wall of the inn. Within the shaded park there was an air of fiesta. A municipal band, in uniforms of blue and red, pumped noisily in the ornate stand. Vendors of *gaseosas*, the pink, green and yellow bottles of soda water making a bouquet within the pails of ice. Carts selling ice cream, peanuts, slices of pineapple and the crisp strips of pork crackling had taken up places along the cement paths. Girls strolled arm in arm around the flowered square and pretended not to notice the boys who ogled them. As the people from the country flooded into the city the square filled and overflowed. In the dark faces of the *campesinos* there was infinite patience. The oldest among them had listened to the words of *politicos* before and had few illusions. The younger betrayed an eager excitement. They stood beside their sleepy burros, held the hands of their children, whispered to their wives or sweethearts, made shy purchases from the carts, commented on the clothing of the city people. In their faces there was a concealed eagerness to believe that a miracle, without real violence, would be performed for them this day. They waited to be told the land was once again theirs.

Juan turned from the window and glanced at his watch. "It is time, General," he said to San Martin. "Do you have your speech?"

"I will speak to the people from my heart." San Martin blew out his cheeks. "It needs no notes."

"Good." Juan grinned. "Let the heart speak then."

They filed up a staircase to a second-story balcony decorated with flags. From here Juan looked down upon the multicolored tide of people whose faces were now turned upward to see the men who made this new revolution. A murmur with the sound of a light wind swept across the plaza. Juan took the standing microphone.

"The old among you know me." He spoke slowly. "Once before I led a revolution. Now I come again. I speak to you as the military head of a new provisional Government. Because I am only a soldier I have made General San Martin the civil head of the revolution and declare him *presidente* until such time as the popular will of the people can be expressed. Presidente Ojeda has not kept the promises made. Once again your land has been taken away and given to the *patrons*. Because I was the son of a fisherman and understand how it is to be stepped upon, I have pledged myself and my life, if necessary, to the righting of this wrong. We will move upon the Capitol, all of us together, and put in Presidente Ojeda's place a Government of sympathy and understanding." He turned to San Martin. "All right, General."

San Martin made no effort to conceal his anger. His face was a scowling mask. A tiny pulse of fury leaped at the side of his neck. His hands clenched as though he would strike. In the streets below there was complete silence.

"I do not like the way *you* make me *presidente.*" The whisper was harsh but keyed so it would not carry into the loud-speakers. "You take much upon yourself. The revolution is mine, bought and paid for with my money. I alone will make the appointments. It is something for you to remember, my friend."

To the crowd the two men appeared in amiable conversation. Realizing the thousands of eyes upon him, San Martin managed a politician's smile.

"You are *presidente.*" Juan took his arm with a gesture of cordiality. "It is what you wanted. What difference can it make who speaks the words? Your *niños* are waiting. Give it to them from the heart. Since it will all be a lie anyhow, make it a good, big one. It may save us all much fighting." He pressed the microphone into San Martin's trembling hand.

XXIV.

AND now, in San Rafael's capital city, the phenomena of revolution spread and multiplied as a bed of poisonous weeds. Thousands of simple, law-abiding persons were suddenly infected with a fever of lawlessness which raced unchecked as an epidemic through the population.

Old grudges, the memory of a fancied insult, flared into open violence. Ancient prejudices of color and race were heated into dark passions. Youthful gangs prowled the parks and side streets in snarling, vicious packs and vented a feral hostility on anyone they chanced to meet. There were senseless beatings, assaults and rape committed in the hours of daylight. The metropolis seethed with the pent fury of a volcano. Against this the city and Federal Police were all but helpless. There were simply not enough men to control a population suddenly berserk.

Servants, with years of service in a family, abruptly left their positions and disappeared. Taxi drivers took the cabs of their employers, loaded their families into the cars and drove off into the country. The entire staffs of the large hotels encircling the bay either walked away from their jobs or refused to perform any service. They stood about or lounged in the lobbies; preempted the cabañas and swimming pools; chased the chefs from their kitchens with knives and cleavers and fed themselves, their friends, relatives and families from the stores. Boats were cut adrift from their moorings, water mains opened to flood the streets, mail trucks overturned and their contents fired. Stores were looted, markets destroyed, idiotic vandalism raced through the schools, the University, museums and libraries. The days and nights were filled with the high wailing of sirens as the police raced from one outbreak to another.

In the country the discontent did not immediately mount to this irresponsible frenzy. By nature patient and stubborn the people simply refused to do any work at all. The barest trickle of food was shipped to urban markets. The Communists worked with a quiet intensity, playing upon the hopes and fears of the credulous. The paint-smeared slogan: TIERRA O MUERTE—land of death—appeared on walls and fences. The professional agitators were interested in nothing but the creation of chaos. Out of this condition something always developed to their advantage. They chanted the praise of San Martin and de Cespedes as true liberators and urged their rural audiences to make of themselves a great wall against which the dictator Ojeda must eventually break himself. For the moment the Communists were willing to forget San Martin's record of tyranny in his own country. He was the fuse which must set off the explosion. Later they would seek the ways and means of disposing of him.

The one man who might have put an end to the malignant convulsions, Jorge Ojeda, did nothing. He raised no voice nor made a move to control the spasms of destruction and lawlessness. He remained detached, watching the fury mount with a clinical interest. It was almost as though he wanted the island to ravage and exhaust itself and was willing to perish with it. He remained within the walled grounds of the Presidential Palace and was indifferent to the pleading of his Cabinet Ministers to exert the authority of his office, the magic of his name and prestige. He received the American Ambassador with formal politeness and committed himself to no action. He listened gravely to his harassed Director of the Federal Police, Raúl Betancourt, who begged him to call upon the militia and declare martial law.

"It is a revolt of the ants. Let them consume each other."

He studied the reports of the metropolitan rioting and the growing ferment in the country as a doctor might consult the chart of a patient who suffered from an interesting malady. His concern over the riots, bloodshed, internecine explosion was maddeningly objective. Nothing Colonel Betancourt said moved him to any action or expression of concern. He walked the palace grounds in meditative silence or stood, sometimes, on a high balcony from where he could look down in Jovian brooding upon the roiling city. He invited the holocaust.

Confused and angry, Colonel Betancourt paced up and down at his headquarters. His department was being subjected to all but unendurable pressures. The press made daily demands he do something. *Hoy!* boldly resumed publication and screamed in its columns for the arrest of President Ojeda and his Cabinet. The great American, Dutch and British corporations with large capital investments in the island demanded protection. The law-abiding minority protested weakly but they were without a real voice. Overstepping his authority, Colonel Betancourt announced a relaxation of all travel restrictions. The American Embassy remained open on a twenty-four-hour basis, issuing visas and tourist permits to the United States for those who could afford to leave the eruptive island. Additional flights were scheduled by the air lines in an effort to absorb the traffic. Because of the danger of water front strikes and sabotage, steamship lines rerouted their vessels to skip San Rafael. The flow of American and other foreign goods on which the country depended halted abruptly. Medicines and foodstocks reached a dangerous low.

Colonel Betancourt was a man with a sincere love of his country. He was, also, a man long accustomed to proceeding along the channels of discipline. For a time he waited for a summons from Ojeda. The country teetered on the edge of panic. The sporadic outbreaks were only a weather gauge of a political hurricane which was brewing. Unhappily, he issued certain confidential directives to key personnel and then made an unprecedented call without invitation at the palace.

He waited now within the great, formal reception room, understanding he had committed himself to certain things; troubled by the inevitable consequences. At the sound of a step he glanced toward the entranceway.

Ojeda crossed the huge expanse of marble floor and Betancourt regarded him with astonishment. He walked not as a man burdened with the problem of a country on the brink of complete revolt. There was no sign of strain or tension on his face. His carriage was erect, his step firm. The only indication of emotion was a slight frown. This was erased as he offered his hand to the officer.

"Sit down, Colonel." He indicated one of the ornately uncomfortable chairs and drew one up for himself. "Your promotion could have been made at a happier time."

Betancourt controlled himself with difficulty. Ojeda was treating the situation as though it were nothing more than a students' demonstration. He lit a cigarette in an effort to hide his agitation and mounting anger. Ojeda watched him gravely.

"The Federal Police, Excellency, can no longer control the situation within the city. In the country," he shrugged helplessly, "no one knows exactly what is happening; how strong the opposition, how deep the strain of revolution."

"I am aware of that, Colonel."

"Then sir, you must take some authoritative action. Every hour of neglect permits the situation to expand. We will be unable to contain it. Without your directive the Army is indifferent. The *Ruales* are completely demoralized. My reports indicate the garrisons stand idly by or meekly surrender to the revolutionists. Here in the city the militia—" He lifted his shoulders with helpless resignation. "I am almost afraid now to request you to call it out. It is made up, after all, of civilians, and the civil population is ready for riot. My own men are uncertain, reluctant to act, for they feel there is no real will on your part to bring an end to what is happening. We have reached the point now where stability may be achieved only through decisive action on your part or, perhaps, an appeal to the O.A.S. or the United States for direct intervention." He left the suggestion there.

"If I told you, Colonel, I no longer care what happens on San Rafael"— Ojeda posed the question as though it were one of academic interest only— "what would you say?"

"I would say, Excellency, you are a reckless and dangerous man. I would urge you to step out of office and permit the formation of a provisional Government."

"You mean I should turn it over to General de Cespedes and San Martin?"

"I do not like either of them." Betancourt was prompt with his reply. "But, in this situation almost anything would be better than what we have. If that is disrespectful then, sir, you force me to it."

"If I step out of office, Colonel . . ." Ojeda permitted himself a faint smile. "Have you a suggestion as to where I go from there?"

"Then you must take command of the situation."

Ojeda shook his head. "To what end, Colonel? To secure myself"—he was lost in meditation for a moment—"*tierra o muerte?*" He mused on the slogan. "It has a fine ring. Once," he continued, "a long time ago I said someday a man would appear and give the country people a phrase to chant. He would suborn and connive. That when I had to make a choice I would take the Presidio rather than a safe refuge somewhere. I find my life singularly empty of meaning now, Colonel. There is nothing for which I really want to fight."

Raúl Betancourt took a deep breath. Then he rose from the chair. Ojeda studied him from beneath lowered eyelids. Then, as though he understood what was in the officer's mind, he nodded.

"I think, Colonel Betancourt," the words came slowly and with a sympathetic understanding, "under the circumstances I would do the same thing."

[308]

"You give me no alternative, Excellency." Betancourt was unhappy. Unconsciously one hand rested lightly on the heavy automatic he carried. "I must place you under palace arrest."

Ojeda made no move beyond leaning slightly back in his chair, his eyes studying the ornately scrolled work of the vaulted ceiling. Then he dropped his hands to the chair's arm rests with a faint slap of finality.

"I am already a prisoner to myself, Colonel." He made the admission wearily.

Betancourt had a moment of irresolution. He had expected, perhaps, a furious outbreak of words and, even, physical resistance. He could not understand this passive indifference.

"You, of course, had this in mind before you came here?" Ojeda seemed almost amused.

"Yes, Excellency." Betancourt was miserable. "My men have relieved the sentries at the gate, the guard at the doors. There was no resistance from your soldiers, *presidente*. They almost seemed grateful for a display of authority. Your staff, the secretaries and servants will also be confined to the palace grounds. All possible measures will be taken for your safety."

"To what end, Colonel?" Ojeda was ironically amused. "To insure a short, safe ride to the Presidio?"

"It does not have to come to that, *presidente*." Betancourt was almost pleading.

Ojeda lit a cigarette and regarded the officer sympathetically. "You know, of course, you are stealing the moment of supreme drama from General de Cespedes and San Martin. I suspect Pepito has already rehearsed the action before a mirror—in full uniform, of course—and memorized the command he would give for my detention. In your place, Colonel, I would have me shot and done with. Why do you temporize?"

"I am not sure." Betancourt was embarrassed. "Perhaps because I still hope you will change your mind. The words for your detention have not been heard outside this room. If you will reconsider, we can think of them as never having been spoken. In return I ask only you give me, give San Rafael, the ex-Marine sergeant, a man of purpose, of determination. There was a day when I would have said you were bad for this little country. Now it needs the tough, inflexible hand of Jorge Ojeda."

Ojeda shook his head. "You make an appeal to my natural vanity, Colonel. I won't deny that. There was a time when I thought my life had purpose. I was never too sure about its meaning, but drive and goal it had. Perhaps those are the only two things which have any real meaning. Without them we crawl about as aimlessly as blind slugs. I do not put too much faith in the vague promises of a reward to come. They are dangled like a carrot on a stick to keep the meek submissive."

Listening, Betancourt wondered what had happened to dull the once sharp edge of this man's will to survive. He was far too intelligent not to understand where this passive resignation led him. Listening, watching, Betancourt was possessed by the uneasy feeling he was confronted by a mystic; one with the black people in the island's hills who were said to be able to will their own death when sorrow and infirmity made life unendurable.

"Have you ever loved a man or a woman deeply, Colonel?" The irrelevancy of the question startled Betancourt.

"I think so, *presidente*." He was uneasy.

"Once lost," Ojeda was, Betancourt knew, talking to himself, "it is not to be recaptured as a bright butterfly is taken in a net. When you have allowed love to fall from your hands then they are forever empty. Once I would not have believed this."

For a moment Betancourt caught himself questioning the sanity of the man facing him. These were the vague maunderings of an unbalanced mind. What had love or the absence of it to do with man's duty to himself? A woman, if it was a woman, seemed to the officer to be a little thing for which to sacrifice even so small a country as San Rafael. That a man would willingly go to the Presidio's wall because he was without love was unthinkable. He knew, of course, about the *presidente's* attachment to Ferris Dessaline. *La huera*. That there were family obstacles to this union was obvious. He could only surmise that the formidable old lady atop her green hill, secure in her heritage, had interposed her will. Señorita Dessaline. Beautiful, yes. Mentally Betancourt shrugged. Love came easily in this tropical land. He had no real understanding of how deep the attachment or what had happened to destroy it so completely.

"Did you know Juan de Cespedes and I were boys together?"

Betancourt was confused by the question. It followed the pattern of detached musing. Again Ojeda seemed to divine what was in the Colonel's mind. He shook his head.

"I am not rambling, Colonel." He smiled. "These thoughts come to me and I speak them." He stood up. "You have been patient. On another day and at another time I would have resisted what you are doing. Today such action strikes me as an empty gesture. This is no pose of self-immolation. I never suspected my life would end with indifference. The truth is, though, I no longer give a damn. My heart has the sound of an empty barrel being struck."

Betancourt hesitated. What was to be done must be done without equivocation.

"I regret, Excellency," he was anxious to be understood, "certain restrictive measures are necessary. Your movements and contacts must be restrained. I cannot risk your doing something now without my knowledge. Your telephone will be monitored. No calls save to my office will be permitted. Your freedom will be confined to the palace itself. When you move outside you must accept the presence of one or more of my men in your walks about the grounds."

"These are unnecessary precautions, Colonel." Ojeda was almost amused. "I am not a senile, irresponsible man."

"I am not certain. Senility no. Irresponsibility yes. I am willing to accept almost anything for the formation of a stable government."

"In your place, Colonel, I would make a deal with Juan de Cespedes."

"It is in my mind, *presidente.*"

"Good!" With a gesture of warmth Ojeda placed his arm on the officer's shoulder. They walked together toward the doors. "You know," he continued in a conversational mood, "this has the elements of high comedy or drama. I am not certain which. I present a problem even when I do nothing."

"Yes, *presidente.*" The admission was touched with humor. "I don't actually know what to do with you."

"That is one of the things which you must discuss with General de Cespedes. I am certain he will have a solution."

Outside, the gardens and terraces shone with the bright morning's sun upon them. The air was fresh and sharply spiced with the odors of flowers and shrubs. The two mastiffs who usually occupied places near the uniformed sentries seemed uneasy and suspicious of the plainclothes men from Betancourt's department. They stood with stiff-legged inquiry, turning their great heads alertly toward Ojeda. He called a soft command and they came to stand questioningly beside him. He bent to pull with gentle affection at their ears.

"General de Cespedes may be your answer, Colonel. He is a resourceful man. We were together for a long time. I know him well. At least, I thought so. His ambition, if this can be called that, somehow escaped me."

Betancourt hesitated. Ojeda put out his hand. The officer took it almost gratefully and then stepped back to snap a salute.

"Thank you for your courtesy, *presidente.* This has been a difficult few minutes for me." He allowed himself a brief smile. "I have never arrested the Head of State before."

Juan was suspicious and moving cautiously with the forces at his disposal. Despite San Martin's jubilant assurance that the revolution was now an accomplished fact, he was wary of Jorge Ojeda's seeming indifference to what was occurring in the country. Against a sudden move by the Government he had split his forces, leaving a detachment to hold La Questa and

San Sebastian. With the others he extended himself, kilometer by kilometer, along the road toward the capital. Always he searched the sky for the planes which might come with small bombs and machine guns. Always there was the danger of an ambush. The motorized column strung itself along the highway where banana trees and the thick fern growth, higher than a man, offered places of concealment. From where he was, Juan had no way of knowing how complete the demoralization of the Army was. He, Major Oruna and San Martin listened at night to the broadcasts from the capital, hoping to find in them a note of panic. There was none. Not even a mention of the revolutionary forces. Apparently, a tight censorship had been exercised over the radio stations. It was, Major Oruna agreed with Juan, a little disconcerting to have their presence ignored. San Martin urged a fast run to the capital's outskirts, the suburban districts with the thousands of small, middle-class homes. Once there, if Ojeda wanted to resist, he pointed out, the *presidente* would have to risk the lives of the civilian population in street-to-street fighting. He didn't believe Ojeda would do this. Juan was skeptical. If he decided to fight, Jorge Ojeda would not make an estimate of the cost beforehand. He would do what was necessary.

The original landing force of something over two hundred men had been augmented to five hundred through the enlistment of defecting *Ruales* and most of the small garrisons at San Sebastian and La Questa. They were well equipped and supplied and with fast, motorized transportation. With the revolutionary army there was now a civilian band which seemed to regard the expedition as an excuse for a great fiesta. They tagged along with the armed men, dressed in their brightest clothing, carrying parcels of food, bunches of fruit, jugs of rum, live chickens and goats. They sang and shouted the revolutionary slogan, TIERRA O MUERTE, and seemed indifferent to or unaware of danger from the sky or jungle. They became an increasing problem as each village yielded additional men, women, children, youths and girls. They fought among themselves when drunk. The girls coquetted with the troops and there were constant, jealous clashes when the column halted for the night. Major Oruna in desperation appealed to Juan to use his influence to send them home.

Juan rejected the plea. "They may come in handy when we start to take San Rafael itself. We will let them march in front. If there is any of the Army left to Ojeda or he calls the militia, I do not think they will fire on these civilians. We'll put the women and the children in the first rank. It may save us some fighting."

San Martin was delighted by the raggle-taggle following. He accepted this noisy gipsy band as a personal tribute. Taking a phrase Ojeda had employed, he addressed them as *my children*. He pinched the bright cheeks of the young girls, complimented the women on a scarf or a strip of ribbon, noted the sturdiness or bellowing lungs of a youngster, spoke seriously of the good life to come to the men and boys. In each town and settlement along the way he insisted on addressing the curious crowds which gathered to stare wonderingly at the soldiers of the revolution. To them all he promised land, freedom from taxes, little work and great comfort. There was no limit to his grandiloquent extravagances. Each kilometer filled him with additional confidence and self-importance.

Juan was growing increasingly impatient with San Martin for he had no conception of how resolute a man Jorge Ojeda could be. In his mind the revolution was won and San Martin already sat in the President's chair. Also, Juan was making a quiet study of this Major Oruna. San Martin saw in him only an officer, a subordinate. Juan recognized a man of quiet purpose. He laughed a little to himself thinking how the three of them must be secretly conspiring in their minds against each other. Three Humpty-Dumptys perched on a wall furtively thrusting at each other. For the moment, Juan thought, he held the margin of power. He was of the country. The rural people were familiar with his name and his connection with the revolution of Quatero years back. Reluctantly San Martin had accepted the unpleasant fact that he must, temporarily, remain in the background. He was, after all, an alien. So, watched suspiciously by San Martin and Oruna, he had taken the authority and command over the volunteers. It was General de Cespedes who gave the orders, issued the directives for their deployment and disposition; who nursed the unstable corps and cultivated the few obvious leaders within their ranks. There had been no real resistance. Now and then a patrol of *Ruales*, frightened and in a state of indecisive panic, fired wildly into the air and then threw away their rifles and ran or came forward, hands raised high in an abject gesture of surrender. Juan hid his disgust and assumed a paternal benevolence. He accepted their words of allegiance and inducted them into his makeshift army. He needed all the support he could get. When they reached the capital there could be no question of control of the armed forces. He must have the complete respect and obedience of these armed men once San Rafael was taken. Everything depended on this. The country people were indifferent to what was happening. No one had fired their imagination. This was an affair of the *politicos*, perhaps they might turn some small advantage to themselves by guessing right in this contest for power. They were borne to no patriotic frenzy but merely hoped something good would happen; their land might be returned. That was their only interest in the outcome of this revolution.

Oruna was no novice in this business of gathering support to further his own ends. He was aware of what Juan did but at the moment found himself in a strategically impossible situation. Without the prestige of Juan de Cespedes the country might, in fear and uncertainty, turn against the invaders.

The revolution would be regarded as an occupation by foreigners. Oruna accepted what was happening as unavoidable. But in moments of private consultation with San Martin he warned the General against Juan's increasing influence.

With a foxy gesture San Martin had held a finger tip against his nose. "We will take care of the General, Major, when the time comes. Right now he must be endured. Watched but endured. He is invaluable to the success of our operation." He spread his hands with a mock gesture of resignation. "In good time, Major Oruna, all debts will be collected. I have not forgotten nor forgiven the insolence in the matter of Serafina while I was a helpless prisoner in San Rafael. My first task, though, is to have him name me the provisional Head of Government. For this we need him and this bastard army which has cost me a fortune. After that—" He popped his tongue against the roof of his mouth with the sound of an abrupt end to the ambitions of Juan de Cespedes.

The red Mercedes was halted outside the palace gates. The quiet man in civilian blue serge stood beside the car and listened with a grave courtesy as Ferris Dessaline remonstrated angrily.

"Unfortunately, señorita, it is not permitted for you or anyone to enter. Those are my orders."

There was something coldly sinister in the men who had taken the places of the smartly uniformed and polished guard usually on duty. Ferris studied them.

"I insist upon speaking with the President." Her tone was sharp and demanding.

"Colonel Betancourt is the only one who can arrange that, señorita."

"Are you telling me without telling me Presidente Ojeda is a prisoner here?"

"To my knowledge such a word has not been used, Señorita Dessaline. Perhaps it is the *presidente's* wish he not be disturbed. I only follow my instructions. It is a matter of deep regret I must deny your request." He saluted and stepped back a pace to indicate the conversation was terminated.

Ferris waited for a moment, arms crossed upon the wheel. Then she nodded and spun the car in a tight circle. If permission to see the President had to come from Raúl Betancourt then it could only mean Jorge Ojeda was under palace arrest by order of the Federal Police. The notion was absurdly fanciful. Jorge Ojeda would never submit to this indignity. Yet, certain facts were inescapable. She had not seen nor heard from him. The palace sentries had been replaced. For a moment she almost braked the car to a skidding halt. It was even possible Jorge Ojeda was no longer alive. The wildest of rumors had been circulating through the city during the past few days. Insurrection was mounting and the *presidente* had done nothing to halt it. Why? Because Jorge Ojeda had been stripped of the power to act. He could already be one with the many dark secrets behind the Presidio's walls.

Instead of taking the road which would lead her home she turned the car into one of the broad *avenidas* which thrust out, spokelike, from the city's central plaza. She had known Raúl Betancourt for years. His family was as old on San Rafael as the Dessalines. Raúl would tell her. Maybe.

Headquarters of the Federal Police was a severely modern building which bore no insignia. It stood apart from the grouping of municipal and government buildings and seemed almost sedately prim by comparison.

Betancourt came to the anteroom of his office immediately Ferris's name was sent to him by a secretary. She stood, waiting impatiently. He crossed with a flashing smile of pleasure and admiration.

"Raúl." She offered him her hand with reservation. "I want to talk with you. Please."

"Of course. How are you, Ferris, Madame Dessaline?"

She made no reply to the conventional courtesy but walked ahead of him through the open door and waited as he followed and closed it behind him.

"Have you, Federal Police, made President Ojeda a prisoner?"

For a second he hesitated. "Yes. Sit down, Ferris. Cigarette?"

She shook her head and sank into a chair, regarding him coldly. "Tell me why such a thing was necessary. Why it has been done in secrecy. The public has been told nothing. Are you ashamed of what you have done?"

"I regret the action was necessary but I am ashamed of nothing."

"You should be. He trusted you. He told me so." She made no effort to control her anger.

"You know what is happening." He seated himself behind the desk. "San Rafael is about to devour itself, rip its guts open. Ojeda will do nothing. I must find a man who will, who can."

"Raúl Betancourt?" The accusation was tipped with scorn.

He shook his head. "I have no ambition to take Jorge Ojeda's place. But I must, in his words, make a deal. Unless I do, the island will tear itself apart in civil war. A dozen factions will be fighting for control and power. Nothing will be secure, no one safe."

"Jorge Ojeda told you to make a deal with these mongrel revolutionists? He placidly submitted to arrest? I don't believe you." She lashed at him with the words.

"Why should I lie to you, Ferris?"

For a moment she stared at him, outrage struggling with reason. Then her head inclined in silent agreement. There was no reason for Raúl Betancourt to lie.

"I saw him this morning," Betancourt continued. "I offered him an alternative. That of some decisive action on his part. He refused. Something has happened to him. In his own words. He said he no longer gave a damn what happened. He left me no choice."

"Well, what does happen?" The question was an appeal. "Does he go quickly to the Presidio? Is San Rafael to be taken over by your Federal Police? Is that what you are planning?"

"I have no plan. I have a hope for stability. At the moment my choice is limited by time. There is no one to rally a demoralized country. No authority beyond my own. The army has been suborned, ranking generals imprisoned. I trust none of them. So, I must approach the only man who commands a force capable of laying a foundation for order. Juan de Cespedes." He spoke the name without enthusiasm.

"Juan! A clown. A man who has betrayed his friend. You would trust him?" Astonishment forced her voice to rise. "What a despicable choice to make. A vain rooster of a man with his ridiculous medals and cheap women. Are you insane?"

"Again," Betancourt's smile was wan, "I refer you to *el presidente*. He said: 'In your place I would make a deal with Juan de Cespedes.'"

"I don't understand. Why?" She spoke aloud but so softly Betancourt understood the question was not for him to answer. She studied the clasped hands as they lay in her lap. Then, her gaze lifted to the officer. "Will you let me see him, Raúl?"

"No."

The shortness of the reply startled her. Wonderingly she stared at him. "Why?"

Betancourt stood up. He walked across the room and back and his eyes were those of a troubled and unhappy man. He fought with himself, striving for dispassionate honesty, wondering if what he was about to say was compounded of the base motives of prejudice and envy. They could well be there. He hoped not.

"I asked why, Raúl?" she reminded him.

"Because I am your friend. Because I like and even admire Jorge Ojeda. I might even be jealous of him, I'm not sure."

"That is a strange thing to say." She was puzzled.

"I talked with a man this morning. A man I did not know. He is helplessly, hopelessly, I believe, in love with you. Ferris Dessaline."

"Hopelessly? Helplessly? Those are strange words." She studied him, not understanding, asking for an explanation. "I have loved Jorge Ojeda as he has loved me but not helplessly, hopelessly. Why do you say that?"

"Because what you reach for is hopeless. Jorge Ojeda is a *mestizo*." There was a complete absence of comprehension in her expression. "Do you understand what I am saying, Ferris?" The tone was unaccountably harsh. "His mother was a Haitian Negress. His father Spanish."

She stared at him as though he spoke in a language which, for her, had no meaning. Then, slowly, understanding asserted itself. In her eyes there was the image of torture and agony.

"Oh, my God." The words were breathed as a prayer.

"I have had to wonder if you knew. If he had told you." He traced an aimless figure on the desk's surface with a finger. "When you came today, asking to see him, I knew he hadn't."

"Oh, my God!" The words were softly moaned. She seemed to rock a little in silent torment and appeared not to have heard him speak. "What did I do to him? What have I done to us both?" She lifted stricken eyes to Betancourt.

"I think he would have told you." Betancourt was unhappy in the part he had chosen for himself. "There is a rare honesty in him. But," his eyes were sad, "it isn't easy for a man to destroy himself; to tear up his love as though it were an old letter."

She stared at him with dumb misery. She had the sensation of being drained of all emotion. It left her weak, nauseated. She wanted to cry. There was the hot scalding of tears which would not come.

"You are certain of this, Raúl?" She pleaded.

"Colonel Pio, my predecessor in the Department, was a thorough man. There is, in our files, complete, documented information on everyone of importance on San Rafael. The President is included. There is no mistake."

"Who else knows of this?" The question was dull, mechanical. Then she flushed and was ashamed, knowing the secret fear which had prompted it.

"In the Department?" Betancourt understood and was reassuring. "No one. Colonel Pio compiled the file himself. He even typed it up and locked it away to keep it secret. So he told me. Outside?" He hesitated. "I imagine certain persons in the American Embassy have the information. I suspect the island blacks know. They have an instinct."

She cringed inwardly at his casual use of the word *blacks*. It was ugly, formless; a thing to be hidden away and kept out of sight as something shameful. She thought of Massau and the figure he had carved from the jade. Massau had known. It was even possible he had wanted to tell her in this way.

"Why did you tell me, Raúl?" She was in control of herself now.

"I'm not certain." He sighed. "I suppose I could attribute some noble motive to myself. I'm not sure it would be valid." He was uncomfortable with the explanation to be made. "It would be useless for me to deny the unreasoning prejudice that exists. I suppose"—he forced himself to the words—"being white I did not like to think of you giving yourself to a

Negro. That isn't very noble or enlightened, is it? I drew upon a common bond even though, at the moment, I am a little ashamed of its existence."

She nodded her understanding. Staring at her clasped hands she unconsciously noted how white the knuckles were in their locked pressure. After a moment she stood up.

He left his chair. "I have to ask. I suppose I want to share the guilt. Do you still want to see Ojeda?"

"What would I say?" She stared at him, lost in her bewilderment and despair. "Do I say: It's all right. I know you are a—a mulatto." Teeth closed upon her lip as she forced a word become hateful. "Do I say: Love conquers all. What you are makes no difference. When I know this isn't, can't be true. Can I deny to him something which is as much a part of me as the color of my hair, my eyes, my body? I wish I could. Give me a cigarette, Raúl."

He took one from a box on the desk and held a match. She drew upon it, heavily, gratefully.

"I won't be able to talk of this with anyone else, Raúl," she apologized. "My inability to say those things isn't a matter of courage, honesty or reason. It goes deeper than that. It is something I have been conditioned to believe. Generations have built the wall. I can't go over it in a single leap. Maybe I'm afraid to try. I don't know. There have been these marriages. Miscegenation has become a fashionable word. All the parlor liberals make it a part of their vocabulary. But no one knows or hears of the secret agony and humiliations they have produced. Perhaps in time. My daughter's daughter." She stopped and shook her head. "No. I don't honestly believe that either. Without being aware of it she will absorb the same prejudices. Maybe," her eyes were dull, "we secretly like it that way. It is safe, comfortable, easy to understand. Everything is in black and white."

She stood for a moment, staring irresolutely at the floor. Then she turned and walked from the office and into the day's hot sunlight. She was crying and made no effort to hide the tears.

XXV.

FROM the first hours of daylight the crowds had been gathering along the great, wide stretch of Avenida de Independencia. Now, as the hour approached noon, they were massed in solid ranks on the curb's edge. They turned their faces northward, straining a little for a first glimpse, but made no move to press forward against the widely spaced police who stood with their backs toward them.

There was no real excitement, no air of carnival or jubilation. A few hopeful vendors made a halfhearted attempt to peddle balloons or sell the colored ices and *refrescos* from their little carts. The people had come, as crowds will always form, because the day offered a diversion, a break in the monotonous routine of their lives. Also, to insure the ranks of spectators, an order had gone out from the Department of Federal Police declaring this a holiday. All businesses were closed, all municipal employees released with instructions to report to group captains. Others lined the avenue because they had been urged there by their parish priests, the leaders of their social clubs, the merchants and shopkeepers, hotel and café operators for whom they worked. The pressure had come from all quarters to give this the appearance of a popular demonstration of approval for what was happening. There had been some open opposition. Groups of chanting, snake-dancing students had forced their way to the *avenida*. They carried hastily lettered signs: RESIST THE FOREIGN INVADER. SAN RAFAEL YES. SAN MARTIN NO. The police had charged in, swinging blackjacks and wicked rattan whips which could lay open the flesh with a single blow. Order had been restored. So the people waited on this day of liberation.

The time, though, was one of speculative apprehension. Most of them were not quite sure from what they were being liberated. Some even felt a little guilty and wondered about the man who, it was freely said, was a lonely prisoner in the Presidential Palace. This, most of them could not understand. Who had placed him there and why? Those who thought about such things noted that there had been no real revolt against the *presidente* within the city. The great statue in the water front park and smaller busts in the central plaza and smaller squares were unmolested and undefiled. Why then had he not come to some sort of terms with the rebellious *campesinos* and withstood what was happening? It was true that there had been violent disorders within the city but surely the *presidente* could have brought these things under control had he wished to do so. He had needed only to walk out on the streets and permit the people to see him.

For days the press and radio had tried to prepare the city for this day. Over and over there had been announcements to the effect that the Government had capitulated to the demands of the revolutionists. The change in the order of things was to be made peacefully, without demonstrations or fighting. A bad thing, and there were many who were no longer certain of this, was to be succeeded by something better. A provisional Government was to be formed, stability restored. The capital would be spared the flaming terror of street fighting and destruction which militant opposition would create. The most persuasive speakers from the Ministry of

Propaganda had alternated at the microphones. The newspapers were told what they could print and how their editorials should reflect approval. Historical and patriotic societies had been persuaded to lend their support. The names of the old island families were used to give the bloodless rebellion respectability. In the University, where ferment was always present, the classes were suspended. All schools were closed. The new Government had promised free elections. Nothing was said of President Ojeda. He had ceased to exist. What remained was to gather the dissident factions into a unified front.

Raúl Betancourt had been tireless. Every resource of the Federal Police had been used. Where an appeal to reason met with apathy the widely feared power of the organization had been employed.

Betancourt's department had taken over complete control of all sources of public information. The all but leaderless and completely demoralized remnants of the Army were now officered by hard, efficient members of the police. Those of rank who had protested had been quietly and summarily jailed. The metropolitan police had been inducted into the Federal organization. Had he elected to use the power at hand Raúl Betancourt could have made himself complete master of the capital on this day. Instead, he had thrown all of his effort into the task of convincing San Rafael that an orderly revolution was what it wanted. The thousands of persons stacked along the *avenida* were a quiet manifestation of his success. It was in a state of indifference. There would be no resistance but neither would there be a hysterical welcome for the troops waiting outside the city and the strange coalescence of the Generals de Cespedes and San Martin. No matter how strenuously the Ministry of Propaganda had tried to explain this union, the people still regarded it as a political abortion. Working in Betancourt's favor was the fact that the city was no longer in the mood to tolerate the epidemic of lawlessness which had fevered it to the point of exhaustion. It was ready to accept almost anything for the sake of order.

The American Embassy was alarmed and confused by what was happening. San Rafael was a key hinge in the power door which the United States guarded in the Caribbean. Ojeda had sometimes embarrassed Washington as had Batista and Trujillo, but at least, the State Department had known where he stood. God alone knew what might evolve from this combination of de Cespedes and San Martin. Washington waited, hoping Betancourt would appeal to the Organization of American States for assistance. Overtures had even been secretly made to him through the Embassy. He had refused them. There was in him a fierce spirit of nationalism. To ask for outside assistance would be an almost unbearable humiliation for San Rafael and open the way to too many unpredictable influences. He preferred to deal directly with de Cespedes and San Martin.

For three days the Army of the Revolution had bivouacked on the out-skirts of San Rafael. Its ranks were swollen hourly by the country people who massed in a great, patient circle about the armed forces. During this time Betancourt had sought an agreement with Juan de Cespedes and San Martin.

General San Martin wanted a triumphant occupation of the capital. It would have pleased him to have had to take the city by force. He insisted that only through a display of power could the people be made to recognize and accept authority. Betancourt argued patiently against this. He was secretly alarmed by the thousands of *campesinos* who were gathered as sul-len carrion hunters with the Army. To allow this undisciplined horde to enter the city in the van of a not too dependable armed force was to invite pillage and riot on a frightening scale. San Martin seemed indifferent to this danger. He wanted a show of force. Disguising his contempt for the man, Betancourt was patient. There was, he pointed out, no need for such punitive measures. They would accomplish nothing but chaos. The Gov-ernment which succeeded Ojeda must offer something constructive. It was not enough simply to promise the people land. There were large urban populations to be considered; the economic life of the island; the stability of its currency, the protection of manifold foreign investments.

Reluctantly, San Martin agreed to a compromise. The revolutionary forces under the command of General de Cespedes must be supplemented by what remained of San Rafael's Army. The men and officers were to be inducted into the corps of revolutionists. They must take an oath of loyalty to the new, provisional Government which would be named by General de Ces-pedes. The march upon the capital must include civic groups, students, business organizations, as an indication of popular approval. San Martin's imagination soared. He saw a parade miles in length, led by the Army of the Revolution. Behind it would come the bands of the Fire and Police Depart-ments, battalions of civil service workers, school children, fraternal orders. Only in this way, he argued, would it be demonstrated to the world how solidly was the support of the people for the revolution.

From a chair in which he lounged Juan eyed San Martin with sardonic amusement. "You ought to leave someone in the city to watch you enter, General. The way you have it planned everyone will be in the parade." He whistled softly.

San Martin flushed. He had frantically searched his mind for a way of getting rid of Juan the moment he had exhausted his usefulness. An in-finite capacity for intrigue kept warning him not to trust this de Cespedes. Yet, he could not do without him. For the moment he must bear the man's insolence and store away his resentment.

Juan, for the most part, had only listened to the conferences between

Betancourt, San Martin and Major Oruna. San Martin's vanity was now swollen out of all proportions. He actually began to see himself as a deliverer of the oppressed. His demands on Betancourt's patience were endless. He seemed unaware of the fact that the only man exercising any power in San Rafael at the moment was the Director of the Federal Police.

When the sessions were in recess Juan spent his time with the troops. By sheer, dogged effort he had whipped them into the semblance, at least, of a disciplined unit. He forced them to constant drill and inspections, for they chafed under the erosive interlude of inactivity. There had been no real opposition and the venture seemed without drama or purpose. Few had any honest convictions. Others, refugees from Cuba who had enlisted in the hope this might be the first step in the liberation of their own island, were disillusioned. They began to see the venture for what it was—an expedition for the self-aggrandizement of a single man. In their loneliness and uncertainty they turned to Juan de Cespedes. He carried the rank of a General but in him they recognized the soldier. He spoke to them in the language of the barracks. If he was tough and demanding, the tone of his command was not imperious but that of an efficient, battlewise combat man. They respected him and found reassurance in his authority.

Juan was secretly astonished by what he had accomplished since that night on the beach at La Semana. There these troops had been a loosely organized, bastard outfit. A single pistol shot would have thrown them into a panic. He had nursed them patiently. The occupation of San Sebastian and La Questa he had magnified as major military operations in which they had displayed valor and daring. The civilian following which they had attracted as they moved toward the capital had given them confidence. It had, also, acted as a catalytic agent, crystallizing those in uniform, setting them apart and giving them an identity. Unconsciously they held themselves a little straighter. The noncommissioned men and junior officers snapped their commands in a tone of confidence and were intolerant of slovenliness in the presence of the silently watchful civilians. The *Ruales* and small garrisons of the regular Army which had joined brought with them the imprint of the earlier training and this, also, had imperceptibly filtered through the ranks. If, Juan thought, they had no fierce enthusiasm for the job at hand they did, at least, have now some small pride in themselves. They looked to only one man for authority. Juan de Cespedes.

Only briefly had Juan an opportunity of talking with Raúl Betancourt alone. He had taken the police officer on an inspection tour of the camp. It was necessary that Betancourt realize the depth of contention here. The man had said nothing as he accompanied Juan down the battalion line. But his quick mind photographed what he saw: well-equipped men, the jeep-mounted machine guns, the vehicles taken at San Sebastian clean and expertly driven. And, beyond the makeshift parade ground, the stolid ranks of the country people. There, he conceded unhappily, was the strength of the revolution.

After the formations had been dismissed, Betancourt stood smoking a cigarette, lost in gloomy meditation.

"Why?" He asked the question abruptly. "Why have you done this? You who always stood at the right hand of Presidente Ojeda?"

"Because I am what you would call an adventurer, an opportunist." Juan was airily indifferent to Betancourt's bitter scorn. "I saw a good thing and I took it. I am no longer satisfied to be a General." He lit a cigarette of his own and watched the flame of the match as it burned to his fingers. "You have to take me for what I am and make the best deal possible. You have a tough department, Colonel. But, I am still Minister of Defense. No one has rescinded that. Besides, I have what you have just seen. It is enough to take San Rafael with or without your Federal Police. By the way, I heard over the radio you had been promoted to Colonel. It was unfortunate what happened to Pio."

Betancourt eyed him coldly. "I don't want to deal with you, General. Before I came here I pleaded with Presidente Ojeda to take action. He is indifferent to what is happening. I am not. This is my home, my country. I will not see it torn to pieces to satisfy your ambition."

"Walk with me for a little, Colonel." Juan dropped his cigarette to the ground.

For a moment Betancourt hesitated. Then he fell into step beside Juan. They strolled slowly from the encampment and past the rows of country people who had massed themselves along a road leading to a nearby village.

"Tomorrow we will occupy the Capitol, Colonel. It will be an easy walk in the sun. There is nothing to stop me. You can have it either way you want. With shooting or a parade. From the Capitol I will announce a temporary, military dictatorship until the excitement dies down. You will assist me in this. I have great respect for your department."

"What do you intend to do with San Martin?" Betancourt conceded his grudging support.

"I will have him shot, probably." Juan shrugged. "Oruna, also. This Oruna is tough and shrewd. In his mind he sees me against the wall."

"I have entertained the same pleasant thought, General." A smile flickered for a moment in Betancourt's eyes. Then it died. "And Ojeda? Will you have him executed, also?"

Juan whistled with soft contemplation. "This Jorge Ojeda is going to be a problem. With any other man I could say: Dip into the till. Take what you want and get out. But Jorge?" He shook his head. "Jorge Ojeda has no place to go. He is in love with a woman he can't have. I have always felt

[323]

this. He has been betrayed by his *compadre*. We were brothers. This doesn't leave him much. That is why he no longer gives a damn what happens to him or San Rafael."

"You will not last in his place, General." Betancourt made the statement flatly.

"I'll last long enough. Nothing else is important." Juan shrugged. "I was once a fisherman. Always I keep an eye out for the weather."

The radio was softly tuned. Even so, the voice of the announcer crackled with excitement. In a mobile unit he followed the Army of the Revolution. In almost incredulous words he described the troops as they swung into the long Avenida de Independencia—the massed thousands of spectators, the long, trailing line of the country people as they followed in a silent procession, their bare feet slapping against unfamiliar paving.

In the homes of the city, in the suburbs, in the island's towns and villages, by short wave to the United States and the Latin-American countries, the rapid-fire elocution of the radio reporters was carried. It was listened to in Havana, Ciudad Trujillo, Guatemala and El Salvador. The impossible had been accomplished by the improbable. Here was the bloodless revolution. The capital of San Rafael was being occupied without a shot fired. The strong man, The Benefactor, had capitulated without resistance. In awed tones the reporters dwelt upon the incredible number of people from the country who followed the line of march. This was the irresistible pressure of a great, silent, inarticulate beast again following the carrot of hope. Once again they had been promised their land. Once again they believed what they wanted to believe. Over the crackling words came the fitful sound of bands, of marching tread. Over and over the name of General Juan de Cespedes was mentioned as he rode in a jeep at the head of the column. A new man of determination had appeared.

Jorge Ojeda stood before the full-length mirror of his dressing room in the palace. His valet waited, holding the coat of white linen. They both listened to the radio and their eyes met in the mirror for an instant. Then Ojeda extended his arms slightly behind him for the sleeves.

"There is still time, Excellency." The valet unconsciously keyed his voice to a conspirator's whisper. "There is, as you know, a way out of this place. The tunnel from the *bodega* in the basement."

Ojeda slipped into the coat. "I have often wondered which of the *presidentes* had that tunnel dug." He half smiled. "He must have been a man of many small fears and trembling uncertainties. Think, my old friend, how it must be to enter this palace in triumph and leave it as a frantic mole, scurrying in fear underground."

"Better a lively mole than a dead *presidente*." The valet stepped away and with a canting of his head gave critical approval to the coat's drape. "We have a good tailor, Excellency. Anyhow," he shrugged, "I didn't think you would go."

Ojeda lit a cigarette. He walked to the radio and turned up its volume, listening with an almost quizzical interest to the staccato reporting.

"I wonder"—he asked the question of himself—"if Pepito has the real guts for what lies ahead."

"General de Cespedes has tried to copy you in many ways, Excellency. He is a mirror in which you are often reflected. I have watched him. Would you like a drink?"

"A little sherry. Have one yourself." He studied the man as he poured the wine. "Did you know, *joven*? In olden times the servants of a chief frequently threw themselves into their master's grave and were buried with him. It was an act of devotion."

The valet brought the wine on a small tray. He was unimpressed. "A foolish custom, *presidente*, I would think, since the chief was not there to admire or reward the sacrifice. Anyhow, it seems to me that even though he has company with him a man goes to the wall alone. He is aware of nothing but his naked self."

"*Salud!*" Ojeda drank part of his wine.

The valet nodded and drained his glass. "By staying here, Excellency, you leave General de Cespedes no choice. I do not think he will like doing what must be done. This is a big place but in it there is room for only one *presidente*." He shook his head. "I keep thinking of the tunnel."

There was a light knock on the door. The valet crossed the room to answer.

The secretary, Carlos Ponti, stood on the threshold. His features were strained, anxious. When he spoke he had difficulty in controlling the emotion in his voice.

"Will you have luncheon on the terrace as usual, *presidente*? It awaits your orders." He pretended not to hear the radio. "Perhaps you would like it here?"

"Outside. On the terrace, Carlos. Have a small radio brought to the table."

"*Presidente* . . ." Ponti hesitated. When he spoke again it was with a note of desperate, pleading urgency. "There is still time. On my own I have done certain things. A plane is waiting at the airport. Colonel Betancourt's officers, one of whom is a cousin to me, would occupy themselves with other things. A car would go swiftly from the palace." He made the suggestion hopefully.

Ojeda finished his wine and put the glass aside. "And where does this plane land me, Carlos? On the moon? It is a trip I would not care to make alone. Come." He walked over and placed an arm over the young man's shoulders. "Have your meal this day with me."

"I feel no hunger, Excellency." Ponti was dejected.

Ojeda smiled and his arm dropped away. "Let me tell you something, Carlos. I am just discovering it. There is a strange feeling of intoxication which possesses the zealot. He becomes no longer earth-bound. To walk upon the spikes or hot stones elevates his spirit. He is filled with a mysterious exaltation. It transports him. I suspect the true martyr secretly enjoys the fire. It is foolish to venerate him since he is pleasing himself. It is something to remember. At this moment I think Pepito, General de Cespedes, is secretly embarrassed and unhappy. I derive a certain amount of satisfaction from the thought. Now—let's have lunch together and listen to the events of this hour."

In the walled garden the day was caressingly warm and fragrant. No sound intruded save that which came from a small transistor radio on a low table within easy reach of Ferris's hand. She lay back in a reclining chair, a forearm crossed to shield her eyes and the shadowed unhappiness in them.

In her favorite chair Madame Dessaline knitted absently as she listened to the broadcast. Secretly, she thought of herself as a latter-day Madame Defarge who purled and knitted as the heads fell. She glanced now and then at her granddaughter.

"I want you to know I take no mean or ugly satisfaction in what is happening."

"That's good," Ferris replied unemotionally.

"I am an old woman and have seen this drama played many times. One scoundrel succeeds another. Somehow San Rafael survives them all. It is the island's history."

"Jorge Ojeda is no scoundrel." Ferris did not change her position. Her tone was listless. "Many things perhaps, but no scoundrel. He could have torn San Rafael apart in bloody pieces to save himself. Or he could have run as the others have. At this hour he is a lonely man." The voice dropped to a whisper.

Madame Cleo turned the ball of soft Angora in her hands. "I have never asked what happened. Thank God, you came to your senses in time."

"Have I?" The doubt was quietly voiced.

"You will recover from this infatuation. Love is not the end of all things or the loss of it irreparable. It reoccurs as does the fever of malaria, unexpectedly and with violence. I have suffered from its chill."

"If you don't mind, I'd rather not talk about it. A thing for which I had no preparation occurred. I could not meet it." Without lifting her arm from her face she twisted over and snapped the radio's switch off. "Everything I had been taught to believe was assaulted without warning. True or not, I believe what I have been taught—conditioned—to believe. I accept what I am and the traditions in which I have been reared. I can't toss this aside overnight. But," she was weary, "I ask myself questions now I never asked before."

Madame Cleo resumed her knitting. She could make no sense out of the words. "I think," she suggested, "it would be a good thing if you went abroad for a while. In my day a sea voyage was regarded as a specific for unhappy love affairs. I wonder," she mused interestedly, "whether, in this age of jet-transport, flying would have the same lenitive effect. I shouldn't think so."

Ferris smiled wanly despite herself. Madame Cleo defied time, logic and emotion. Perhaps that was the reward of age. One boarded a ship and went to Europe. This was the heartease. How wonderful the imperturbable complacency which accumulated with time.

The investiture of the capital city was swiftly and efficiently completed for there was no real opposition. The metropolitan district was weary of disorder, of the fears and uncertainties which had plagued it. There were alarming shortages of almost everything. The port docks were idle, tourists nonexistent. Anything which promised even a temporary stability was welcome. As the Army of the Revolution marched and rolled down the Avenida de Independencia the crowd which had gathered to watch broke apart and scattered. Many returned to their homes, thoughtful and uneasy. Others fell in behind the procession and followed it to the central plaza and the gleaming white buildings of Government. What remained of the military forces within the city accepted the occupation, recognizing the authority of force. There was no one to inspire them to resistance. Betancourt's Federal Police, with picked squads selected by Juan de Cespedes, took over all the vital systems of communication and transport. The municipal police remained at assigned posts. Their headquarters and precinct stations were manned by members of the Federal Department until the loyalty of the captains, lieutenants and desk sergeants was thoroughly assessed. The harshest of punishment was decreed for looting and vandalism. A curfew was established and riot squads patrolled the streets.

Curiously enough the occupation was without drama. A pall of indifference lay over the capital. There was a feeling of suspended animation, of vacuum. Along the line of march there had been no demonstrations of approval for what was happening. Now there was no cheering ovation for General Juan de Cespedes as he alighted from his jeep and, with General San Martin and Major Oruna beside him, mounted the Capitol's steps. There was even something quietly sullen in the faceless mass of humanity which crowded every inch of the plaza and spilled back into the streets.

[327]

Juan could feel it as a giant's hand upon his back. Even General San Martin had ceased to beam his set expression of benevolent paternalism. He seemed subdued and apprehensive and with difficulty kept himself from glancing back over his shoulder.

At the top of the flight of steps microphones had been set up. The flash bulbs of the photographers made bright sun spots as picture after picture was taken. Within the shadows of the colonnades Colonel Betancourt waited with a half dozen of his subordinate officers. Inside the building, along the central corridor, picked troops stood at guard with bayonets on their rifles. In the little time allotted him, Colonel Betancourt had taken all possible security measures.

Juan took a position before the microphones. For a moment he studied the packed scene. The troops were drawn up below. The silence was a thing to be felt. The crowd waited for him to speak. There was an ominous hush. Juan felt a tightening within him as though a fist twisted at his guts. In his heart he knew he did not have the stature for this moment. He was without the superb assurance, the acute sense of drama which Jorge Ojeda had displayed on a day not unlike this one.

When he did speak he forced his words to a sharp edge of authority. The people were to return quietly to their homes. The Army would feed and care for the hundreds of people from the country until they could be returned to their towns and villages. Martial law would not be declared unless the people themselves made such measures necessary. A provisional Government would be formed, a new Cabinet of Ministers named. For their own security the people of San Rafael would accept the authority of the Minister of Defense, who spoke now in the name of the Revolution.

The words were carried by loud-speakers to the farthest reaches of the plaza and by radio into all parts of the island. Juan did not mention Presidente Ojeda nor did he offer any recognition of General San Martin who stood beside him. As Juan finished speaking San Martin scowled and glanced worriedly at Major Oruna. This was not the scene he had created in his mind. He was being ignored, publicly insulted and debased, relegated to no more than a follower of Juan de Cespedes who, by deliberate omission, was repudiating his presence. He cursed de Cespedes in whispers of unbridled temper.

Juan stood for a moment. There was no applause, not even a murmuring of sound. He turned away and began walking toward the open doors. There was nothing San Martin and Oruna could do but follow. Betancourt and his officers fell into step behind them.

When the doors of the Cabinet Room had closed upon them, San Martin was inarticulate in his rage. A froth of spittle appeared at the corners of his mouth. He screamed his fury with incoherent sound. Juan sat on a corner of the table and watched the spectacle. Major Oruna paid no attention to San Martin. He studied Juan contemplatively.

San Martin fought himself for control. When he could finally speak, his voice was hoarse and his breath came in gusty, wheezing sighs.

"Am I nothing, a stumbling peon in this bastard army which I paid for? The hundreds of thousands of dollars spent for nothing. Why did you not do what was promised—name me the provisional President as agreed? Now was the time. Now the opportunity. What is it you want for yourself? Do you think I am to be put aside? Shoved into the background to endure this damnable place as some hunted refugee? I warn you—I am General Chivas San Martin. I have spit upon your betters." His face had turned to a mottled color of purple and red. Heavy veins appeared on his forehead and pulsated. "I will have what I paid for. Now. Today. You will announce my appointment as administrator for the island. From there it is an easy step to the Presidency. I am not to be satisfied with less. Do you understand? I will not be duped and made a fool of by you. My instinct warned me you were not to be trusted." He gasped for breath.

"You'll have a stroke, General, if you're not careful." Juan eyed him indifferently.

"The revolution is mine." San Martin's voice was a thin scream. "It was planned by me. Paid for by me. You are nothing but a hired gangster. I will have you shot in public." The words trailed away weakly.

Juan lit a cigarette. "Who will do the shooting, General? You? Major Oruna?" He shook his head, unimpressed. "If the Army belongs to anyone it is mine. I made it so. Today, at least, it takes its orders from me. Tomorrow?" He shrugged. "Who knows about tomorrow?"

At a sound, San Martin whirled nervously. The double doors were flung open. Colonel Betancourt stood within the frame. Behind him were his officers of the Federal Police. Behind them a squad of soldiers blocked the corridor.

"I am arresting you, General San Martin." Betancourt spoke quietly. "And you, Major Oruna. In the name of the provisional military Government of San Rafael—for conspiracy."

In an insane frenzy San Martin threw himself forward, clawing and screaming at Juan.

"Assassin. Filth. Thief." The words were yelled by a man insane with rage and frustration.

Juan hit him across the mouth and nose with the back of one hand. San Martin screamed with pain and covered his face with his hands. A crimson stain began to spread between the fingers.

Major Oruna's hand dropped to the butt of the side arm he wore. His glance moved from Betancourt to the police and the soldiers. Then he shrugged with a philosophical acceptance of the situation.

Betancourt spoke again as though he read from a paper. "Formal charges will be drawn and presented by the Government. You will have a trial. Now, if you please"—he stepped aside—"General San Martin."

San Martin took his hands away from his face and stared at the blood-stained palms as though he did not recognize them as his own. His mouth opened and closed soundlessly and he was crying without shame. The tears made bloody rivulets down his face. He glanced appealingly at Juan and then shuffled forward with the halting movement of a palsied man.

Betancourt nodded to his men. Two stepped forward to support the tottering San Martin. Major Oruna looked at Juan and shook his head with something close to a grudging admiration.

"I didn't think you would have time to do it so fast, General." He brushed aside the officers and followed San Martin into the corridor. The doors closed.

Colonel Betancourt remained behind. Juan walked to the end of the room and opened a cabinet. From it he took a bottle of cognac.

"A drink, Colonel?" He spoke without turning.

"I don't like you, General. I see no reason to pretend I do by drinking with you."

"Come here a minute, Colonel." Juan filled a small glass with the brandy and stood at the window. "It isn't necessary you like me."

With obvious distaste for this interview Betancourt crossed the room. Only the country people remained in the plaza. They had settled themselves on the grass and beneath the trees. Their children raced and played, babies cried and were taken to bare breasts by their mothers. Some had opened and spread out their small packets of food. They were waiting to be told what they must do.

Before the Capitol's steps a company of the troops maintained their stations. They stood at ease. An officer with the bars of a captain on his shoulder stood talking with a lieutenant and two noncommissioned officers. At the corners of the plaza other soldiers patrolled in twos.

Juan and Betancourt stood looking down upon the scene.

"Whether you like me is unimportant, Colonel." Juan made the statement flatly. "But you must work with me right now. I put no real faith in this Army. Only one thing it has—the habit of accepting authority. Right now I am the authority. I am the Minister of Defense, appointed by President Ojeda. If there is an over-all command, I am it. You are a policeman and your department is outnumbered. Those are the facts as of today. How it will be the day after tomorrow is something you and I must decide. We have five hundred, maybe a thousand *campesinos* to take care of; feed and send back to their homes. We have a dozen bastard *juntas*, including the Communists, who right now are conspiring to take advantage of the situation. If we leave the jug empty someone will fill it for us. So, Colonel, you need me. If you want it cold—I can get along without you but you can't survive without me and the military force I command."

"What is it you want?" Betancourt unbent slightly.

"I want you to accept the facts as they are and stop concerning yourself with whether you like or dislike me. I don't want this job."

"Why did you take it? Why did you permit what San Martin plotted to expand? Colonel Pio warned President Ojeda against you from the beginning."

Juan shook his head. "If I answered those questions you wouldn't believe me. Anyhow—let's get back to the business at hand. I am ordering, through you, the release of those officers who are in the Presidio." He waved away the objection he knew was forming in Betancourt's mind. "I know they plotted against Ojeda but, again, we must make use of what we have. I want them returned to their commands. Only by doing this can we pull the regular Army together and restore its discipline. This mongrel force we have, the volunteers and deserters, can't be trusted for long. We must replace them. Today I am the military dictator. Tomorrow?" He rubbed a smile from his lips. "Tomorrow, after San Rafael recovers from what has happened, the people are going to ask: Who is this son of a bitch Juan de Cespedes? You see?" He was ingenuously frank. "I am no Jorge Ojeda."

Betancourt acknowledged the statement with a little smile. "I'm still not sure I want to like you, General. But, as you say, we must work with what we have."

"There is one more thing to be done. Jorge Ojeda. I want him taken from the palace and confined in the Presidio."

Betancourt stared at him. "You insist on this?" He made no effort to disguise his contempt. "No alternative occurs to you?"

Juan was indifferent to the scorn. "What do you do with an ex-President? Do you pension him off to sit in the park and feed the pigeons and, maybe, plot another revolution?" He shook his head. "Besides, let me tell you something. Given a little time the people will turn their anger and discontent against Ojeda. They will blame him for everything that has happened. They will say he sat in the palace and did nothing. There is no longer room for Ojeda here. I know this man. He will take no easy way out."

"So, you arrange one for him?" Betancourt's sarcasm was not disguised. "You are, in your own words, a son of a bitch, General. But I will do as you demand because, at the moment, I have no choice."

Juan did not turn from the window as Betancourt left the room. He remained standing there, staring thoughtfully at the plaza. There was something ominous in the silent patience of the people as they sat upon the ground. He had the feeling that there was too little time left.

XXVI.

THE window high in the wall and beyond the reach of even a tall man's finger tips, framed a small square of the blue sky. The opening was unbarred and now and then a hovering sea hawk held itself motionless just outside, appearing for an instant as it might in a camera's lens. The only sound which entered the cell was the wild shrilling of the sea birds when the prison's garbage was thrown on an outgoing tide.

A stone ledge covered with a thin pallet and rough blankets was the only resting place. Here a man might sit or lie. There was no chair, no stool. At night an oil lamp on a bracket shed a yellow light. In the early morning, a shaft of sunlight lanced down from the window and brought with it a small warmth in which to stretch and raise one's face. There were, Ojeda knew, small cubicles in the level below this one into which no sign of day had shown itself for centuries. Heavy studs for the ancient chains and leg irons were still visible in the stone. He was wryly amused by the idea that he occupied the Presidio's Presidential suite. The door of his cell was unlocked and stood open. Outside there was a long, narrow corridor. It was closed off at one end by the solid masonry of a wall, and by a heavy iron gate at the other. Along this passage he walked in the afternoon, counting the steps and roughly translating them into feet and yards. It was his only exercise. Through the gate he could sometimes hear the sounds of the guard being changed. This and the orderly who brought his meals were the only indications that he did not exist in this place alone.

On the walls of the cell a history of sorts had been written. Names and dates were scratched into the porous rock. Studying them he wondered what tools had been used. Perhaps the tongue of a belt buckle, the edge of a coin, the tine of a fork or a nail supplied by a sympathetic guard. Because the time of waiting seemed without end, he tried to pass it by attempting to recreate the image of the long-forgotten men who had occupied this silent place. Who, for instance, was or had been Francisco Alezar? He had dug his name boldly and deep and with it the date—1697. What had been his crime? The length of his imprisonment had been a little short of fourteen weeks. He had marked them off in a series of six vertical lines with the seventh lying across them at an angle. He had survived only to the third day of the fourteenth week. The calendar ended abruptly with three straight scratches. In what manner had Francisco Alezar walked from this cell to his death? There were other names, other dates, covering the walls. In this fashion had each of the prisoners sought some small measure of immortality. He mused on how they had faced their final hours in this grim fortress. Probably as did Jorge Ojeda with a secret fear for the unknown, stoicism, a little hope, some regret and with it resignation. It is no easy thing to come to terms with the end of all familiar things and only an idiot could view it with complacency.

He had been confined here for three days now. Colonel Betancourt had come to the palace to make the arrest personally in the name of the Provisional Government. He had done this, Ojeda sensed, without malice or satisfaction. It was a tacit act of respect, even courtesy. He had offered no hypocritical words of apology or regret, but there was an obvious reluctance on his part to do what must be done. He had been trained to accept authority no matter how violently he might disagree with the principles involved. He had been ordered to arrest the President by General de Cespedes. This was his duty, the obligation of his office.

There had been, and Ojeda thought about this now with a brief smile of appreciation, a prelude of delicate comedy during which time neither had mentioned the real purpose of Betancourt's call at the palace. With a grave politeness the officer had accepted the President's invitation to have coffee. It had been served in the intimately comfortable library, where they sat in the deep chairs of soft leather facing each other with the relaxed ease of a social visit. They had talked, almost casually, of the capital's occupation; the growing problem of housing and feeding the hundreds of *campesinos* who had trailed the army. They discussed the curious apathy of the urban population and their seeming indifference to what had happened. These things they spoke of as though they had occurred at another place or even at another time. Little news had been released to the press and radio beyond the fact that as a measure of safety both General San Martin and Major Oruna had been arrested on a charge of conspiracy.

Betancourt had smiled a little over the employment of this word. "Conspiracy? Against whom, Excellency? You?"

"It is a convenient locution, Colonel." Ojeda lit a cigarette from the butt of the one he had been smoking. "Anyhow, it was a thing Juan had to do. If he had tried to shove San Martin down the people's throats they would have gagged and spit him out. Juan is no fool but he is still balanced on a tightrope."

Betancourt put aside his empty cup. "You know, of course, *presidente*, why I am here?" He employed the title unconsciously.

"I have been expecting you, Colonel." Ojeda nodded. "Perhaps not you personally, but someone to do what has to be done."

"I take no pleasure in it." Betancourt displayed a momentary embarrassment. "Even now I find it hard to dislike you. But," he paused, "what you have represented on San Rafael, the dictatorial power of one man over the lives and thinking of others, is evil and a thing to be destroyed. General de Cespedes seems determined to walk in your footsteps."

"There will always be men of ambition in contention, Colonel. The attractiveness of complete power will not vanish with my execution. An Ojeda is succeeded by a de Cespedes. A de Cespedes?" He shrugged. "Who knows? A Betancourt, perhaps. The names do not matter."

Betancourt shook his head. "Not I. I am satisfied to be a police officer."

"Pepito, Juan, was once satisfied to be a General. Today? I am not sure what he wants."

"There is no real strength in this revolution led by General de Cespedes." Betancourt displayed a brief impatience. "You could have stamped it out. As of today General de Cespedes has the support of the Army. There is no other real authority. But he sits in an uneasy chair. What has been bought once can be bought again. The General Staff officers he has released have always been jealous of his position. They will conspire against him. It has been said, with how much truth I am not sure, that in a time of crisis a man of strength and determination appears. I don't think that man is General de Cespedes. I have the strange feeling he has no real desire to be San Rafael's strong man. I think he is secretly unhappy with what he has accomplished and uneasy over tomorrow."

Ojeda put out his cigarette and stood up. "I keep you from your duty, Colonel."

"There is no hurry." Betancourt was courteous.

"Just the same, let's have it done with. By the way, how do we make the trip to the Presidio?" He smiled at the fancy in his mind. "Was it in Pepito's instructions that I be dragged through the streets in chains?"

Betancourt also rose. There was a trace of dry amusement in his expression. "I have an idea, *presidente,* General de Cespedes was secretly afraid you would refuse to leave the palace. He was vague in his orders. Deliberately so, I think. He is still not too sure of his position."

Ojeda chuckled. "I don't know whether a deposed *presidente* has ever engaged in a sit-down strike. Save for the fact it might make things awkward for you, I might try it. *Vamonos?*"

"I came in my own car, my personal car without the insignia of the Federal Police." Betancourt left the decision to Ojeda.

"By all means. Let's go as inconspicuously as possible. I can send for such things as I will need. Although I don't think Pepito will keep me in residence in the Presidio for long."

On the way from the palace, through the high gates and along the graceful curving of the road, neither man spoke. Not until they had passed unnoticed through the poorer section of the city and the open market area and were nearing the Presidio did Betancourt ask the question in his mind.

"Is it possible, *presidente*, you are as indifferent to what is happening as you seem?"

Ojeda did not reply immediately. When he did speak, the words were in the nature of a confession in which he found a certain grim amusement.

"At the moment, Colonel," he explored the idea, "I think I enjoy the possible heroics of the situation. I am not indifferent. I dislike the certainty that I am to be shot. But, since it seems pretty obvious that is exactly what is going to happen I am trying to conduct myself with as much grace as possible. No. I am not looking forward to it. I remember," he mused, "reading something once in a book by Hemingway. I forget which one. He wrote, as I recall, that if a man dies well today he will not have to do it tomorrow. Since death is inevitable anyhow, that is a reassuring thought. I frequently turned to it when I ordered the execution of others. You see, it simply adds or subtracts a little time to what will happen anyhow." He hesitated and then continued. "It may surprise you, but I feel no real anger toward Juan de Cespedes. He does what I would do in his place. What I have had to do many times over the years to protect myself. It is the loss of Juan as a man I have loved beyond my power to explain that turns the screw. There was between us something rare. We shared many things; but, above all, laughter. That I miss now. The other business is an anticlimax."

The small car halted at the far end of the ancient drawbridge. Where once a portcullis had hung there were now heavy gates of steel. The sentries there froze to attention at the approach of Betancourt and Ojeda and stared ahead without recognition. Then, as though someone had been watching and waiting for this moment, the doors were swung open from the inside. From the squared court there was the sharp bark of a command and the garrison which had been drawn up came to attention.

The prison's commander wheeled from his position, advanced half a dozen paces to halt and salute. He held the gesture of respect until Ojeda nodded and spoke his name.

"Captain Parada."

"*Presidente.*" The officer then turned to salute Betancourt although he was in the familiar blue serge civilian garb of the Federal Police. "Colonel Betancourt."

Betancourt drew a paper from his inside coat pocket. "This is the order for the arrest and detention of Presidente Ojeda, signed by General de

Cespedes in the name of the Provisional Government. He is to be confined in the Presidio until the date of execution." Betancourt recited the words unemotionally.

Almost reluctantly the Captain accepted the paper. He glanced doubtfully from Betancourt to Ojeda.

"We don't have to be so formal about this." Ojeda made the remark with an absence of interest. His glance roved over the courtyard as though he were a tourist seeing the place for the first time. "It is awkward enough for everyone as it is. Dismiss the garrison, Captain Parada." He gave the order with an unconscious assumption of authority. Then he smiled a quick apology. "Forgive me, Captain. I am not yet completely adjusted to a changed situation."

When the broad, flagged area was cleared, the three men stood alone. There was no sound within the walled fortress and time here was again without meaning. It was Betancourt who broke the silence.

"*Adios, presidente.*"

Ojeda extended his hand. "*Adios, coronel.*"

Betancourt nodded to the garrison's commander and turned away with the shadow of an unhappy expression on his face.

Ojeda and Captain Parada watched as the officer crossed the courtyard. The gates closed after him with a harsh, metallic sound. Parada turned questioningly to Ojeda as though to ask for instructions.

"I am your prisoner, Captain." Ojeda spoke with an understanding for the officer's dilemma. "You are not mine. Do your duty and don't make it difficult for us both."

"I have no suitable place for you, *presidente.*"

"I am familiar with the accommodations in the Presidio, Captain."

"My own quarters if you will accept them?" The offer was made hopefully.

Ojeda shook his head with a quick smile. "No, Captain. That would only stretch an uncomfortable situation. After all, the Presidio has been host to many Presidents. Anyhow, the chances are I won't be here for long. We'll make do with what we have."

So, he had come to this cell with its single window. He refused the offer of a cot, accepting the thin mattress and blankets on the stone ledge. He was not quite certain why he did this, for the damp chill of hundreds of years was locked within the walls. He felt it in his bones at night. The narrow hall outside provided what exercise he needed. He walked it daily. Once, out of curiosity, he put his hand to the gate at the far end and found it was not locked or bolted. The sentry just outside pretended not to notice as he opened and closed it.

"You have no key for this, *joven?*" Ojeda put the question mildly.

"It has lost itself, *presidente.*" The young soldier lifted his shoulders, indicating his astonishment over the mysterious disappearance of the key. "Perhaps," he suggested, "it is an act of God. Who knows?"

After that whenever Ojeda approached the gate the sentry found a reason to disappear for a few minutes up a short passageway of stairs, leaving the gate unguarded.

Ojeda had read no newspapers these past three days. He had refused the offer of a portable radio in the cell. He was without interest in what was happening beyond the walls and the time of waiting had become all but unendurable. Driven to a point of anger he asked for Captain Parada. The officer came at once.

"When is this thing to be, Captain?" Ojeda's question was sharp, impatient.

"I do not know, *presidente.* I have received no orders beyond what Colonel Betancourt brought me." Then he spoke with the intimate humor of one man to another. "Are you in a hurry, *presidente?* Few persons would be."

Ojeda relaxed. There was some truth in what Parada had said. Was he looking forward to this thing? He wasn't sure. He caught himself thinking of that Francisco Alezar who had so carefully noted the passing of the days. Had he become restless in this place and scratched the final day on his calendar with relief?

Now night had come again and the curtain of darkness was drawn across the high window. The orderly had brought the evening meal. It was finished and Jorge Ojeda lay upon the pallet, smoking and staring at the ceiling. He realized he was succumbing to the mysterious inertia which comes with confinement. The body became almost indifferent to time and discomfort. It felt no need for action and was satisfied to be passive. It simply asked to be let alone to lie and, perhaps, decay as a useless vegetable. The mind, though, was something else again. It would not pause but was a restless hunter. It pursued the years, tracing and retracing them along dimly remembered paths. It contested ceaselessly with the lethargy of the flesh, wanting to drive it. Across the paths of time it coursed as a well-trained hunting dog will cast over a field. Here and there it halted at the sharp scent of a memory, alert and interested the way a setter might come to a point. Then it moved on tirelessly. It drew up abruptly though, Ojeda realized, at the invisible barrier, the fence which divided yesterday from tomorrow. He found he could think of many things. It was possible to recall scenes, smells, tastes, sensations and emotions. But when he tried to imagine how it would be to stand in the hot sun tomorrow or the next day, his back against the scarred and pitted wall of the Presidio, the mind balked, the brain refused to function. Idly, he sought to force it. What was the pain of steel-jacketed bullets? How was it to look into the vacant eyes of leveled rifles? What did a man think of in that instant between the time the order to fire was given and life ended? There must be a moment, a split second, when the last conscious thought formed. The brain refused to define it and he finally gave up trying to drive it beyond the point where it so stubbornly halted.

He heard the faint sound of creaking hinges as the gate at the far end of the corridor was swung open. The orderly, he thought, coming to find out if there was anything he needed for the night. Matches? Cigarettes? To make a check of the oil in the lamp which made a saffron pool of light on the floor. The steps were those of an unhurried stride. The sound was unfamiliar. The soldier who usually came walked with a soft, padding shuffle. Curious, he raised himself on an elbow.

Juan halted at the open door of the cell. He was alone and out of uniform, in dungarees and a turtle-neck sweater with an old, stained yachting cap canted on his head. There was the butt of an automatic thrusting up from a holster on a webbed belt at his waist.

They regarded each other for a moment and then there was the faintest kindling of excitement in Juan's eyes.

"*Presidente.*" He spoke the words softly. There was an unmistakable thrusting of tongue against cheek.

Ojeda swung his legs down from the ledge and sat up. He dropped the cigarette to the floor and placed his foot upon it.

"At night, Pepito?" he asked. "This one you are going to do yourself?"

"Don't be a damned fool." There was an impatient sharpness in the reply. "Tonight we get out of here, *compadre.*" His glance flicked over the bare cell. "I have had things to do. This was the safest place I could think of for you until I was ready. In the palace, God knows what might have come into your head. I think you want to be a martyr. I couldn't take a chance."

Ojeda remained seated on the bunk. He studied Juan. "Where?" he asked. "How?" The questions formed themselves without conscious thought. "To what place do we go from here?"

"We can talk about that later. I've gone to a hell of a lot of trouble for this. I stuck my neck out good." His eyes measured Ojeda. "Do you come or do I take you?" He grinned then at the idea. "Even when we were kids I was tougher than you at this kind of fighting. Don't make me do it the hard way." He moved to one side, leaving the opening clear. "*Andele, chamaco!*"

Ojeda walked from the cell and Juan dropped in beside him. They stood for a moment in the dim, silent corridor; so close together their shoulders touched. It was this contact more than what was happening that sent a warming flood of spirit through him. What he felt was neither relief nor gratitude. For, he thought, the mind of man rejects the idea of his destruction. Even to the final second it refuses to believe it can happen. So, he had not honestly sat in fear these past three days but in sadness; a sense of loss;

the deep, shrouding melancholy of bereavement, and the knowledge that the man for whom he had felt an affection beyond all comprehension had needlessly, uselessly betrayed him. He wanted to touch him. It was such a simple thing. He wanted to speak but was afraid to trust his voice. Anyhow, he thought, there was nothing which could be said now of what was in his heart.

Juan, sensing this, dug a fist gently into Ojeda's side. He was embarrassed by his own emotions. "We'll talk about it later, eh?" He spoke what was in both their minds. "Now. Let's get the hell out of this place."

They moved down the corridor, through the open gate and up the flight of stone steps which led to the court. It was empty. From an orderly room and here and there in the officers' quarters light was slitted through barred windows. The sound of their footsteps echoed in the silence and was ignored. Once, fleetingly through one of the courtyard-level windows, Ojeda could see half a dozen soldiers gathered around a table. They were playing cards and gave no sign they were aware of any movement outside, although the footsteps were sharply audible.

They could be, Ojeda thought, actors striding across an empty stage but with the scenery set. He couldn't resist an inward smile of appreciation. This was Pepito's delight in the theatrical. He had always had it. Even in that long-ago time when they were running rum from the Bahamas, Juan had not been a mere bootlegger. He had been a pirate, gold ring in ear, parrot on shoulder and, briefly, a black patch over one eye. He had enjoyed playing the scene in just this manner tonight. The release of Jorge Ojeda from the Presidio must be carried out in the manner of a conspiracy, a thing of dark and mysterious intrigue. To have done it any other way would have been to rob it of all flavor.

In the half light Juan glanced up and winked. So intimate was their communion at the moment that he had understood what Ojeda was thinking. He halted, offered a cigarette to Jorge and then lit one for himself. The movements were unhurried, casually deliberate.

"I know what's in your mind, *hermano*. You are saying to yourself: This Pepito is a ham. Maybe. Sure. You could have walked out in the morning. I am San Rafael's Minister of Defense. Maybe I am even its *presidente* for the moment. I'm not sure. Right now I give orders and people jump but I ask myself: For how long? That is the hell of a revolution. You never know when it has stopped. Right now there are maybe half a dozen ranking officers in my army figuring out how to get rid of Juan de Cespedes. And if they got rid of me, *compadre*, before I was ready, you wouldn't have lasted an hour. They would have put both our backs against the wall. So, we do it this way. I tell Captain Parada how I want it to be. I even promote him to a full Colonel just for the hell of it. I've made a lot of promotions.

Everyone is someone for the moment. It keeps them quiet." His expression grew serious. "If I had officially ordered your release there might have been hell to pay. I don't know. Anyhow, where would you have gone? What would you do? Those were questions I couldn't answer."

They started walking again, turning through an ungated archway and a steep flight of steps. Ojeda knew where they led. In the early days of the fort it had been completely surrounded by water. Prisoners were ferried over in a barge. There was a landing stage below, unused for a century or more. The stone was heavily encrusted with barnacles and slimy weed.

They halted at the platform. The craft moored there was painted in the dull color of grayish-blue clay. Heavy fenders protected her as she rose and fell in the light wash. Only a single, dim light burned over the compass. There were four drums of fuel lashed in the after cockpit. Outriggers, the tall slender poles for sail fishing, made a delicate tracing against the sky.

"*La guardia costa?*" Ojeda turned from his brief inspection with a question in his eyes.

"It was." Juan nodded. "She came after us the night Oruna was putting his men ashore. I had her hid away in a cove near La Semana. It was in my mind we would use her. I needed these past three days to have her stripped of the guns and repainted. Now she is a fishing boat. The Minister of Defense gave her to himself. He used to be a fisherman."

Ojeda stood, studying the boat. "And," he spoke without turning, "if I do not go, Pepito? If I say that when I leave this island it is to nothing and I am not sure that is how I want it to be? What will you do? What will you say?"

"I'll say first you are a damn fool. There is nothing here for either of us any longer. Why do you suppose I did what I have done? Because I wanted to be *presidente* in your place?" He shook his head. "There was a time. I'm not sure just when. I sat with myself. Juan de Cespedes with Juan de Cespedes. We talked this thing over. I said to him: Juanito, we have had the best of all this and now it is coming to an end. This place ferments and bubbles. Out of it will come a man. I do not know yet who he is. San Martin. Betancourt. One of the generals. He will have what Jorge Ojeda once had— the drive, the ambition, the purpose. Maybe he is one of the peons. Maybe he is a sergeant, as that Batista was. He is somewhere. He will make a revolution for real as we did a long time ago in the mountains. He will be tougher because he is younger and he will want what Jorge Ojeda has as Jorge Ojeda once wanted it; beyond all cost. When that time comes we will find ourselves standing alone. We will have to take what we can and run as did Morillo, Torralba and San Martin. Or we can stay and stand against the wall. I don't like either of those ideas. So. I make what started out to be an incident real. I say to myself: I show Jorge now how another man will do it, he will believe what he sees. He'll say: Pepito, you are right. We have had the best of this, the icing off the cake. . . . If you don't admit it now you will later. It was not easy to have you think of me what you did, for you are my brother as surely as though my old man were father to us both. There are things I could say to you which would sound strange coming from one man to another, but they are in my heart even if I can't speak them."

"And if I still say I won't go?" Ojeda asked quietly.

"Then I will take the butt of this gun and beat you over the head with it. I will tie you up and throw you in the boat. I will fight you for your life and mine. I won't go without you. Now, *presidente*—do you walk aboard or do we have it out here? I have not gone through this for nothing. You say how it is going to be between the two of us."

Ojeda studied Juan for a moment. He could not deny the truth of what had been said. In him there was an emptiness. There was no longer anything for him here on this island. How far he had come from that hot day on Tampa's Franklin Street. He could recall the Haitian woman's words. *Someday, Boy, you be lak king. I gots the feelin'.* Well, he had had that, also. He had known love and the sickening fear of losing it. He had found honesty in himself and a great understanding in the one who stood facing him. These were no small things to be held in a man's hand even for a little while.

"Well?" Juan was waiting.

"I'll take the bow lines, Pepito." He turned and walked forward along the slip.

And here the islands lay as broken pieces of a long chain. They stretched northeastward from Turks Island Passage to the Northwest Providence Channel and the Little Bahama Bank. The sun broke over them as a great, tangerine-colored balloon and the water lay in huge patches of green, pink, blue and purple. There was no sense of time or its passing. There was no sound save that which they made when they spoke or moved about the boat. It was anchored now within the shelter of a reef. From the stern they fished with hand lines on the bottom for the small Grunts as they swarmed in the weedy depths.

They had worked their way upward through the Bahamas without real purpose or destination. Now and then they put in at one of the island settlements and bought fresh fruit, a chicken or two, a ham of freshly killed pig. Once in a while they passed or sighted an interisland boat, but beyond this they had the sea to themselves. In both of their minds there was the understanding that a time of decision was closing upon them. They had deliberately avoided talking about it.

Ojeda baited his hook with a small piece of conch meat but he held the line in his hand without dropping it over the side.

"We have to make up our minds soon, Pepito."

"You make it up for us both. I have thought too much these past months."
He glanced up. "Making a revolution is no little thing."

"I don't think we are United States citizens any longer. We have an un-
registered boat. If we get into American waters the Coast Guard might pick
us up for questioning."

"So," Juan shrugged, "we tell them you are a *presidente* and I am a
general. Both out of work. Do they deport us back to San Rafael? I don't
think anyone there wants us." He hesitated. "I stole quite a lot of San Martin's money. It is on deposit in Miami. Not too much. Not enough for us
to live as we have but it is enough for a little while."

"If we put into Miami the Immigration authorities may start asking
things we don't want to answer."

Juan took a knife and began scaling and gutting the fish for their breakfast. "How will it be if we ask for political asylum?" He shook his head. "I'm
not sure I like the sound of that word." He washed one of the cleaned fish
and put it aside.

"If we go into Nassau it may be someone there will also ask questions."
Ojeda was turning the alternatives over in his mind.

"You should have thought of all these things before you made yourself a
presidente." The small silvery scales flew with Juan's knife. His hand halted
abruptly. "No one really wants us. No one gives a damn. That's going to be
hard to get used to."

Ojeda went forward to the wheel compartment and came back with a
chart. He spread it out and studied it, frowning. His fingers traced along the
Florida Keys.

"We can stay here." He spoke without glancing up. "Until the fuel is all
gone. The food and what money you brought, also. Or, we go now and take
our chances on what will happen. I have no feeling about it one way or the
other. I think we'll go." He made the decision and rolled the chart up again,
sliding it into the waterproof tube.

Juan finished the last of the fish. He stared at them. "My God!" He spoke
with soft wonder. "The money we could have stolen. Always I am going to
think of that. Being a *presidente* is not a good, steady job. We should have
put something aside for our old age. France. South America. Spain. Portugal.
The smart ones are there with their women and their money safe in Swiss
banks."

"Those things are not enough, Pepito." Ojeda opened a locker and took a
bottle of rum from a half-filled case. He pulled at the wired cork and worked
it out. "I learned that on San Rafael." He poured the rum into two tin cups
and handed one to Juan.

"*Salud*, General!"

"*Salud, presidente!*" Juan replied gravely. He drank and then stared at the remaining liquor. "It may be, *compadre,* that the old man told the truth. Maybe he was the Duke of Alba's cousin after all. I find it easier to believe now that I, a general and the Minister of Defense, sit here and clean little fish."

Ojeda smiled to himself. Time had not blurred the old one's image. He wondered if the small cottage still weathered upon the dunes where the wild sea oats bent to the wind's command and the purple of morning glories spread as a ragged carpet on white sand.

"As the *viejito* said." He spoke with quiet meditation. "'We take from God only what we need.' That I have done. There was a hunger in me. I reached to satisfy it. There was a fear and a loneliness. Both are gone now. I have no real wish to look beyond today."

"I don't know if it can be that simple." Juan poured a stream of bright, yellow cornmeal into a tin plate and began rolling the fish in the grains. "What we have had is not easily put aside and forgotten." He looked up abruptly. "We are a couple of middle-aged men, *compadre.* I don't like the sound of that. The fire is out. We should have put a little kindling aside to start it again. With what do we warm our hands during the long evenings to come? Maybe, we had better just stay here and let the boat rot beneath us. I'm not sure there is a place for us beyond these islands. I have a feeling there isn't much of a market for an ex-*presidente* and a Minister of Defense. We might even end in someone's jail." His eyes brightened. "But, we had it, *chamaco.* We had it all the way. No matter what happens now."

Ojeda picked up the bottle and the golden rum was a flashing stream into the cups again. "What you talk of is tomorrow. I have never worried too much about it. I'll take now what comes and say as I have always said: This is the way it was to be. We will make the best of today." He stood up and his eyes swept over the empty sea. "So, we will have some of those *pescado* fish with *frijole* beans. Maybe we'll even get a little drunk together and lie in the sun with the food and rum warm in our bellies. If we shut our eyes and listen well it is even possible the Duke of Alba's cousin will come and make gipsy music on an old accordion for us while we sleep."